My Little Pony

Friends Forever

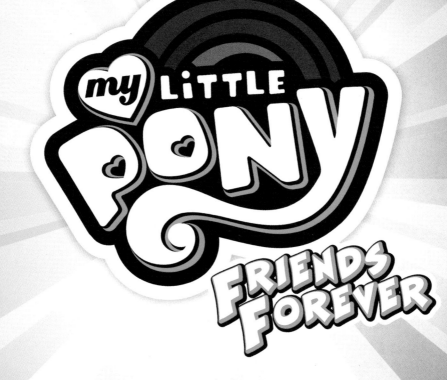

MY LITTLE PONY
FRIENDS FOREVER

PINKIE PIE & CHEESE SANDWICH

Written by
Thom Zahler

Art by
Agnes Garbowska

Color Assist by
Lauren Perry

Letters by
Neil Uyetake

TWILIGHT SPARKLE & STARLIGHT GLIMMER

Written by
Rob Anderson

Art by
Jay Fosgitt

Colors by
Heather Breckel

Letters by
Neil Uyetake

Fountaindale Public Library
Bolingbrook, IL
(630) 759-2102

Special thanks to Meghan McCarthy, Eliza Hart, Ed Lane, Beth Artale, and Michael Kelly.

For international rights, contact licensing@idwpublishing.com

ISBN: 978-1-63140-918-9

20 19 18 17   1 2 3 4

Licensed By: Hasbro

Ted Adams, CEO & Publisher • Greg Goldstein, President & COO • Robbie Robbins, EVP/Sr. Graphic Artist • Chris Ryall, Chief Creative Officer • David Hedgecock, Editor-in-Chief • Laurie Windrow, Senior Vice President of Sales & Marketing • Matthew Ruzicka, CPA, Chief Financial Officer • Lorelei Bunjes, VP of Digital Services • Jerry Bennington, VP of New Product Development

www.IDWPUBLISHING.com

Facebook: facebook.com/idwpublishing • Twitter: @idwpublishing • YouTube: youtube.com/idwpublishing
Tumblr: tumblr.idwpublishing.com • Instagram: instagram.com/idwpublishing

Rainbow Dash & Soarin

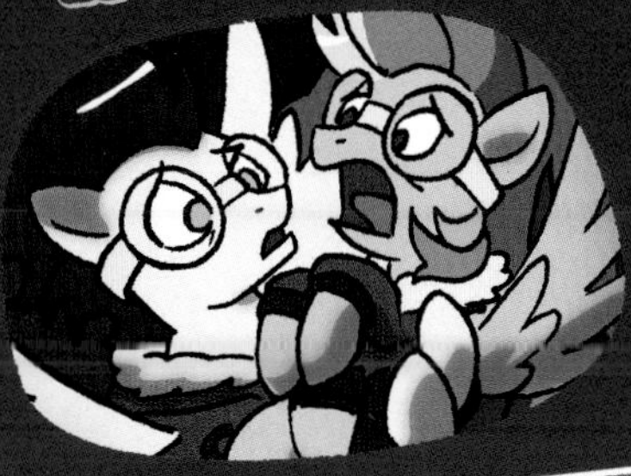

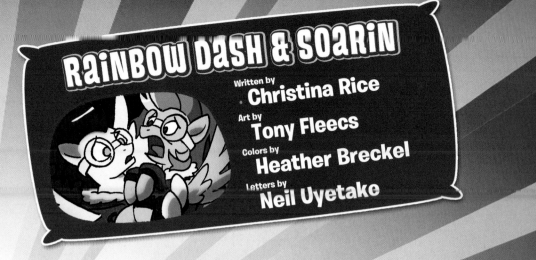

Written by
Christina Rice
Art by
Tony Fleecs
Colors by
Heather Breckel
Letters by
Neil Uyetake

Rarity & Trixie

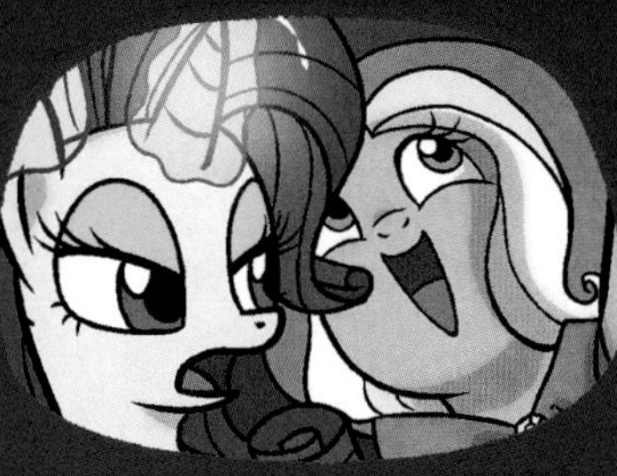

Written by
Jeremy Whitley
Art by
Agnes Garbowska
Colors by
Heather Breckel
Letters by
Neil Uyetake

Princess Celestia & Princess Luna

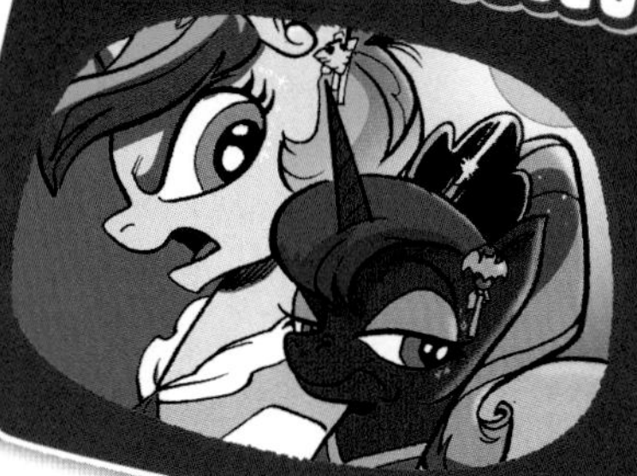

Script and Art by
Andy Price
Colors by
Heather Breckel
Letters by
Neil Uyetake

Cover by
Tony Fleecs

Series Edits by
Bobby Curnow

Collection Edits by
Justin Eisinger & Alonzo Simon

Collection Design by
Neil Uyetake

Publisher
Ted Adams

Pinkie Pie & Cheese Sandwich

art by
Agnes Garbowska

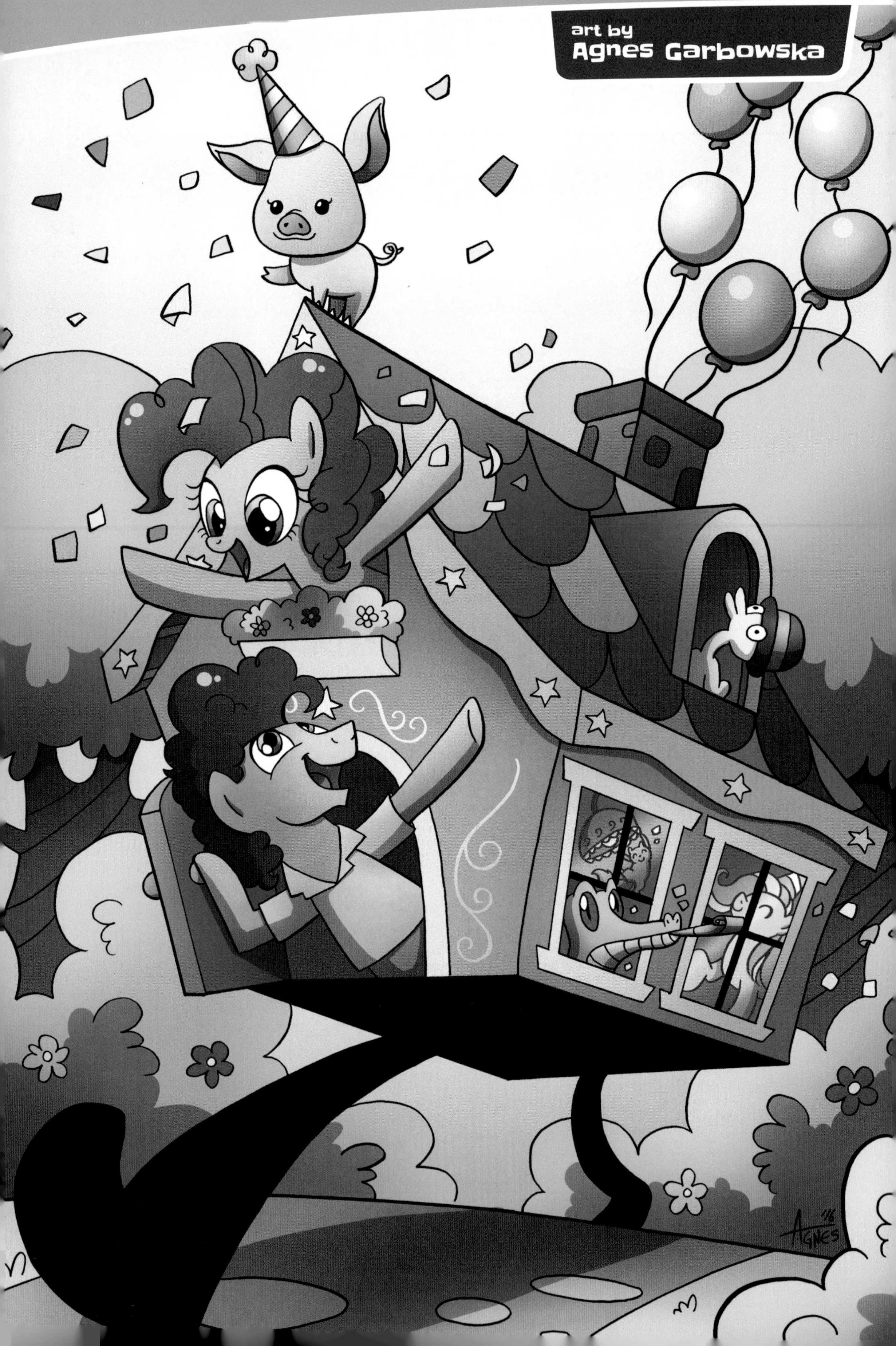
Agnes '16

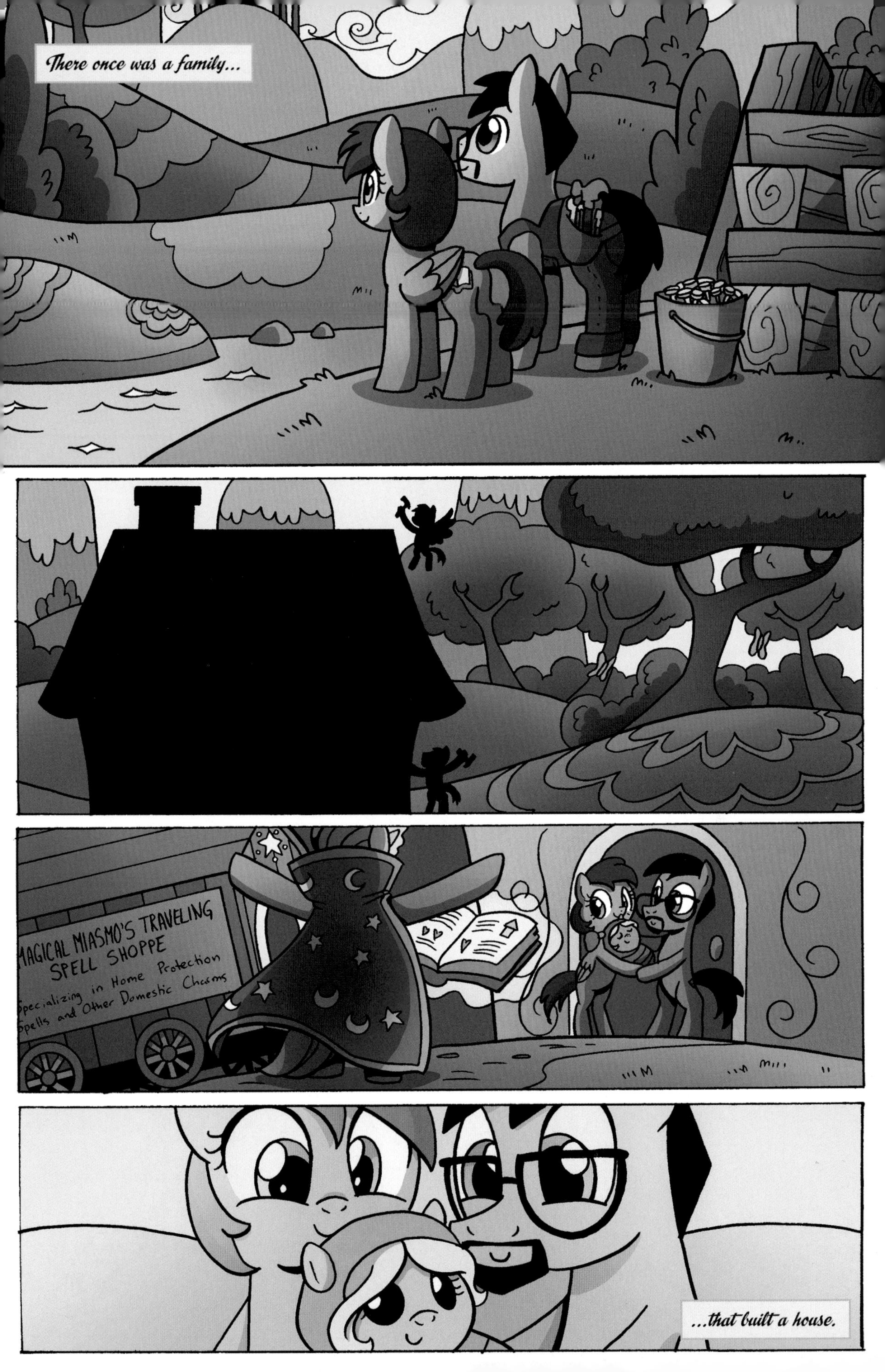
There once was a family...
MAGICAL MIASMO'S TRAVELING SPELL SHOPPE
Specializing in Home Protection Spells and Other Domestic Charms
...that built a house.

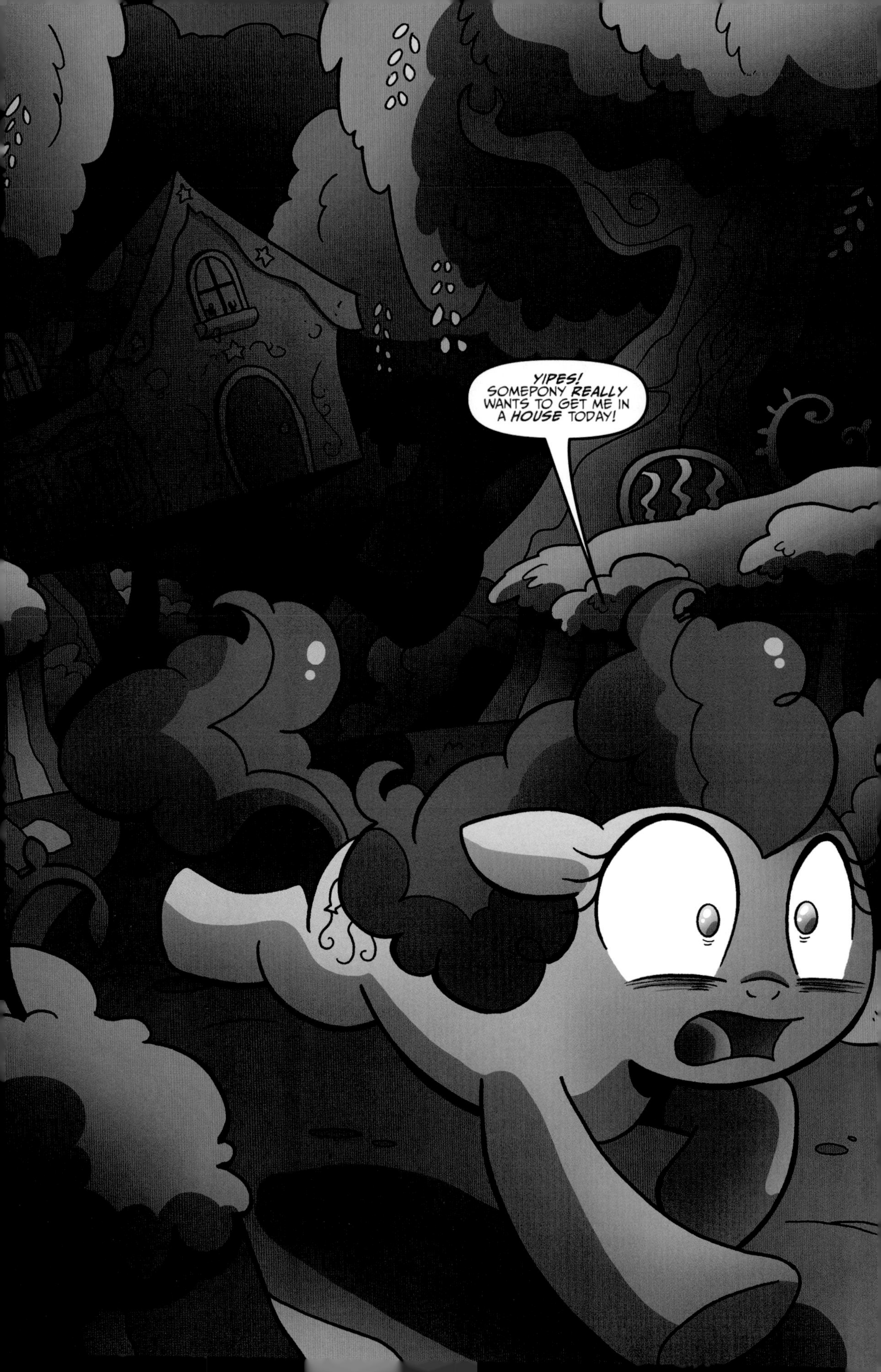
YIPES! SOMEPONY REALLY WANTS TO GET ME IN A HOUSE TODAY!

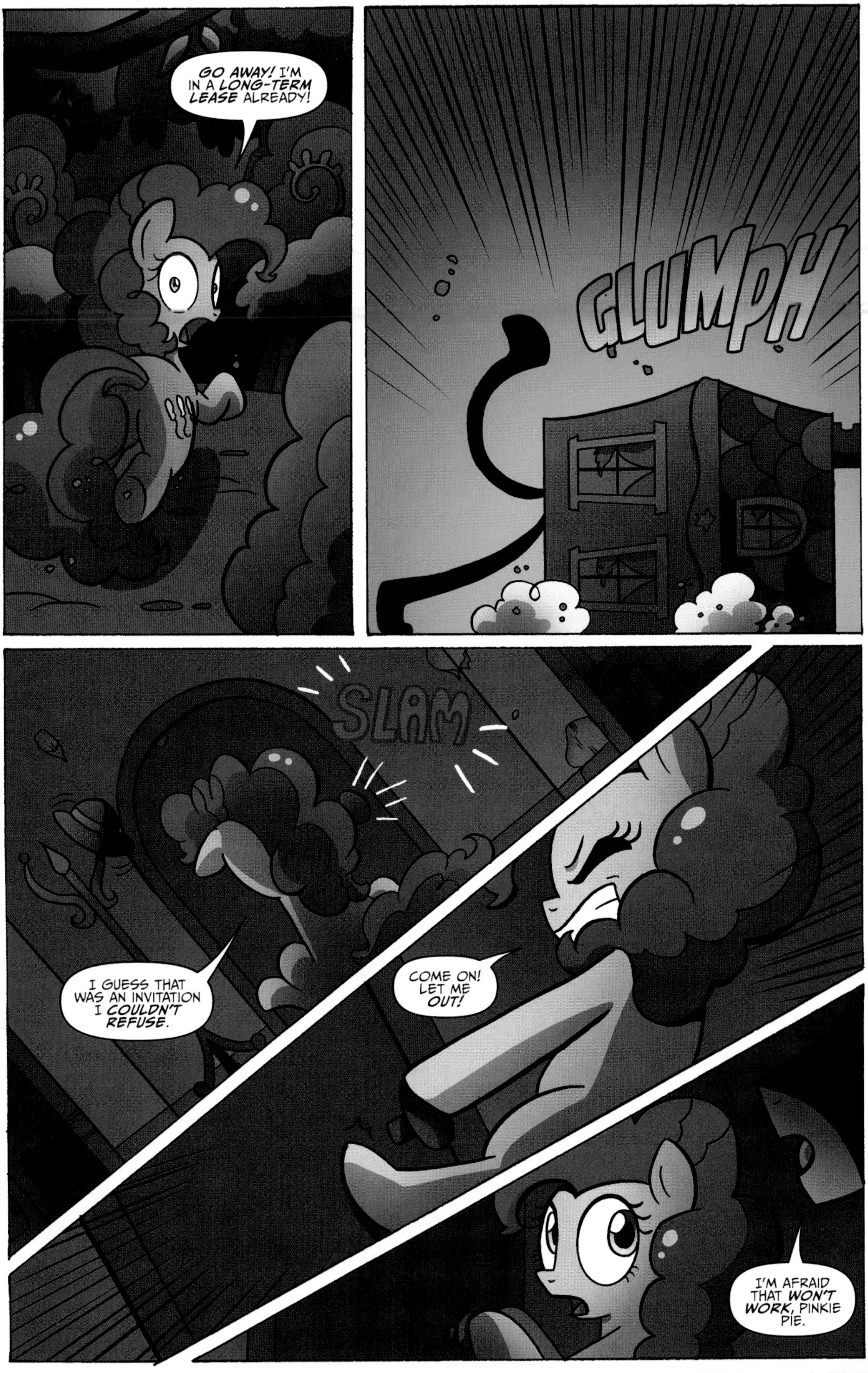
GO AWAY! I'M IN A LONG-TERM LEASE ALREADY!
GLUMPH
SLAM
I GUESS THAT WAS AN INVITATION I COULDN'T REFUSE.
COME ON! LET ME OUT!
I'M AFRAID THAT WON'T WORK, PINKIE PIE.

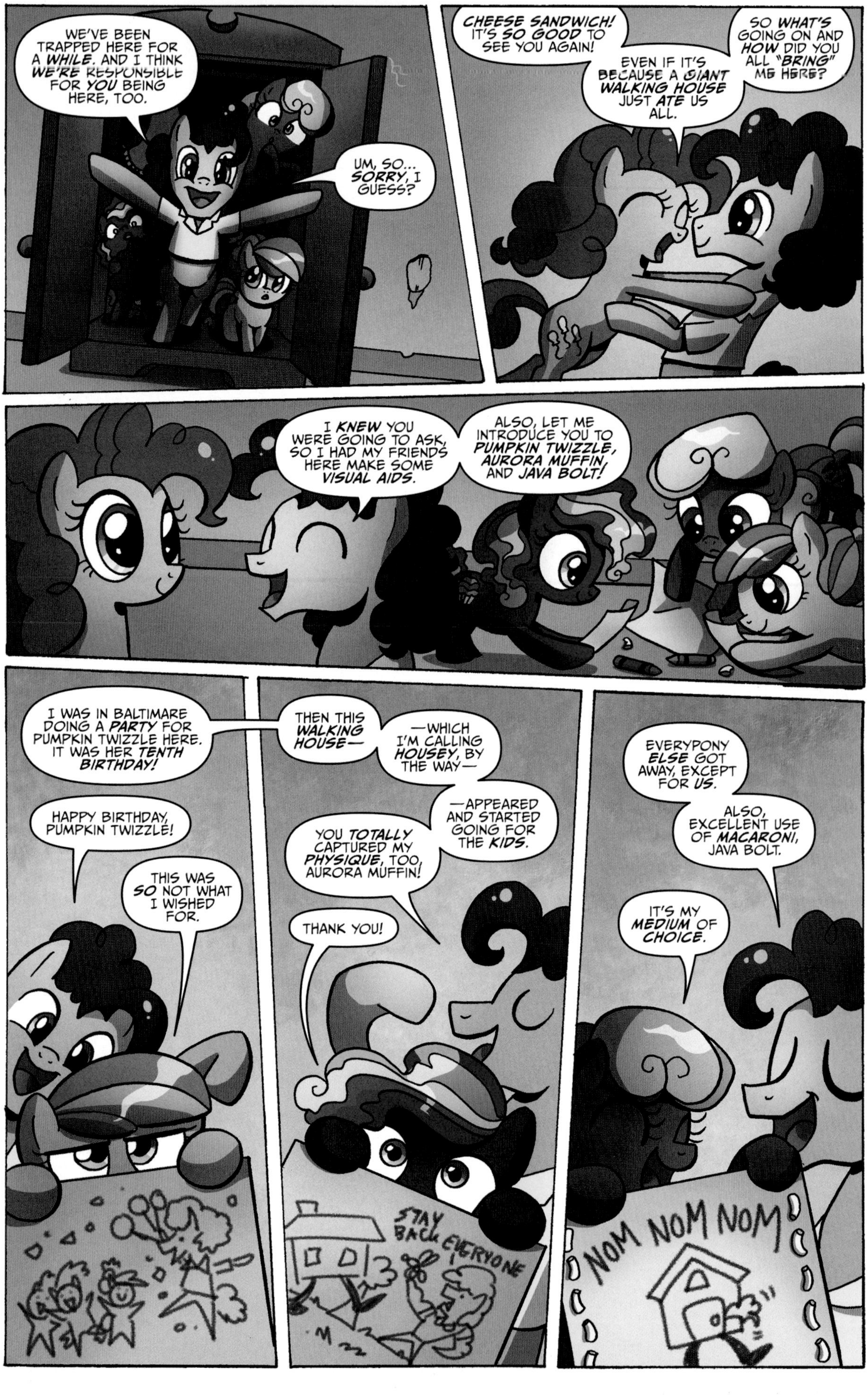
WE'VE BEEN TRAPPED HERE FOR A WHILE. AND I THINK WE'RE RESPONSIBLE FOR YOU BEING HERE, TOO.
UM, SO... SORRY, I GUESS?
CHEESE SANDWICH! IT'S SO GOOD TO SEE YOU AGAIN!
EVEN IF IT'S BECAUSE A GIANT WALKING HOUSE JUST ATE US ALL.
SO WHAT'S GOING ON AND HOW DID YOU ALL "BRING" ME HERE?
I KNEW YOU WERE GOING TO ASK, SO I HAD MY FRIENDS HERE MAKE SOME VISUAL AIDS.
ALSO, LET ME INTRODUCE YOU TO PUMPKIN TWIZZLE, AURORA MUFFIN, AND JAVA BOLT!
I WAS IN BALTIMARE DOING A PARTY FOR PUMPKIN TWIZZLE HERE. IT WAS HER TENTH BIRTHDAY!
THEN THIS WALKING HOUSE—
—WHICH I'M CALLING HOUSEY, BY THE WAY—
—APPEARED AND STARTED GOING FOR THE KIDS.
HAPPY BIRTHDAY, PUMPKIN TWIZZLE!
THIS WAS SO NOT WHAT I WISHED FOR.
YOU TOTALLY CAPTURED MY PHYSIQUE, TOO, AURORA MUFFIN!
THANK YOU!
STAY BACK EVERYONE
EVERYPONY ELSE GOT AWAY, EXCEPT FOR US.
ALSO, EXCELLENT USE OF MACARONI, JAVA BOLT.
IT'S MY MEDIUM OF CHOICE.
NOM NOM NOM

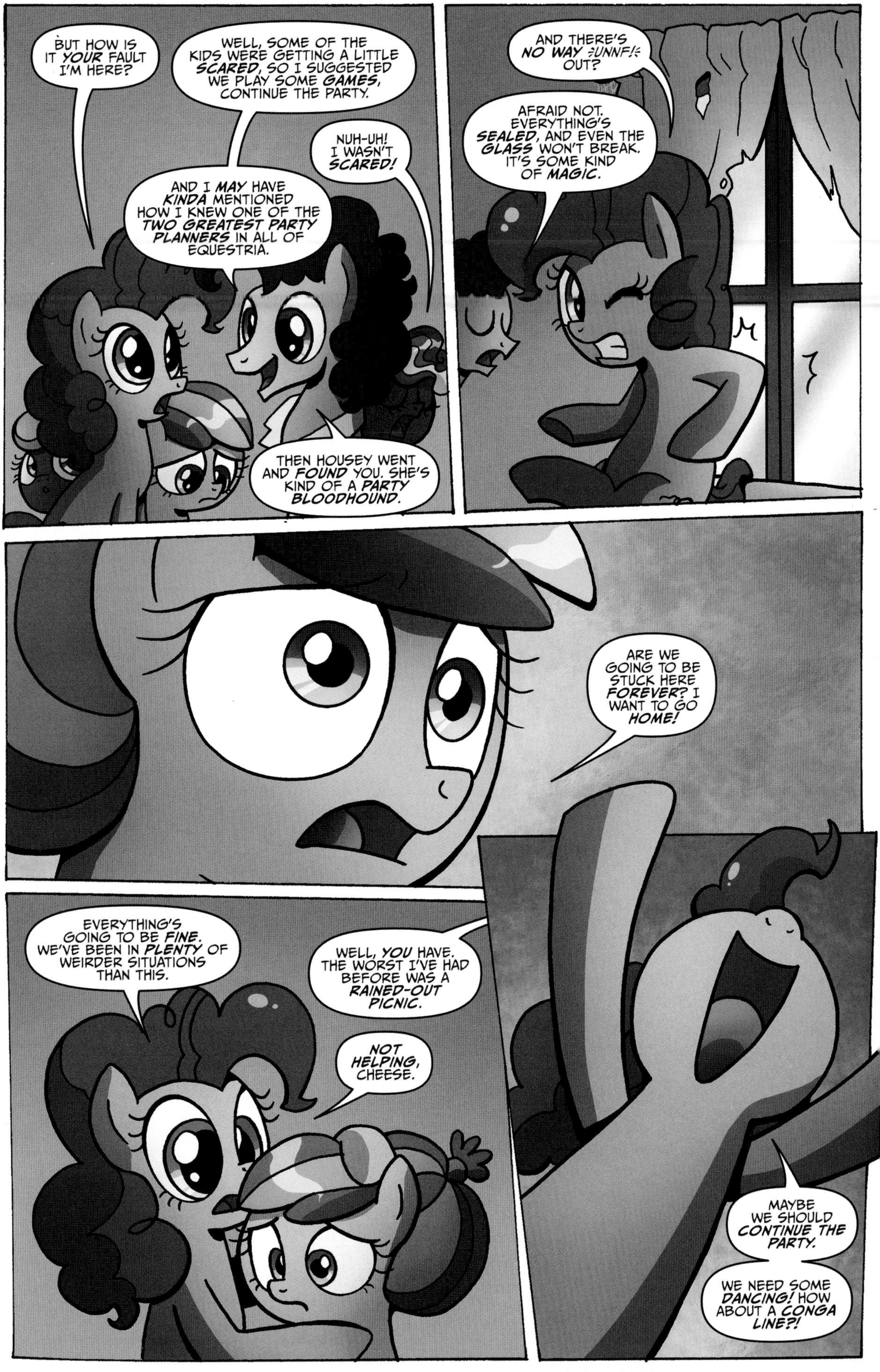

BUT HOW IS IT *YOUR* FAULT I'M HERE?
WELL, SOME OF THE KIDS WERE GETTING A LITTLE *SCARED*, SO I SUGGESTED WE PLAY SOME *GAMES*, CONTINUE THE PARTY.
NUH-UH! I WASN'T *SCARED!*
AND I *MAY* HAVE *KINDA* MENTIONED HOW I KNEW ONE OF THE *TWO GREATEST PARTY PLANNERS* IN ALL OF EQUESTRIA.
THEN HOUSEY WENT AND *FOUND* YOU. SHE'S KIND OF A *PARTY BLOODHOUND*.
AND THERE'S *NO WAY* ~UNNF!~ OUT?
AFRAID NOT. EVERYTHING'S *SEALED*, AND EVEN THE *GLASS* WON'T BREAK. IT'S SOME KIND OF *MAGIC*.
ARE WE GOING TO BE STUCK HERE *FOREVER?* I WANT TO GO *HOME!*
EVERYTHING'S GOING TO BE *FINE*. WE'VE BEEN IN *PLENTY* OF WEIRDER SITUATIONS THAN THIS.
WELL, *YOU* HAVE. THE WORST I'VE HAD BEFORE WAS A *RAINED-OUT PICNIC*.
NOT HELPING, CHEESE.
MAYBE WE SHOULD *CONTINUE THE PARTY*.
WE NEED SOME *DANCING!* HOW ABOUT A *CONGA LINE?!*

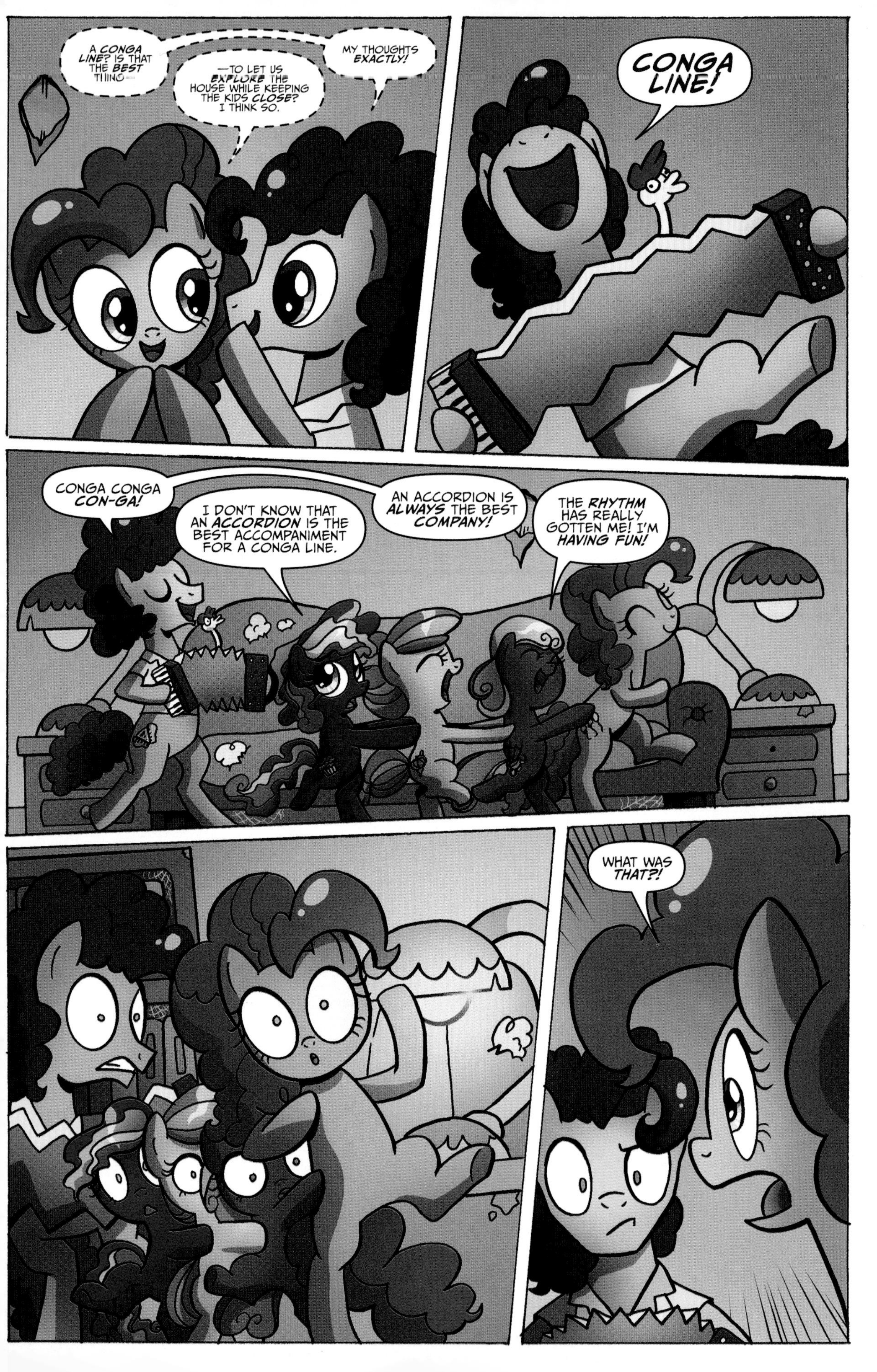
A CONGA LINE? IS THAT THE BEST THING—
—TO LET US EXPLORE THE HOUSE WHILE KEEPING THE KIDS CLOSE? I THINK SO.
MY THOUGHTS EXACTLY!
CONGA LINE!
CONGA CONGA CON-GA!
I DON'T KNOW THAT AN ACCORDION IS THE BEST ACCOMPANIMENT FOR A CONGA LINE.
AN ACCORDION IS ALWAYS THE BEST COMPANY!
THE RHYTHM HAS REALLY GOTTEN ME! I'M HAVING FUN!
WHAT WAS THAT?!

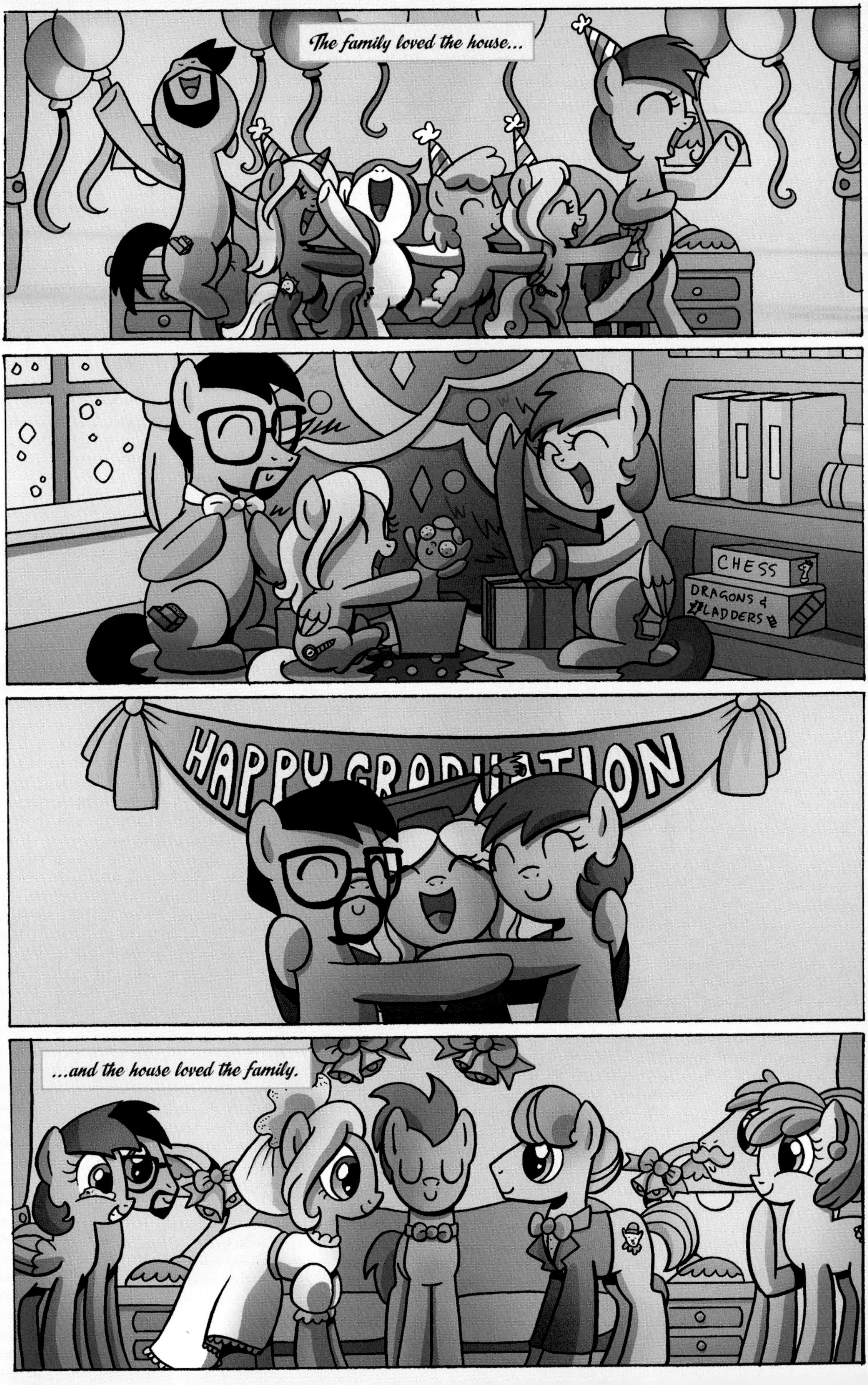
The family loved the house...
CHESS
DRAGONS & LADDERS
HAPPY GRADUATION
...and the house loved the family.

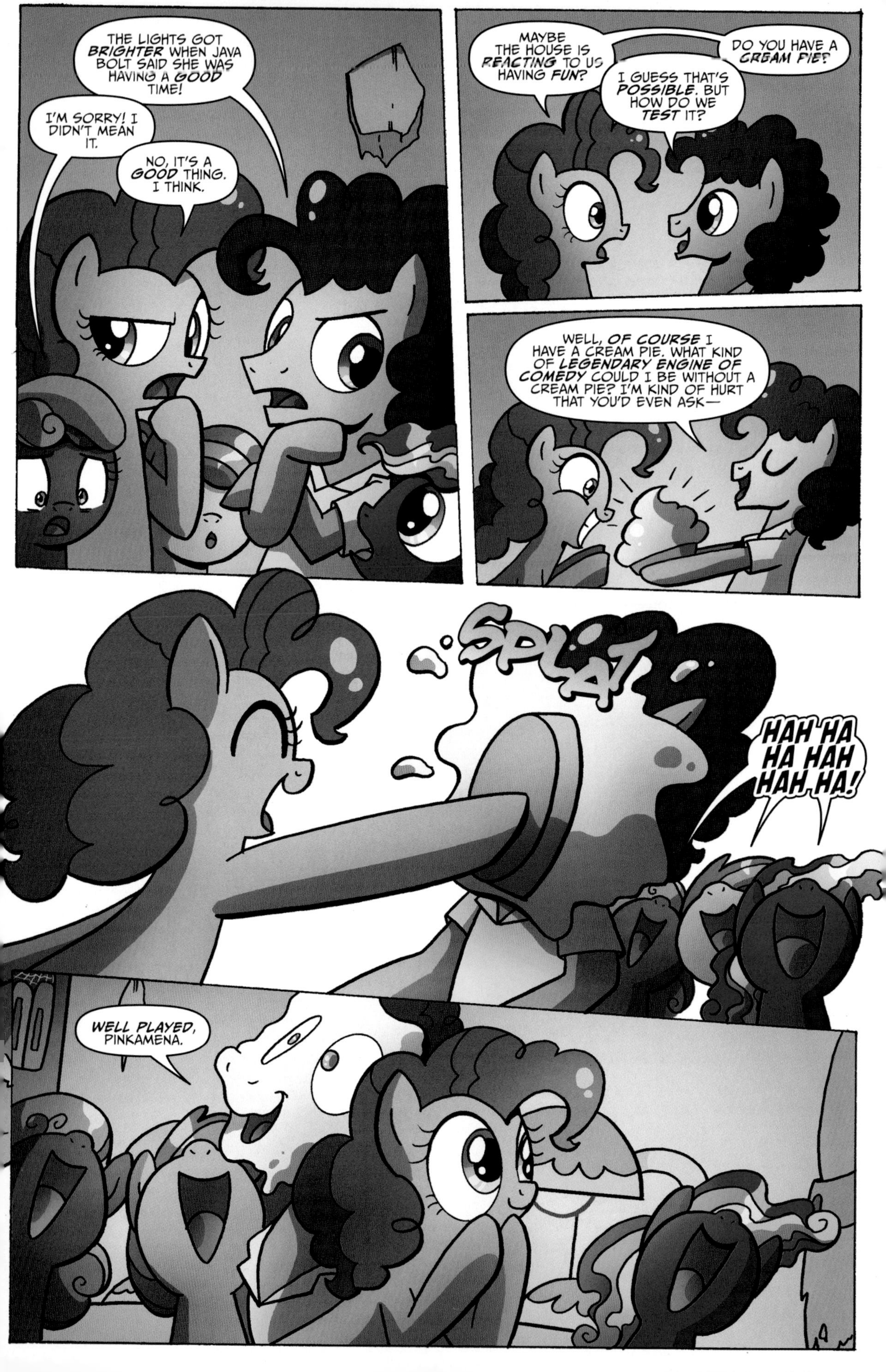

THE LIGHTS GOT BRIGHTER WHEN JAVA BOLT SAID SHE WAS HAVING A GOOD TIME!
I'M SORRY! I DIDN'T MEAN IT.
NO, IT'S A GOOD THING. I THINK.
MAYBE THE HOUSE IS REACTING TO US HAVING FUN?
I GUESS THAT'S POSSIBLE. BUT HOW DO WE TEST IT?
DO YOU HAVE A CREAM PIE?
WELL, OF COURSE I HAVE A CREAM PIE. WHAT KIND OF LEGENDARY ENGINE OF COMEDY COULD I BE WITHOUT A CREAM PIE? I'M KIND OF HURT THAT YOU'D EVEN ASK—
SPLAT
HAH HA HA HAH HAH HA!
WELL PLAYED, PINKAMENA.

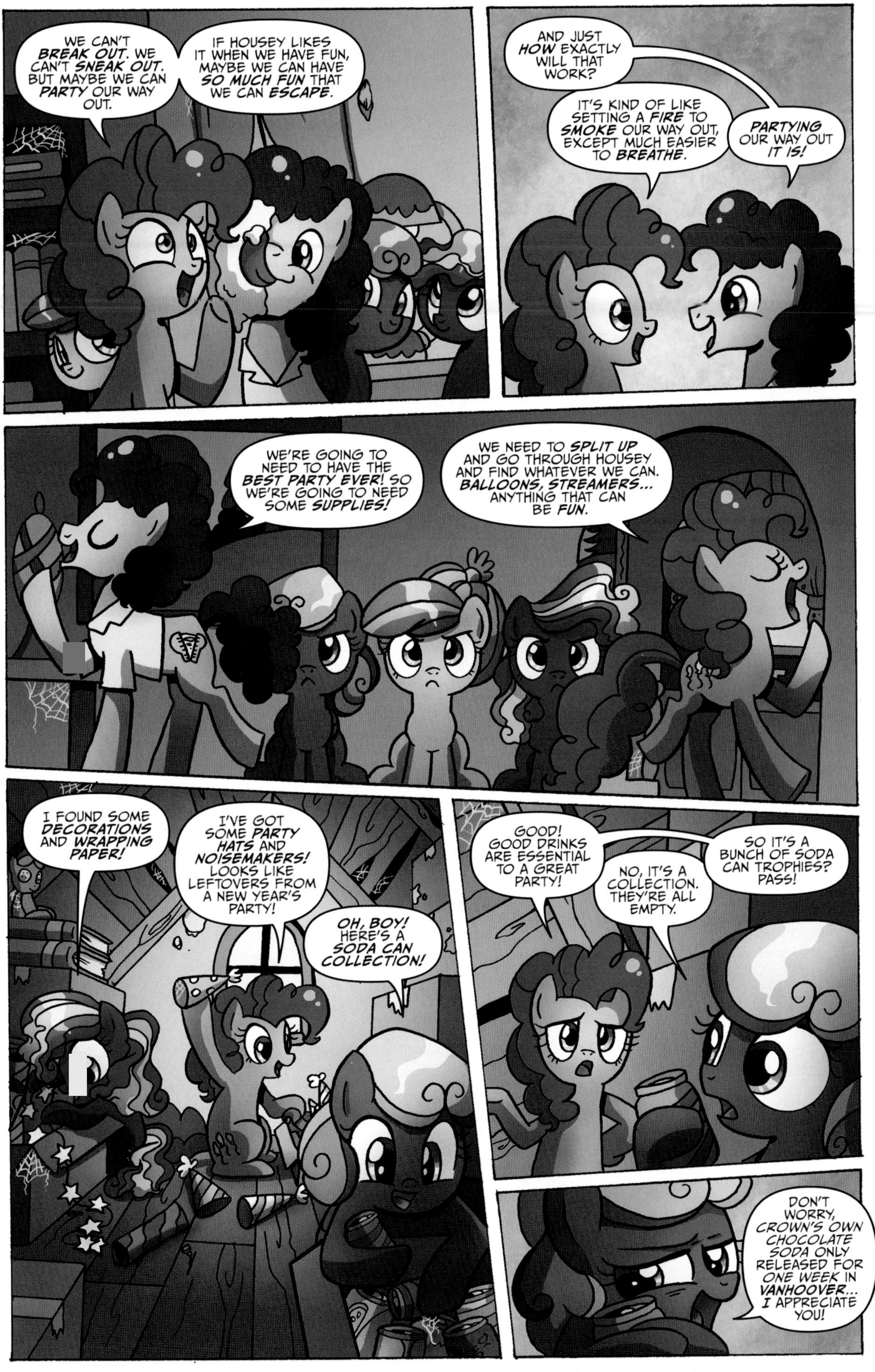
WE CAN'T BREAK OUT. WE CAN'T SNEAK OUT. BUT MAYBE WE CAN PARTY OUR WAY OUT.
IF HOUSEY LIKES IT WHEN WE HAVE FUN, MAYBE WE CAN HAVE SO MUCH FUN THAT WE CAN ESCAPE.
AND JUST HOW EXACTLY WILL THAT WORK?
IT'S KIND OF LIKE SETTING A FIRE TO SMOKE OUR WAY OUT, EXCEPT MUCH EASIER TO BREATHE.
PARTYING OUR WAY OUT IT IS!
WE'RE GOING TO NEED TO HAVE THE BEST PARTY EVER! SO WE'RE GOING TO NEED SOME SUPPLIES!
WE NEED TO SPLIT UP AND GO THROUGH HOUSEY AND FIND WHATEVER WE CAN. BALLOONS, STREAMERS... ANYTHING THAT CAN BE FUN.
I FOUND SOME DECORATIONS AND WRAPPING PAPER!
I'VE GOT SOME PARTY HATS AND NOISEMAKERS! LOOKS LIKE LEFTOVERS FROM A NEW YEAR'S PARTY!
OH, BOY! HERE'S A SODA CAN COLLECTION!
GOOD! GOOD DRINKS ARE ESSENTIAL TO A GREAT PARTY!
NO, IT'S A COLLECTION. THEY'RE ALL EMPTY.
SO IT'S A BUNCH OF SODA CAN TROPHIES? PASS!
DON'T WORRY, CROWN'S OWN CHOCOLATE SODA ONLY RELEASED FOR ONE WEEK IN VANHOOVER... I APPRECIATE YOU!

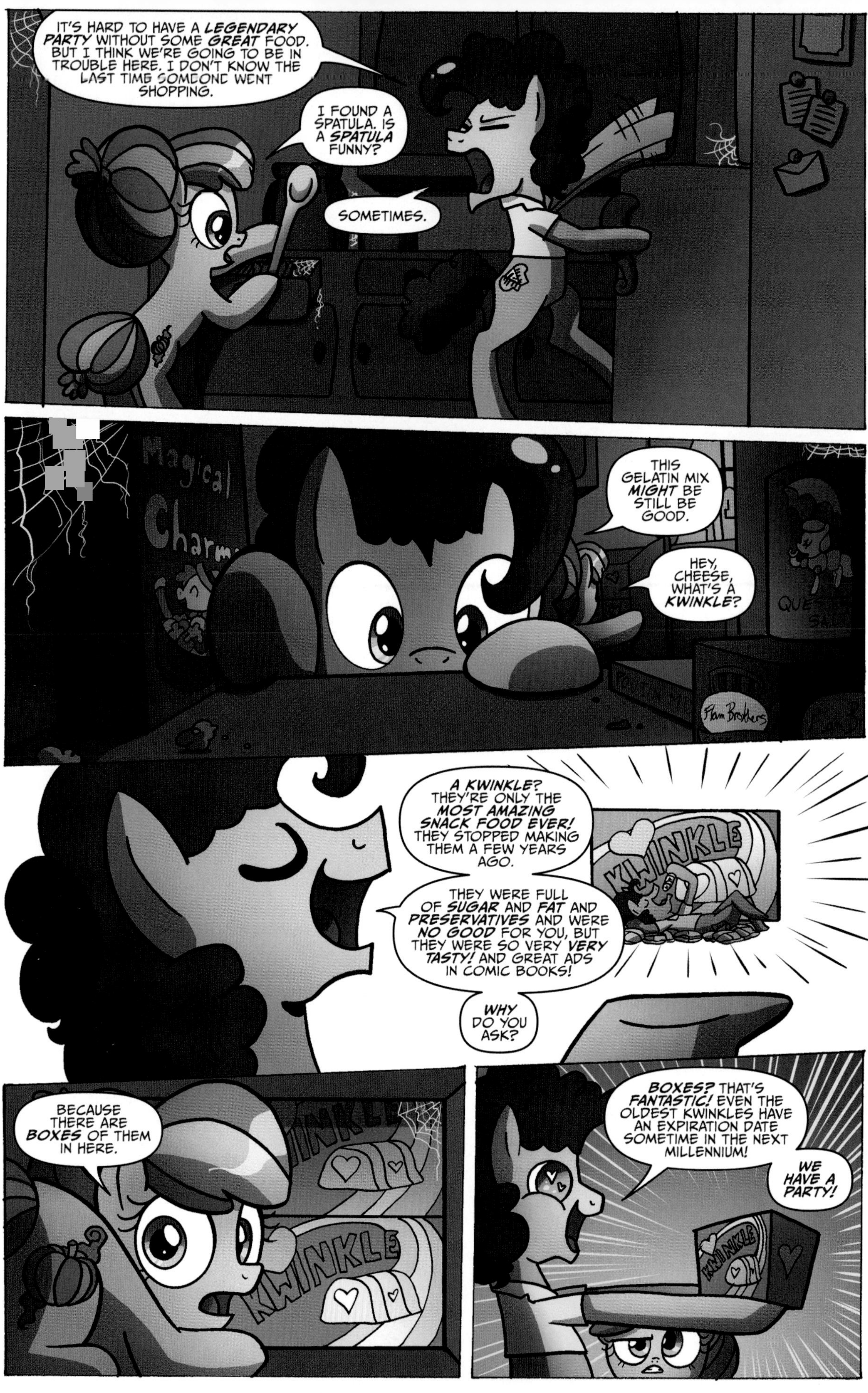

IT'S HARD TO HAVE A LEGENDARY PARTY WITHOUT SOME GREAT FOOD. BUT I THINK WE'RE GOING TO BE IN TROUBLE HERE. I DON'T KNOW THE LAST TIME SOMEONE WENT SHOPPING.
I FOUND A SPATULA. IS A SPATULA FUNNY?
SOMETIMES.
Magical Charm
THIS GELATIN MIX MIGHT BE STILL BE GOOD.
HEY, CHEESE, WHAT'S A KWINKLE?
Flam Brothers
A KWINKLE? THEY'RE ONLY THE MOST AMAZING SNACK FOOD EVER! THEY STOPPED MAKING THEM A FEW YEARS AGO.
KWINKLE
THEY WERE FULL OF SUGAR AND FAT AND PRESERVATIVES AND WERE NO GOOD FOR YOU, BUT THEY WERE SO VERY VERY TASTY! AND GREAT ADS IN COMIC BOOKS!
WHY DO YOU ASK?
BECAUSE THERE ARE BOXES OF THEM IN HERE.
KWINKLE
BOXES? THAT'S FANTASTIC! EVEN THE OLDEST KWINKLES HAVE AN EXPIRATION DATE SOMETIME IN THE NEXT MILLENNIUM!
WE HAVE A PARTY!
KWINKLE

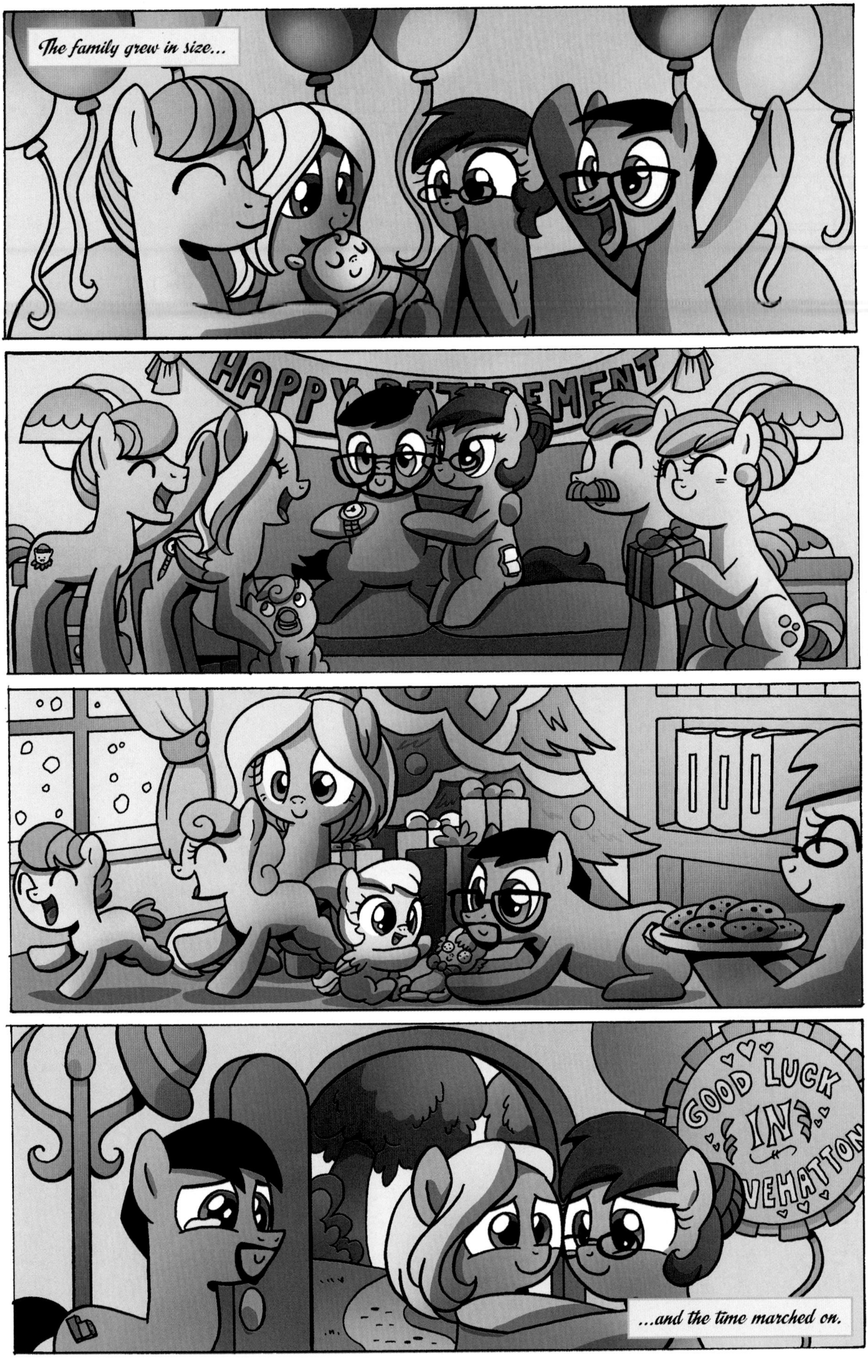
The family grew in size...
HAPPY
GOOD LUCK IN
...and the time marched on.

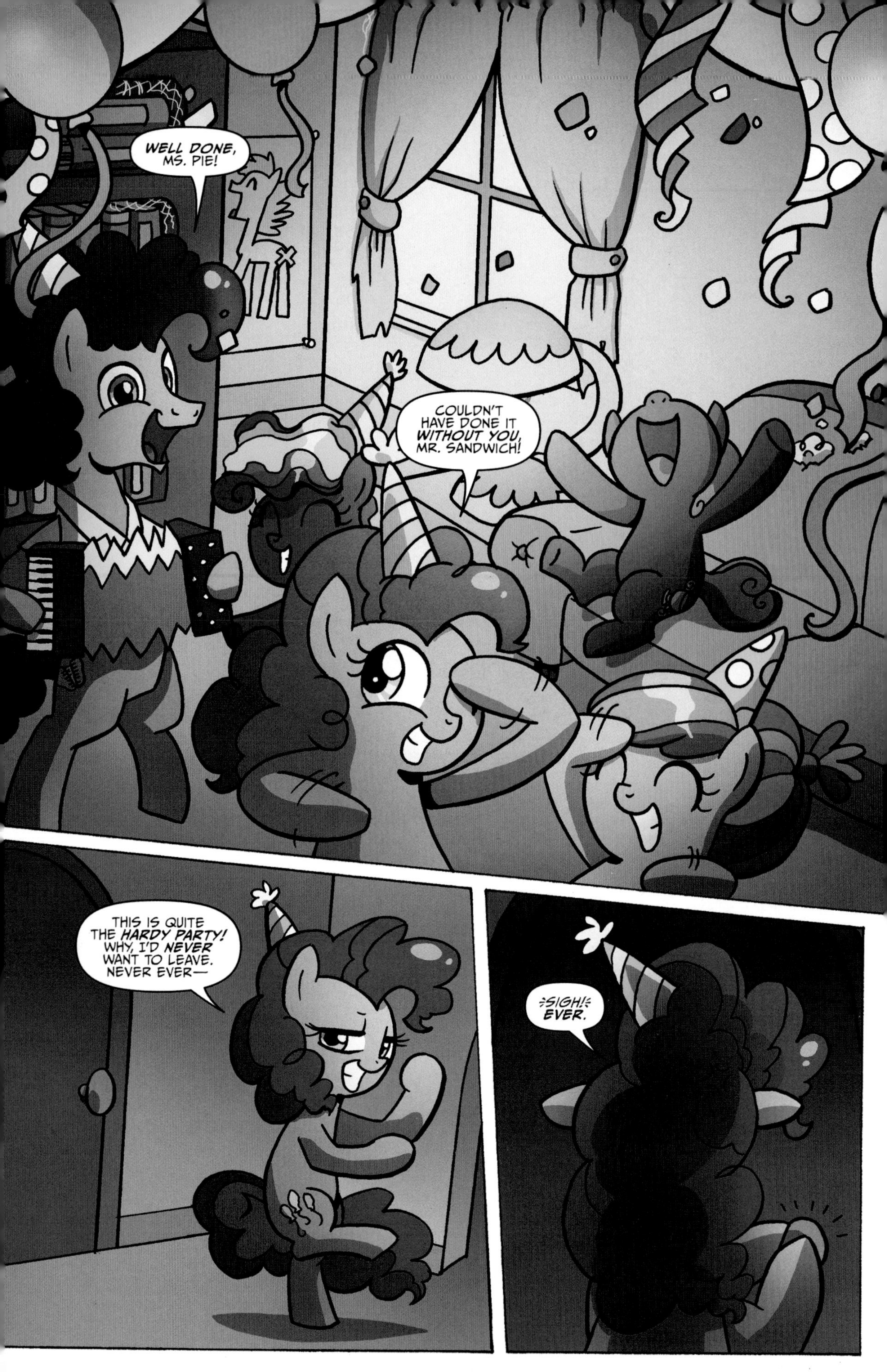
WELL DONE, MS. PIE!
COULDN'T HAVE DONE IT WITHOUT YOU, MR. SANDWICH!
THIS IS QUITE THE HARDY PARTY! WHY, I'D NEVER WANT TO LEAVE. NEVER EVER—
SIGH! EVER.

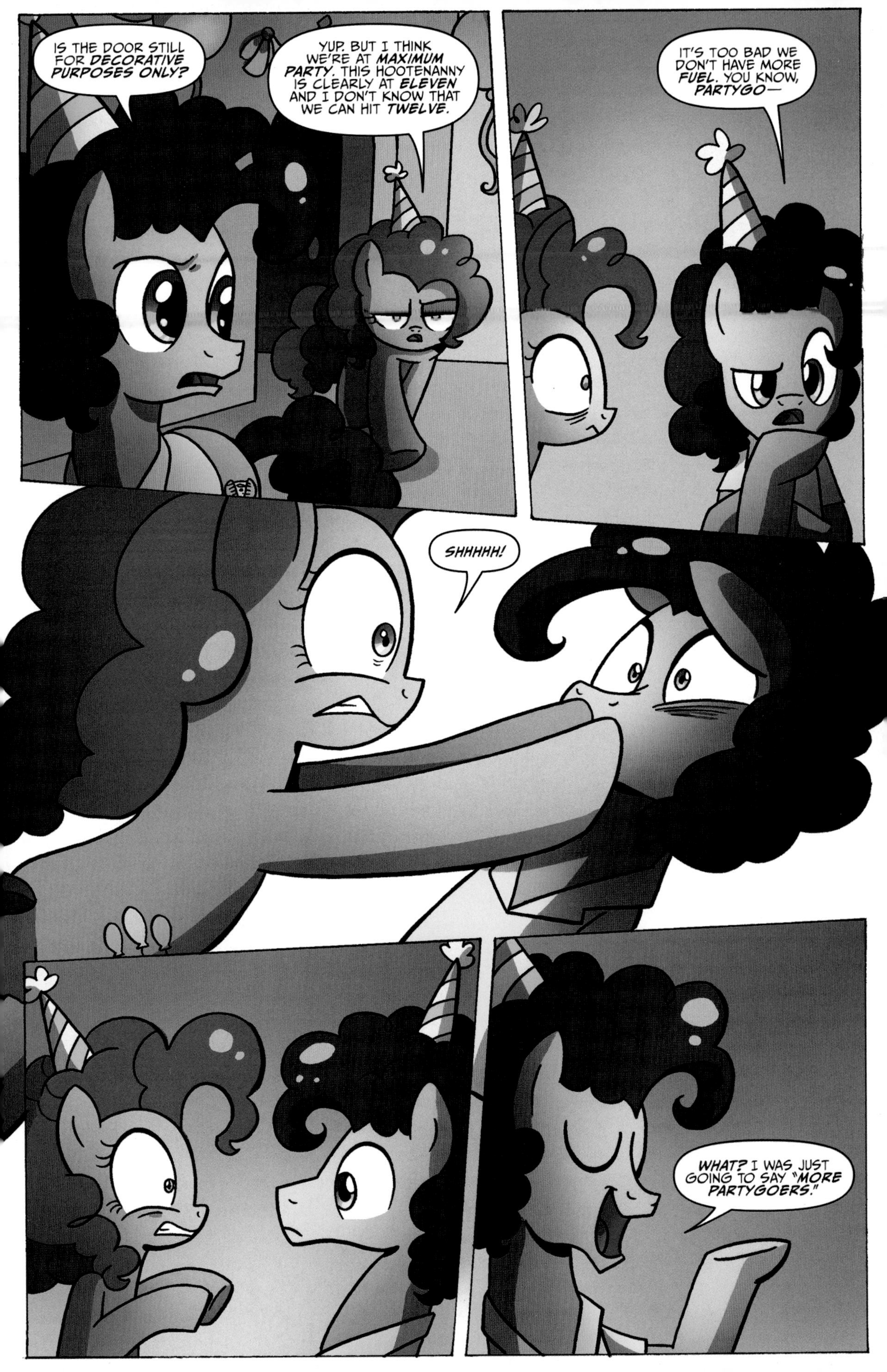
IS THE DOOR STILL FOR DECORATIVE PURPOSES ONLY?
YUP. BUT I THINK WE'RE AT MAXIMUM PARTY. THIS HOOTENANNY IS CLEARLY AT ELEVEN AND I DON'T KNOW THAT WE CAN HIT TWELVE.
IT'S TOO BAD WE DON'T HAVE MORE FUEL. YOU KNOW, PARTYGO—
SHHHHH!
WHAT? I WAS JUST GOING TO SAY "MORE PARTYGOERS."

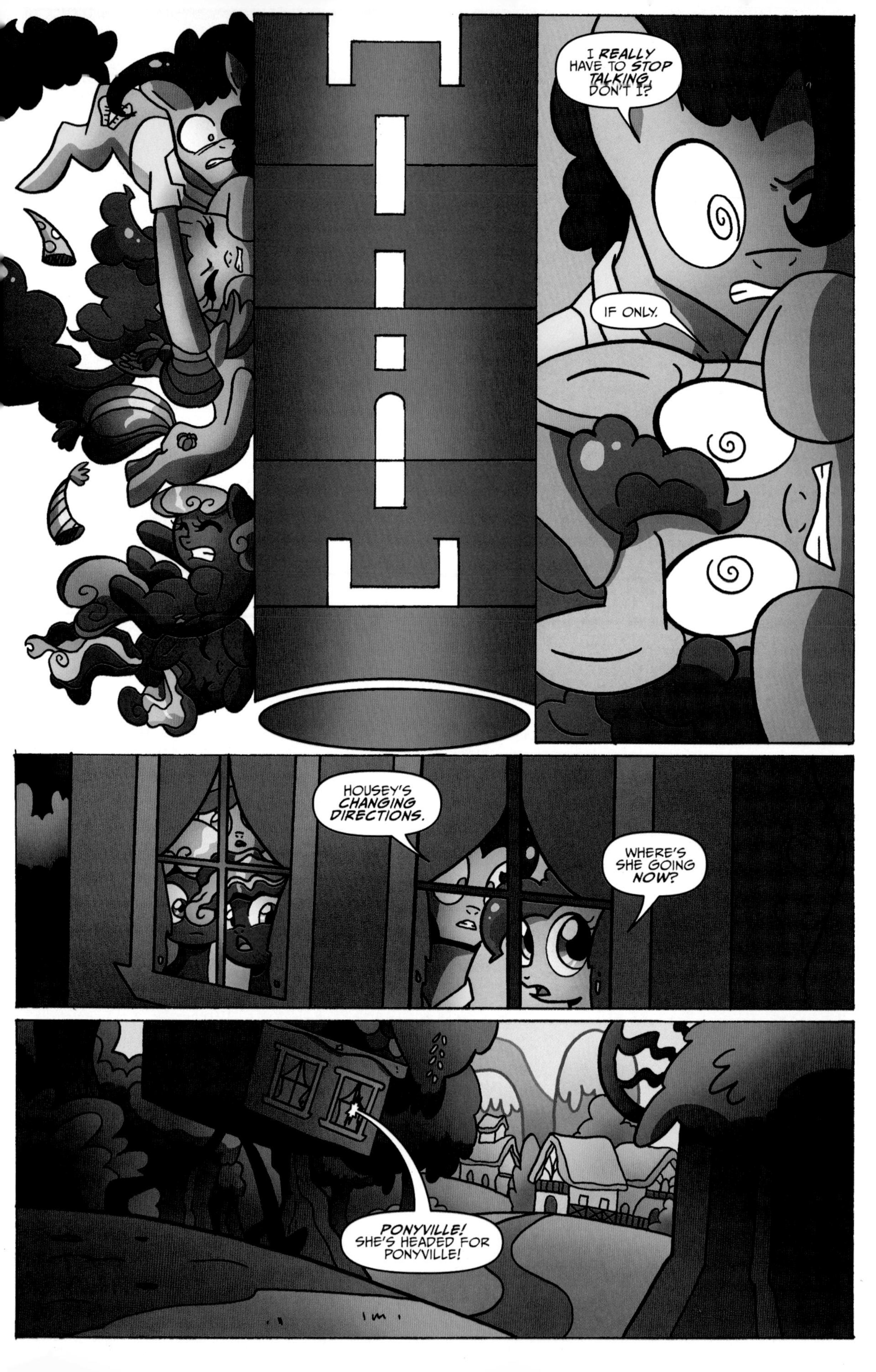
I REALLY HAVE TO STOP TALKING, DON'T I?
IF ONLY.
HOUSEY'S CHANGING DIRECTIONS.
WHERE'S SHE GOING NOW?
PONYVILLE! SHE'S HEADED FOR PONYVILLE!

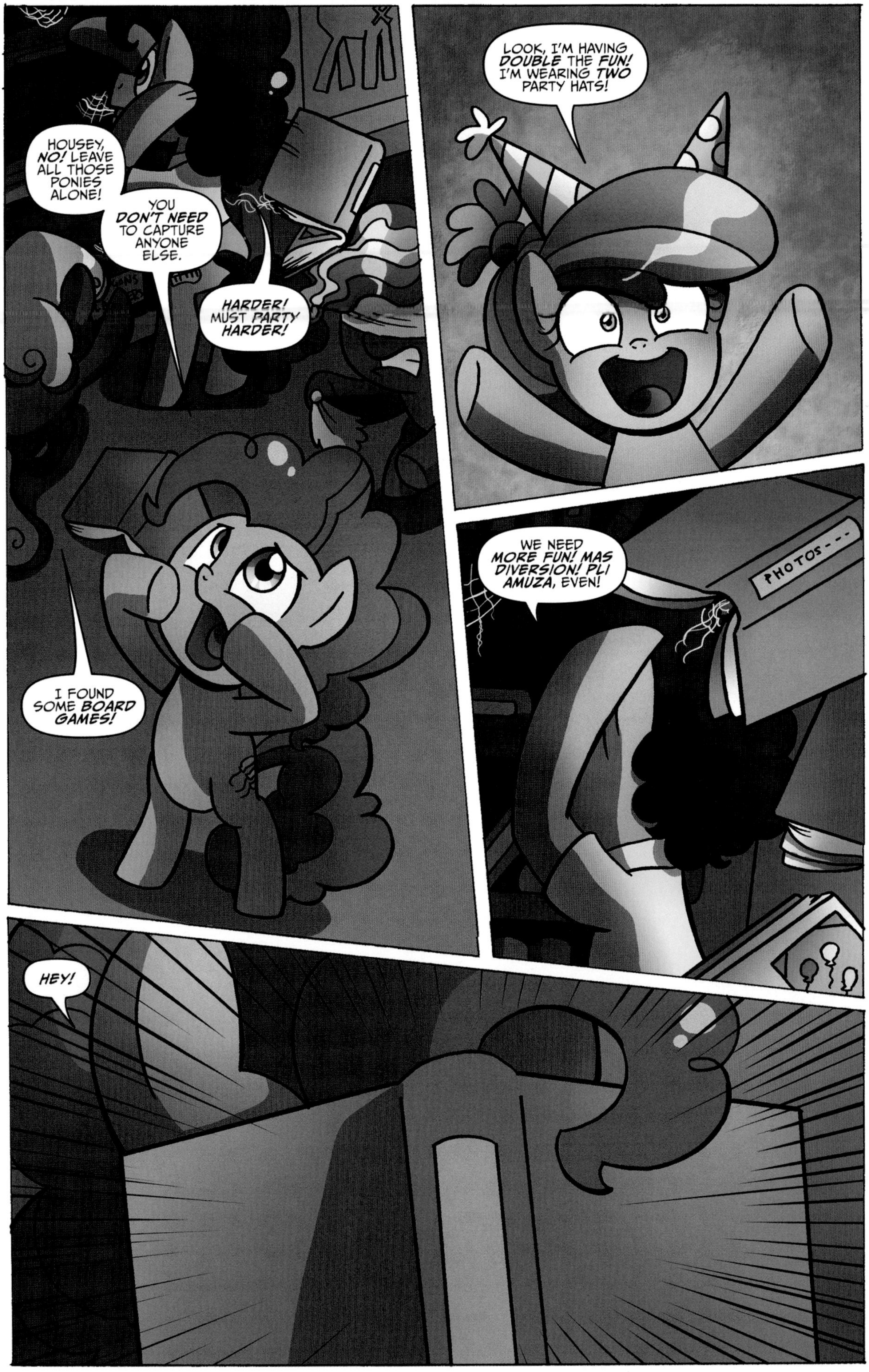
HOUSEY, NO! LEAVE ALL THOSE PONIES ALONE!
YOU DON'T NEED TO CAPTURE ANYONE ELSE.
HARDER! MUST PARTY HARDER!
LOOK, I'M HAVING DOUBLE THE FUN! I'M WEARING TWO PARTY HATS!
I FOUND SOME BOARD GAMES!
WE NEED MORE FUN! MAS DIVERSION! PLI AMUZA, EVEN!
PHOTOS
HEY!

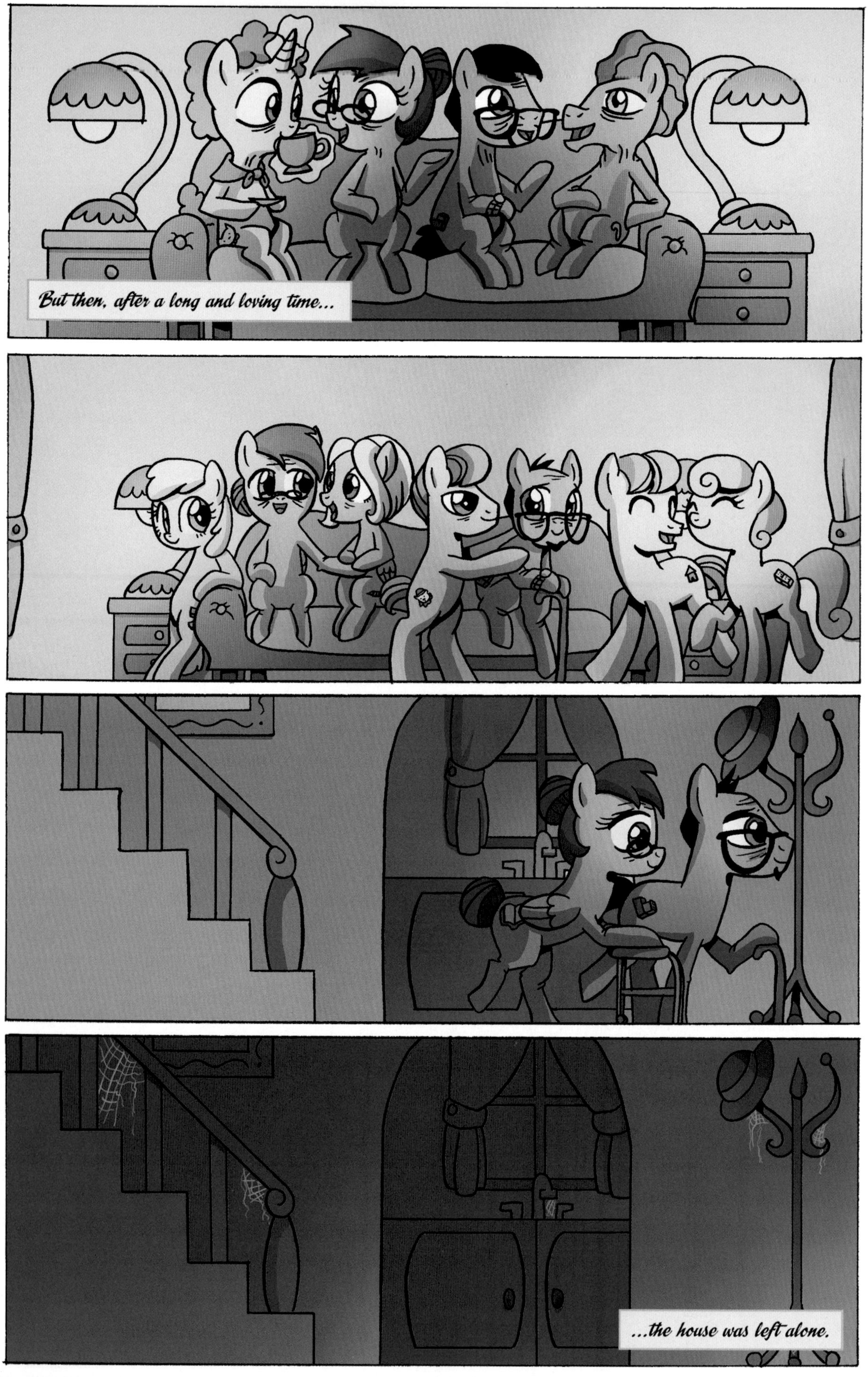
But then, after a long and loving time...
...the house was left alone.

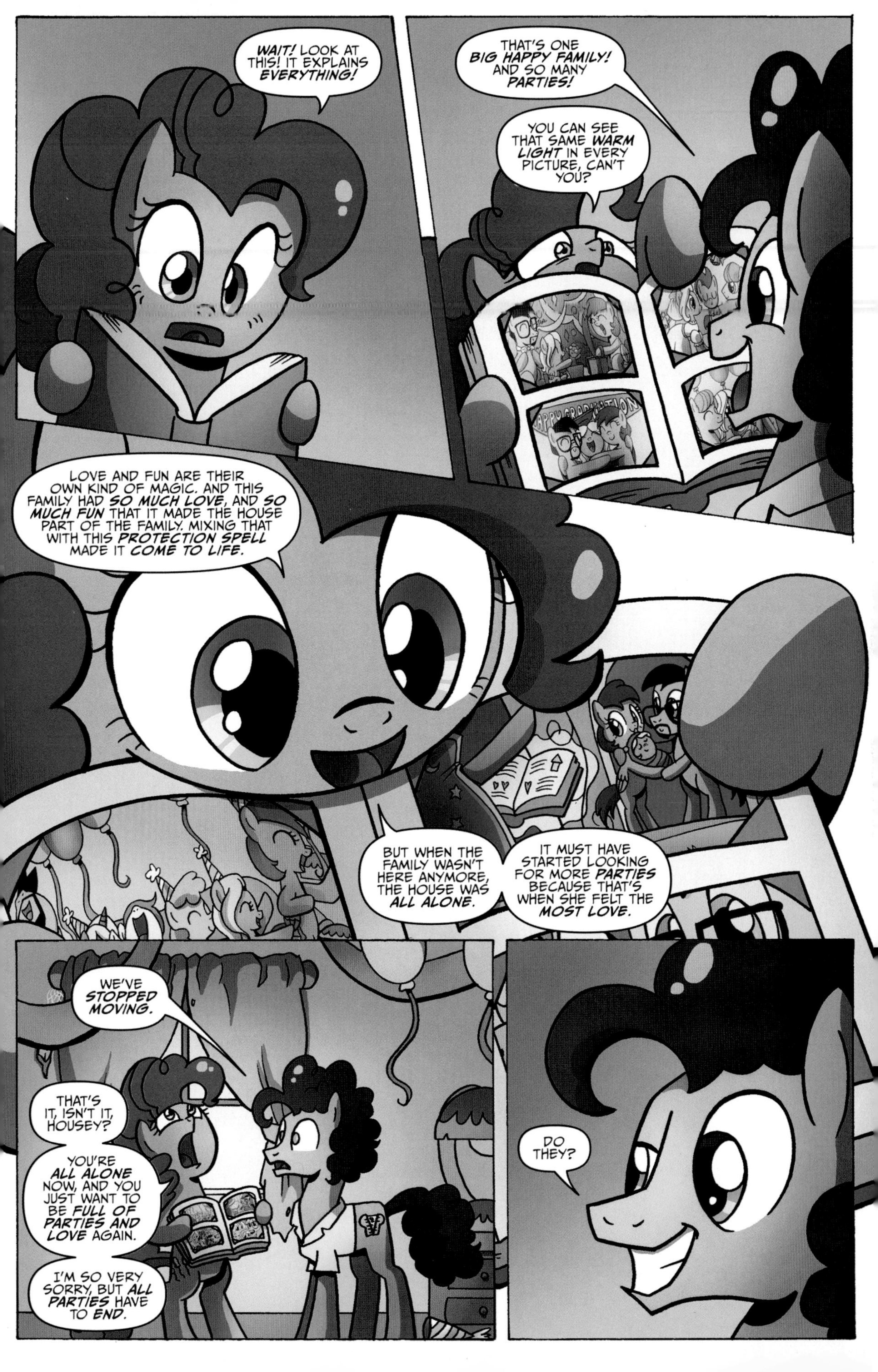
WAIT! LOOK AT THIS! IT EXPLAINS EVERYTHING!
THAT'S ONE BIG HAPPY FAMILY! AND SO MANY PARTIES!
YOU CAN SEE THAT SAME WARM LIGHT IN EVERY PICTURE, CAN'T YOU?
LOVE AND FUN ARE THEIR OWN KIND OF MAGIC. AND THIS FAMILY HAD SO MUCH LOVE, AND SO MUCH FUN THAT IT MADE THE HOUSE PART OF THE FAMILY. MIXING THAT WITH THIS PROTECTION SPELL MADE IT COME TO LIFE.
BUT WHEN THE FAMILY WASN'T HERE ANYMORE, THE HOUSE WAS ALL ALONE.
IT MUST HAVE STARTED LOOKING FOR MORE PARTIES BECAUSE THAT'S WHEN SHE FELT THE MOST LOVE.
WE'VE STOPPED MOVING.
THAT'S IT, ISN'T IT, HOUSEY?
YOU'RE ALL ALONE NOW, AND YOU JUST WANT TO BE FULL OF PARTIES AND LOVE AGAIN.
I'M SO VERY SORRY, BUT ALL PARTIES HAVE TO END.
DO THEY?

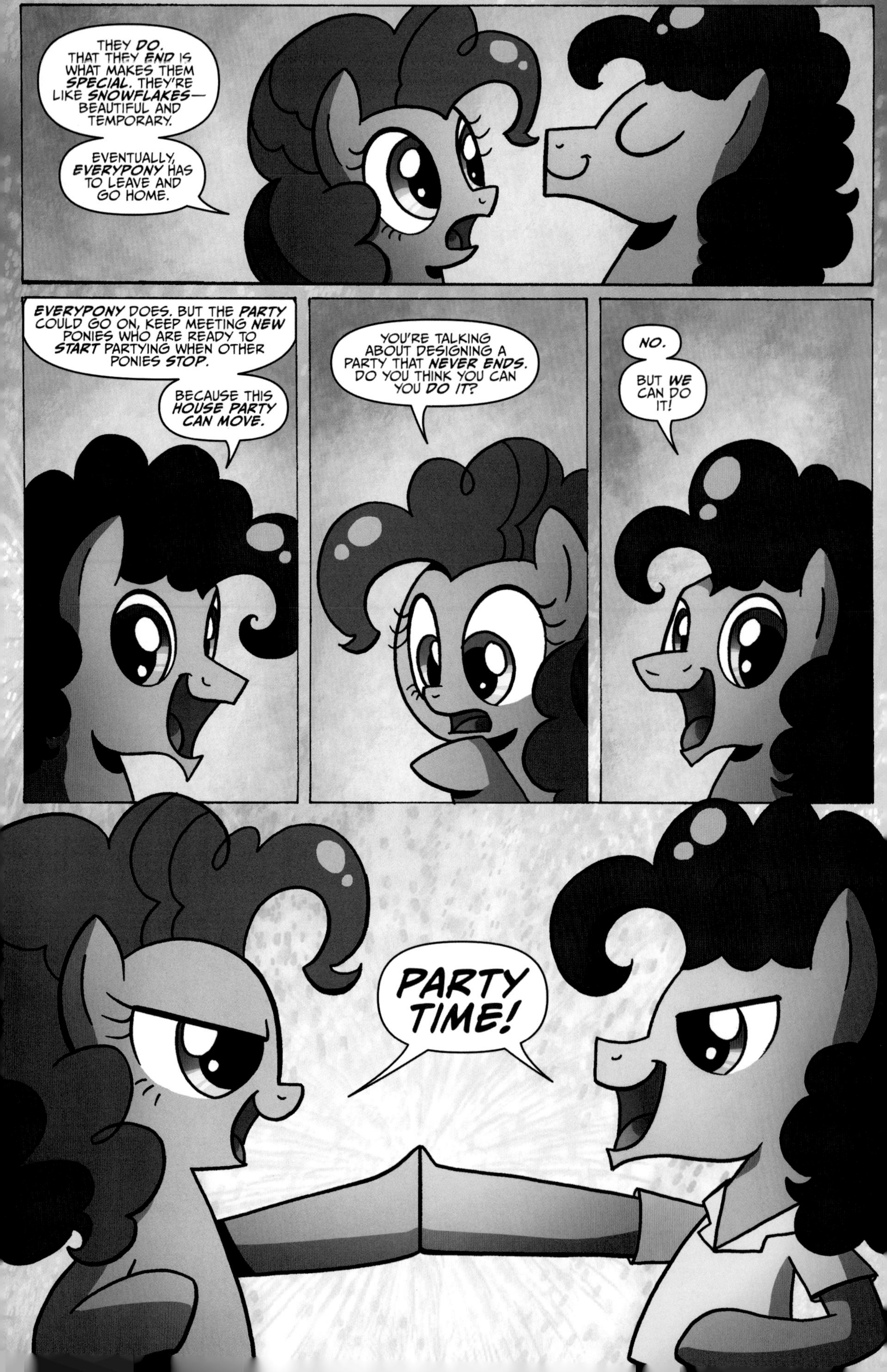
THEY *DO.* THAT THEY *END* IS WHAT MAKES THEM *SPECIAL.* THEY'RE LIKE *SNOWFLAKES*— BEAUTIFUL AND TEMPORARY.
EVENTUALLY, *EVERYPONY* HAS TO LEAVE AND GO HOME.
EVERYPONY DOES. BUT THE *PARTY* COULD GO ON, KEEP MEETING *NEW* PONIES WHO ARE READY TO *START* PARTYING WHEN OTHER PONIES *STOP.*
BECAUSE THIS *HOUSE PARTY CAN MOVE.*
YOU'RE TALKING ABOUT DESIGNING A PARTY THAT *NEVER ENDS.* DO YOU THINK YOU CAN YOU *DO IT?*
NO.
BUT *WE* CAN DO IT!
PARTY TIME!

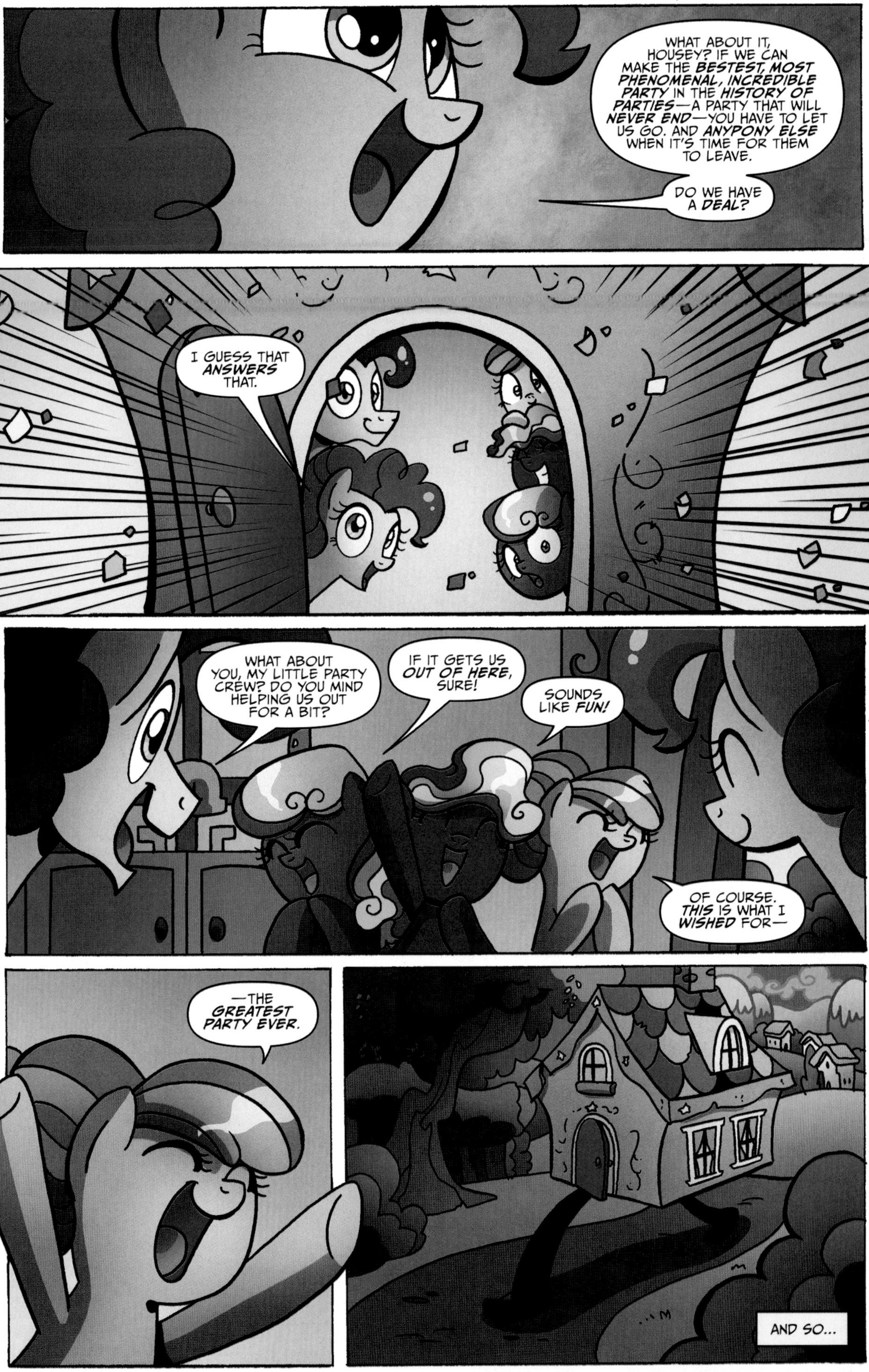
WHAT ABOUT IT, HOUSEY? IF WE CAN MAKE THE BESTEST, MOST PHENOMENAL, INCREDIBLE PARTY IN THE HISTORY OF PARTIES—A PARTY THAT WILL NEVER END—YOU HAVE TO LET US GO. AND ANYPONY ELSE WHEN IT'S TIME FOR THEM TO LEAVE.
DO WE HAVE A DEAL?
I GUESS THAT ANSWERS THAT.
WHAT ABOUT YOU, MY LITTLE PARTY CREW? DO YOU MIND HELPING US OUT FOR A BIT?
IF IT GETS US OUT OF HERE, SURE!
SOUNDS LIKE FUN!
OF COURSE. THIS IS WHAT I WISHED FOR—
—THE GREATEST PARTY EVER.
AND SO...

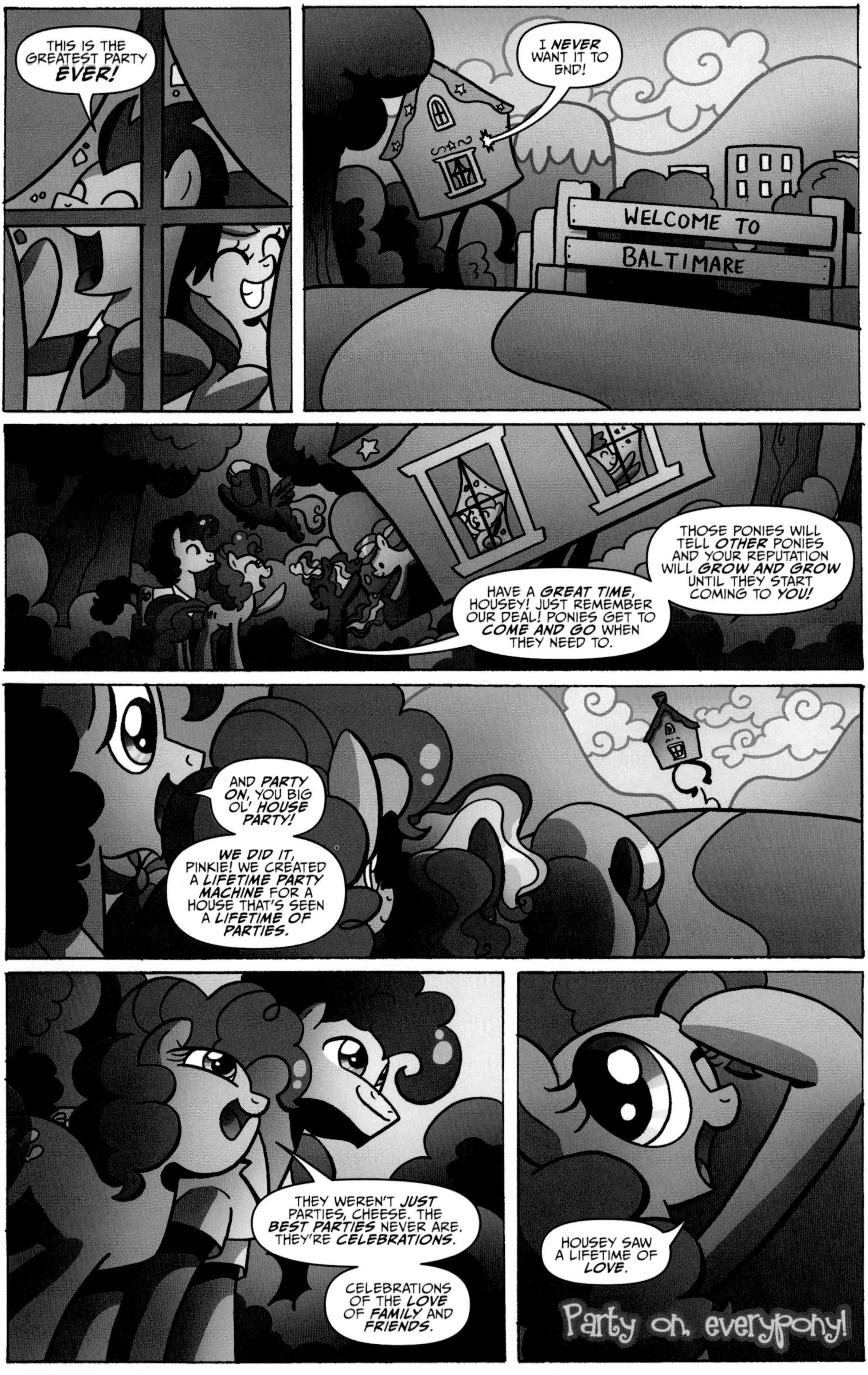

THIS IS THE GREATEST PARTY **EVER!**
I **NEVER** WANT IT TO END!
WELCOME TO BALTIMARE
HAVE A **GREAT TIME**, HOUSEY! JUST REMEMBER OUR DEAL! PONIES GET TO **COME AND GO** WHEN THEY NEED TO.
THOSE PONIES WILL TELL **OTHER** PONIES AND YOUR REPUTATION WILL **GROW AND GROW** UNTIL THEY START COMING TO **YOU!**
AND **PARTY ON**, YOU BIG OL' **HOUSE PARTY!**
WE DID IT, PINKIE! WE CREATED A **LIFETIME PARTY MACHINE** FOR A HOUSE THAT'S SEEN A **LIFETIME OF PARTIES.**
THEY WEREN'T **JUST** PARTIES, CHEESE. THE **BEST PARTIES** NEVER ARE. THEY'RE **CELEBRATIONS**.
CELEBRATIONS OF THE **LOVE** OF **FAMILY** AND **FRIENDS**.
HOUSEY SAW A LIFETIME OF **LOVE**.
Party on, everypony!

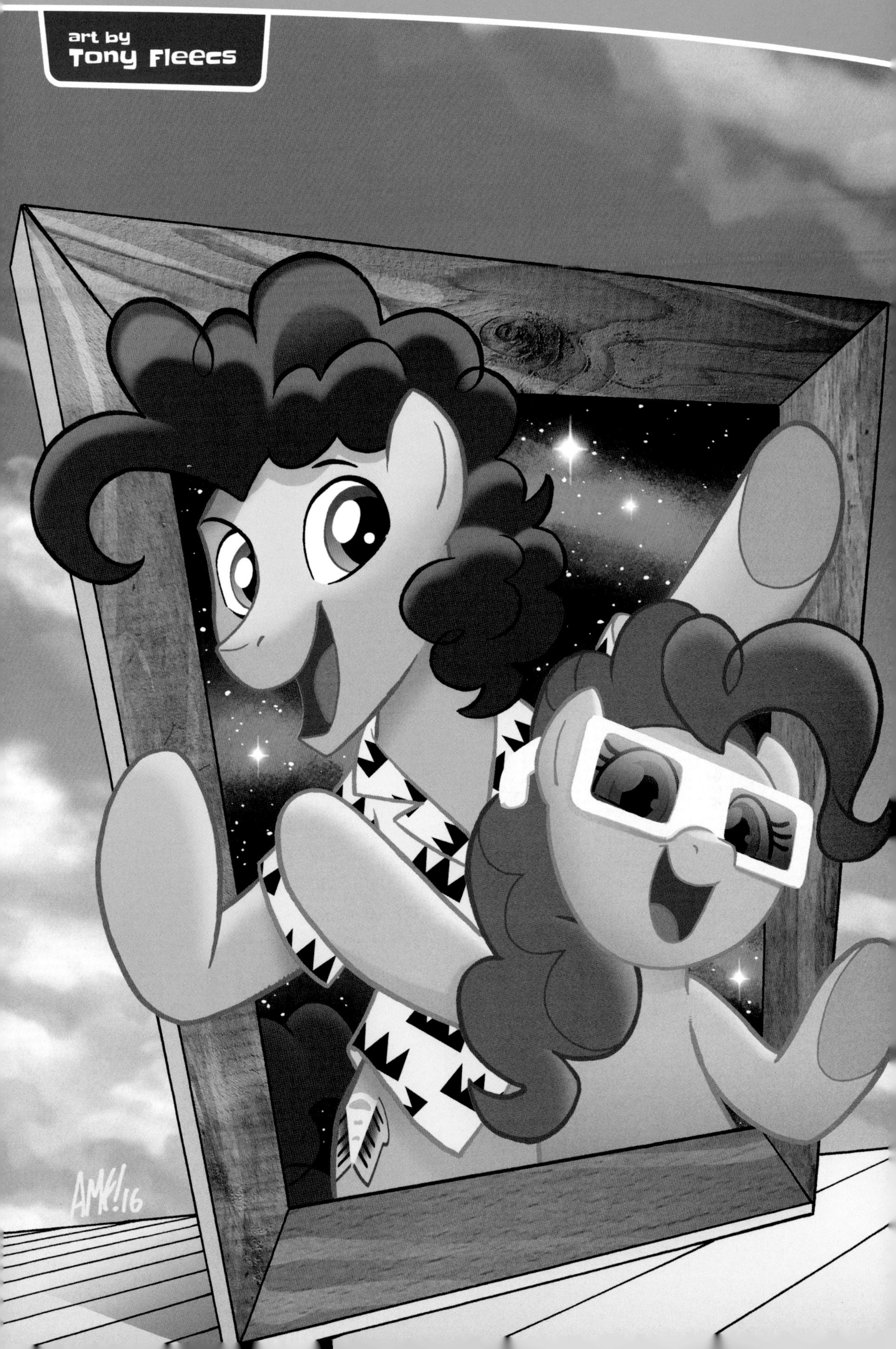

art by
Tony Fleecs

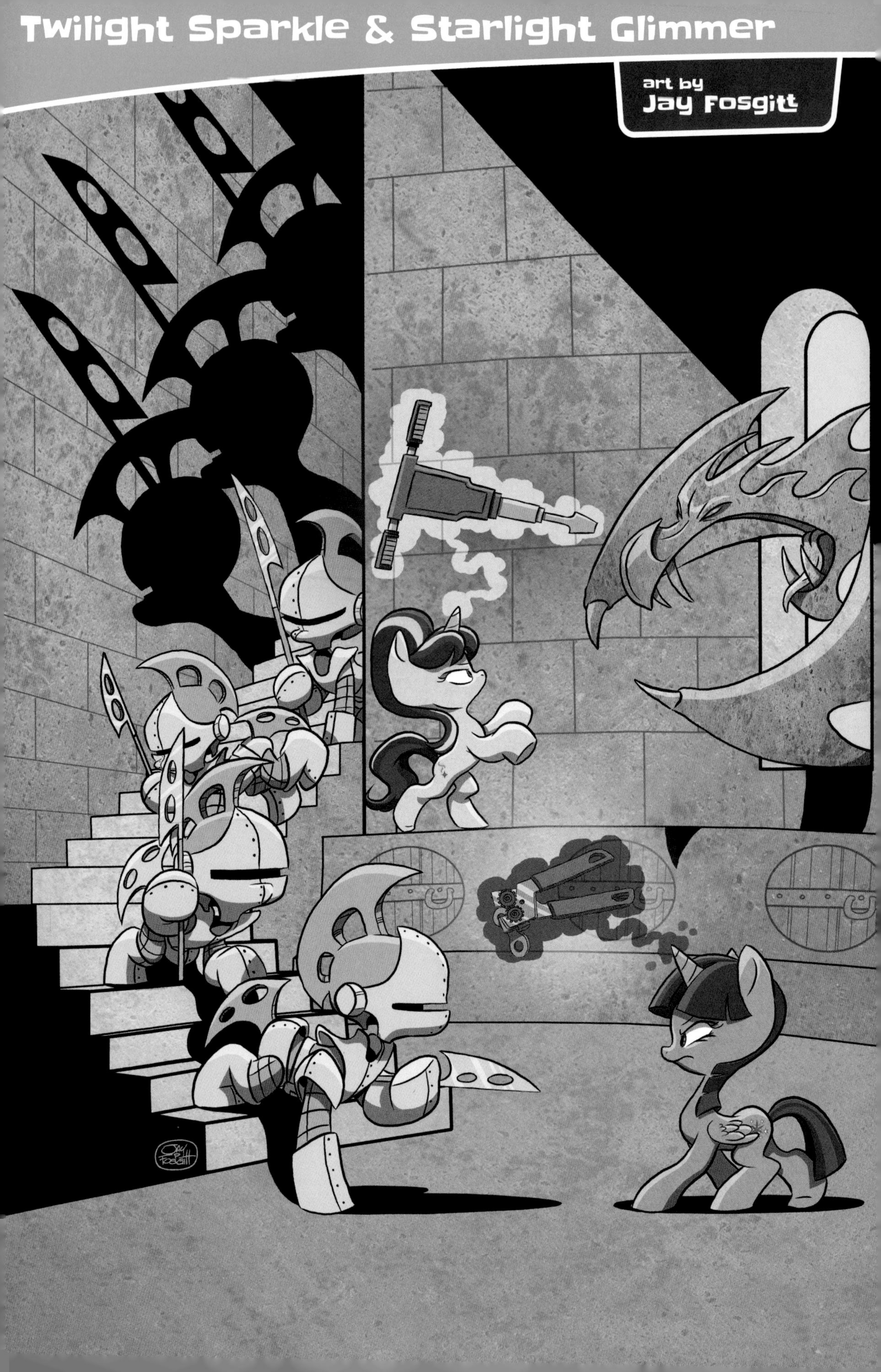
Twilight Sparkle & Starlight Glimmer
art by
Jay Fosgitt

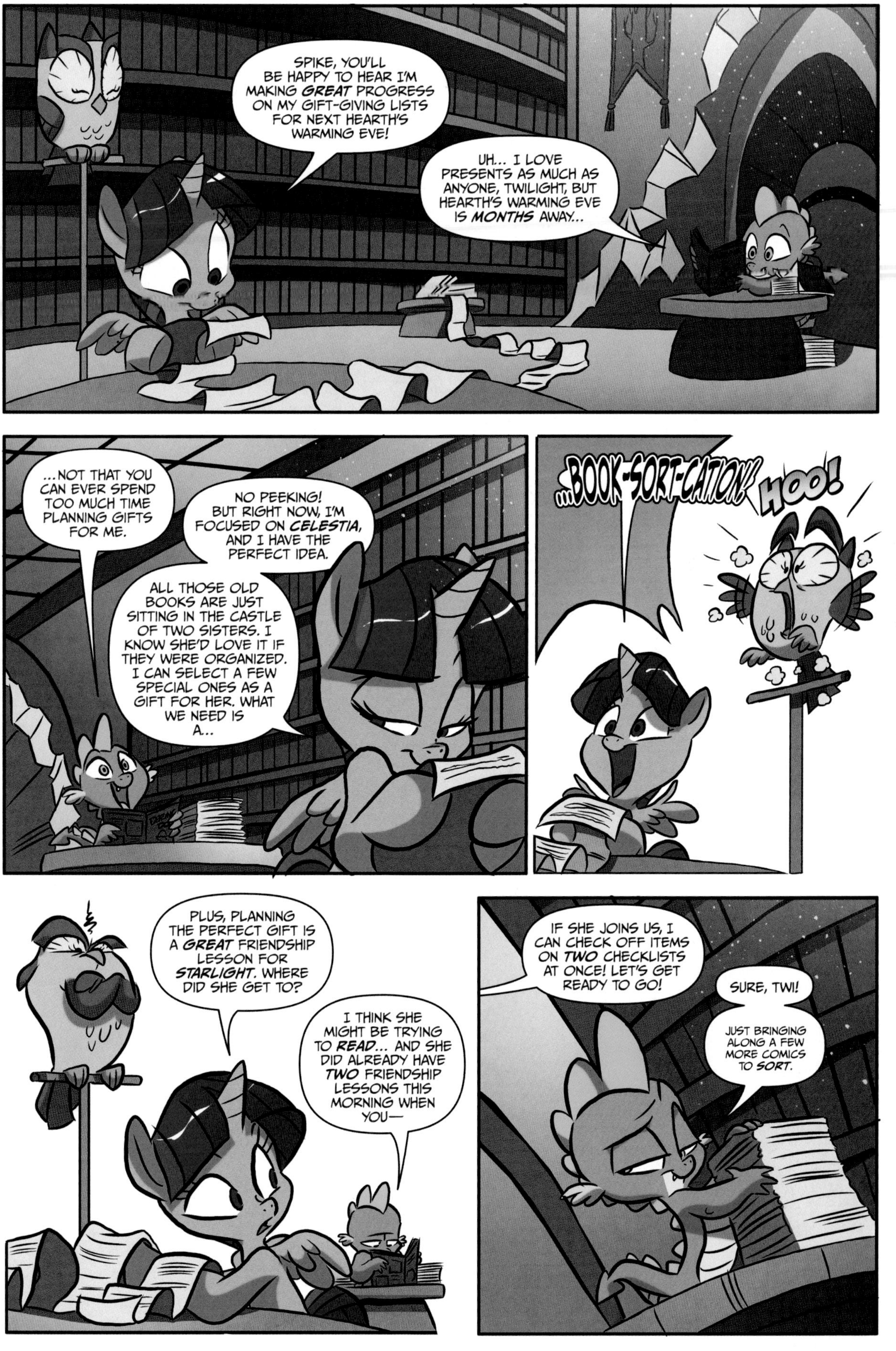

SPIKE, YOU'LL BE HAPPY TO HEAR I'M MAKING GREAT PROGRESS ON MY GIFT-GIVING LISTS FOR NEXT HEARTH'S WARMING EVE!
UH... I LOVE PRESENTS AS MUCH AS ANYONE, TWILIGHT, BUT HEARTH'S WARMING EVE IS MONTHS AWAY...
...NOT THAT YOU CAN EVER SPEND TOO MUCH TIME PLANNING GIFTS FOR ME.
NO PEEKING! BUT RIGHT NOW, I'M FOCUSED ON CELESTIA, AND I HAVE THE PERFECT IDEA.
ALL THOSE OLD BOOKS ARE JUST SITTING IN THE CASTLE OF TWO SISTERS. I KNOW SHE'D LOVE IT IF THEY WERE ORGANIZED. I CAN SELECT A FEW SPECIAL ONES AS A GIFT FOR HER. WHAT WE NEED IS A...
...BOOK-SORT-CATION!
HOO!
PLUS, PLANNING THE PERFECT GIFT IS A GREAT FRIENDSHIP LESSON FOR STARLIGHT. WHERE DID SHE GET TO?
I THINK SHE MIGHT BE TRYING TO READ... AND SHE DID ALREADY HAVE TWO FRIENDSHIP LESSONS THIS MORNING WHEN YOU—
IF SHE JOINS US, I CAN CHECK OFF ITEMS ON TWO CHECKLISTS AT ONCE! LET'S GET READY TO GO!
SURE, TWI!
JUST BRINGING ALONG A FEW MORE COMICS TO SORT.

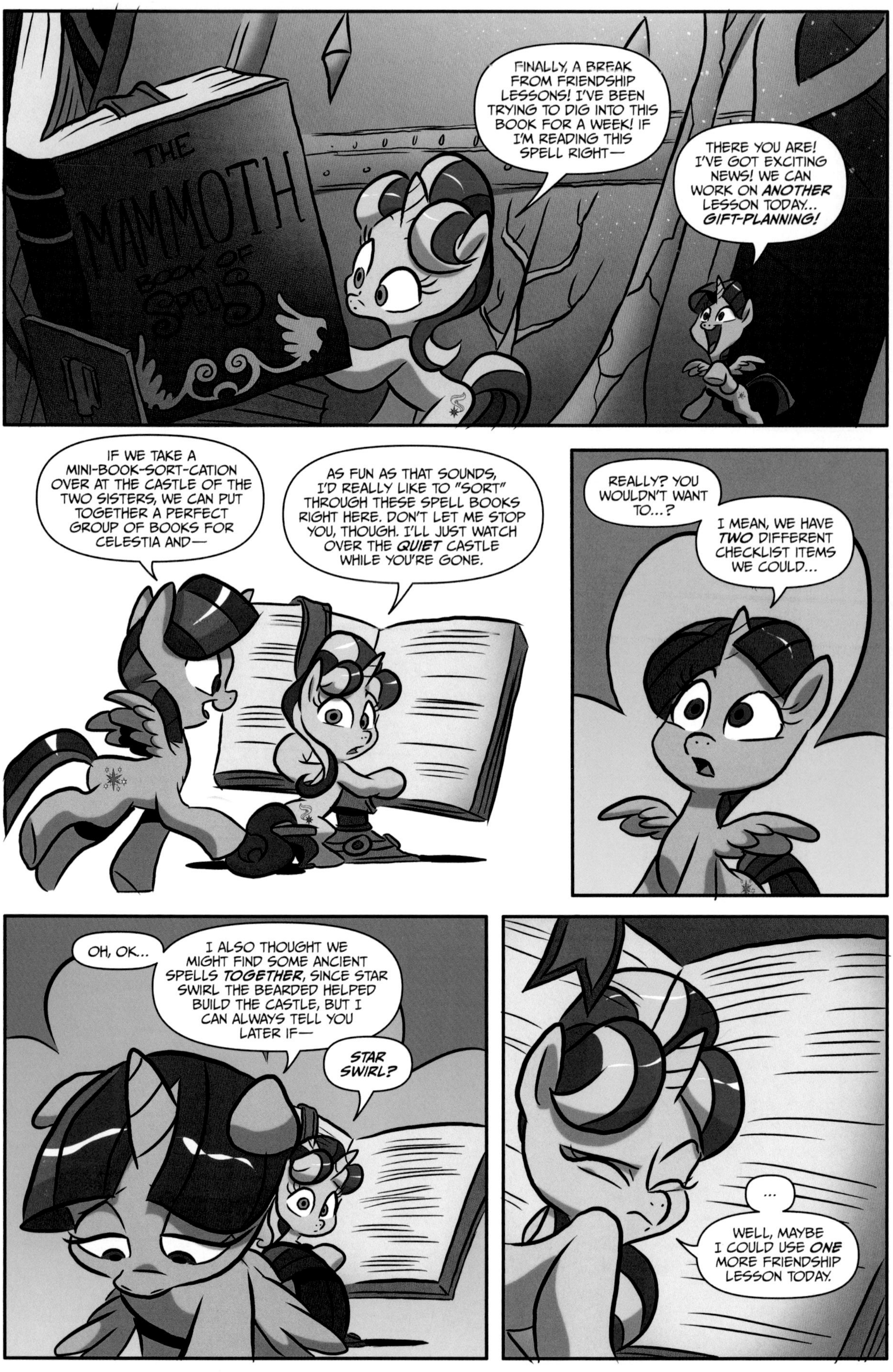
THE MAMMOTH BOOK OF SPELLS
FINALLY, A BREAK FROM FRIENDSHIP LESSONS! I'VE BEEN TRYING TO DIG INTO THIS BOOK FOR A WEEK! IF I'M READING THIS SPELL RIGHT—
THERE YOU ARE! I'VE GOT EXCITING NEWS! WE CAN WORK ON ANOTHER LESSON TODAY... GIFT-PLANNING!
IF WE TAKE A MINI-BOOK-SORT-CATION OVER AT THE CASTLE OF THE TWO SISTERS, WE CAN PUT TOGETHER A PERFECT GROUP OF BOOKS FOR CELESTIA AND—
AS FUN AS THAT SOUNDS, I'D REALLY LIKE TO "SORT" THROUGH THESE SPELL BOOKS RIGHT HERE. DON'T LET ME STOP YOU, THOUGH. I'LL JUST WATCH OVER THE QUIET CASTLE WHILE YOU'RE GONE.
REALLY? YOU WOULDN'T WANT TO...?
I MEAN, WE HAVE TWO DIFFERENT CHECKLIST ITEMS WE COULD...
OH, OK...
I ALSO THOUGHT WE MIGHT FIND SOME ANCIENT SPELLS TOGETHER, SINCE STAR SWIRL THE BEARDED HELPED BUILD THE CASTLE, BUT I CAN ALWAYS TELL YOU LATER IF—
STAR SWIRL?
...
WELL, MAYBE I COULD USE ONE MORE FRIENDSHIP LESSON TODAY.

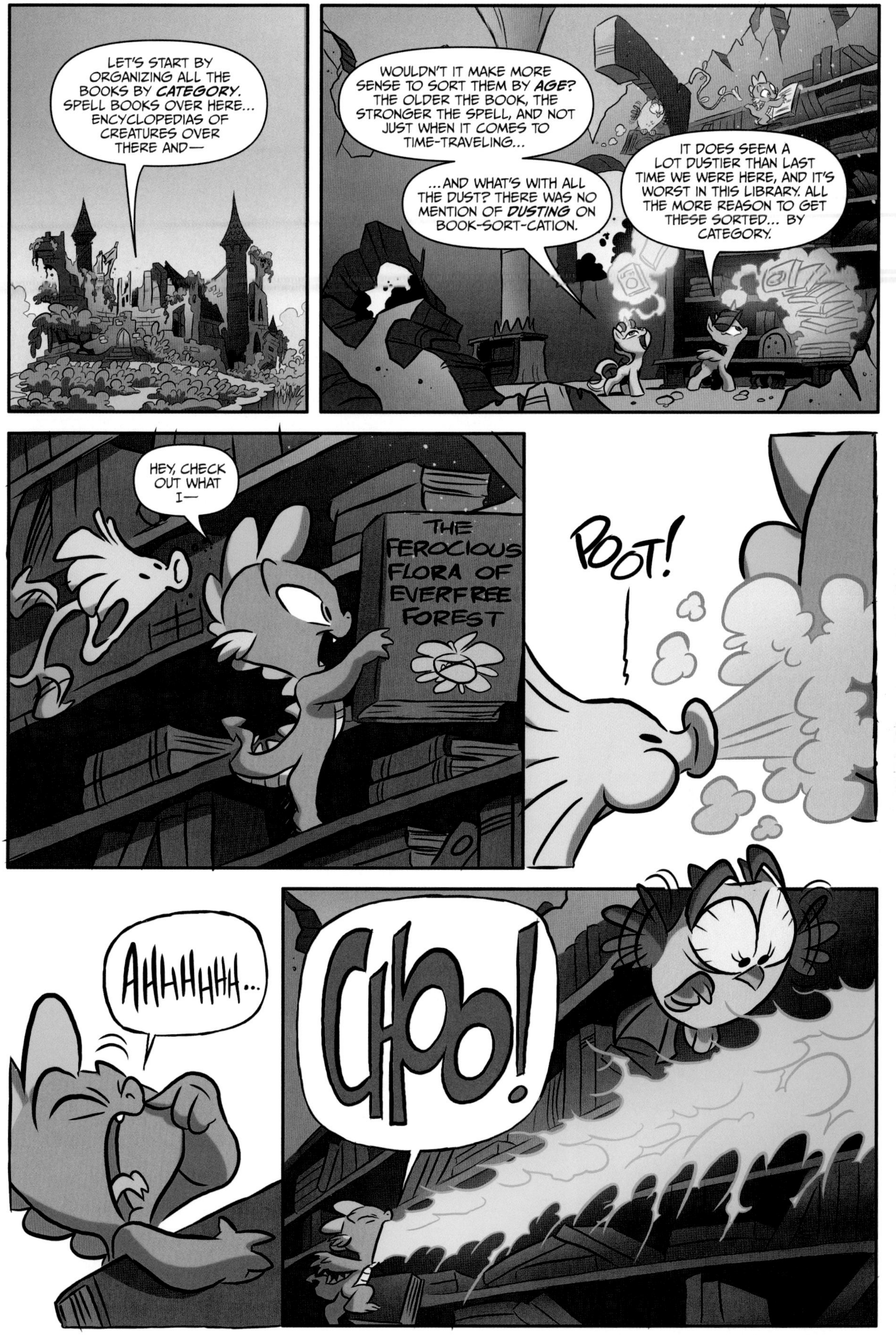
LET'S START BY ORGANIZING ALL THE BOOKS BY CATEGORY. SPELL BOOKS OVER HERE... ENCYCLOPEDIAS OF CREATURES OVER THERE AND—
WOULDN'T IT MAKE MORE SENSE TO SORT THEM BY AGE? THE OLDER THE BOOK, THE STRONGER THE SPELL, AND NOT JUST WHEN IT COMES TO TIME-TRAVELING...
...AND WHAT'S WITH ALL THE DUST? THERE WAS NO MENTION OF DUSTING ON BOOK-SORT-CATION.
IT DOES SEEM A LOT DUSTIER THAN LAST TIME WE WERE HERE, AND IT'S WORST IN THIS LIBRARY. ALL THE MORE REASON TO GET THESE SORTED... BY CATEGORY.
HEY, CHECK OUT WHAT I—
THE FEROCIOUS FLORA OF EVERFREE FOREST
POOT!
AHHHHHH...
CHOO!

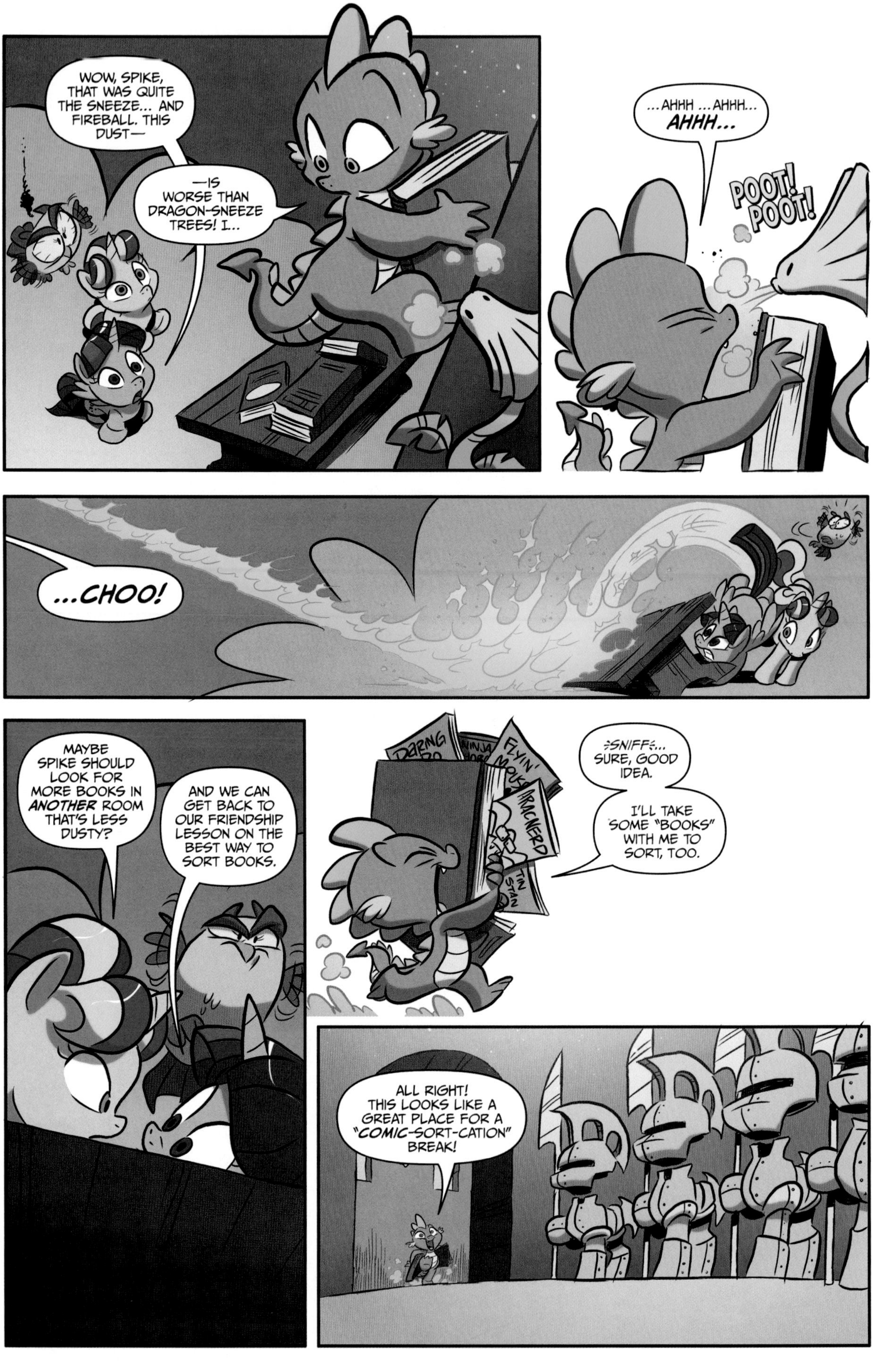
WOW, SPIKE, THAT WAS QUITE THE SNEEZE... AND FIREBALL. THIS DUST—
—IS WORSE THAN DRAGON-SNEEZE TREES! I...
...AHHH ...AHHH... ***AHHH...***
POOT! POOT!
...CHOO!
MAYBE SPIKE SHOULD LOOK FOR MORE BOOKS IN ***ANOTHER*** ROOM THAT'S LESS DUSTY?
AND WE CAN GET BACK TO OUR FRIENDSHIP LESSON ON THE BEST WAY TO SORT BOOKS.
ARACHNERD
TIN STAN
SNIFF... SURE, GOOD IDEA.
I'LL TAKE SOME "BOOKS" WITH ME TO SORT, TOO.
ALL RIGHT! THIS LOOKS LIKE A GREAT PLACE FOR A "***COMIC***-SORT-CATION" BREAK!

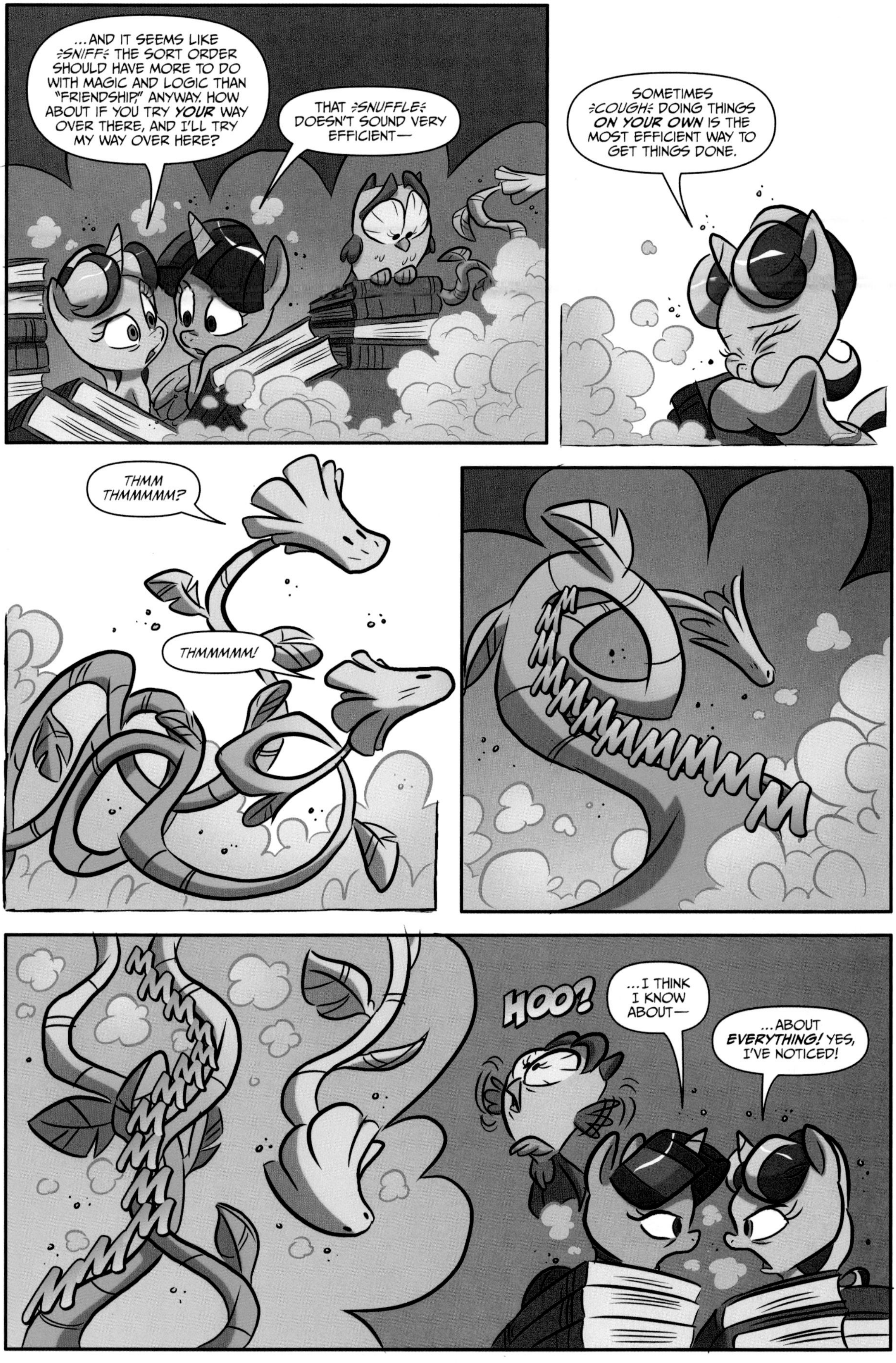
...AND IT SEEMS LIKE ⸗SNIFF⸗ THE SORT ORDER SHOULD HAVE MORE TO DO WITH MAGIC AND LOGIC THAN "FRIENDSHIP," ANYWAY. HOW ABOUT IF YOU TRY YOUR WAY OVER THERE, AND I'LL TRY MY WAY OVER HERE?
THAT ⸗SNUFFLE⸗ DOESN'T SOUND VERY EFFICIENT—
SOMETIMES ⸗COUGH⸗ DOING THINGS ON YOUR OWN IS THE MOST EFFICIENT WAY TO GET THINGS DONE.
THMM THMMMMM?
THMMMMM!
MMMMMMMMMMMMMMM
MMMMMMMMMMMMMM
HOO?
...I THINK I KNOW ABOUT—
...ABOUT EVERYTHING! YES, I'VE NOTICED!

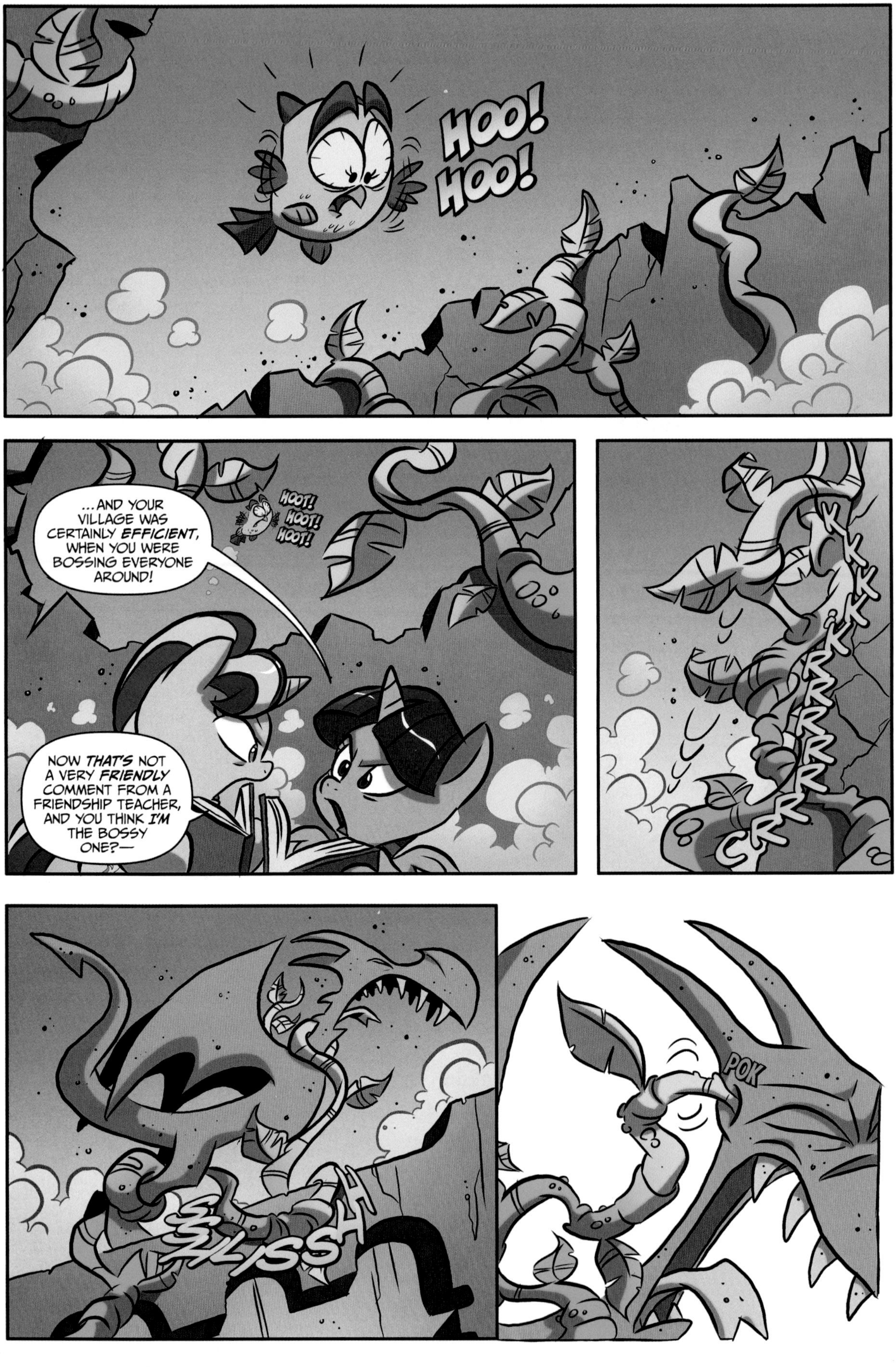
HOO! HOO!
HOOT! HOOT! HOOT!
...AND YOUR VILLAGE WAS CERTAINLY *EFFICIENT*, WHEN YOU WERE BOSSING EVERYONE AROUND!
NOW *THAT'S* NOT A VERY *FRIENDLY* COMMENT FROM A FRIENDSHIP TEACHER, AND YOU THINK *I'M* THE BOSSY ONE?—
CRRRRRRRKKKKK
SHLISSSH
POK

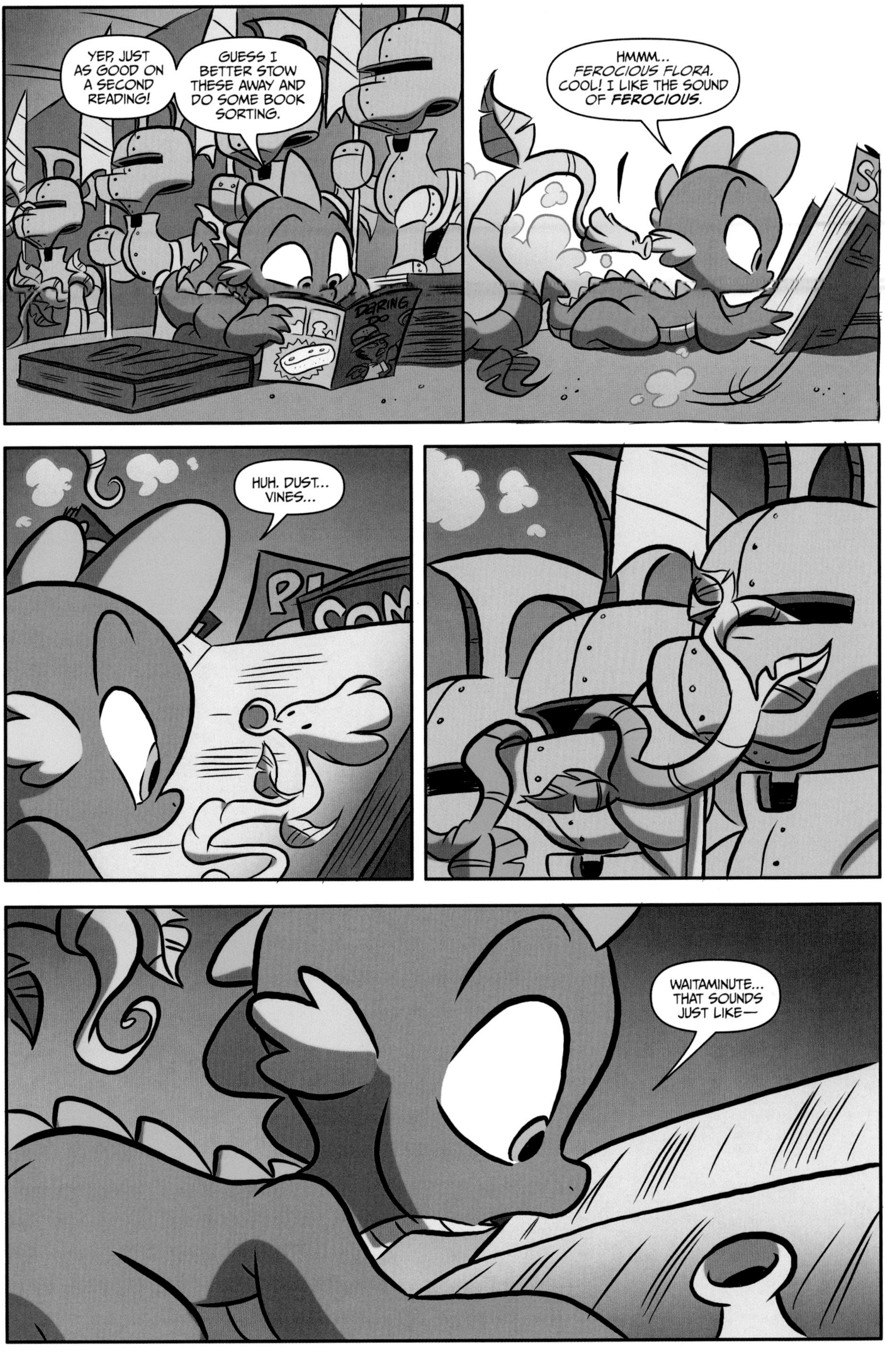
YEP, JUST AS GOOD ON A SECOND READING!
GUESS I BETTER STOW THESE AWAY AND DO SOME BOOK SORTING.
DARING DO
HMMM... *FEROCIOUS FLORA.* COOL! I LIKE THE SOUND OF ***FEROCIOUS***.
HUH. DUST... VINES...
WAITAMINUTE... THAT SOUNDS JUST LIKE—

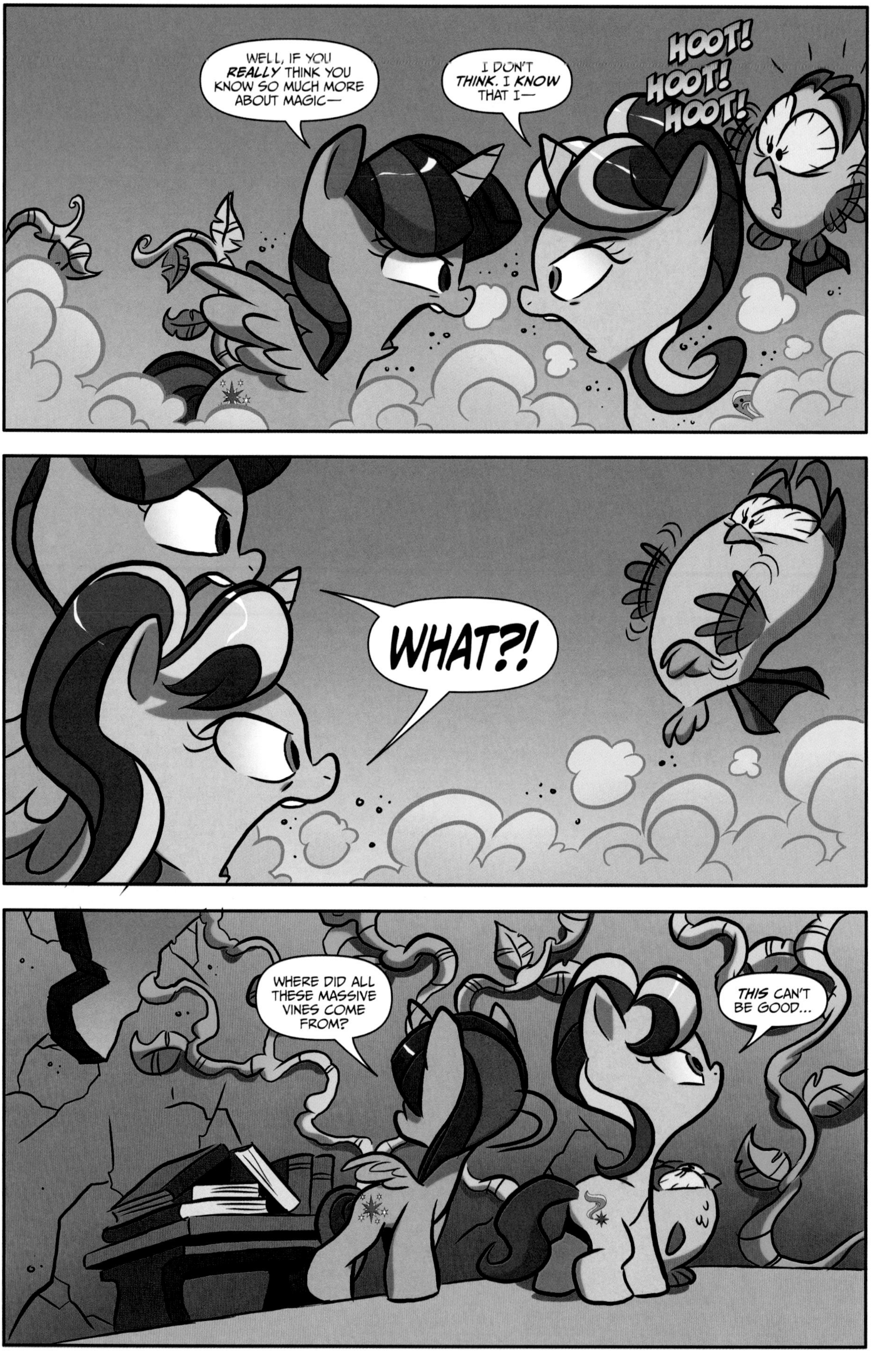
WELL, IF YOU REALLY THINK YOU KNOW SO MUCH MORE ABOUT MAGIC—
I DON'T THINK. I KNOW THAT I—
HOOT! HOOT! HOOT!
WHAT?!
WHERE DID ALL THESE MASSIVE VINES COME FROM?
THIS CAN'T BE GOOD...

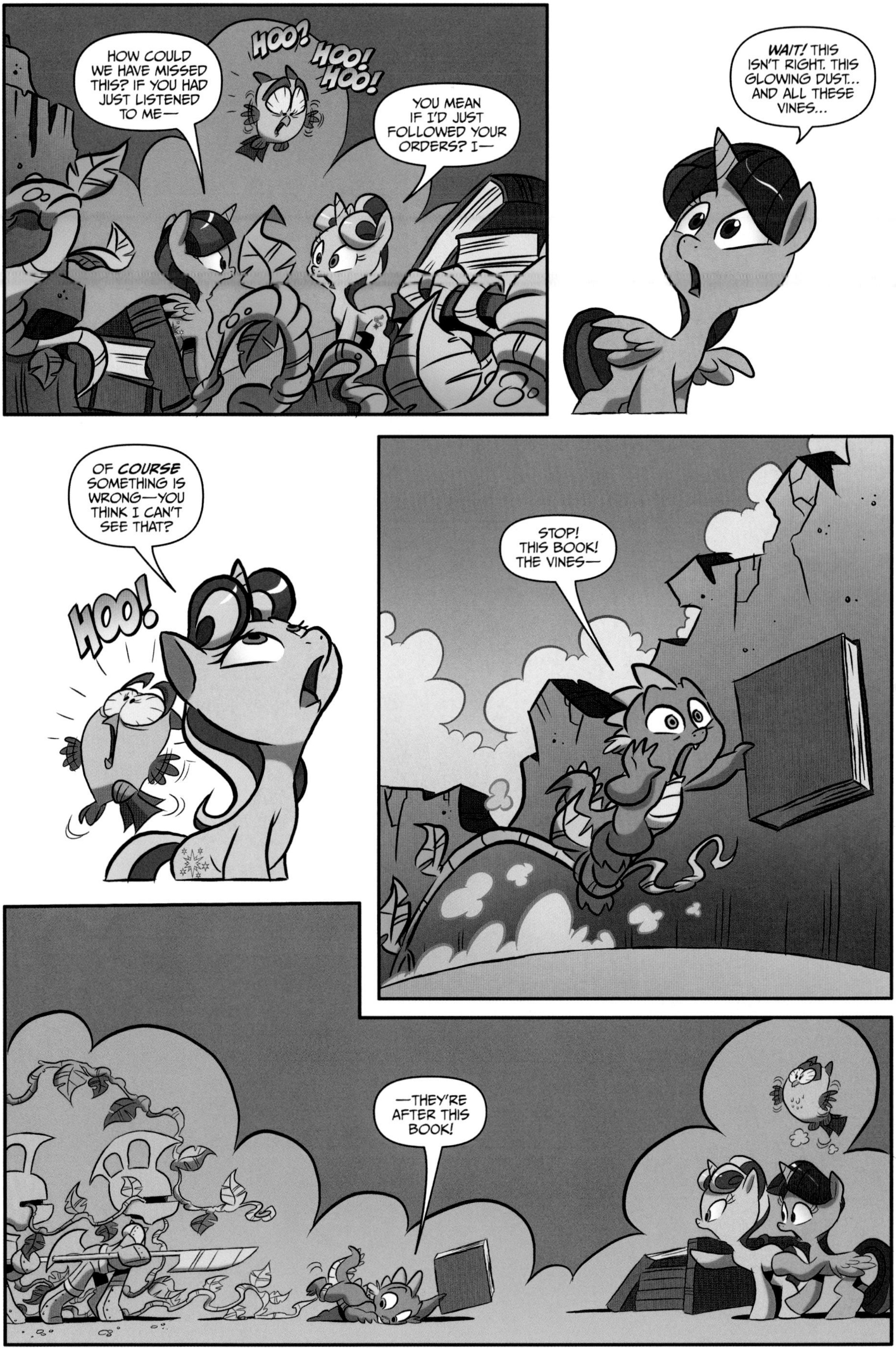
HOW COULD WE HAVE MISSED THIS? IF YOU HAD JUST LISTENED TO ME—
HOO? HOO! HOO!
YOU MEAN IF I'D JUST FOLLOWED YOUR ORDERS? I—
WAIT! THIS ISN'T RIGHT. THIS GLOWING DUST... AND ALL THESE VINES...
OF COURSE SOMETHING IS WRONG—YOU THINK I CAN'T SEE THAT?
HOO!
STOP! THIS BOOK! THE VINES—
—THEY'RE AFTER THIS BOOK!

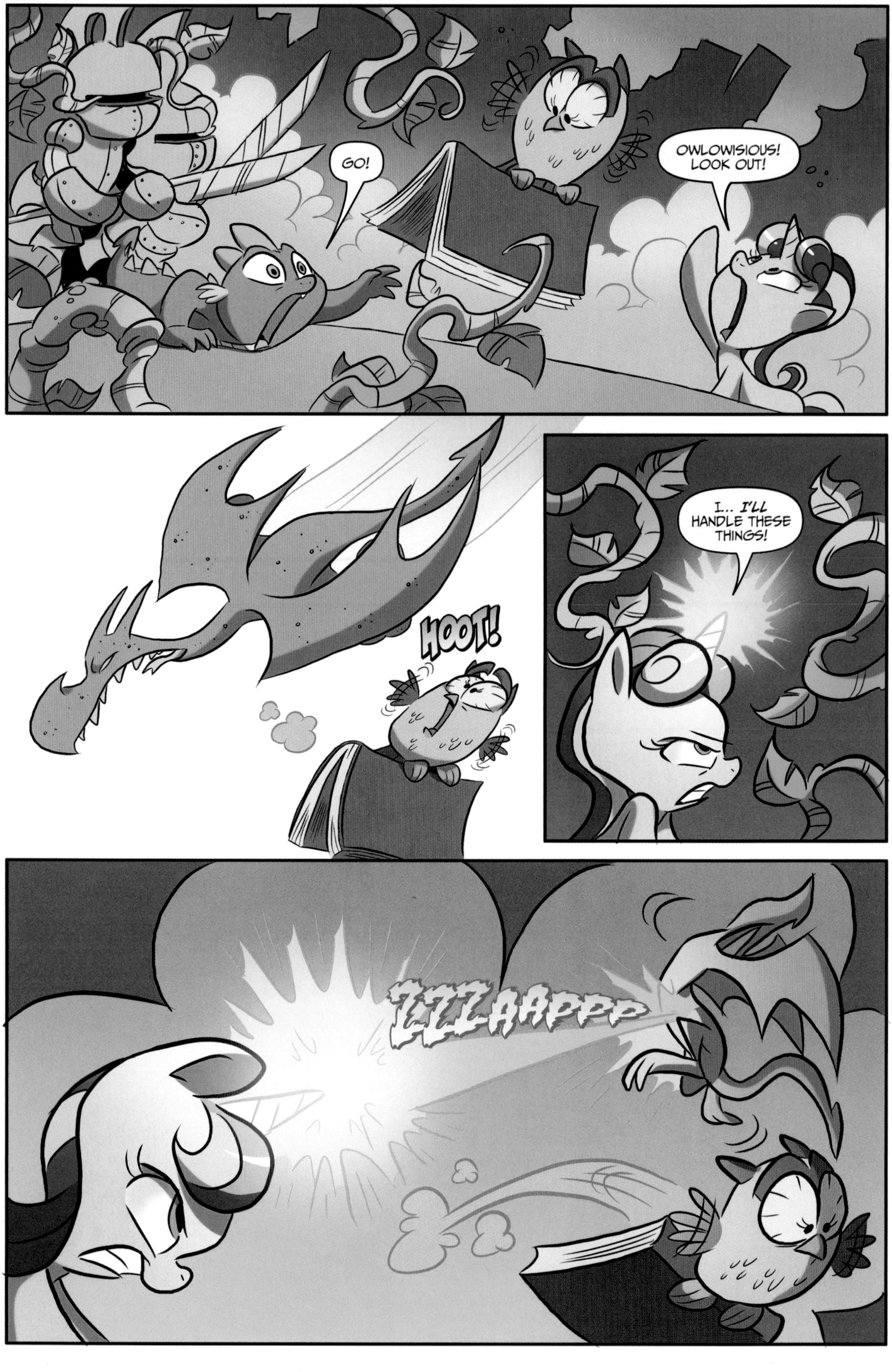
GO!
OWLOWISIOUS! LOOK OUT!
HOOT!
I... I'LL HANDLE THESE THINGS!
ZZZAAPPP

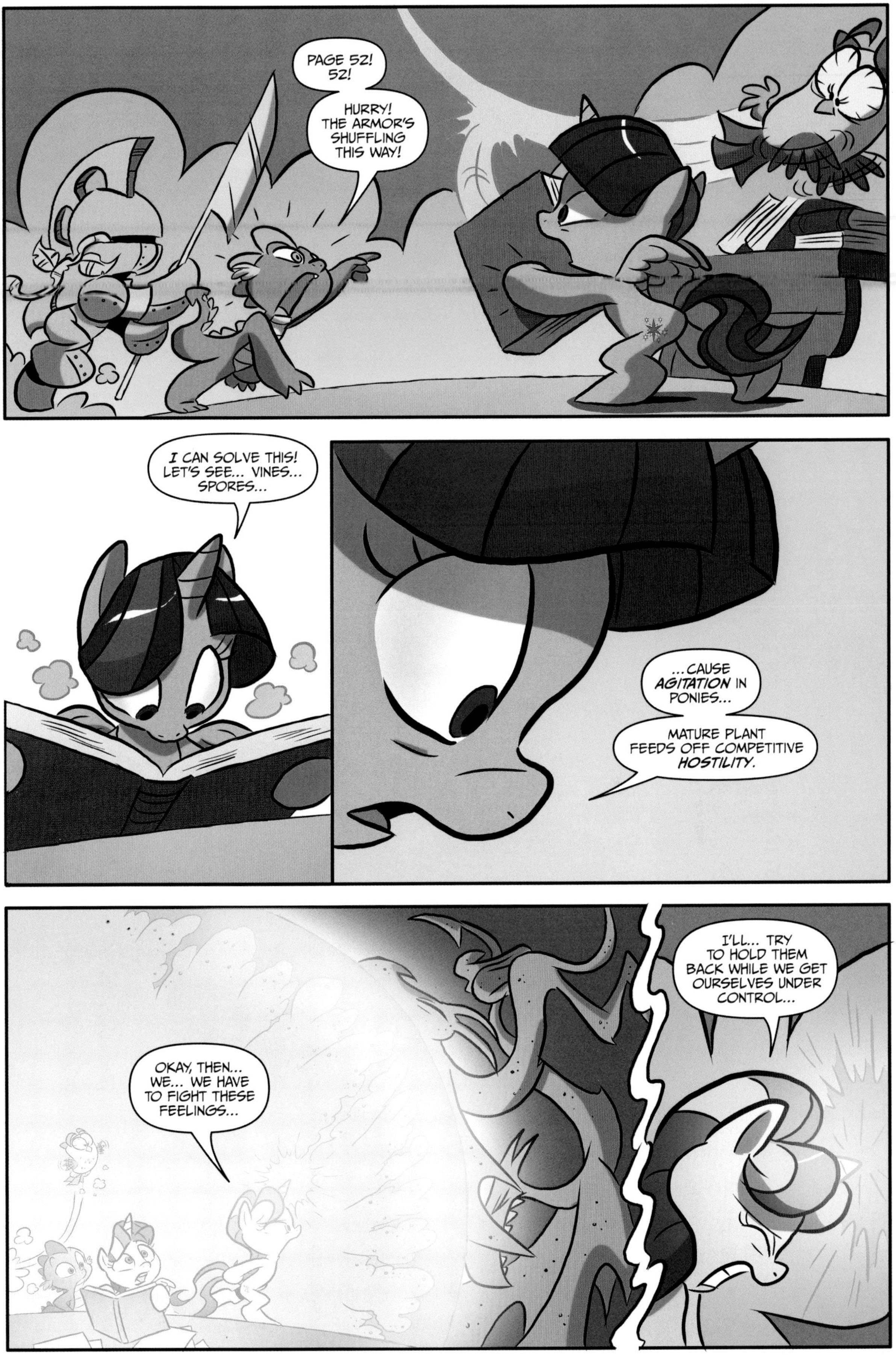
PAGE 52! 52!
HURRY! THE ARMOR'S SHUFFLING THIS WAY!
I CAN SOLVE THIS! LET'S SEE... VINES... SPORES...
...CAUSE *AGITATION* IN PONIES...
MATURE PLANT FEEDS OFF COMPETITIVE *HOSTILITY*.
OKAY, THEN... WE... WE HAVE TO FIGHT THESE FEELINGS...
I'LL... TRY TO HOLD THEM BACK WHILE WE GET OURSELVES UNDER CONTROL...

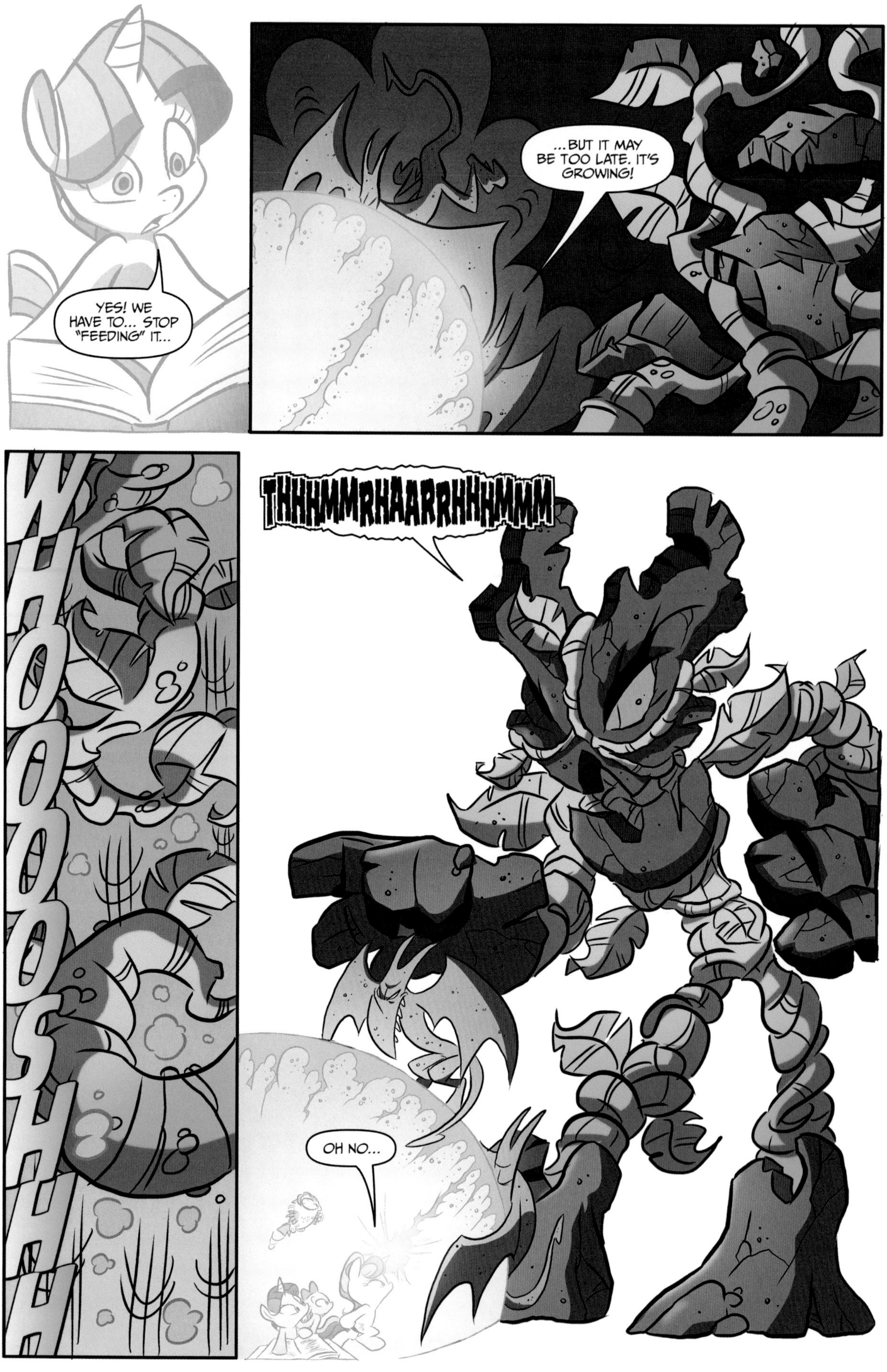
YES! WE HAVE TO... STOP "FEEDING" IT...
...BUT IT MAY BE TOO LATE. IT'S GROWING!
WHOOOOOSHHHH
THHHMMRHAARRHHHMMM
OH NO...

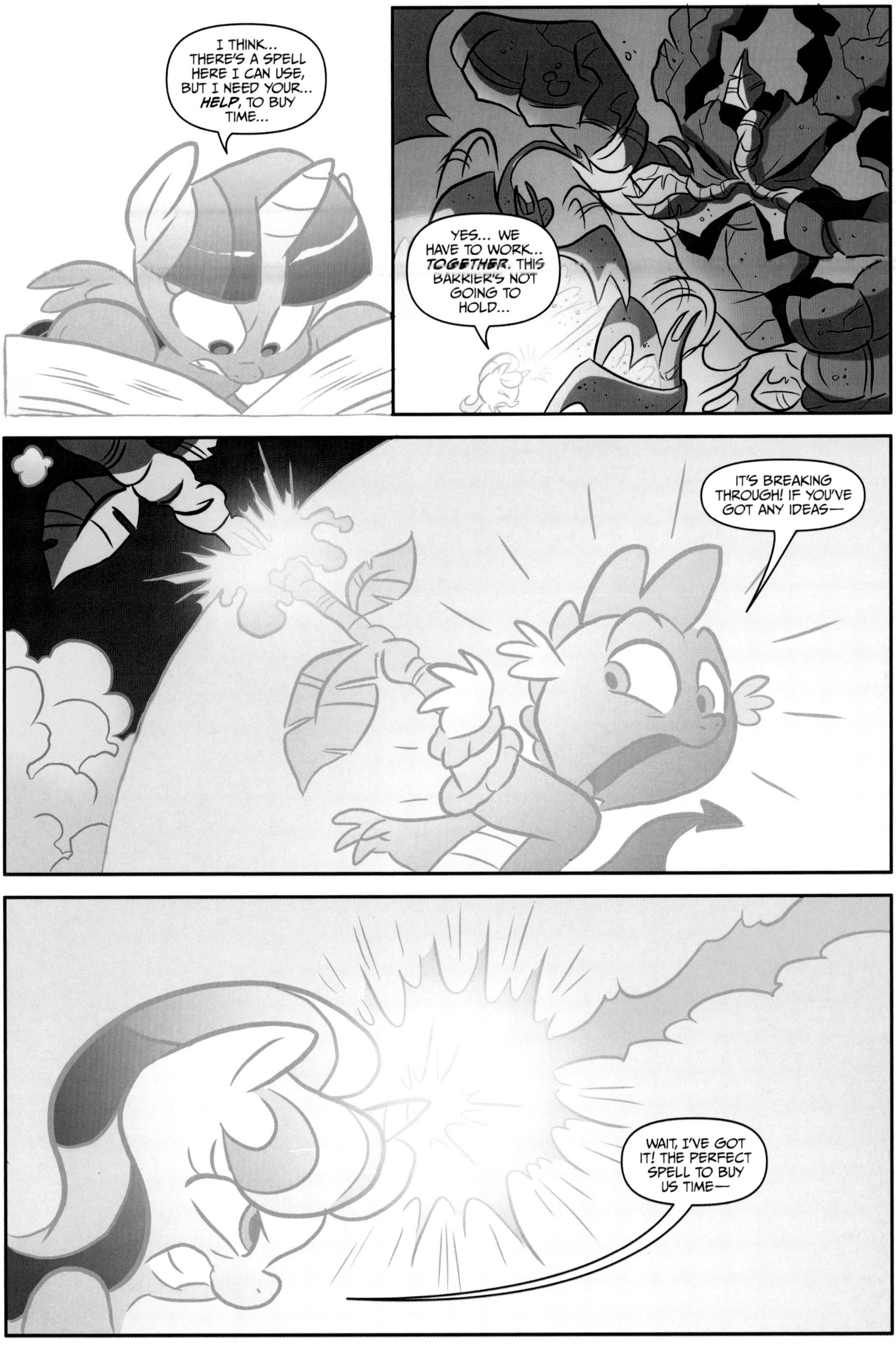
I THINK... THERE'S A SPELL HERE I CAN USE, BUT I NEED YOUR... ***HELP***, TO BUY TIME...
YES... WE HAVE TO WORK... ***TOGETHER***. THIS BARRIER'S NOT GOING TO HOLD...
IT'S BREAKING THROUGH! IF YOU'VE GOT ANY IDEAS—
WAIT, I'VE GOT IT! THE PERFECT SPELL TO BUY US TIME—

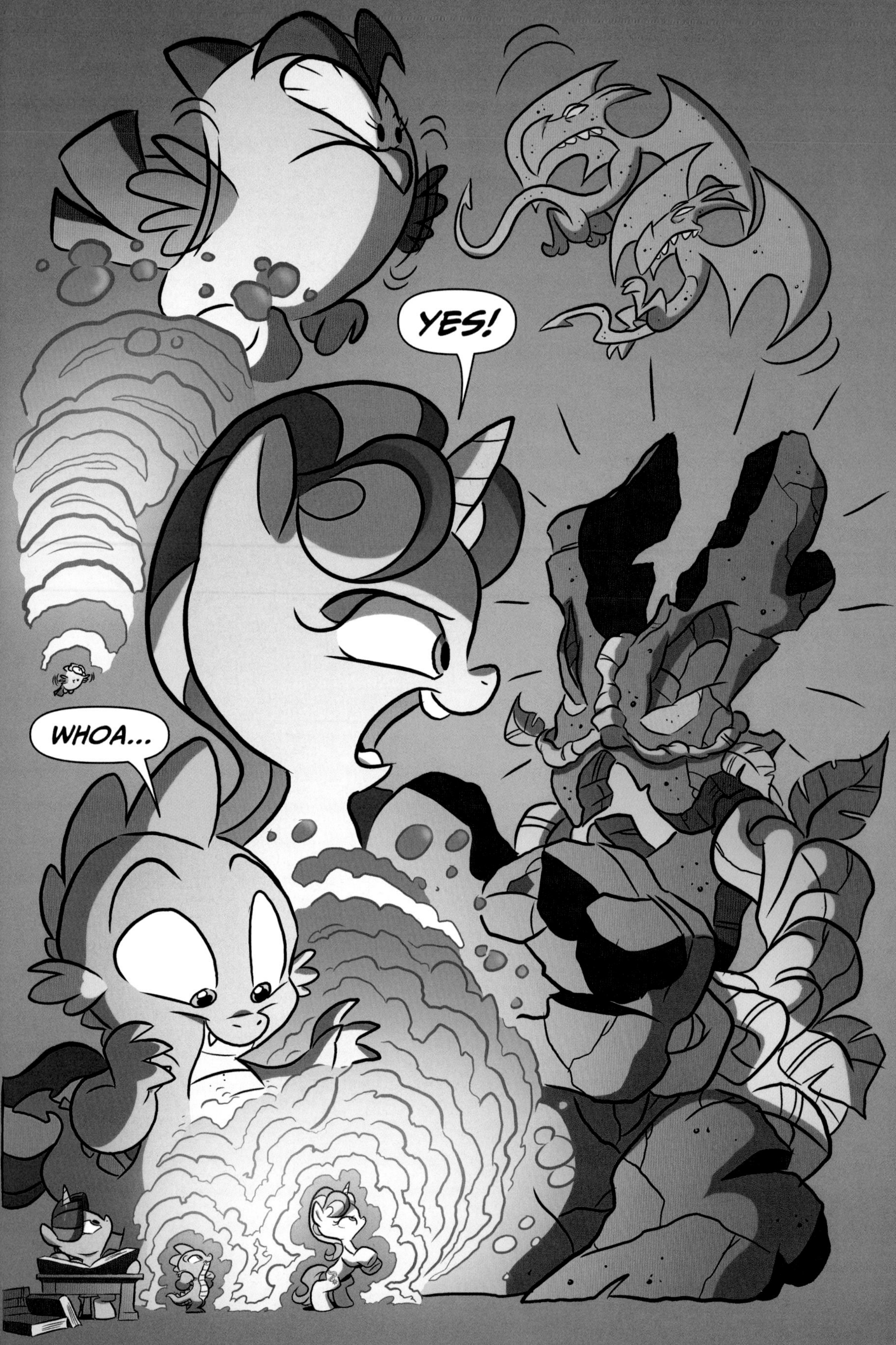
YES!
WHOA...

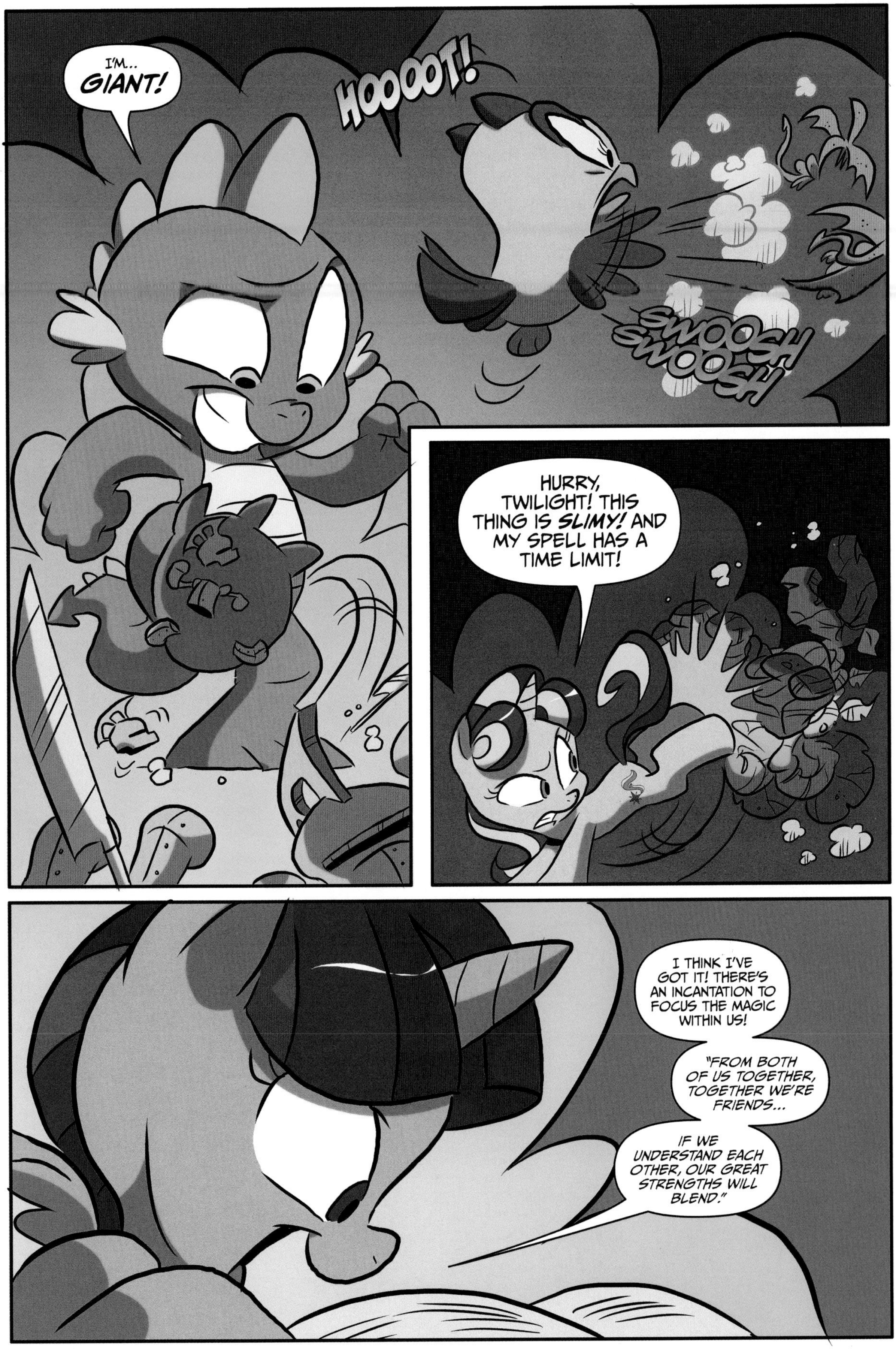
I'M... GIANT!
HOOOOT!
SWOOSH SWOOSH
HURRY, TWILIGHT! THIS THING IS SLIMY! AND MY SPELL HAS A TIME LIMIT!
I THINK I'VE GOT IT! THERE'S AN INCANTATION TO FOCUS THE MAGIC WITHIN US!
"FROM BOTH OF US TOGETHER, TOGETHER WE'RE FRIENDS...
IF WE UNDERSTAND EACH OTHER, OUR GREAT STRENGTHS WILL BLEND."

FLAP
FLAP

ZZZZAAP!!

FWWOOOOSSH

AWWW... WE'RE SHRINKING ALREADY?

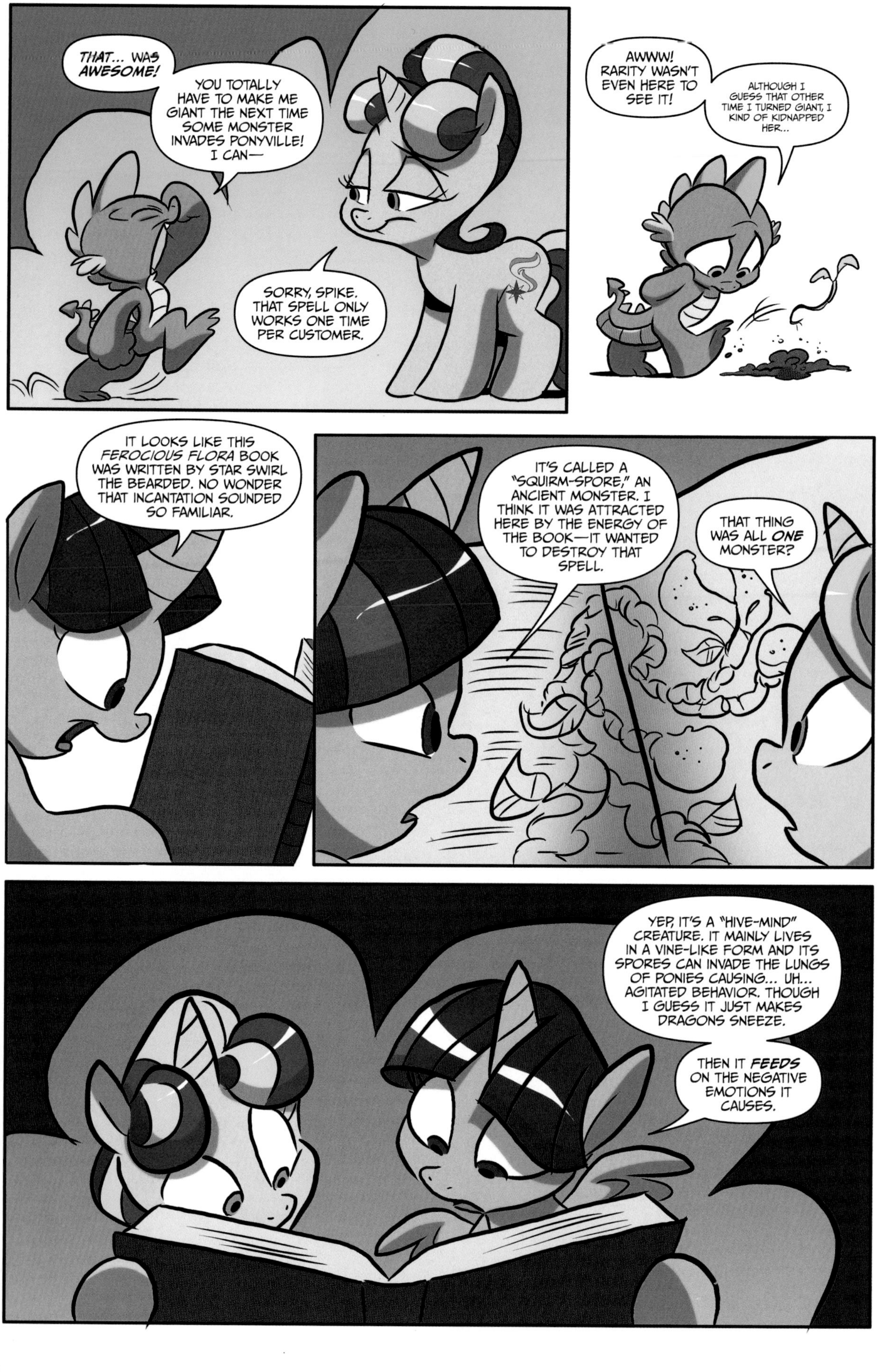
THAT... WAS AWESOME!
YOU TOTALLY HAVE TO MAKE ME GIANT THE NEXT TIME SOME MONSTER INVADES PONYVILLE! I CAN—
SORRY, SPIKE. THAT SPELL ONLY WORKS ONE TIME PER CUSTOMER.
AWWW! RARITY WASN'T EVEN HERE TO SEE IT!
ALTHOUGH I GUESS THAT OTHER TIME I TURNED GIANT, I KIND OF KIDNAPPED HER...
IT LOOKS LIKE THIS FEROCIOUS FLORA BOOK WAS WRITTEN BY STAR SWIRL THE BEARDED. NO WONDER THAT INCANTATION SOUNDED SO FAMILIAR.
IT'S CALLED A "SQUIRM-SPORE," AN ANCIENT MONSTER. I THINK IT WAS ATTRACTED HERE BY THE ENERGY OF THE BOOK—IT WANTED TO DESTROY THAT SPELL.
THAT THING WAS ALL ONE MONSTER?
YEP, IT'S A "HIVE-MIND" CREATURE. IT MAINLY LIVES IN A VINE-LIKE FORM AND ITS SPORES CAN INVADE THE LUNGS OF PONIES CAUSING... UH... AGITATED BEHAVIOR. THOUGH I GUESS IT JUST MAKES DRAGONS SNEEZE.
THEN IT FEEDS ON THE NEGATIVE EMOTIONS IT CAUSES.

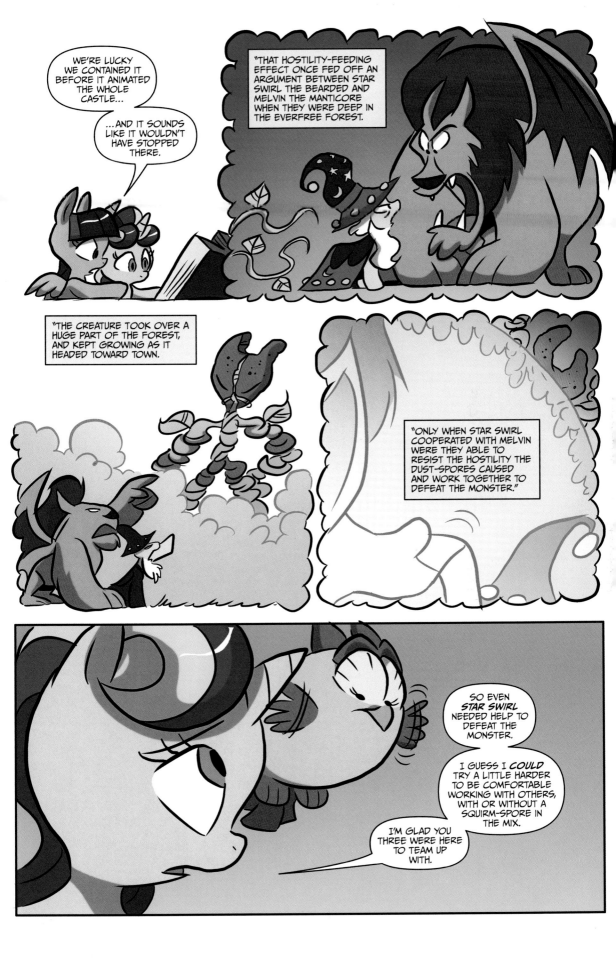

WE'RE LUCKY WE CONTAINED IT BEFORE IT ANIMATED THE WHOLE CASTLE...

...AND IT SOUNDS LIKE IT WOULDN'T HAVE STOPPED THERE.

"THAT HOSTILITY-FEEDING EFFECT ONCE FED OFF AN ARGUMENT BETWEEN STAR SWIRL THE BEARDED AND MELVIN THE MANTICORE WHEN THEY WERE DEEP IN THE EVERFREE FOREST.

"THE CREATURE TOOK OVER A HUGE PART OF THE FOREST, AND KEPT GROWING AS IT HEADED TOWARD TOWN.

"ONLY WHEN STAR SWIRL COOPERATED WITH MELVIN WERE THEY ABLE TO RESIST THE HOSTILITY THE DUST-SPORES CAUSED AND WORK TOGETHER TO DEFEAT THE MONSTER."

SO EVEN *STAR SWIRL* NEEDED HELP TO DEFEAT THE MONSTER.

I GUESS I *COULD* TRY A LITTLE HARDER TO BE COMFORTABLE WORKING WITH OTHERS, WITH OR WITHOUT A SQUIRM-SPORE IN THE MIX.

I'M GLAD YOU THREE WERE HERE TO TEAM UP WITH.

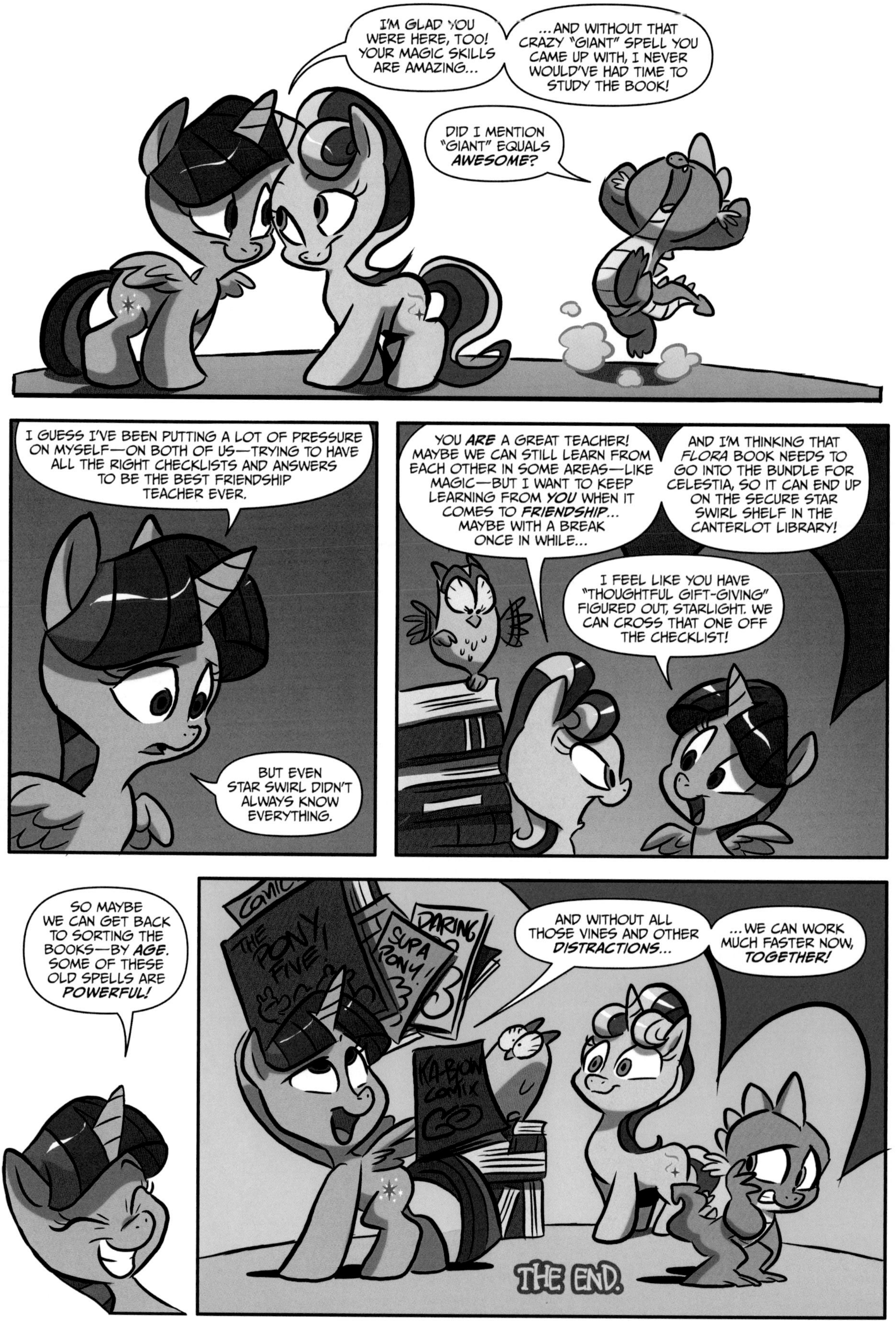
I'M GLAD YOU WERE HERE, TOO! YOUR MAGIC SKILLS ARE AMAZING...
...AND WITHOUT THAT CRAZY "GIANT" SPELL YOU CAME UP WITH, I NEVER WOULD'VE HAD TIME TO STUDY THE BOOK!
DID I MENTION "GIANT" EQUALS AWESOME?
I GUESS I'VE BEEN PUTTING A LOT OF PRESSURE ON MYSELF—ON BOTH OF US—TRYING TO HAVE ALL THE RIGHT CHECKLISTS AND ANSWERS TO BE THE BEST FRIENDSHIP TEACHER EVER.
BUT EVEN STAR SWIRL DIDN'T ALWAYS KNOW EVERYTHING.
YOU ARE A GREAT TEACHER! MAYBE WE CAN STILL LEARN FROM EACH OTHER IN SOME AREAS—LIKE MAGIC—BUT I WANT TO KEEP LEARNING FROM YOU WHEN IT COMES TO FRIENDSHIP... MAYBE WITH A BREAK ONCE IN WHILE...
AND I'M THINKING THAT FLORA BOOK NEEDS TO GO INTO THE BUNDLE FOR CELESTIA, SO IT CAN END UP ON THE SECURE STAR SWIRL SHELF IN THE CANTERLOT LIBRARY!
I FEEL LIKE YOU HAVE "THOUGHTFUL GIFT-GIVING" FIGURED OUT, STARLIGHT. WE CAN CROSS THAT ONE OFF THE CHECKLIST!
SO MAYBE WE CAN GET BACK TO SORTING THE BOOKS—BY AGE. SOME OF THESE OLD SPELLS ARE POWERFUL!
COMIC
THE PONY FIVE
SUPA PONY
DARING
KA-BOOM COMIX
AND WITHOUT ALL THOSE VINES AND OTHER DISTRACTIONS...
...WE CAN WORK MUCH FASTER NOW, TOGETHER!
THE END.

art by
Tony Fleecs

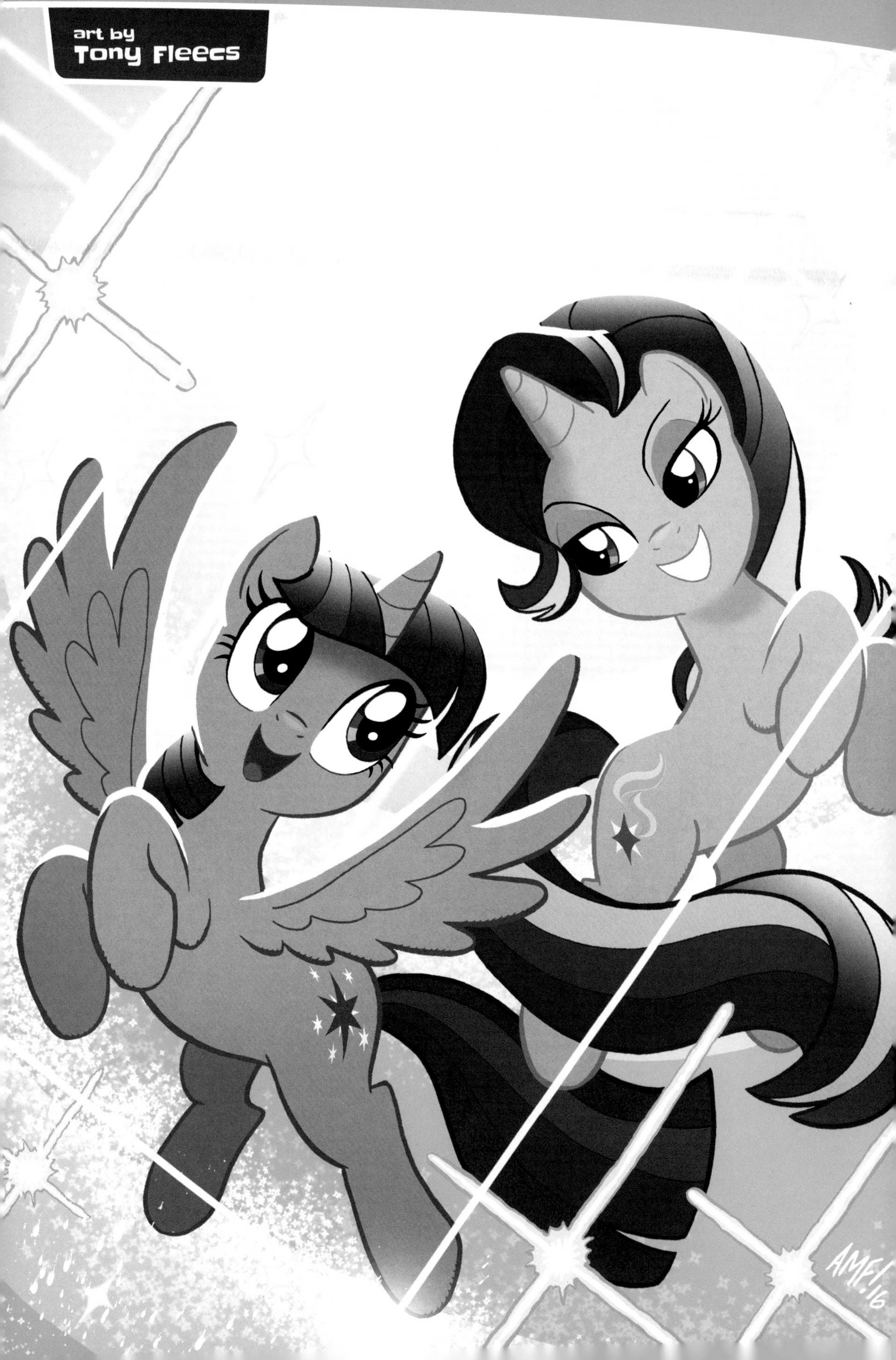
AMF! '16

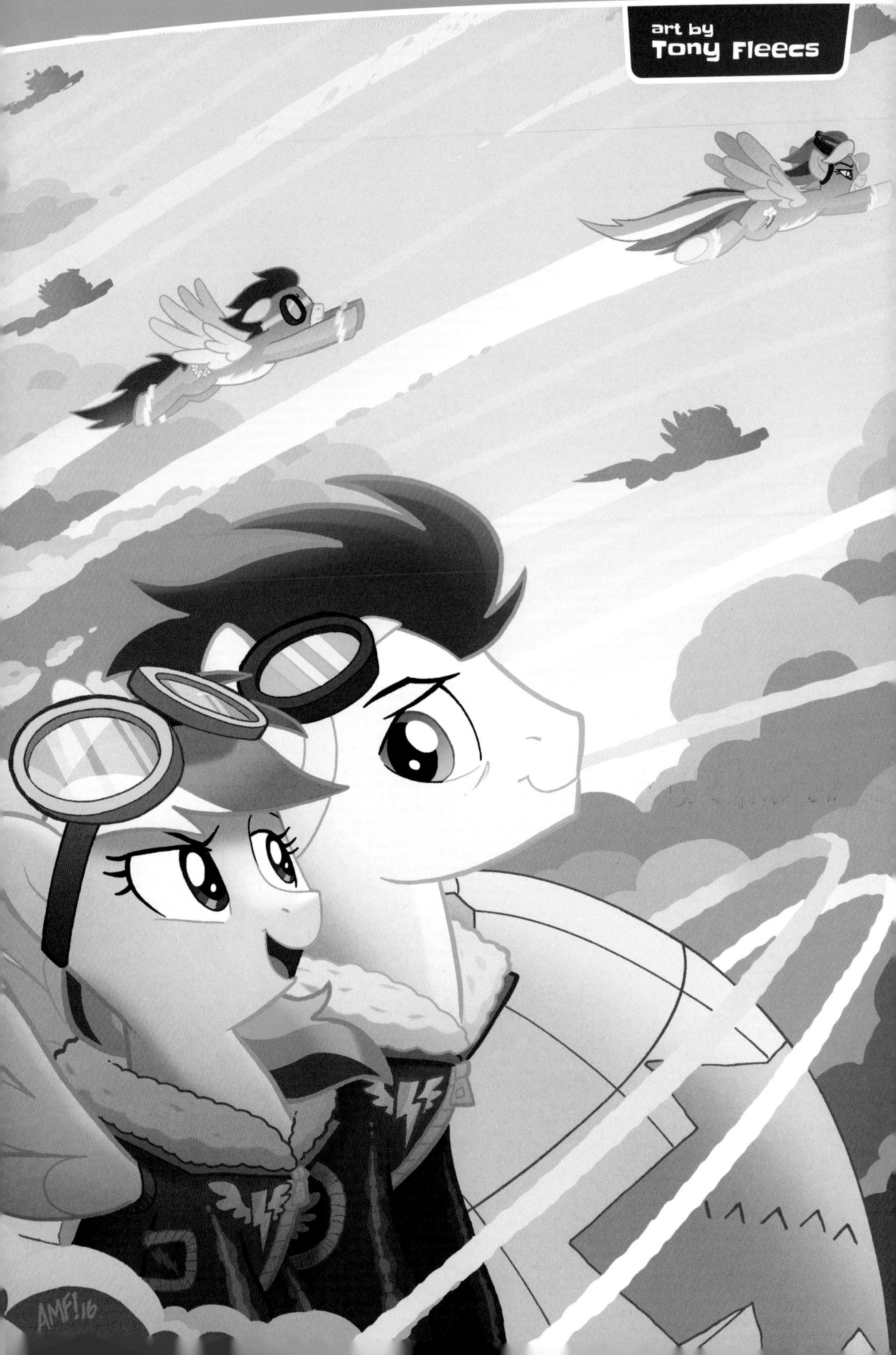
art by
Tony Fleecs
AMF!16

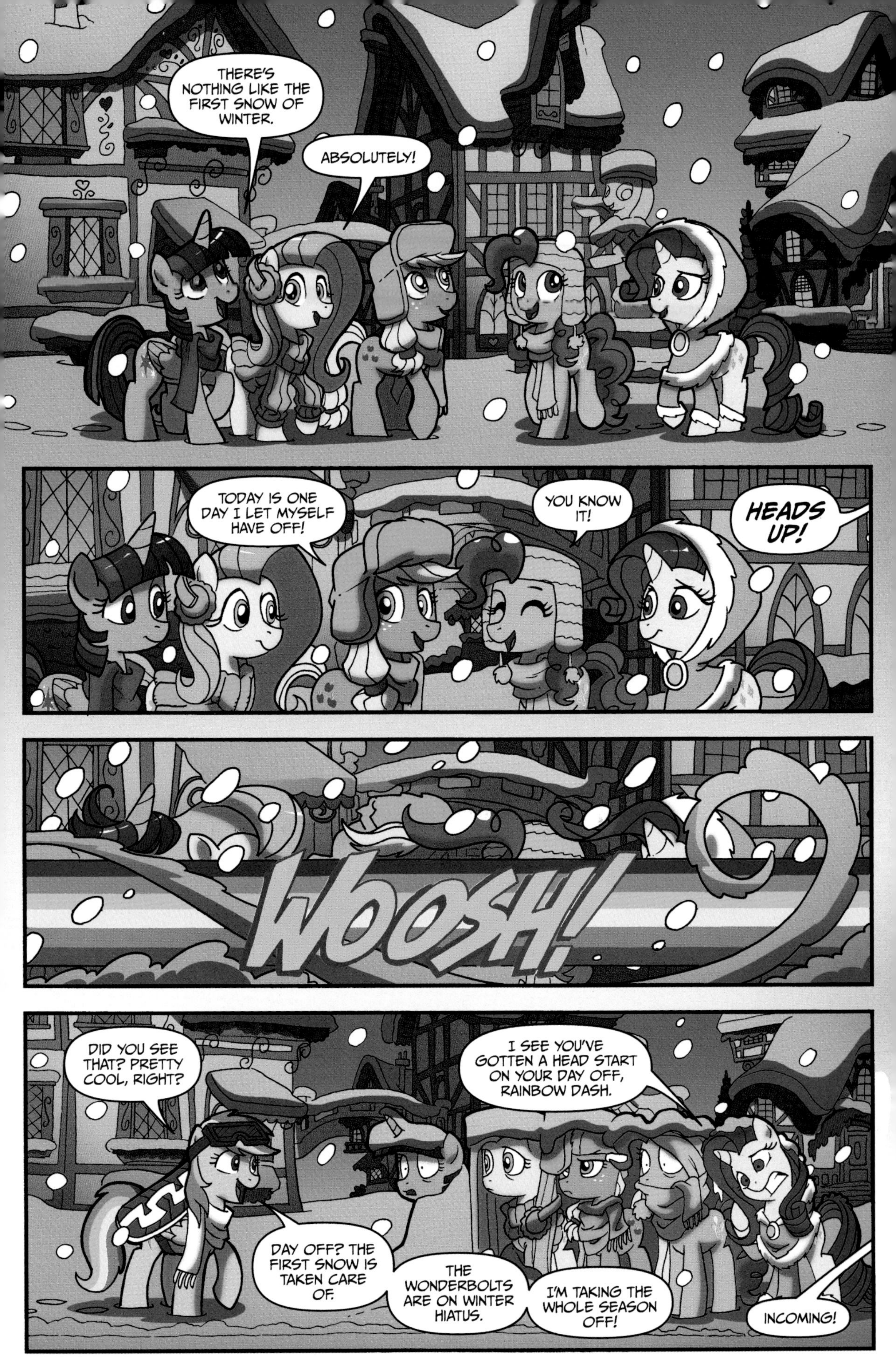
THERE'S NOTHING LIKE THE FIRST SNOW OF WINTER.
ABSOLUTELY!
TODAY IS ONE DAY I LET MYSELF HAVE OFF!
YOU KNOW IT!
HEADS UP!
WOOSH!
DID YOU SEE THAT? PRETTY COOL, RIGHT?
I SEE YOU'VE GOTTEN A HEAD START ON YOUR DAY OFF, RAINBOW DASH.
DAY OFF? THE FIRST SNOW IS TAKEN CARE OF.
THE WONDERBOLTS ARE ON WINTER HIATUS.
I'M TAKING THE WHOLE SEASON OFF!
INCOMING!

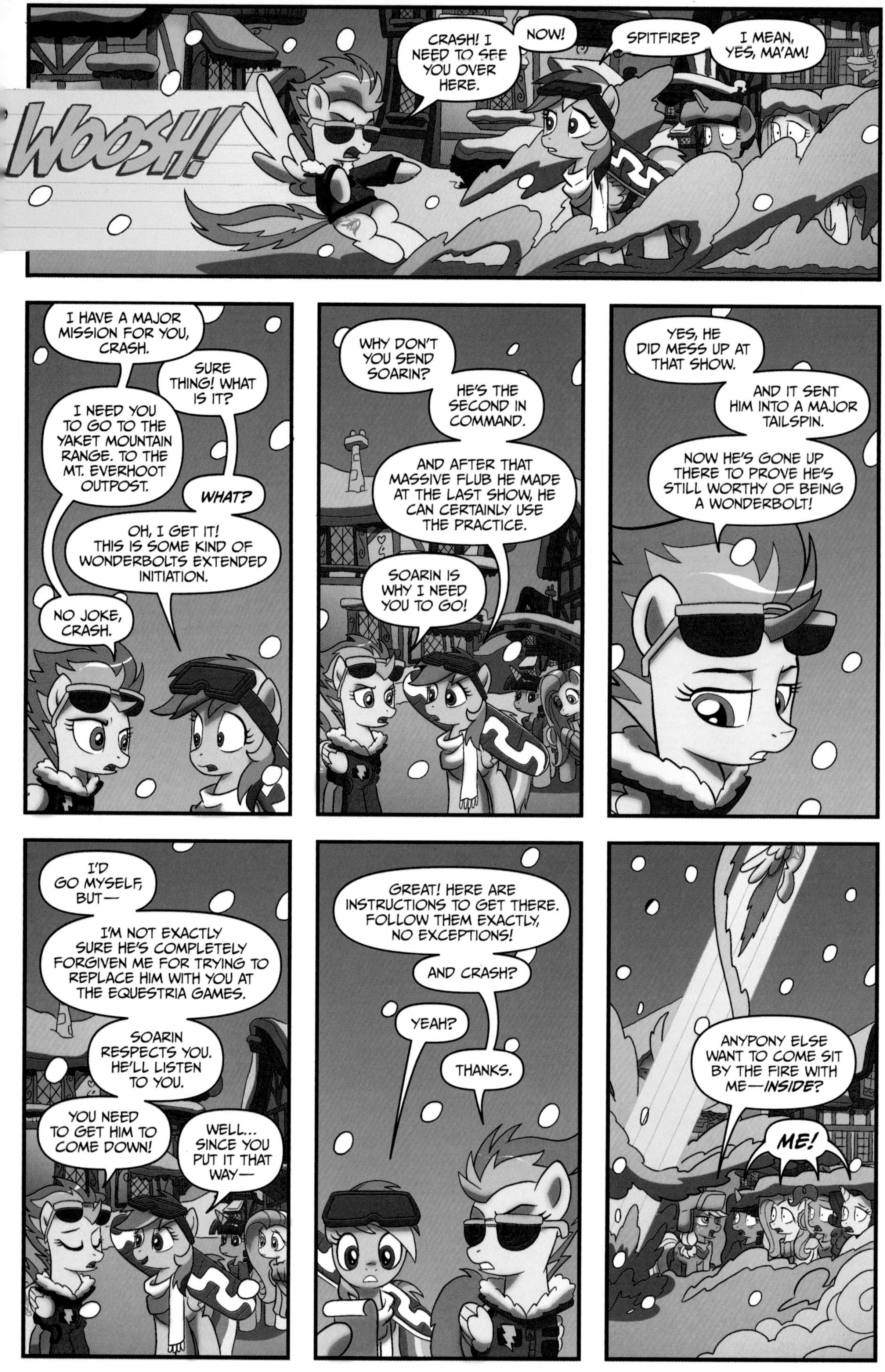
WOOSH!
CRASH! I NEED TO SEE YOU OVER HERE.
NOW!
SPITFIRE?
I MEAN, YES, MA'AM!
I HAVE A MAJOR MISSION FOR YOU, CRASH.
SURE THING! WHAT IS IT?
I NEED YOU TO GO TO THE YAKET MOUNTAIN RANGE. TO THE MT. EVERHOOT OUTPOST.
WHAT?
OH, I GET IT! THIS IS SOME KIND OF WONDERBOLTS EXTENDED INITIATION.
NO JOKE, CRASH.
WHY DON'T YOU SEND SOARIN?
HE'S THE SECOND IN COMMAND.
AND AFTER THAT MASSIVE FLUB HE MADE AT THE LAST SHOW, HE CAN CERTAINLY USE THE PRACTICE.
SOARIN IS WHY I NEED YOU TO GO!
YES, HE DID MESS UP AT THAT SHOW.
AND IT SENT HIM INTO A MAJOR TAILSPIN.
NOW HE'S GONE UP THERE TO PROVE HE'S STILL WORTHY OF BEING A WONDERBOLT!
I'D GO MYSELF, BUT—
I'M NOT EXACTLY SURE HE'S COMPLETELY FORGIVEN ME FOR TRYING TO REPLACE HIM WITH YOU AT THE EQUESTRIA GAMES.
SOARIN RESPECTS YOU. HE'LL LISTEN TO YOU.
YOU NEED TO GET HIM TO COME DOWN!
WELL... SINCE YOU PUT IT THAT WAY—
GREAT! HERE ARE INSTRUCTIONS TO GET THERE. FOLLOW THEM EXACTLY, NO EXCEPTIONS!
AND CRASH?
YEAH?
THANKS.
ANYPONY ELSE WANT TO COME SIT BY THE FIRE WITH ME—INSIDE?
ME!

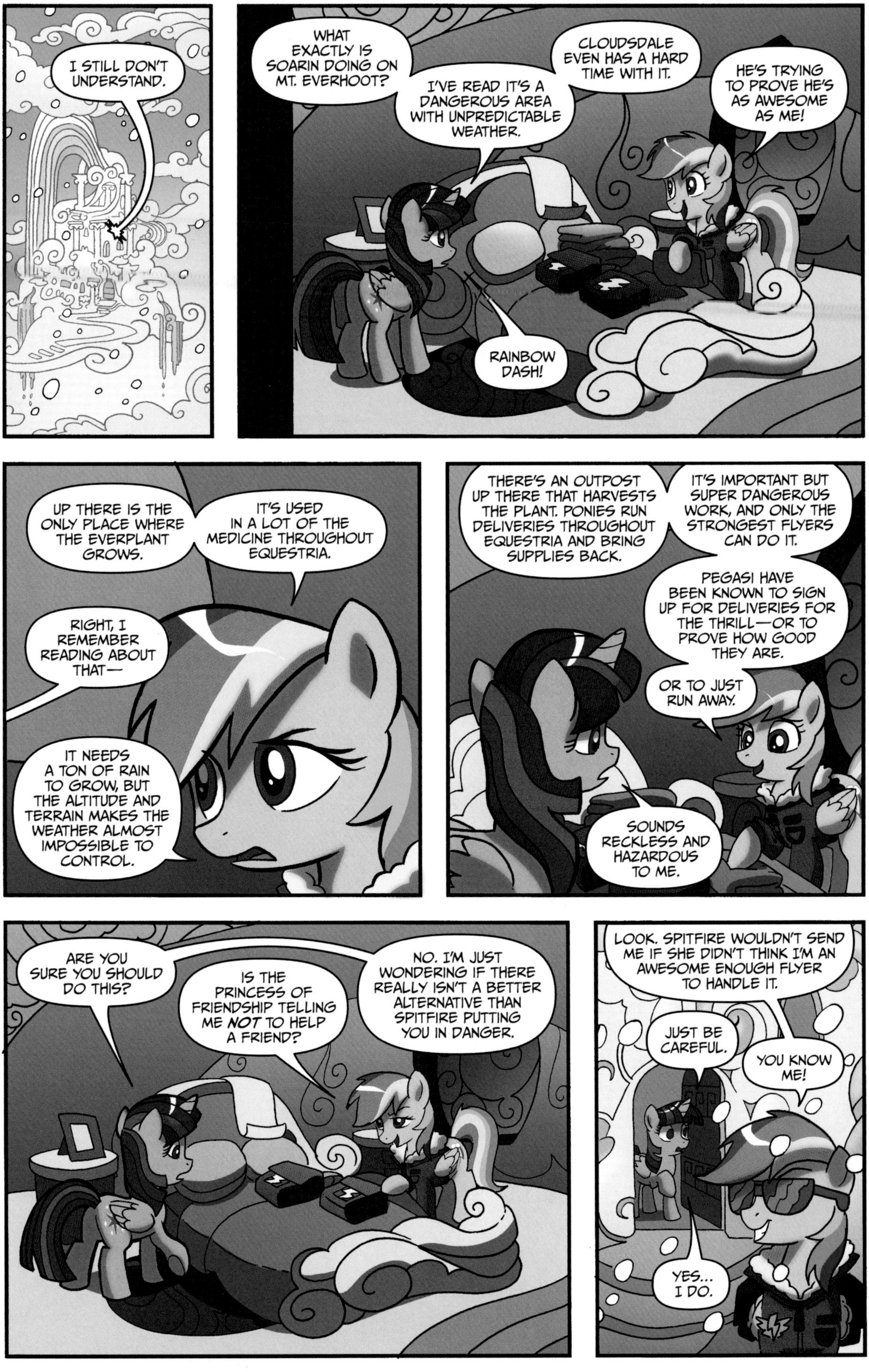
I STILL DON'T UNDERSTAND.
WHAT EXACTLY IS SOARIN DOING ON MT. EVERHOOT?
I'VE READ IT'S A DANGEROUS AREA WITH UNPREDICTABLE WEATHER.
CLOUDSDALE EVEN HAS A HARD TIME WITH IT.
HE'S TRYING TO PROVE HE'S AS AWESOME AS ME!
RAINBOW DASH!
UP THERE IS THE ONLY PLACE WHERE THE EVERPLANT GROWS.
IT'S USED IN A LOT OF THE MEDICINE THROUGHOUT EQUESTRIA.
RIGHT, I REMEMBER READING ABOUT THAT—
IT NEEDS A TON OF RAIN TO GROW, BUT THE ALTITUDE AND TERRAIN MAKES THE WEATHER ALMOST IMPOSSIBLE TO CONTROL.
THERE'S AN OUTPOST UP THERE THAT HARVESTS THE PLANT. PONIES RUN DELIVERIES THROUGHOUT EQUESTRIA AND BRING SUPPLIES BACK.
IT'S IMPORTANT BUT SUPER DANGEROUS WORK, AND ONLY THE STRONGEST FLYERS CAN DO IT.
PEGASI HAVE BEEN KNOWN TO SIGN UP FOR DELIVERIES FOR THE THRILL—OR TO PROVE HOW GOOD THEY ARE.
OR TO JUST RUN AWAY.
SOUNDS RECKLESS AND HAZARDOUS TO ME.
ARE YOU SURE YOU SHOULD DO THIS?
IS THE PRINCESS OF FRIENDSHIP TELLING ME *NOT* TO HELP A FRIEND?
NO. I'M JUST WONDERING IF THERE REALLY ISN'T A BETTER ALTERNATIVE THAN SPITFIRE PUTTING YOU IN DANGER.
LOOK. SPITFIRE WOULDN'T SEND ME IF SHE DIDN'T THINK I'M AN AWESOME ENOUGH FLYER TO HANDLE IT.
JUST BE CAREFUL.
YOU KNOW ME!
YES... I DO.

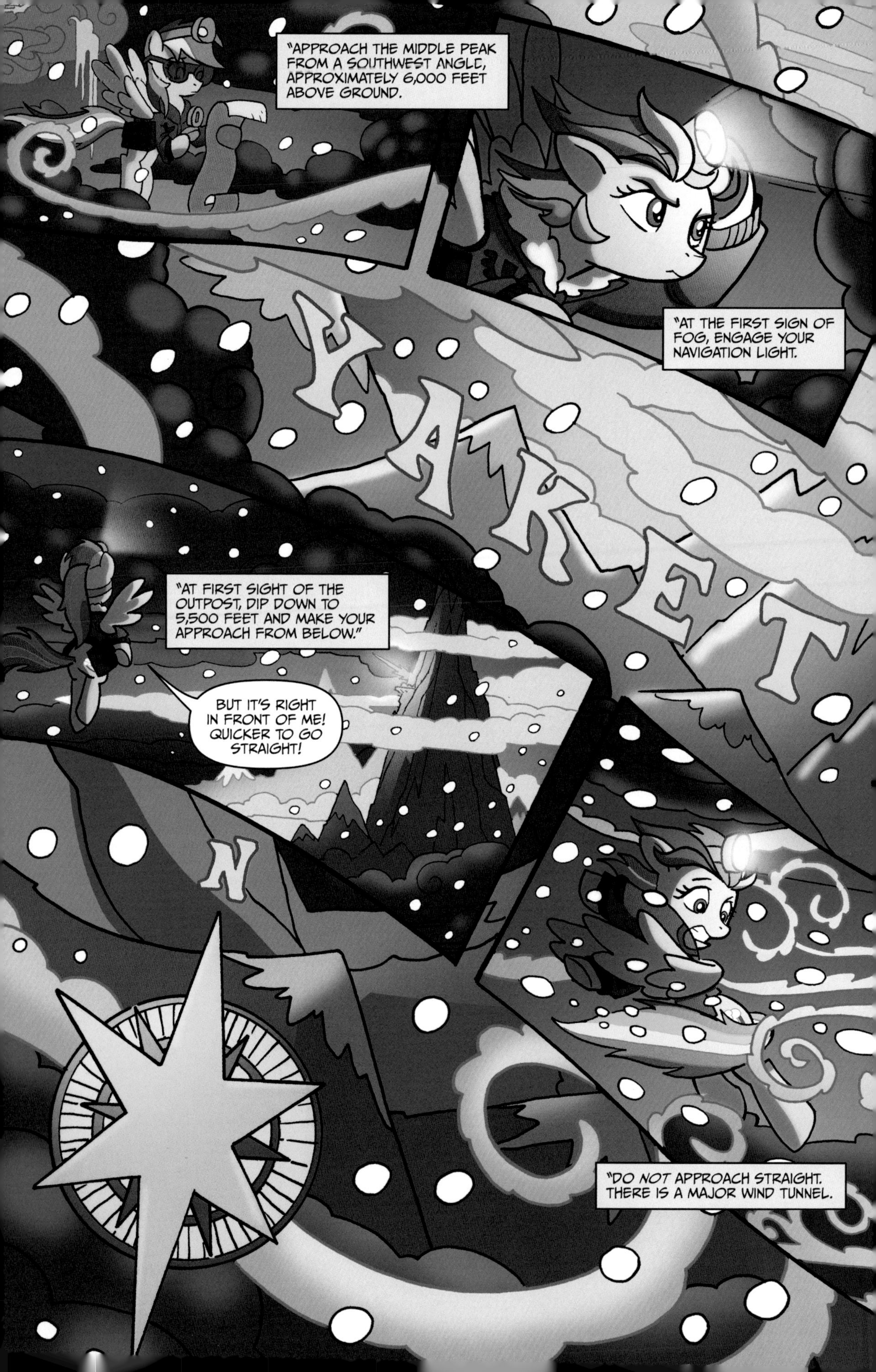
"APPROACH THE MIDDLE PEAK FROM A SOUTHWEST ANGLE, APPROXIMATELY 6,000 FEET ABOVE GROUND.
"AT THE FIRST SIGN OF FOG, ENGAGE YOUR NAVIGATION LIGHT.
YAKETN
"AT FIRST SIGHT OF THE OUTPOST, DIP DOWN TO 5,500 FEET AND MAKE YOUR APPROACH FROM BELOW."
BUT IT'S RIGHT IN FRONT OF ME! QUICKER TO GO STRAIGHT!
"DO NOT APPROACH STRAIGHT. THERE IS A MAJOR WIND TUNNEL.

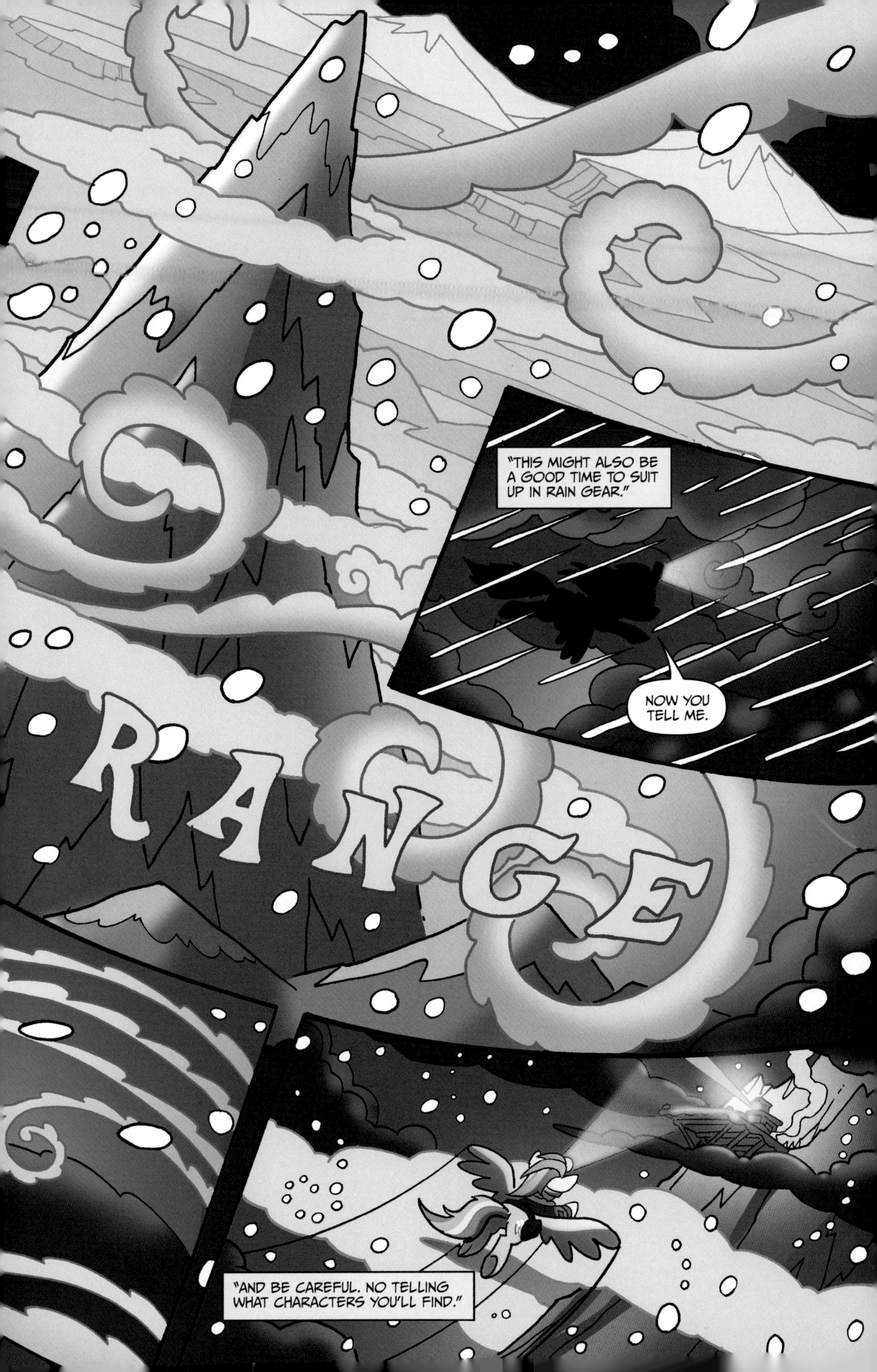
RANGE
"THIS MIGHT ALSO BE A GOOD TIME TO SUIT UP IN RAIN GEAR."
NOW YOU TELL ME.
"AND BE CAREFUL. NO TELLING WHAT CHARACTERS YOU'LL FIND."

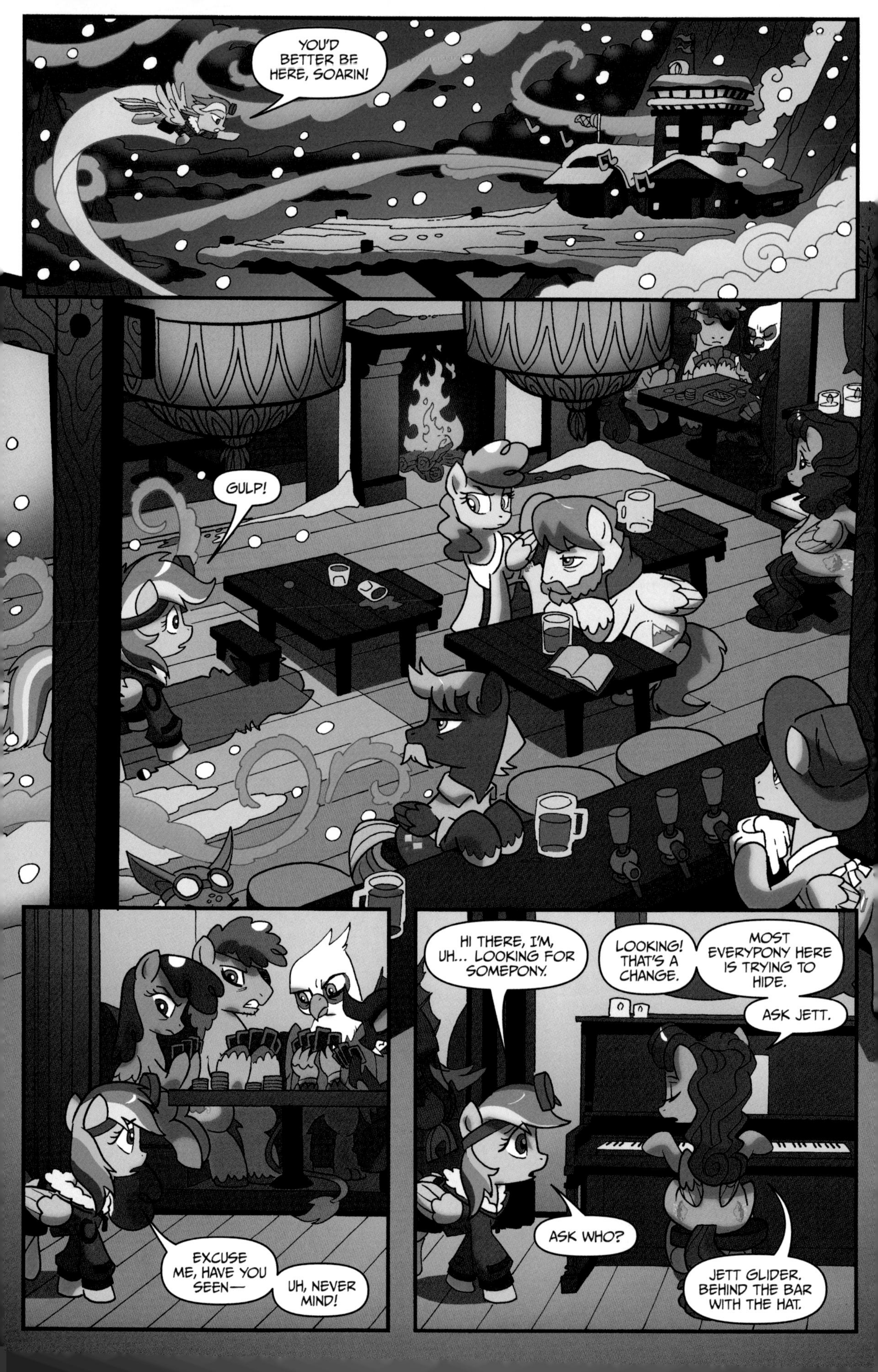
YOU'D BETTER BE HERE, SOARIN!
GULP!
EXCUSE ME, HAVE YOU SEEN—
UH, NEVER MIND!
HI THERE, I'M, UH... LOOKING FOR SOMEPONY.
LOOKING! THAT'S A CHANGE.
MOST EVERYPONY HERE IS TRYING TO HIDE.
ASK JETT.
ASK WHO?
JETT GLIDER. BEHIND THE BAR WITH THE HAT.

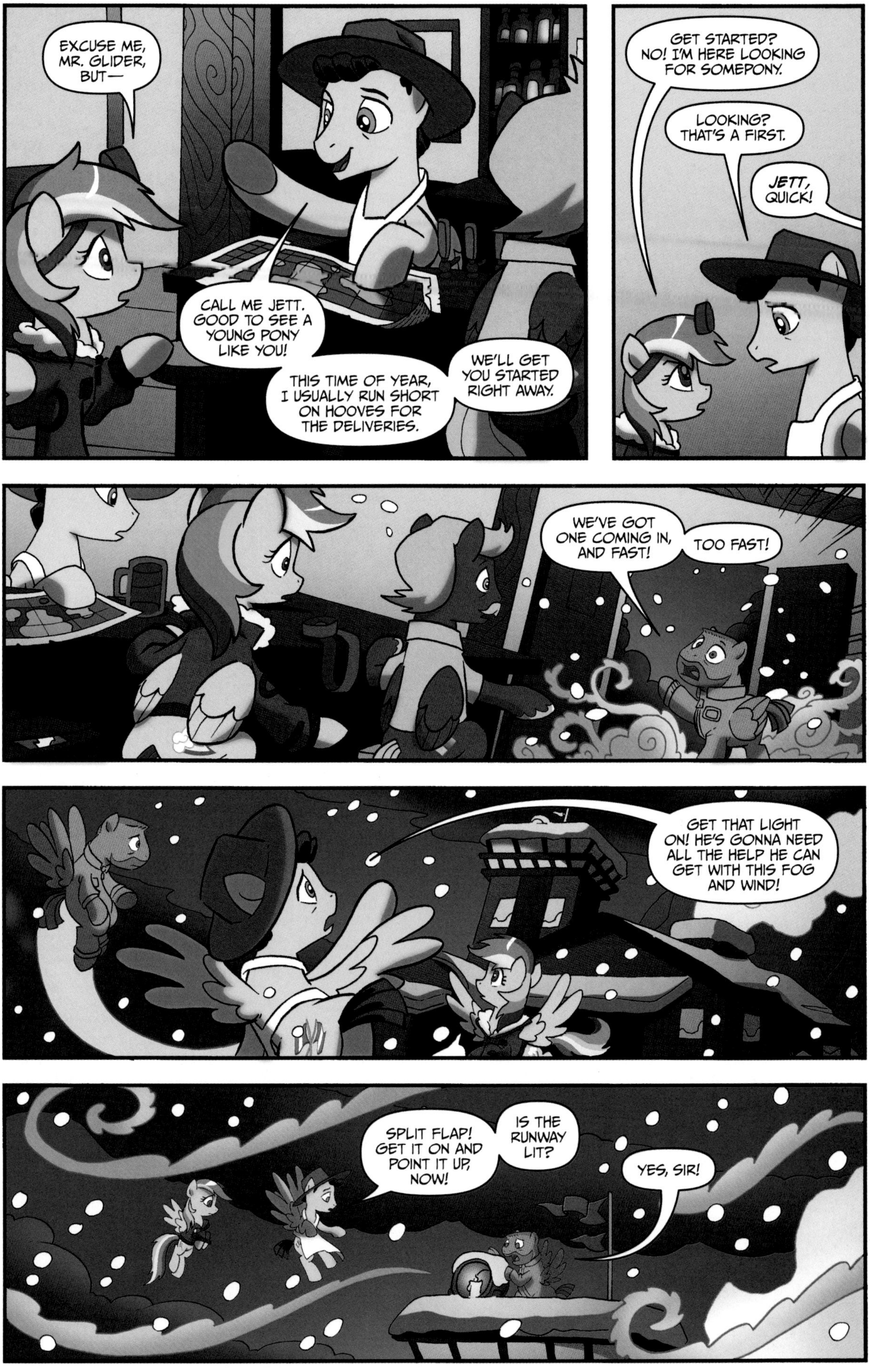
EXCUSE ME, MR. GLIDER, BUT—
CALL ME JETT. GOOD TO SEE A YOUNG PONY LIKE YOU!
THIS TIME OF YEAR, I USUALLY RUN SHORT ON HOOVES FOR THE DELIVERIES.
WE'LL GET YOU STARTED RIGHT AWAY.
GET STARTED? NO! I'M HERE LOOKING FOR SOMEPONY.
LOOKING? THAT'S A FIRST.
JETT, QUICK!
WE'VE GOT ONE COMING IN, AND FAST!
TOO FAST!
GET THAT LIGHT ON! HE'S GONNA NEED ALL THE HELP HE CAN GET WITH THIS FOG AND WIND!
SPLIT FLAP! GET IT ON AND POINT IT UP, NOW!
IS THE RUNWAY LIT?
YES, SIR!

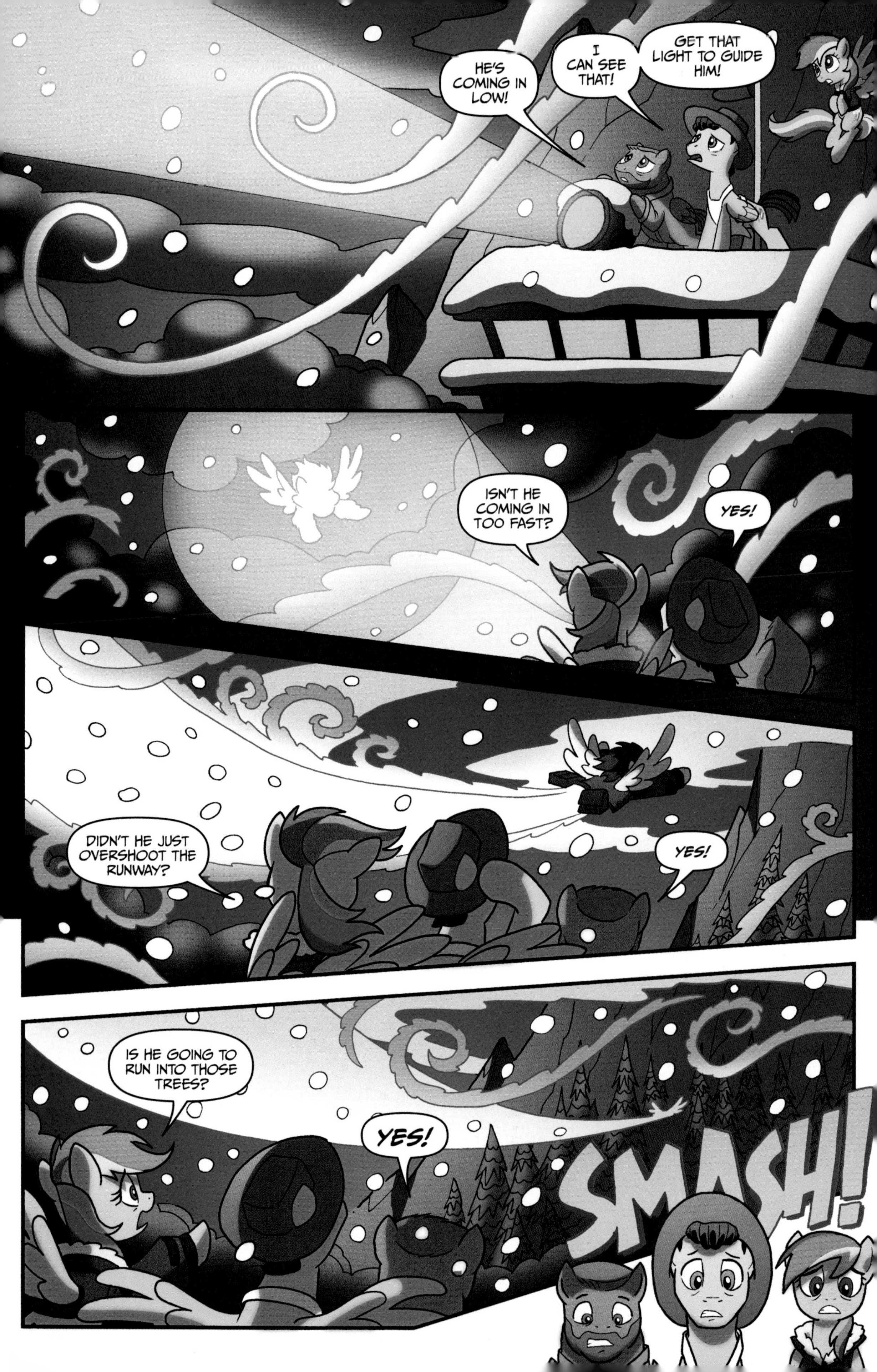
HE'S COMING IN LOW!
I CAN SEE THAT!
GET THAT LIGHT TO GUIDE HIM!
ISN'T HE COMING IN TOO FAST?
YES!
DIDN'T HE JUST OVERSHOOT THE RUNWAY?
YES!
IS HE GOING TO RUN INTO THOSE TREES?
YES!
SMASH!

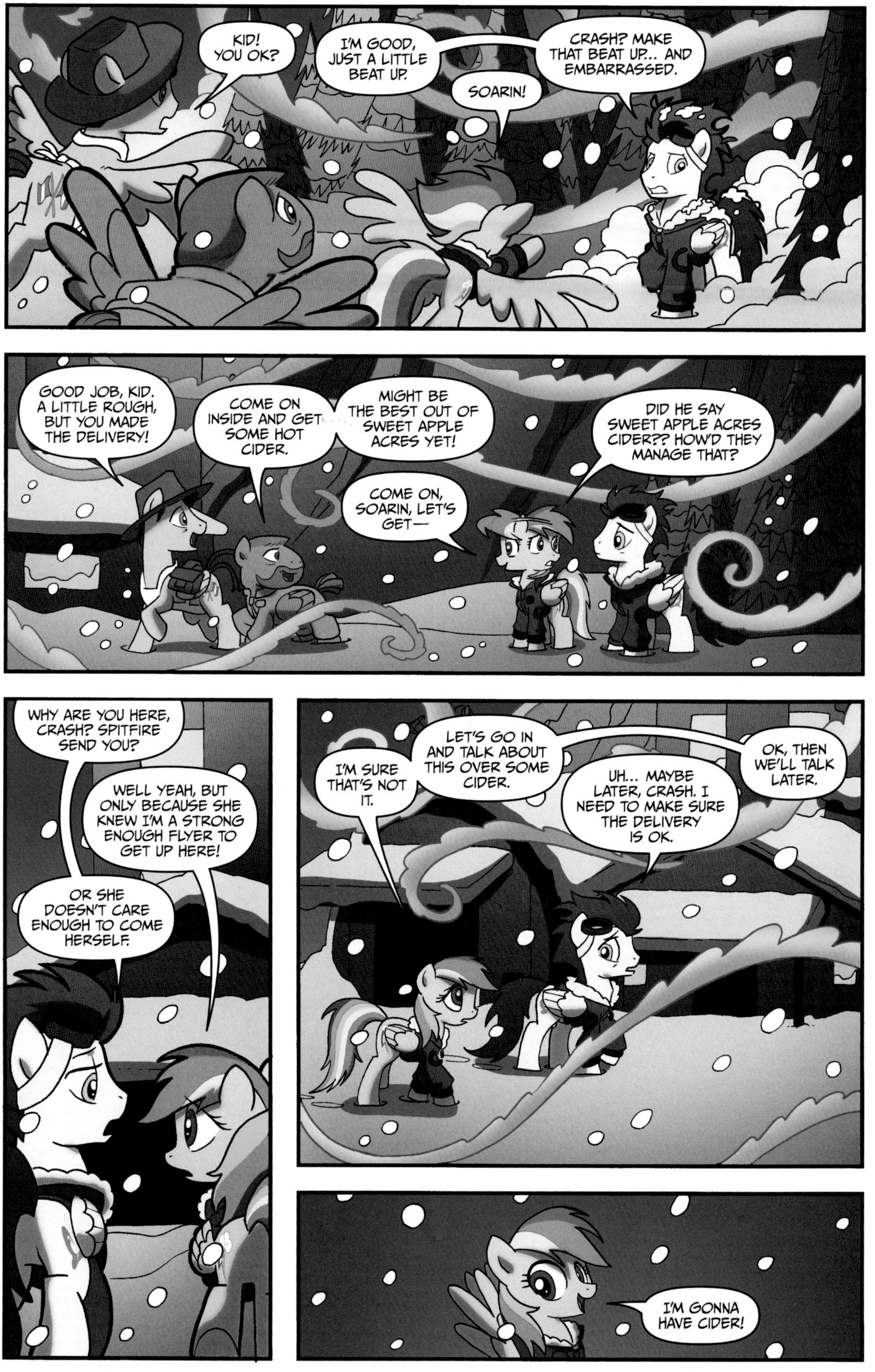
KID! YOU OK?
I'M GOOD, JUST A LITTLE BEAT UP.
SOARIN!
CRASH? MAKE THAT BEAT UP... AND EMBARRASSED.
GOOD JOB, KID. A LITTLE ROUGH, BUT YOU MADE THE DELIVERY!
COME ON INSIDE AND GET SOME HOT CIDER.
MIGHT BE THE BEST OUT OF SWEET APPLE ACRES YET!
COME ON, SOARIN, LET'S GET—
DID HE SAY SWEET APPLE ACRES CIDER?? HOW'D THEY MANAGE THAT?
WHY ARE YOU HERE, CRASH? SPITFIRE SEND YOU?
WELL YEAH, BUT ONLY BECAUSE SHE KNEW I'M A STRONG ENOUGH FLYER TO GET UP HERE!
OR SHE DOESN'T CARE ENOUGH TO COME HERSELF.
I'M SURE THAT'S NOT IT.
LET'S GO IN AND TALK ABOUT THIS OVER SOME CIDER.
UH... MAYBE LATER, CRASH. I NEED TO MAKE SURE THE DELIVERY IS OK.
OK, THEN WE'LL TALK LATER.
I'M GONNA HAVE CIDER!

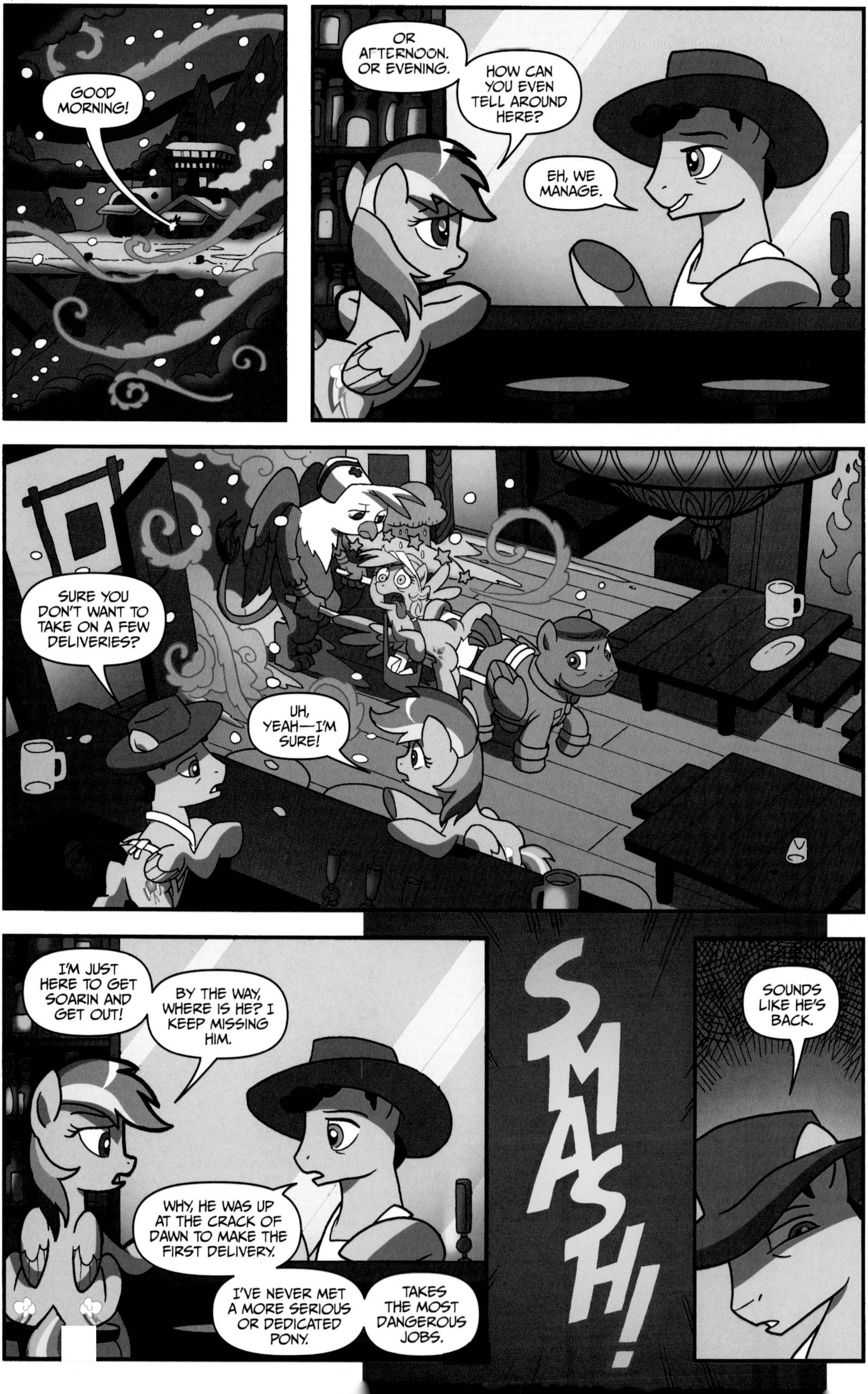
GOOD MORNING!
OR AFTERNOON. OR EVENING.
HOW CAN YOU EVEN TELL AROUND HERE?
EH, WE MANAGE.
SURE YOU DON'T WANT TO TAKE ON A FEW DELIVERIES?
UH, YEAH—I'M SURE!
I'M JUST HERE TO GET SOARIN AND GET OUT!
BY THE WAY, WHERE IS HE? I KEEP MISSING HIM.
WHY, HE WAS UP AT THE CRACK OF DAWN TO MAKE THE FIRST DELIVERY.
I'VE NEVER MET A MORE SERIOUS OR DEDICATED PONY.
TAKES THE MOST DANGEROUS JOBS.
SMASH!
SOUNDS LIKE HE'S BACK.

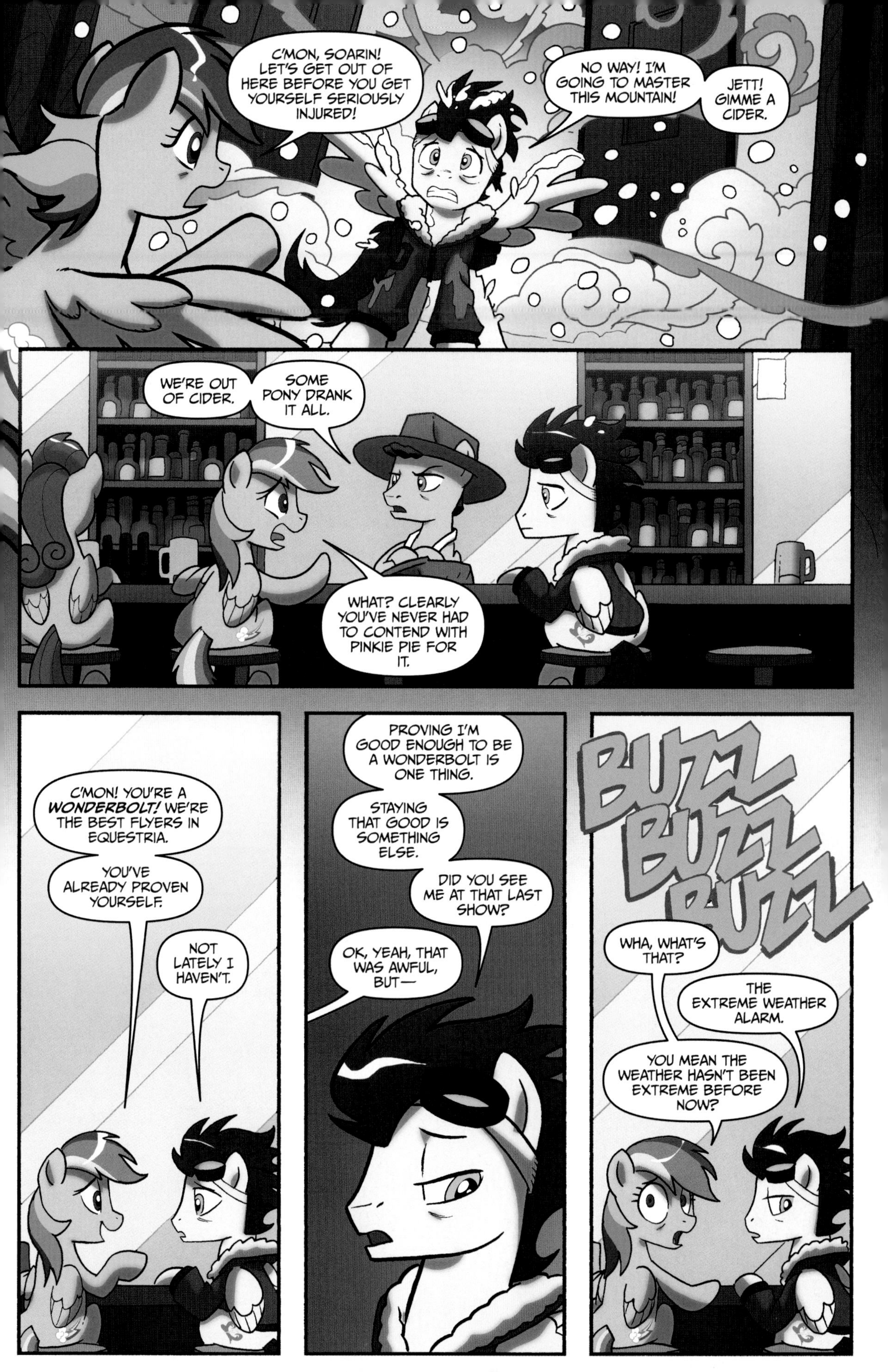
C'MON, SOARIN! LET'S GET OUT OF HERE BEFORE YOU GET YOURSELF SERIOUSLY INJURED!
NO WAY! I'M GOING TO MASTER THIS MOUNTAIN!
JETT! GIMME A CIDER.
WE'RE OUT OF CIDER.
SOME PONY DRANK IT ALL.
WHAT? CLEARLY YOU'VE NEVER HAD TO CONTEND WITH PINKIE PIE FOR IT.
C'MON! YOU'RE A WONDERBOLT! WE'RE THE BEST FLYERS IN EQUESTRIA.
YOU'VE ALREADY PROVEN YOURSELF.
NOT LATELY I HAVEN'T.
PROVING I'M GOOD ENOUGH TO BE A WONDERBOLT IS ONE THING.
STAYING THAT GOOD IS SOMETHING ELSE.
DID YOU SEE ME AT THAT LAST SHOW?
OK, YEAH, THAT WAS AWFUL, BUT—
BUZZ BUZZ BUZZ
WHA, WHAT'S THAT?
THE EXTREME WEATHER ALARM.
YOU MEAN THE WEATHER HASN'T BEEN EXTREME BEFORE NOW?

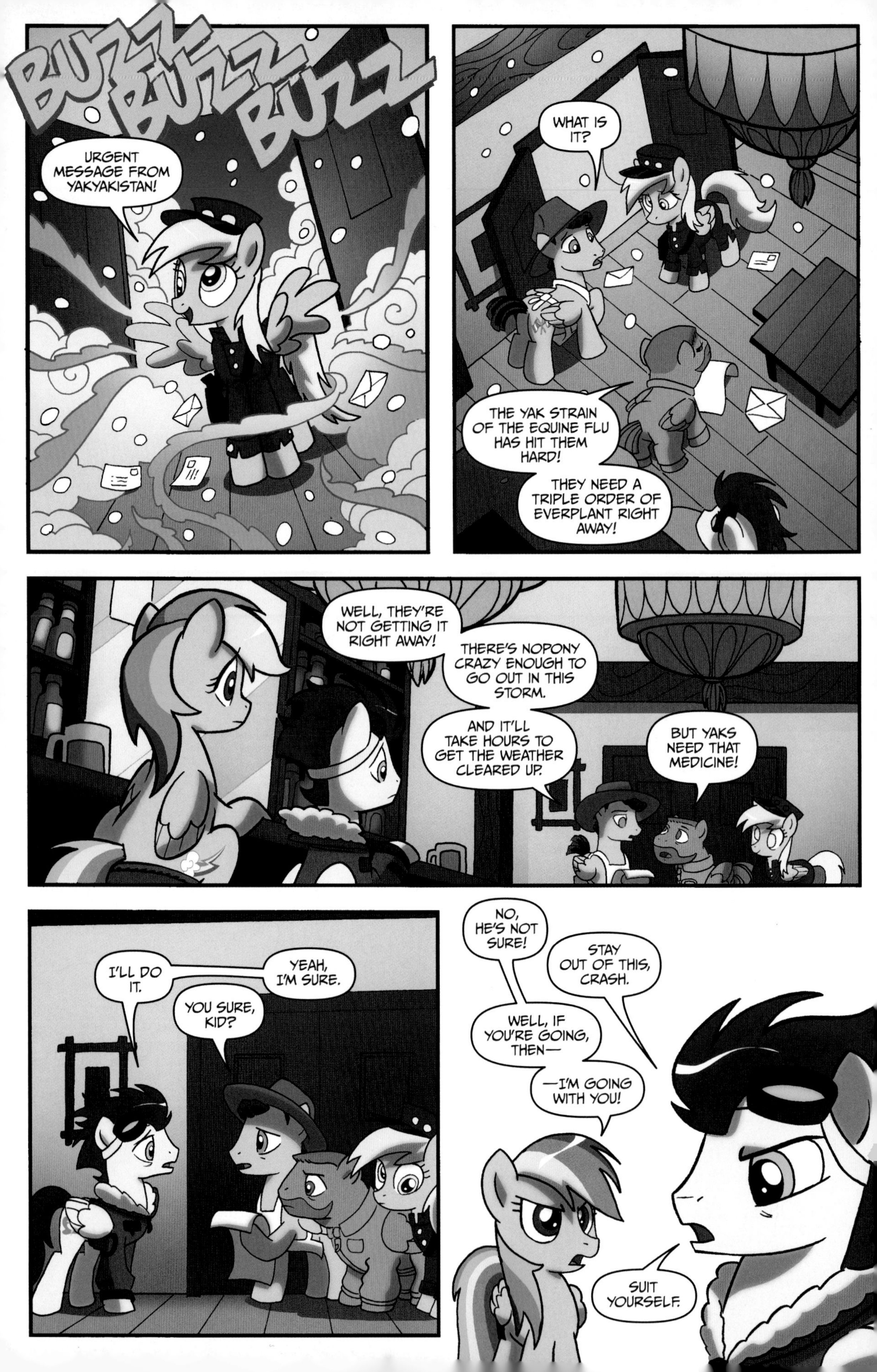
BUZZ BUZZ BUZZ
URGENT MESSAGE FROM YAKYAKISTAN!
WHAT IS IT?
THE YAK STRAIN OF THE EQUINE FLU HAS HIT THEM HARD!
THEY NEED A TRIPLE ORDER OF EVERPLANT RIGHT AWAY!
WELL, THEY'RE NOT GETTING IT RIGHT AWAY!
THERE'S NOPONY CRAZY ENOUGH TO GO OUT IN THIS STORM.
AND IT'LL TAKE HOURS TO GET THE WEATHER CLEARED UP.
BUT YAKS NEED THAT MEDICINE!
I'LL DO IT.
YOU SURE, KID?
YEAH, I'M SURE.
NO, HE'S NOT SURE!
STAY OUT OF THIS, CRASH.
WELL, IF YOU'RE GOING, THEN—
—I'M GOING WITH YOU!
SUIT YOURSELF.

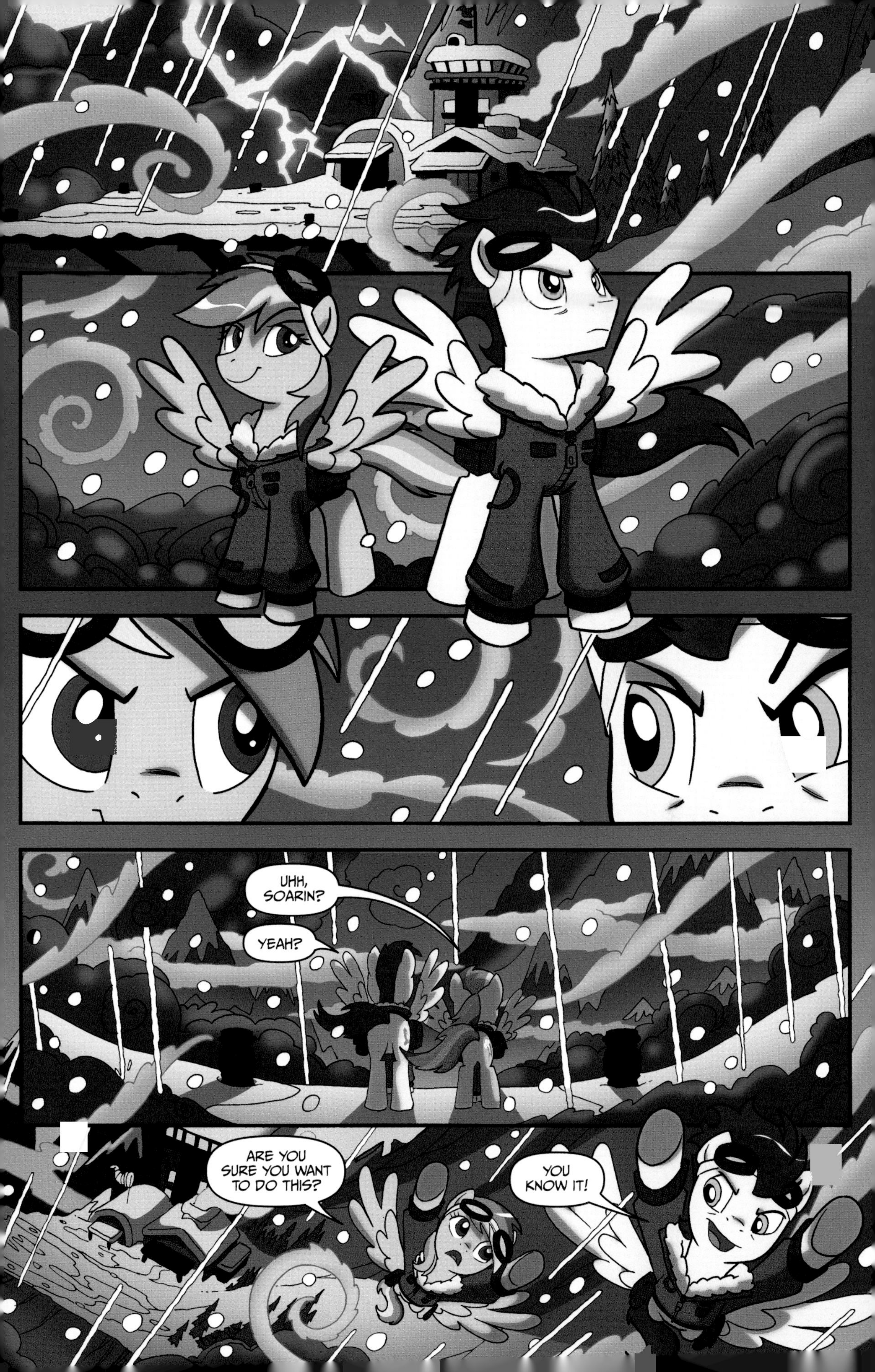
UHH, SOARIN?
YEAH?
ARE YOU SURE YOU WANT TO DO THIS?
YOU KNOW IT!

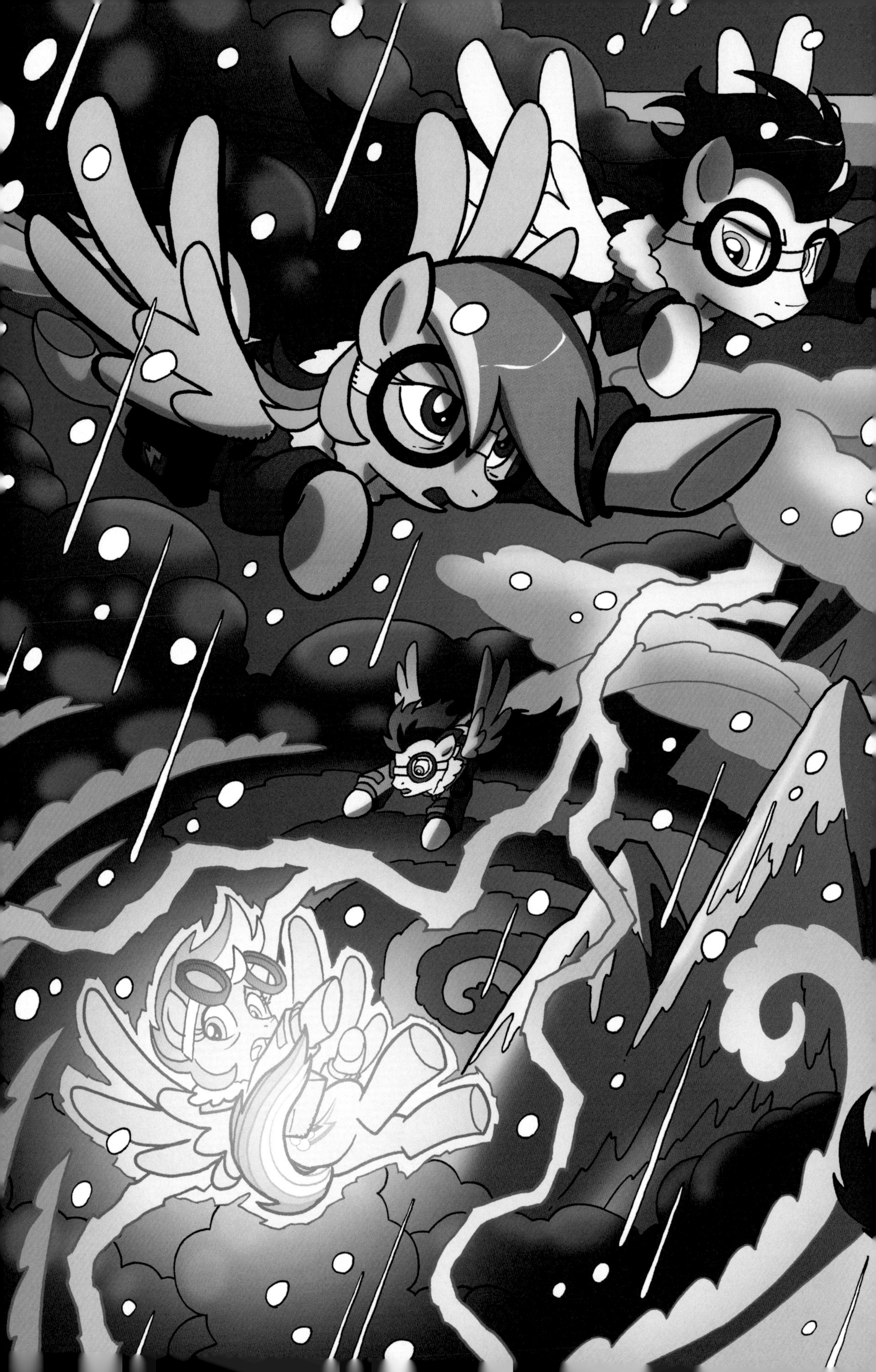

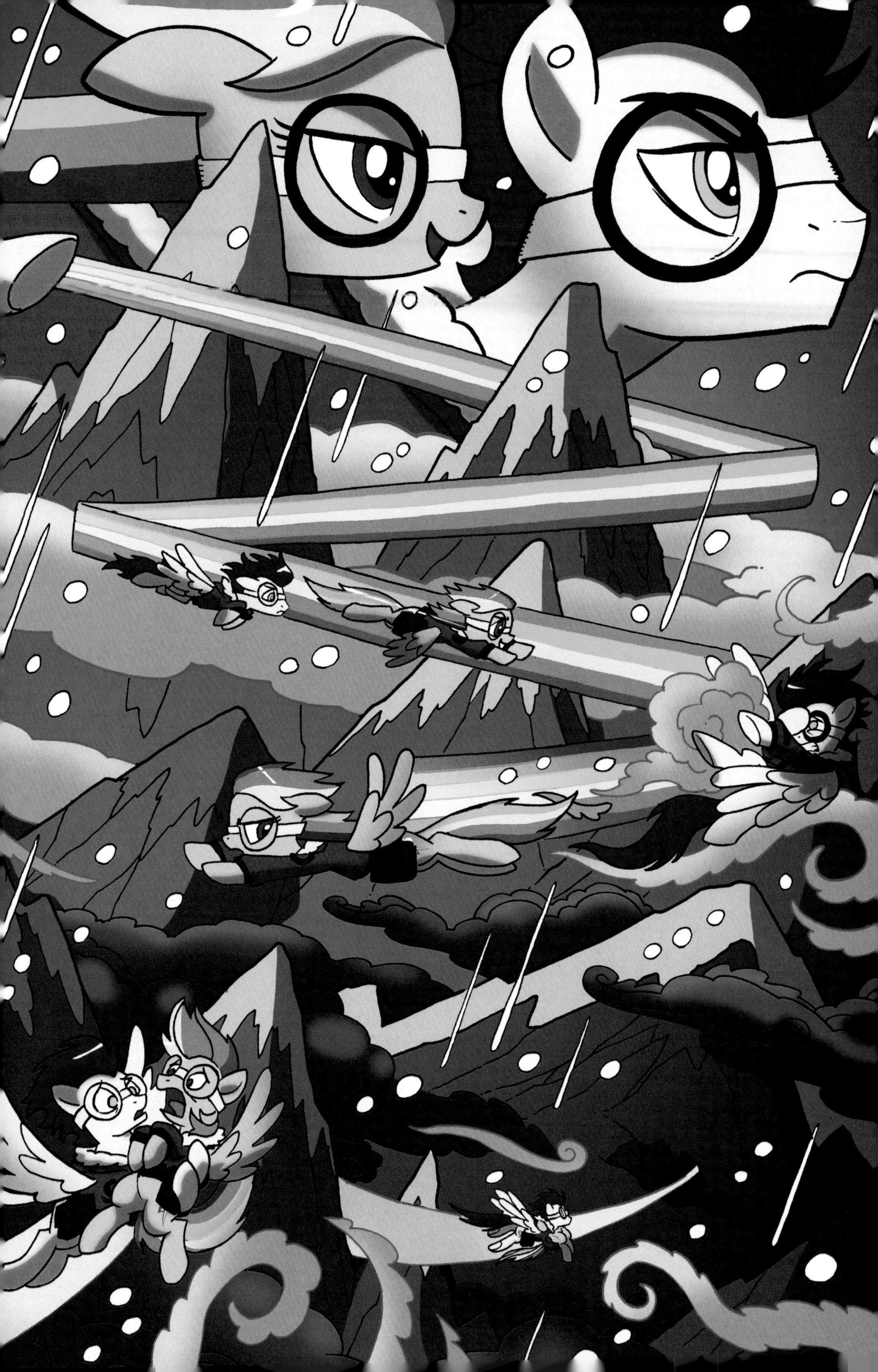

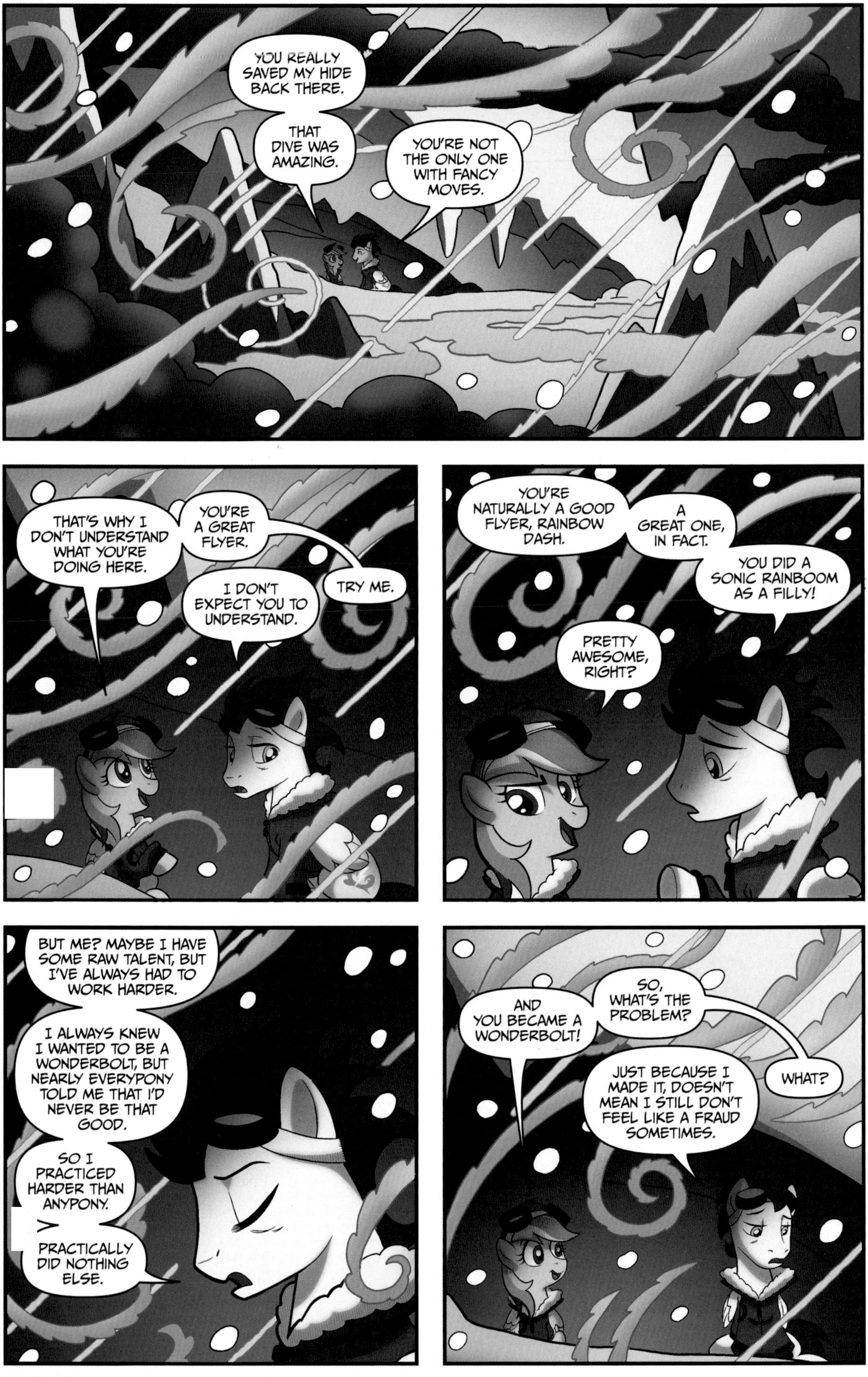
YOU REALLY SAVED MY HIDE BACK THERE.
THAT DIVE WAS AMAZING.
YOU'RE NOT THE ONLY ONE WITH FANCY MOVES.
THAT'S WHY I DON'T UNDERSTAND WHAT YOU'RE DOING HERE.
YOU'RE A GREAT FLYER.
I DON'T EXPECT YOU TO UNDERSTAND.
TRY ME.
YOU'RE NATURALLY A GOOD FLYER, RAINBOW DASH.
A GREAT ONE, IN FACT.
YOU DID A SONIC RAINBOOM AS A FILLY!
PRETTY AWESOME, RIGHT?
BUT ME? MAYBE I HAVE SOME RAW TALENT, BUT I'VE ALWAYS HAD TO WORK HARDER.
I ALWAYS KNEW I WANTED TO BE A WONDERBOLT, BUT NEARLY EVERYPONY TOLD ME THAT I'D NEVER BE THAT GOOD.
SO I PRACTICED HARDER THAN ANYPONY.
PRACTICALLY DID NOTHING ELSE.
AND YOU BECAME A WONDERBOLT!
SO, WHAT'S THE PROBLEM?
JUST BECAUSE I MADE IT, DOESN'T MEAN I STILL DON'T FEEL LIKE A FRAUD SOMETIMES.
WHAT?

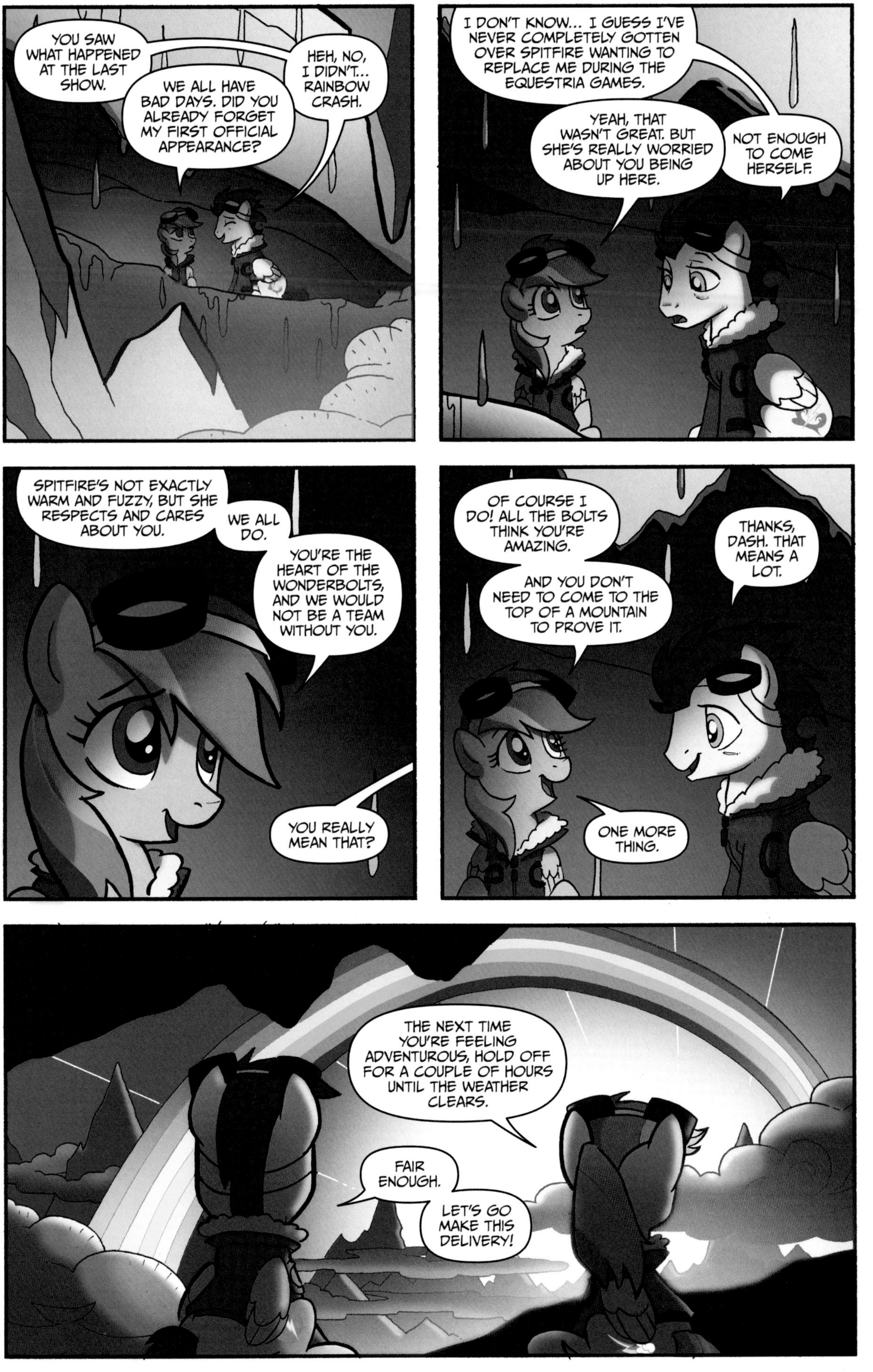
YOU SAW WHAT HAPPENED AT THE LAST SHOW.
WE ALL HAVE BAD DAYS. DID YOU ALREADY FORGET MY FIRST OFFICIAL APPEARANCE?
HEH, NO, I DIDN'T... RAINBOW CRASH.
I DON'T KNOW... I GUESS I'VE NEVER COMPLETELY GOTTEN OVER SPITFIRE WANTING TO REPLACE ME DURING THE EQUESTRIA GAMES.
YEAH, THAT WASN'T GREAT. BUT SHE'S REALLY WORRIED ABOUT YOU BEING UP HERE.
NOT ENOUGH TO COME HERSELF.
SPITFIRE'S NOT EXACTLY WARM AND FUZZY, BUT SHE RESPECTS AND CARES ABOUT YOU.
WE ALL DO.
YOU'RE THE HEART OF THE WONDERBOLTS, AND WE WOULD NOT BE A TEAM WITHOUT YOU.
YOU REALLY MEAN THAT?
OF COURSE I DO! ALL THE BOLTS THINK YOU'RE AMAZING.
AND YOU DON'T NEED TO COME TO THE TOP OF A MOUNTAIN TO PROVE IT.
THANKS, DASH. THAT MEANS A LOT.
ONE MORE THING.
THE NEXT TIME YOU'RE FEELING ADVENTUROUS, HOLD OFF FOR A COUPLE OF HOURS UNTIL THE WEATHER CLEARS.
FAIR ENOUGH.
LET'S GO MAKE THIS DELIVERY!

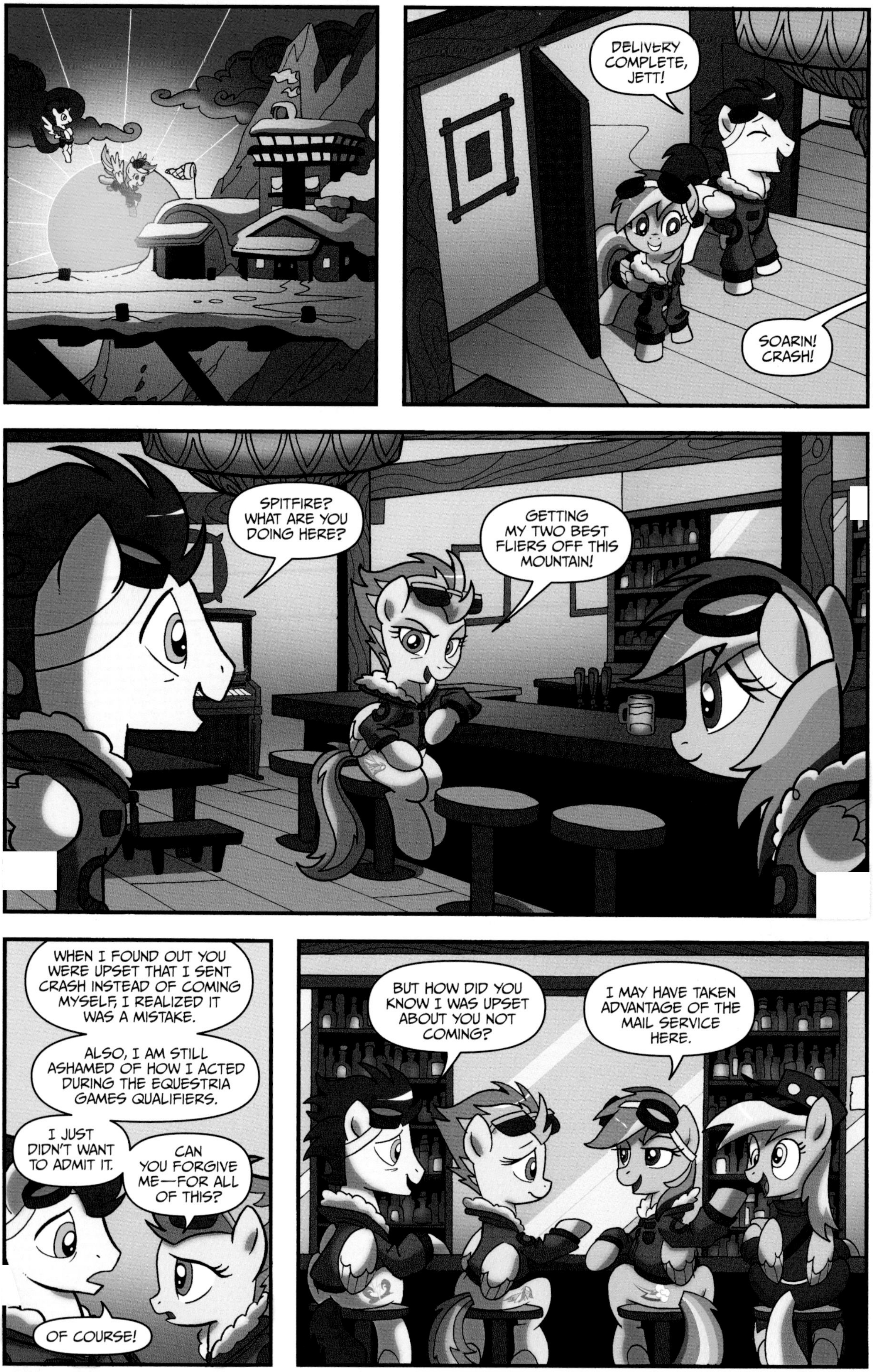
DELIVERY COMPLETE, JETT!
SOARIN! CRASH!
SPITFIRE? WHAT ARE YOU DOING HERE?
GETTING MY TWO BEST FLIERS OFF THIS MOUNTAIN!
WHEN I FOUND OUT YOU WERE UPSET THAT I SENT CRASH INSTEAD OF COMING MYSELF, I REALIZED IT WAS A MISTAKE.
ALSO, I AM STILL ASHAMED OF HOW I ACTED DURING THE EQUESTRIA GAMES QUALIFIERS.
I JUST DIDN'T WANT TO ADMIT IT.
CAN YOU FORGIVE ME—FOR ALL OF THIS?
OF COURSE!
BUT HOW DID YOU KNOW I WAS UPSET ABOUT YOU NOT COMING?
I MAY HAVE TAKEN ADVANTAGE OF THE MAIL SERVICE HERE.

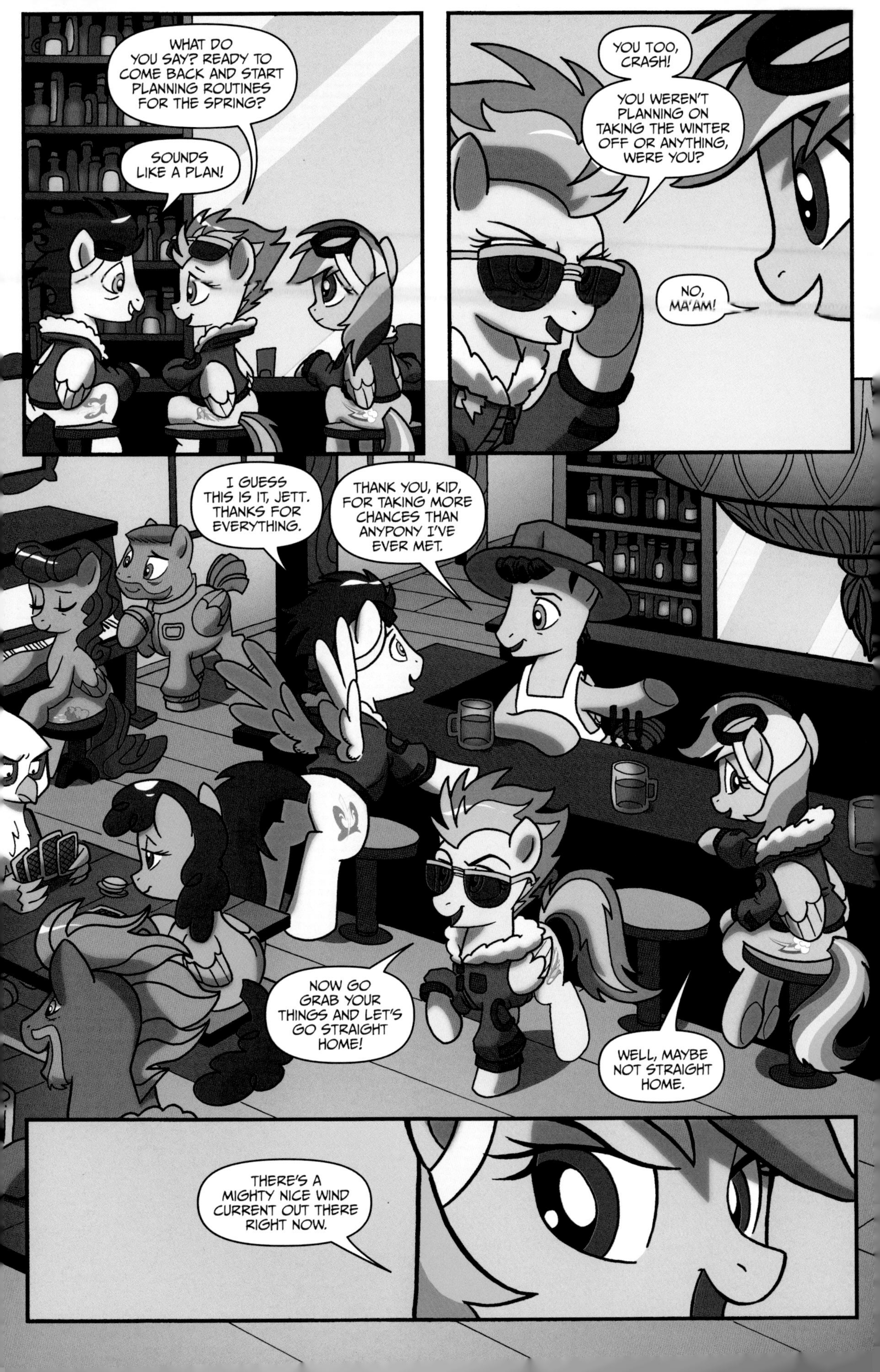
WHAT DO YOU SAY? READY TO COME BACK AND START PLANNING ROUTINES FOR THE SPRING?
SOUNDS LIKE A PLAN!
YOU TOO, CRASH!
YOU WEREN'T PLANNING ON TAKING THE WINTER OFF OR ANYTHING, WERE YOU?
NO, MA'AM!
I GUESS THIS IS IT, JETT. THANKS FOR EVERYTHING.
THANK YOU, KID, FOR TAKING MORE CHANCES THAN ANYPONY I'VE EVER MET.
NOW GO GRAB YOUR THINGS AND LET'S GO STRAIGHT HOME!
WELL, MAYBE NOT STRAIGHT HOME.
THERE'S A MIGHTY NICE WIND CURRENT OUT THERE RIGHT NOW.

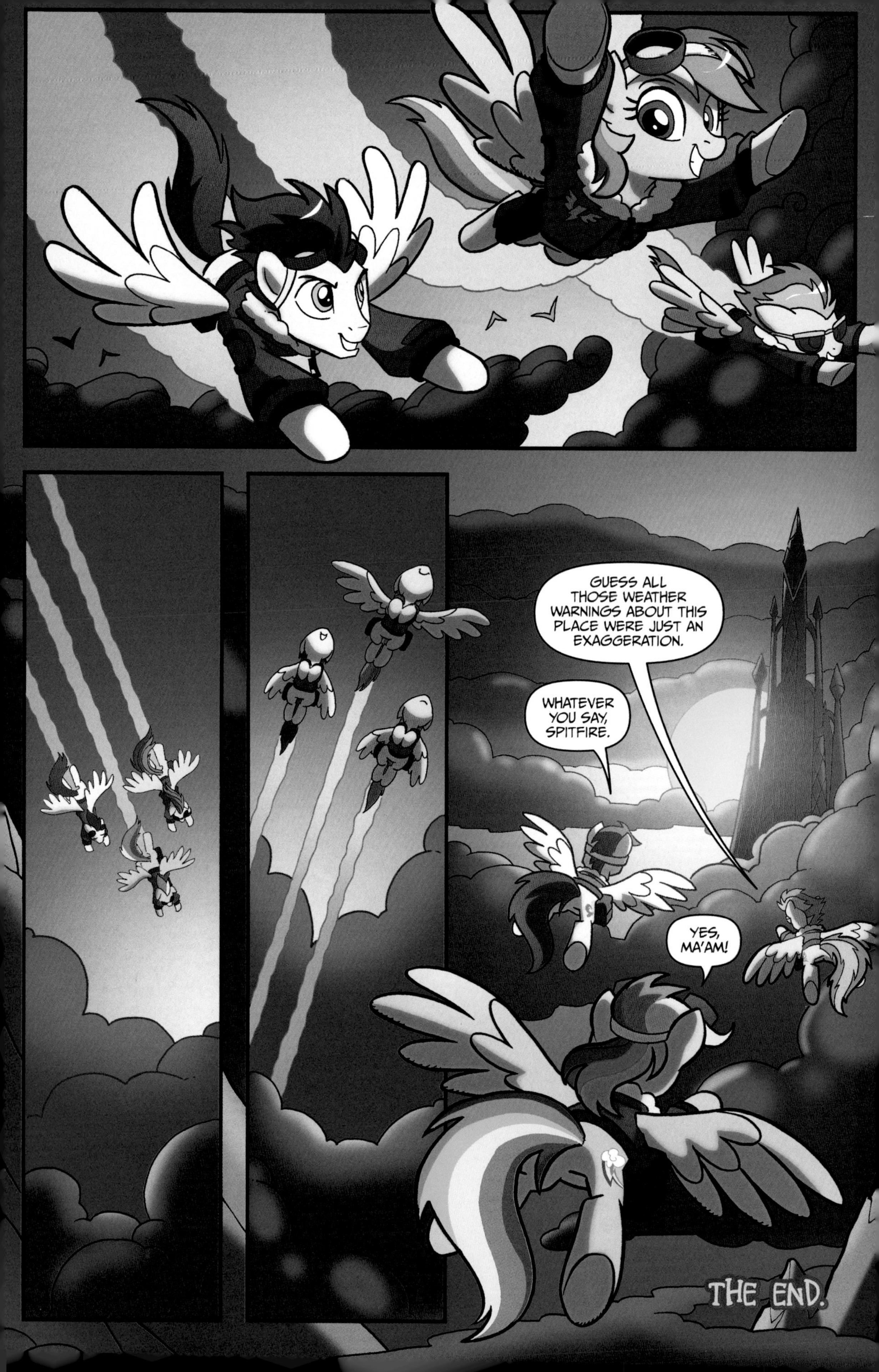
GUESS ALL THOSE WEATHER WARNINGS ABOUT THIS PLACE WERE JUST AN EXAGGERATION.
WHATEVER YOU SAY, SPITFIRE.
YES, MA'AM!
THE END.

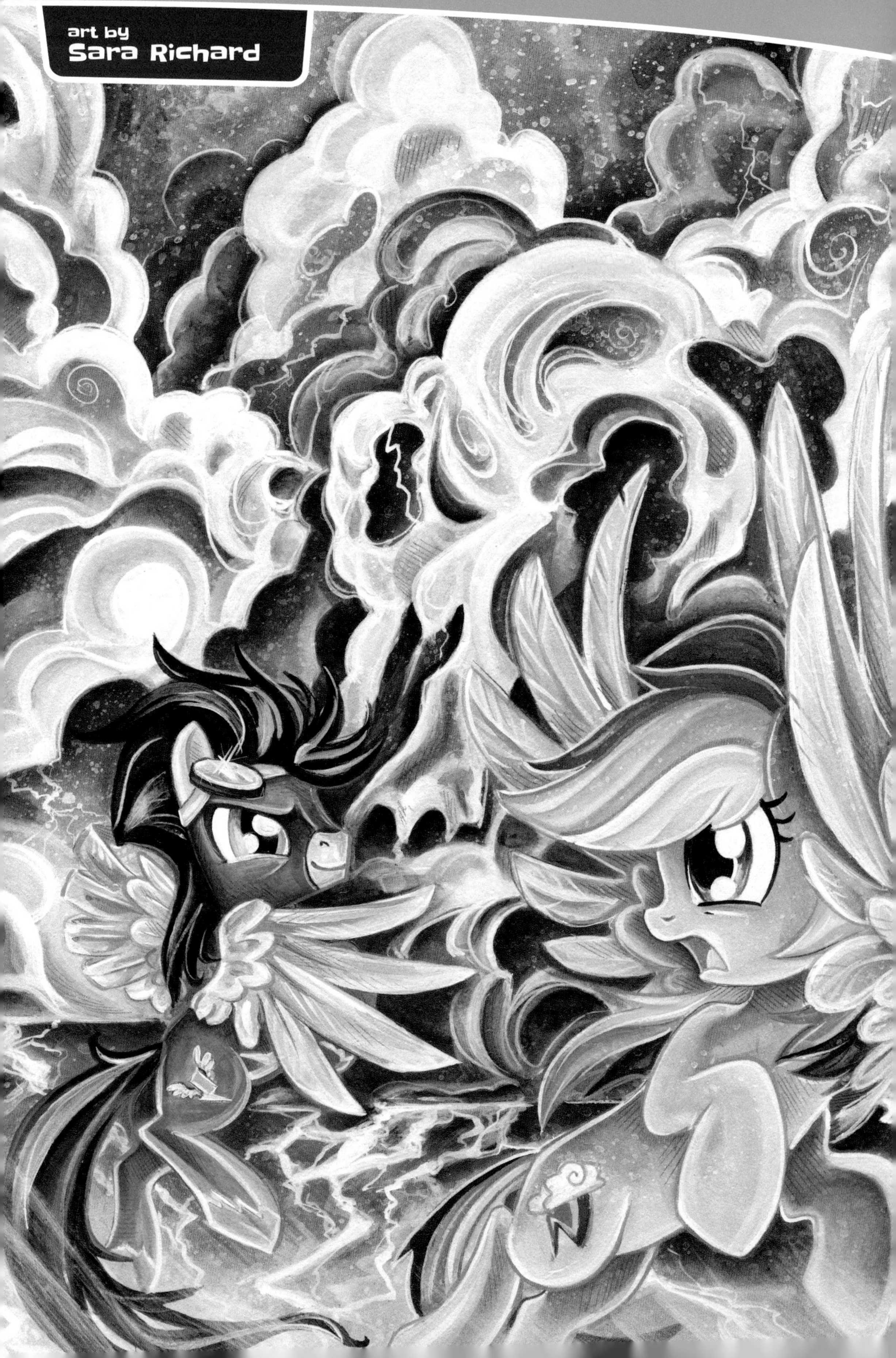
art by
Sara Richard

Rarity & Trixie

art by
Agnes Garbowska

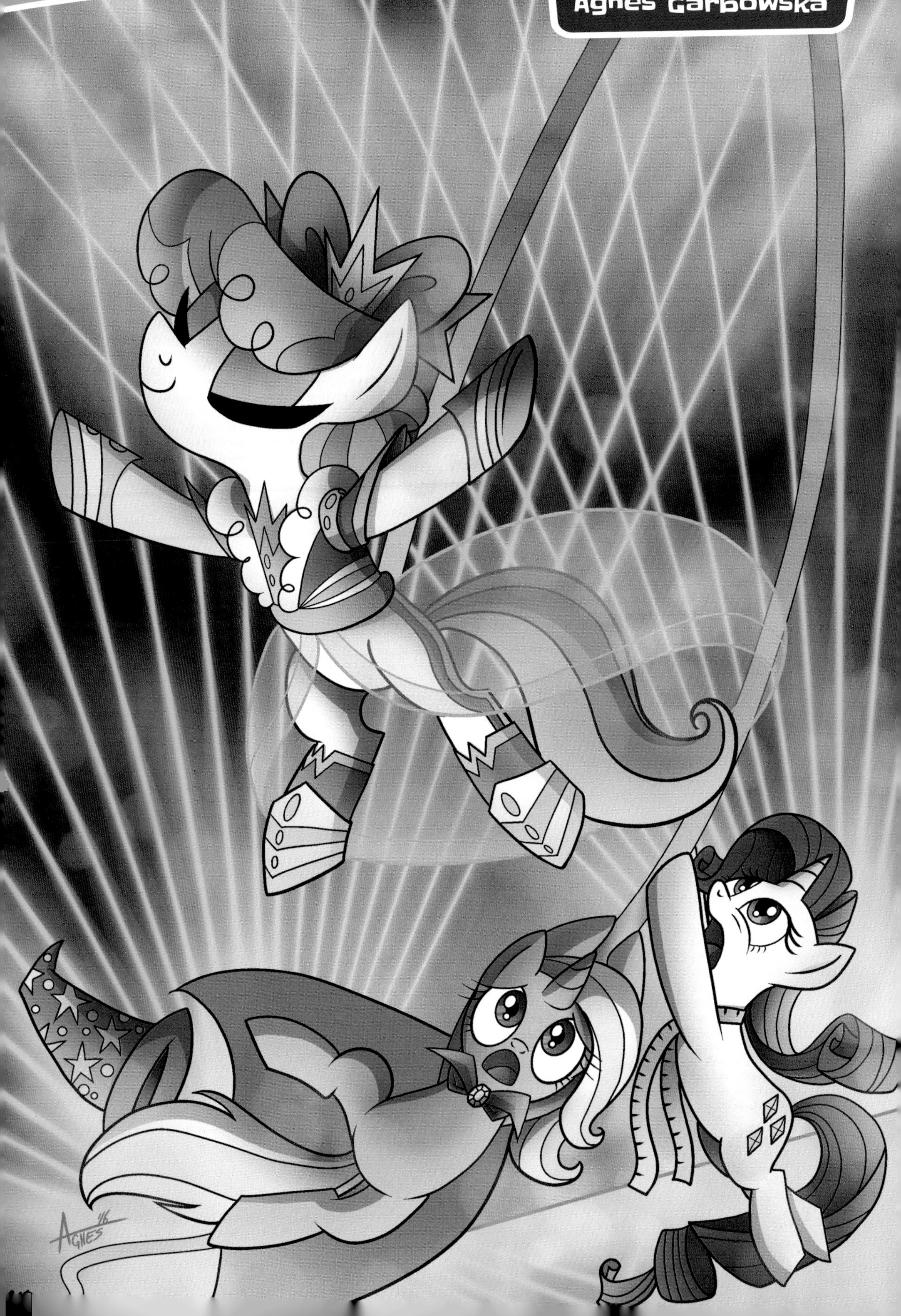

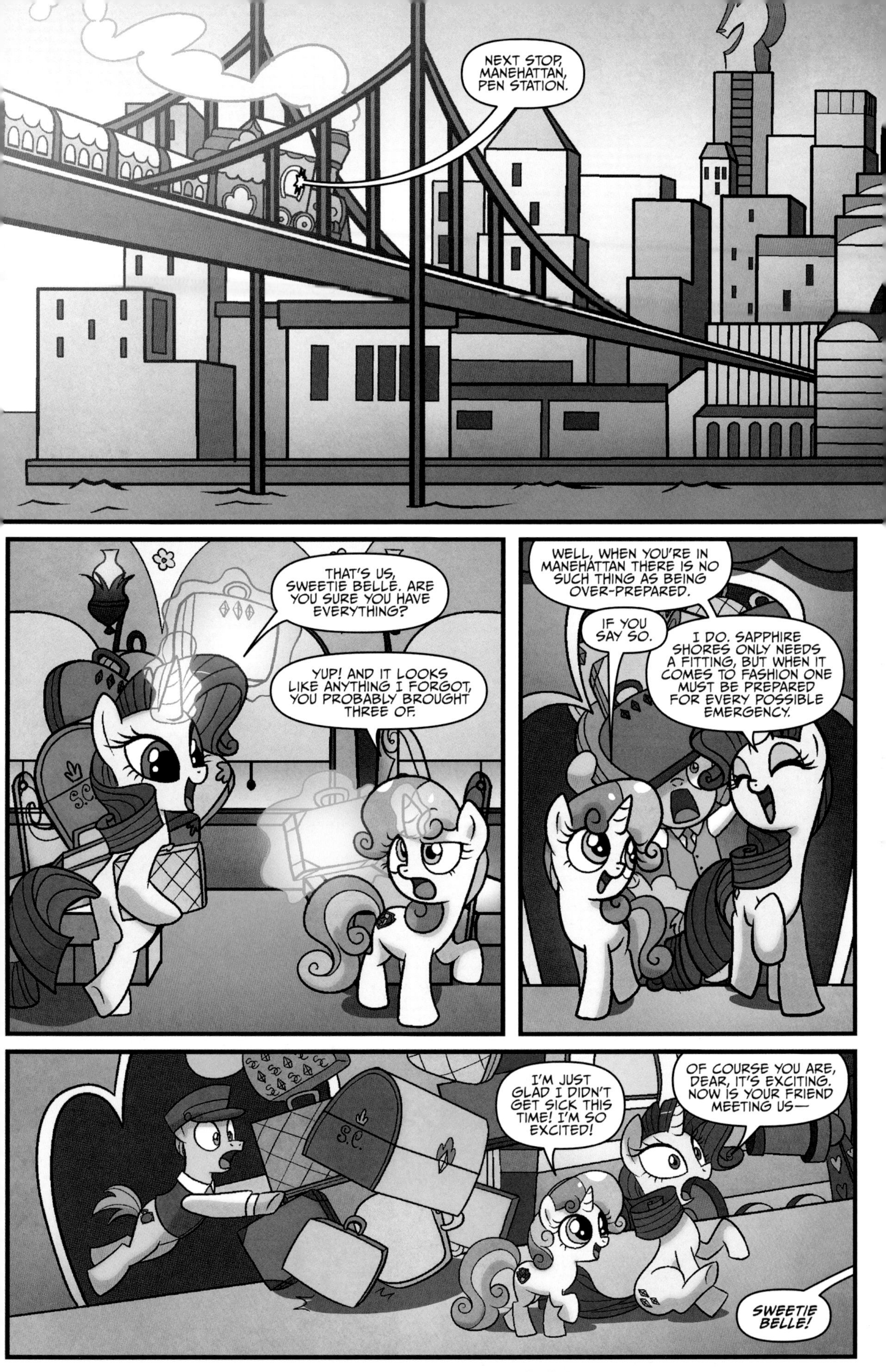
NEXT STOP, MANEHATTAN, PEN STATION.
THAT'S US, SWEETIE BELLE. ARE YOU SURE YOU HAVE EVERYTHING?
YUP! AND IT LOOKS LIKE ANYTHING I FORGOT, YOU PROBABLY BROUGHT THREE OF.
WELL, WHEN YOU'RE IN MANEHATTAN THERE IS NO SUCH THING AS BEING OVER-PREPARED.
IF YOU SAY SO.
I DO. SAPPHIRE SHORES ONLY NEEDS A FITTING, BUT WHEN IT COMES TO FASHION ONE MUST BE PREPARED FOR EVERY POSSIBLE EMERGENCY.
I'M JUST GLAD I DIDN'T GET SICK THIS TIME! I'M SO EXCITED!
OF COURSE YOU ARE, DEAR, IT'S EXCITING. NOW IS YOUR FRIEND MEETING US—
SWEETIE BELLE!

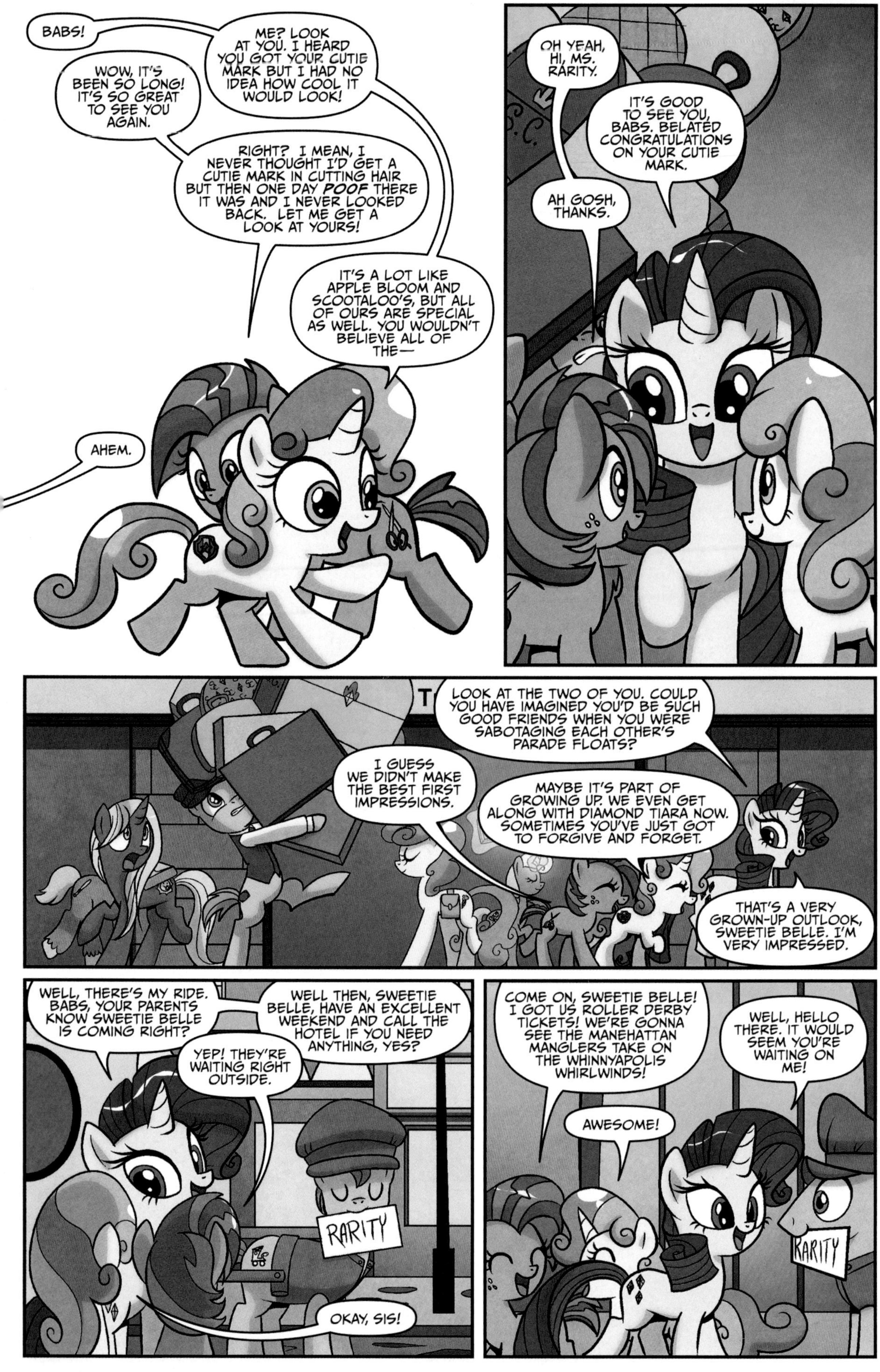
BABS!
WOW, IT'S BEEN SO LONG! IT'S SO GREAT TO SEE YOU AGAIN.
ME? LOOK AT YOU. I HEARD YOU GOT YOUR CUTIE MARK BUT I HAD NO IDEA HOW COOL IT WOULD LOOK!
RIGHT? I MEAN, I NEVER THOUGHT I'D GET A CUTIE MARK IN CUTTING HAIR BUT THEN ONE DAY *POOF* THERE IT WAS AND I NEVER LOOKED BACK. LET ME GET A LOOK AT YOURS!
IT'S A LOT LIKE APPLE BLOOM AND SCOOTALOO'S, BUT ALL OF OURS ARE SPECIAL AS WELL. YOU WOULDN'T BELIEVE ALL OF THE—
AHEM.
OH YEAH, HI, MS. RARITY.
IT'S GOOD TO SEE YOU, BABS. BELATED CONGRATULATIONS ON YOUR CUTIE MARK.
AH GOSH, THANKS.
LOOK AT THE TWO OF YOU. COULD YOU HAVE IMAGINED YOU'D BE SUCH GOOD FRIENDS WHEN YOU WERE SABOTAGING EACH OTHER'S PARADE FLOATS?
I GUESS WE DIDN'T MAKE THE BEST FIRST IMPRESSIONS.
MAYBE IT'S PART OF GROWING UP. WE EVEN GET ALONG WITH DIAMOND TIARA NOW. SOMETIMES YOU'VE JUST GOT TO FORGIVE AND FORGET.
THAT'S A VERY GROWN-UP OUTLOOK, SWEETIE BELLE. I'M VERY IMPRESSED.
WELL, THERE'S MY RIDE. BABS, YOUR PARENTS KNOW SWEETIE BELLE IS COMING RIGHT?
YEP! THEY'RE WAITING RIGHT OUTSIDE.
WELL THEN, SWEETIE BELLE, HAVE AN EXCELLENT WEEKEND AND CALL THE HOTEL IF YOU NEED ANYTHING, YES?
RARITY
OKAY, SIS!
COME ON, SWEETIE BELLE! I GOT US ROLLER DERBY TICKETS! WE'RE GONNA SEE THE MANEHATTAN MANGLERS TAKE ON THE WHINNYAPOLIS WHIRLWINDS!
AWESOME!
WELL, HELLO THERE. IT WOULD SEEM YOU'RE WAITING ON ME!
RARITY

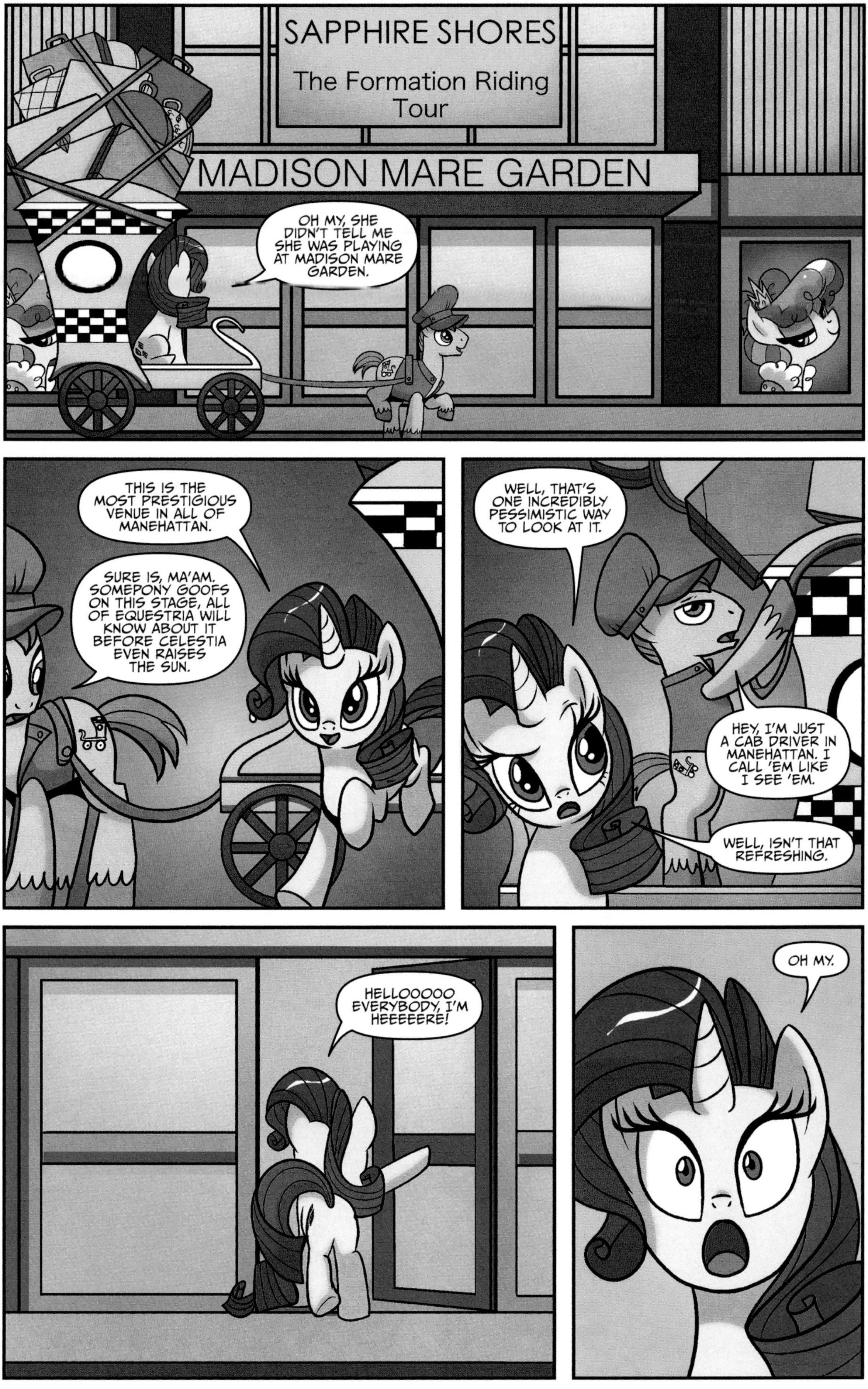
SAPPHIRE SHORES
The Formation Riding Tour
MADISON MARE GARDEN
OH MY, SHE DIDN'T TELL ME SHE WAS PLAYING AT MADISON MARE GARDEN.
THIS IS THE MOST PRESTIGIOUS VENUE IN ALL OF MANEHATTAN.
SURE IS, MA'AM. SOMEPONY GOOFS ON THIS STAGE, ALL OF EQUESTRIA WILL KNOW ABOUT IT BEFORE CELESTIA EVEN RAISES THE SUN.
WELL, THAT'S ONE INCREDIBLY PESSIMISTIC WAY TO LOOK AT IT.
HEY, I'M JUST A CAB DRIVER IN MANEHATTAN. I CALL 'EM LIKE I SEE 'EM.
WELL, ISN'T THAT REFRESHING.
HELLOOOOO EVERYBODY, I'M HEEEEERE!
OH MY.

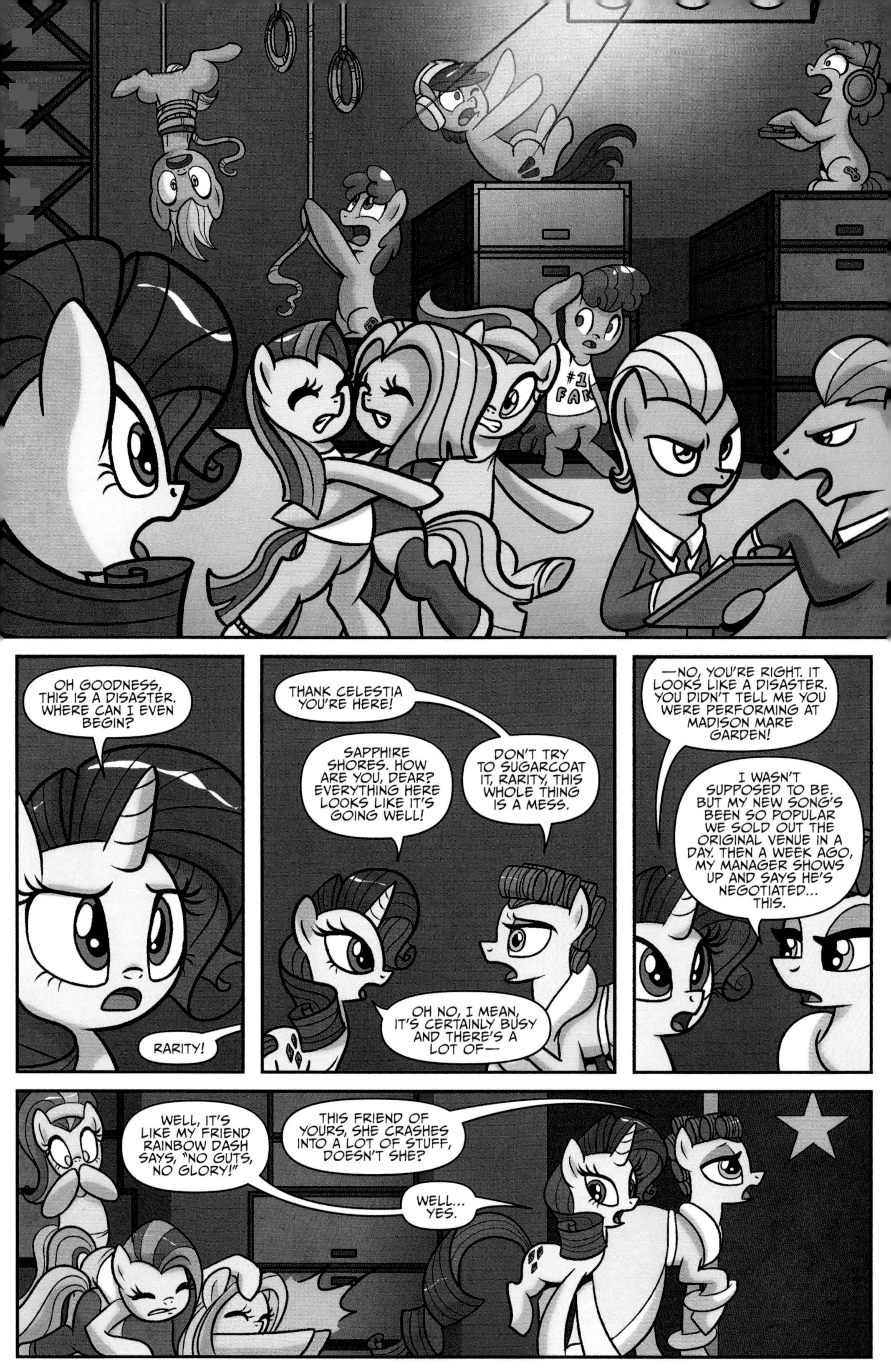

#1 FAN
OH GOODNESS, THIS IS A DISASTER. WHERE CAN I EVEN BEGIN?
RARITY!
THANK CELESTIA YOU'RE HERE!
SAPPHIRE SHORES. HOW ARE YOU, DEAR? EVERYTHING HERE LOOKS LIKE IT'S GOING WELL!
DON'T TRY TO SUGARCOAT IT, RARITY, THIS WHOLE THING IS A MESS.
OH NO, I MEAN, IT'S CERTAINLY BUSY AND THERE'S A LOT OF—
—NO, YOU'RE RIGHT. IT LOOKS LIKE A DISASTER. YOU DIDN'T TELL ME YOU WERE PERFORMING AT MADISON MARE GARDEN!
I WASN'T SUPPOSED TO BE. BUT MY NEW SONG'S BEEN SO POPULAR WE SOLD OUT THE ORIGINAL VENUE IN A DAY. THEN A WEEK AGO, MY MANAGER SHOWS UP AND SAYS HE'S NEGOTIATED... THIS.
WELL, IT'S LIKE MY FRIEND RAINBOW DASH SAYS, "NO GUTS, NO GLORY!"
THIS FRIEND OF YOURS, SHE CRASHES INTO A LOT OF STUFF, DOESN'T SHE?
WELL... YES.

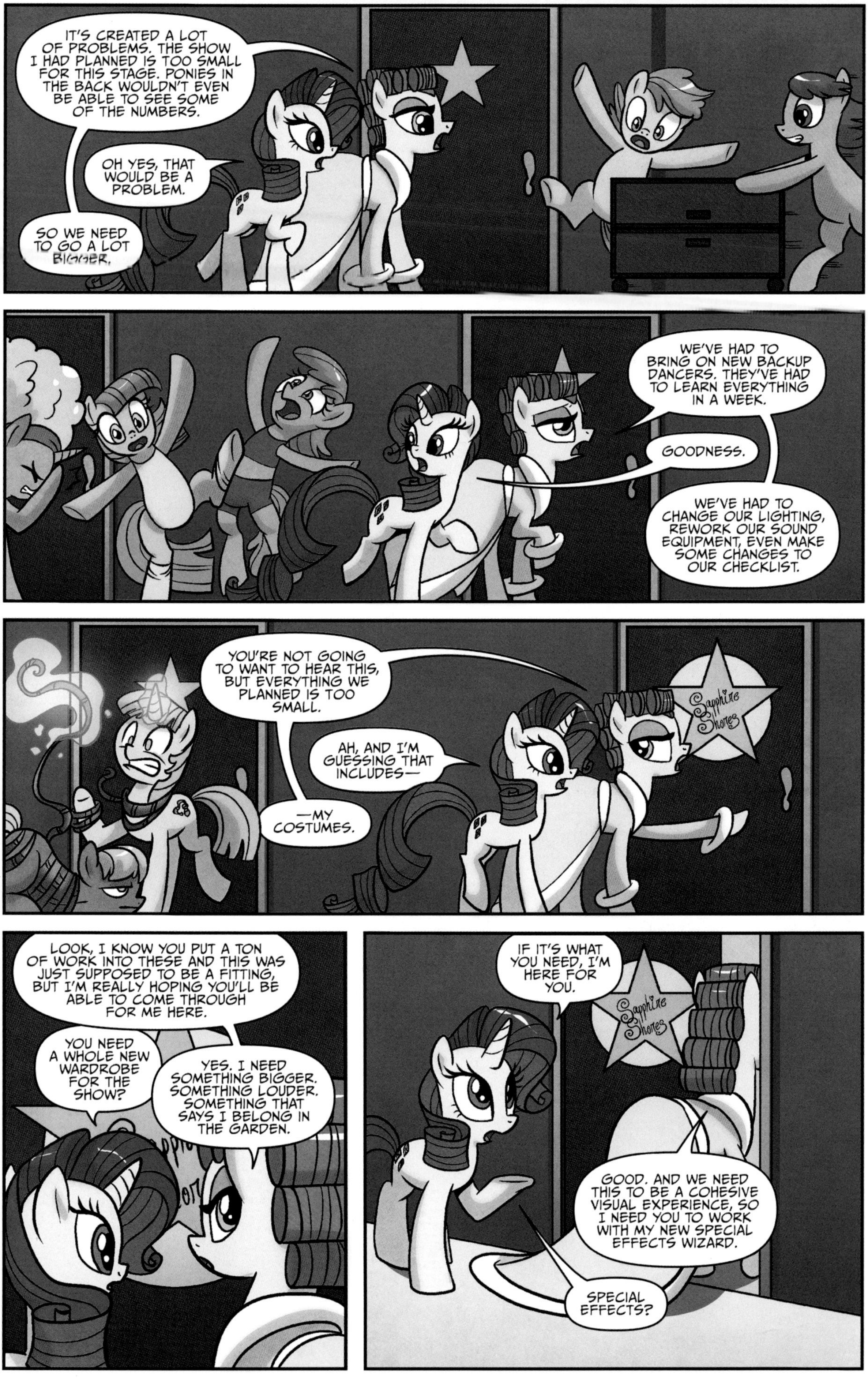

IT'S CREATED A LOT OF PROBLEMS. THE SHOW I HAD PLANNED IS TOO SMALL FOR THIS STAGE. PONIES IN THE BACK WOULDN'T EVEN BE ABLE TO SEE SOME OF THE NUMBERS.
OH YES, THAT WOULD BE A PROBLEM.
SO WE NEED TO GO A LOT BIGGER.
WE'VE HAD TO BRING ON NEW BACKUP DANCERS. THEY'VE HAD TO LEARN EVERYTHING IN A WEEK.
GOODNESS.
WE'VE HAD TO CHANGE OUR LIGHTING, REWORK OUR SOUND EQUIPMENT, EVEN MAKE SOME CHANGES TO OUR CHECKLIST.
YOU'RE NOT GOING TO WANT TO HEAR THIS, BUT EVERYTHING WE PLANNED IS TOO SMALL.
AH, AND I'M GUESSING THAT INCLUDES—
—MY COSTUMES.
Sapphire Shores
LOOK, I KNOW YOU PUT A TON OF WORK INTO THESE AND THIS WAS JUST SUPPOSED TO BE A FITTING, BUT I'M REALLY HOPING YOU'LL BE ABLE TO COME THROUGH FOR ME HERE.
YOU NEED A WHOLE NEW WARDROBE FOR THE SHOW?
YES. I NEED SOMETHING BIGGER. SOMETHING LOUDER. SOMETHING THAT SAYS I BELONG IN THE GARDEN.
IF IT'S WHAT YOU NEED, I'M HERE FOR YOU.
Sapphire Shores
GOOD. AND WE NEED THIS TO BE A COHESIVE VISUAL EXPERIENCE, SO I NEED YOU TO WORK WITH MY NEW SPECIAL EFFECTS WIZARD.
SPECIAL EFFECTS?

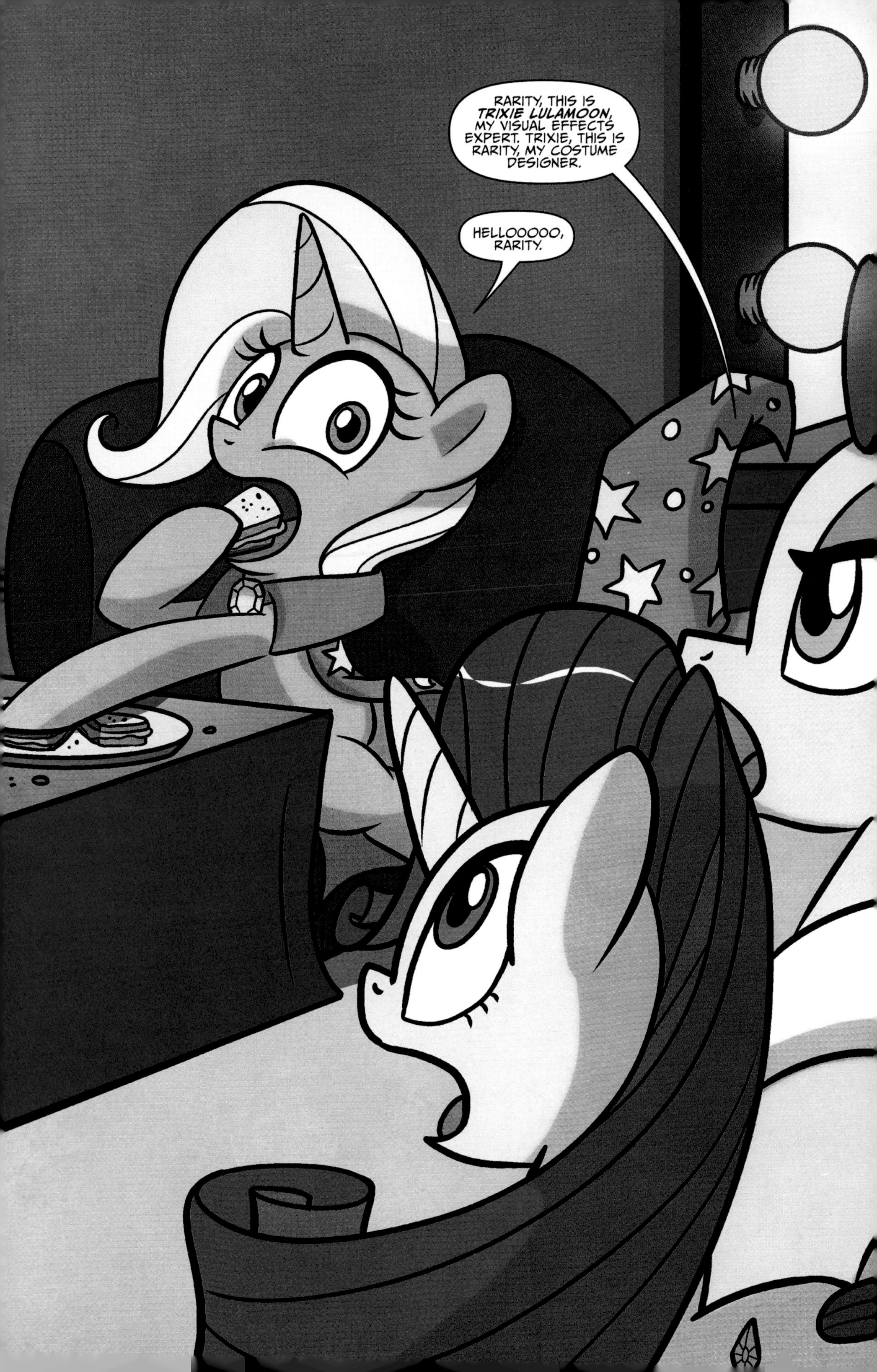
RARITY, THIS IS TRIXIE LULAMOON, MY VISUAL EFFECTS EXPERT. TRIXIE, THIS IS RARITY, MY COSTUME DESIGNER.
HELLOOOOO, RARITY.

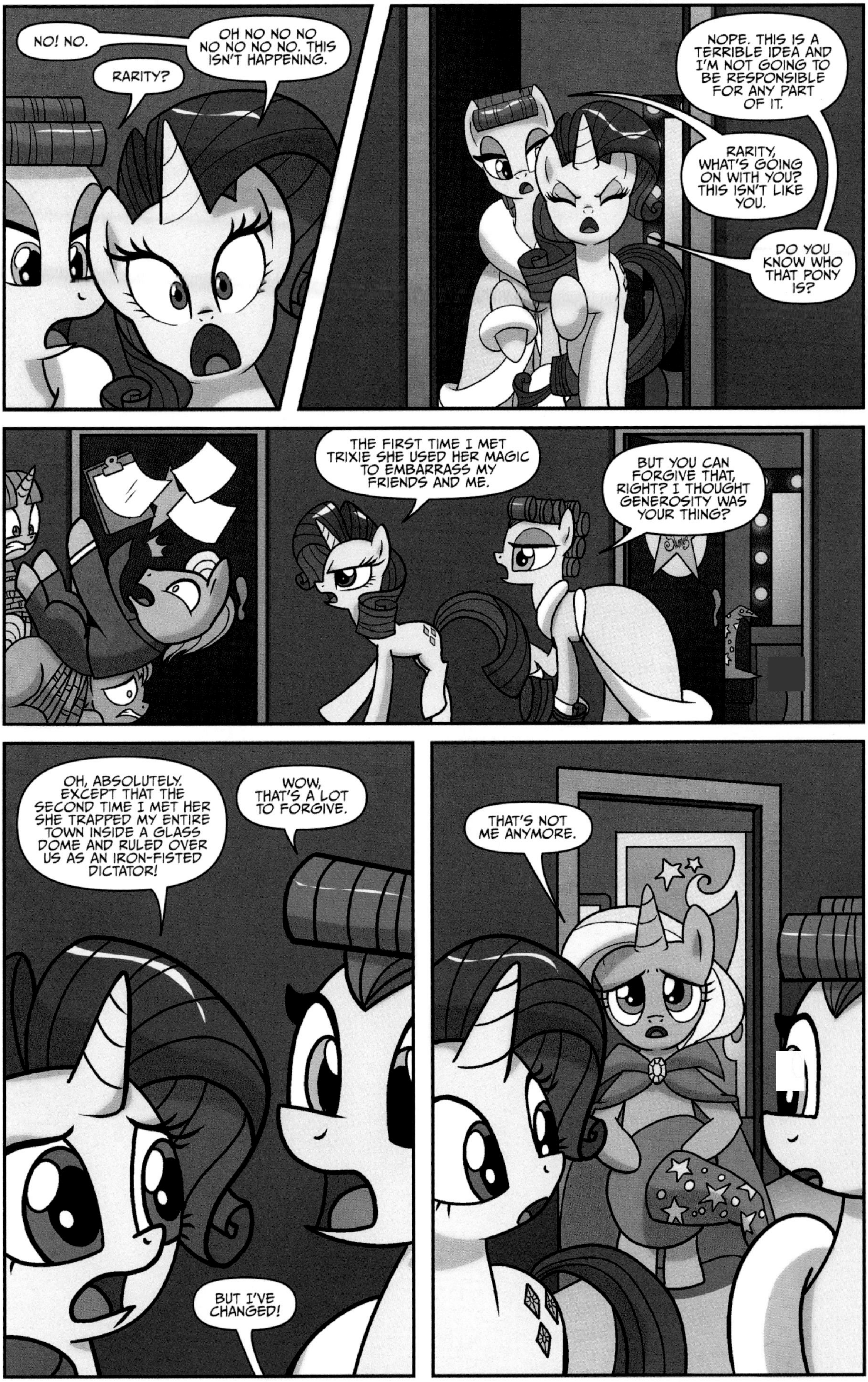
NO! NO.
OH NO NO NO NO NO NO NO. THIS ISN'T HAPPENING.
RARITY?
NOPE. THIS IS A TERRIBLE IDEA AND I'M NOT GOING TO BE RESPONSIBLE FOR ANY PART OF IT.
RARITY, WHAT'S GOING ON WITH YOU? THIS ISN'T LIKE YOU.
DO YOU KNOW WHO THAT PONY IS?
THE FIRST TIME I MET TRIXIE SHE USED HER MAGIC TO EMBARRASS MY FRIENDS AND ME.
BUT YOU CAN FORGIVE THAT, RIGHT? I THOUGHT GENEROSITY WAS YOUR THING?
OH, ABSOLUTELY. EXCEPT THAT THE SECOND TIME I MET HER SHE TRAPPED MY ENTIRE TOWN INSIDE A GLASS DOME AND RULED OVER US AS AN IRON-FISTED DICTATOR!
WOW, THAT'S A LOT TO FORGIVE.
BUT I'VE CHANGED!
THAT'S NOT ME ANYMORE.

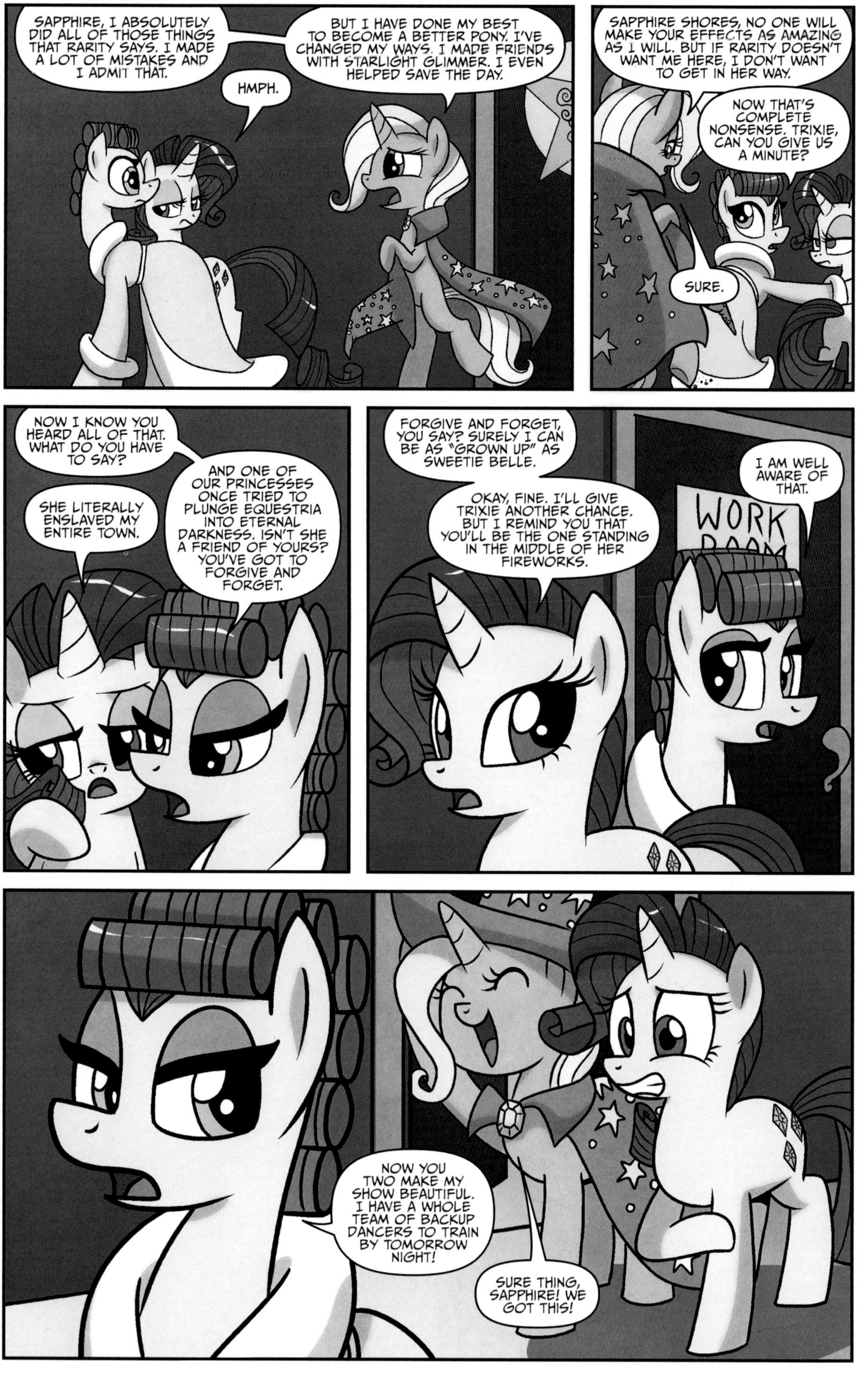
SAPPHIRE, I ABSOLUTELY DID ALL OF THOSE THINGS THAT RARITY SAYS. I MADE A LOT OF MISTAKES AND I ADMIT THAT.
HMPH.
BUT I HAVE DONE MY BEST TO BECOME A BETTER PONY. I'VE CHANGED MY WAYS. I MADE FRIENDS WITH STARLIGHT GLIMMER. I EVEN HELPED SAVE THE DAY.
SAPPHIRE SHORES, NO ONE WILL MAKE YOUR EFFECTS AS AMAZING AS I WILL. BUT IF RARITY DOESN'T WANT ME HERE, I DON'T WANT TO GET IN HER WAY.
NOW THAT'S COMPLETE NONSENSE. TRIXIE, CAN YOU GIVE US A MINUTE?
SURE.
NOW I KNOW YOU HEARD ALL OF THAT. WHAT DO YOU HAVE TO SAY?
SHE LITERALLY ENSLAVED MY ENTIRE TOWN.
AND ONE OF OUR PRINCESSES ONCE TRIED TO PLUNGE EQUESTRIA INTO ETERNAL DARKNESS. ISN'T SHE A FRIEND OF YOURS? YOU'VE GOT TO FORGIVE AND FORGET.
FORGIVE AND FORGET, YOU SAY? SURELY I CAN BE AS "GROWN UP" AS SWEETIE BELLE.
OKAY, FINE. I'LL GIVE TRIXIE ANOTHER CHANCE. BUT I REMIND YOU THAT YOU'LL BE THE ONE STANDING IN THE MIDDLE OF HER FIREWORKS.
I AM WELL AWARE OF THAT.
WORK
NOW YOU TWO MAKE MY SHOW BEAUTIFUL. I HAVE A WHOLE TEAM OF BACKUP DANCERS TO TRAIN BY TOMORROW NIGHT!
SURE THING, SAPPHIRE! WE GOT THIS!

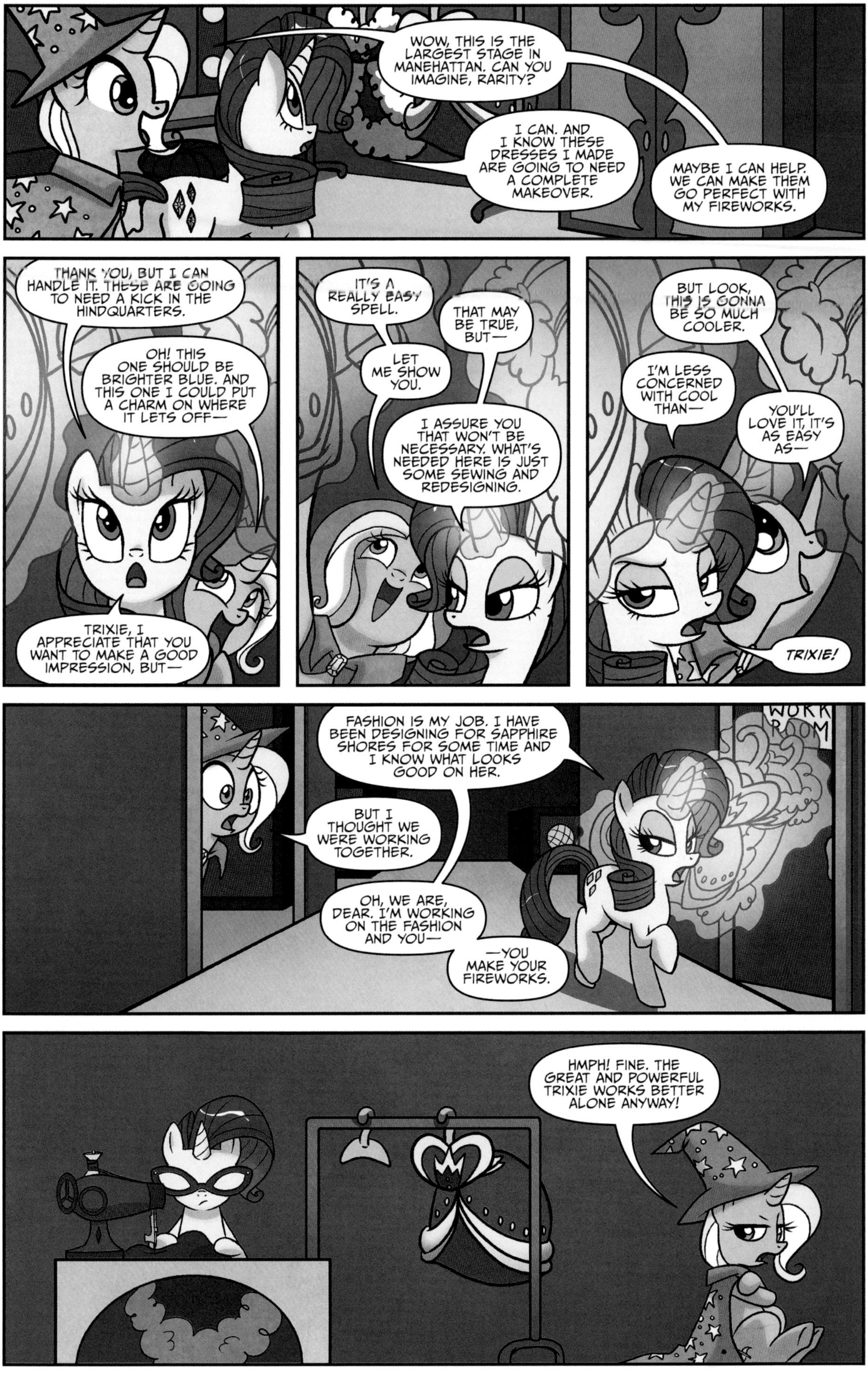
WOW, THIS IS THE LARGEST STAGE IN MANEHATTAN. CAN YOU IMAGINE, RARITY?
I CAN. AND I KNOW THESE DRESSES I MADE ARE GOING TO NEED A COMPLETE MAKEOVER.
MAYBE I CAN HELP. WE CAN MAKE THEM GO PERFECT WITH MY FIREWORKS.
THANK YOU, BUT I CAN HANDLE IT. THESE ARE GOING TO NEED A KICK IN THE HINDQUARTERS.
OH! THIS ONE SHOULD BE BRIGHTER BLUE. AND THIS ONE I COULD PUT A CHARM ON WHERE IT LETS OFF—
TRIXIE, I APPRECIATE THAT YOU WANT TO MAKE A GOOD IMPRESSION, BUT—
IT'S A REALLY EASY SPELL.
THAT MAY BE TRUE, BUT—
LET ME SHOW YOU.
I ASSURE YOU THAT WON'T BE NECESSARY. WHAT'S NEEDED HERE IS JUST SOME SEWING AND REDESIGNING.
BUT LOOK, THIS IS GONNA BE SO MUCH COOLER.
I'M LESS CONCERNED WITH COOL THAN—
YOU'LL LOVE IT, IT'S AS EASY AS—
TRIXIE!
WORK ROOM
FASHION IS MY JOB. I HAVE BEEN DESIGNING FOR SAPPHIRE SHORES FOR SOME TIME AND I KNOW WHAT LOOKS GOOD ON HER.
BUT I THOUGHT WE WERE WORKING TOGETHER.
OH, WE ARE, DEAR. I'M WORKING ON THE FASHION AND YOU—
—YOU MAKE YOUR FIREWORKS.
HMPH! FINE. THE GREAT AND POWERFUL TRIXIE WORKS BETTER ALONE ANYWAY!

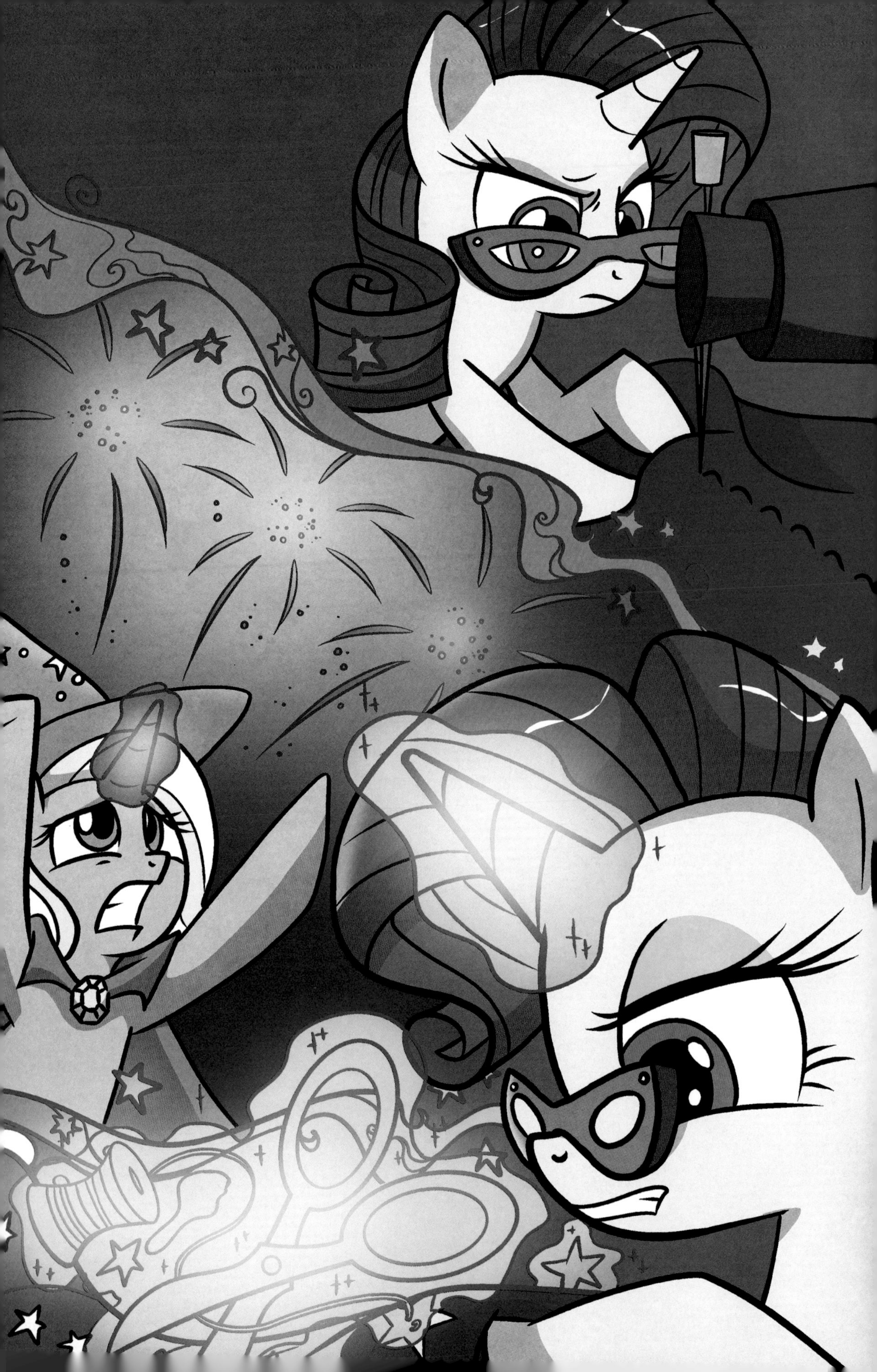

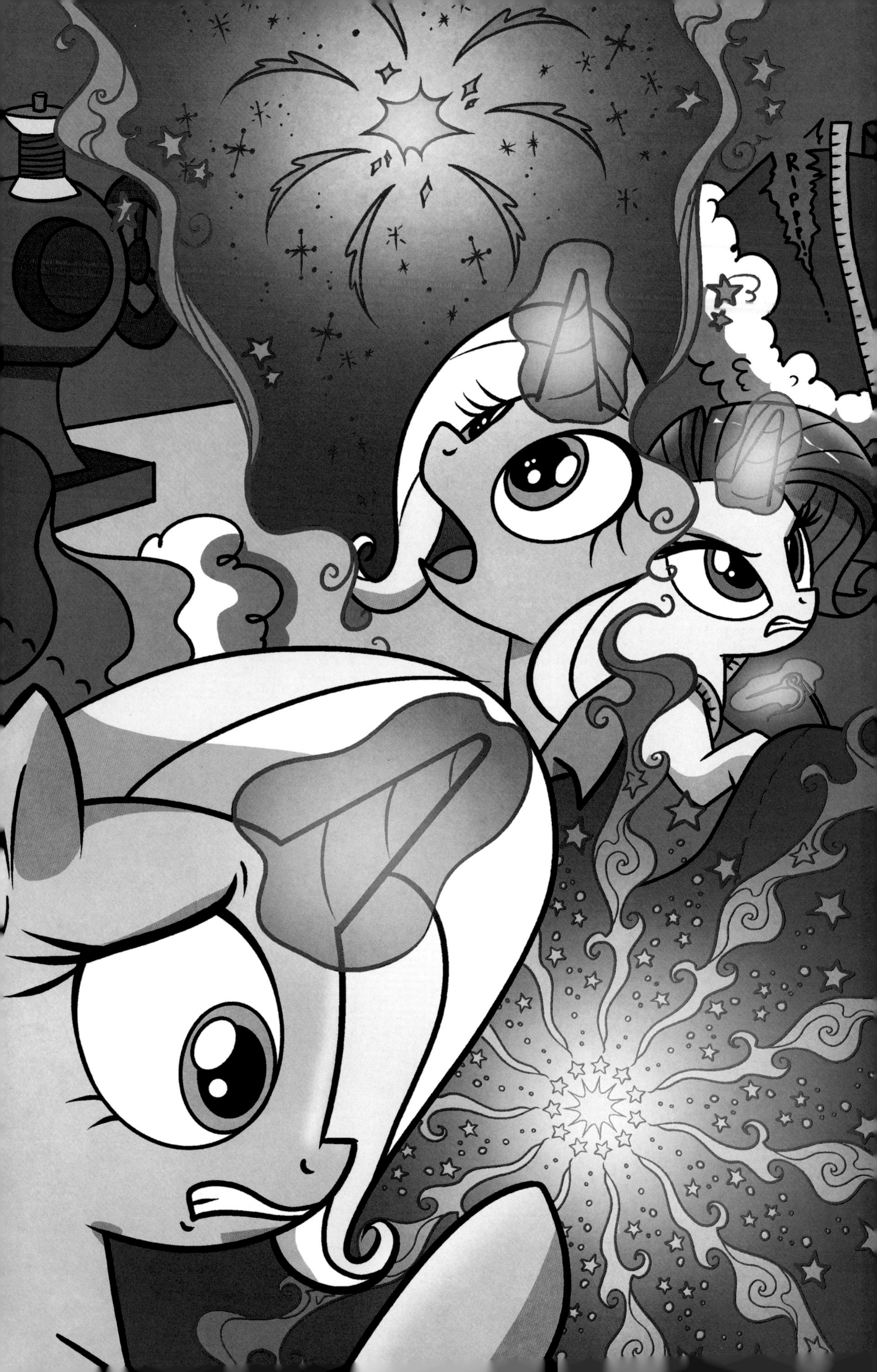
RIPPP!

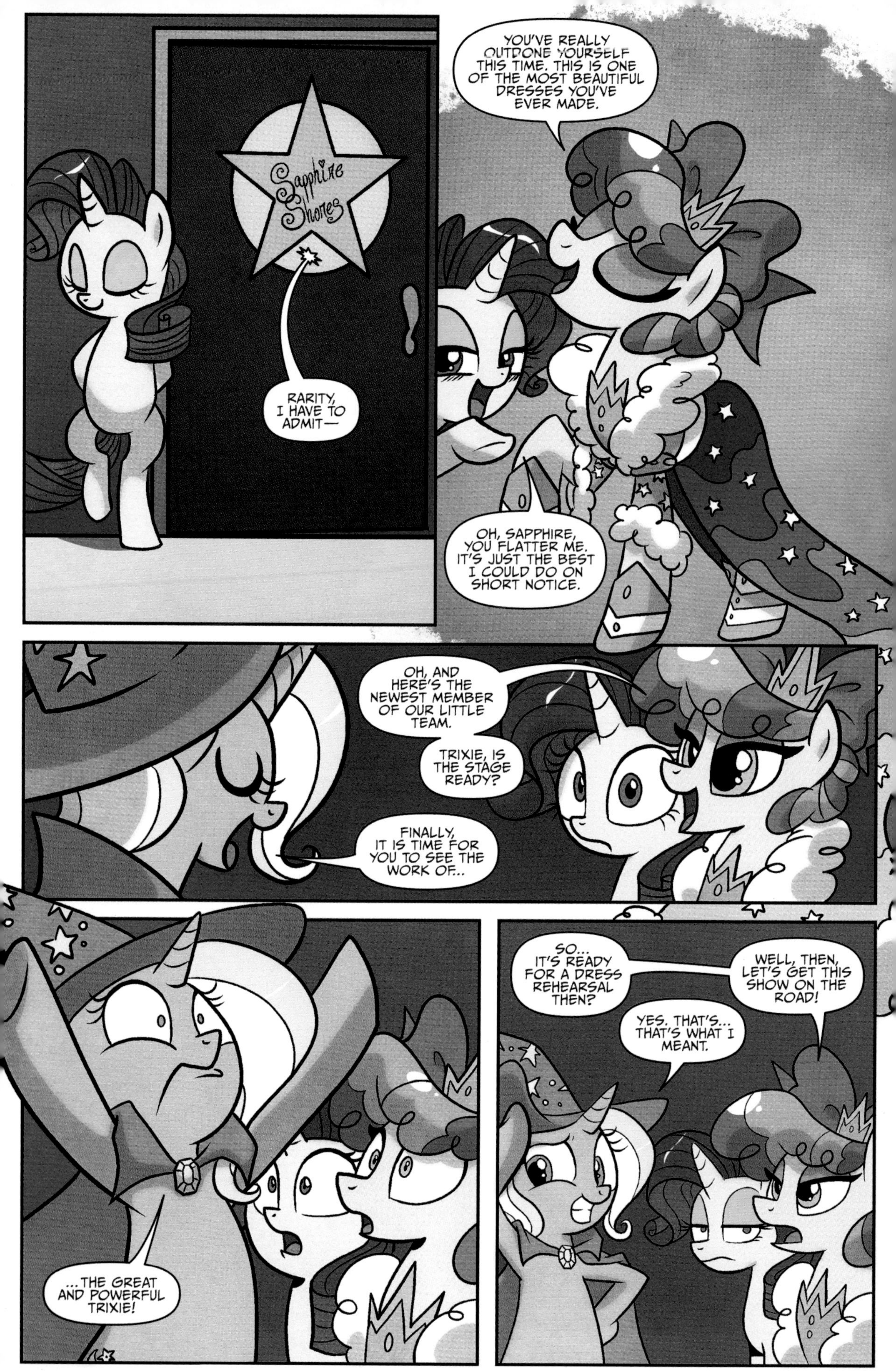
Sapphire Shores
RARITY, I HAVE TO ADMIT—
YOU'VE REALLY OUTDONE YOURSELF THIS TIME. THIS IS ONE OF THE MOST BEAUTIFUL DRESSES YOU'VE EVER MADE.
OH, SAPPHIRE, YOU FLATTER ME. IT'S JUST THE BEST I COULD DO ON SHORT NOTICE.
OH, AND HERE'S THE NEWEST MEMBER OF OUR LITTLE TEAM.
TRIXIE, IS THE STAGE READY?
FINALLY, IT IS TIME FOR YOU TO SEE THE WORK OF...
...THE GREAT AND POWERFUL TRIXIE!
SO... IT'S READY FOR A DRESS REHEARSAL THEN?
YES. THAT'S... THAT'S WHAT I MEANT.
WELL, THEN, LET'S GET THIS SHOW ON THE ROAD!

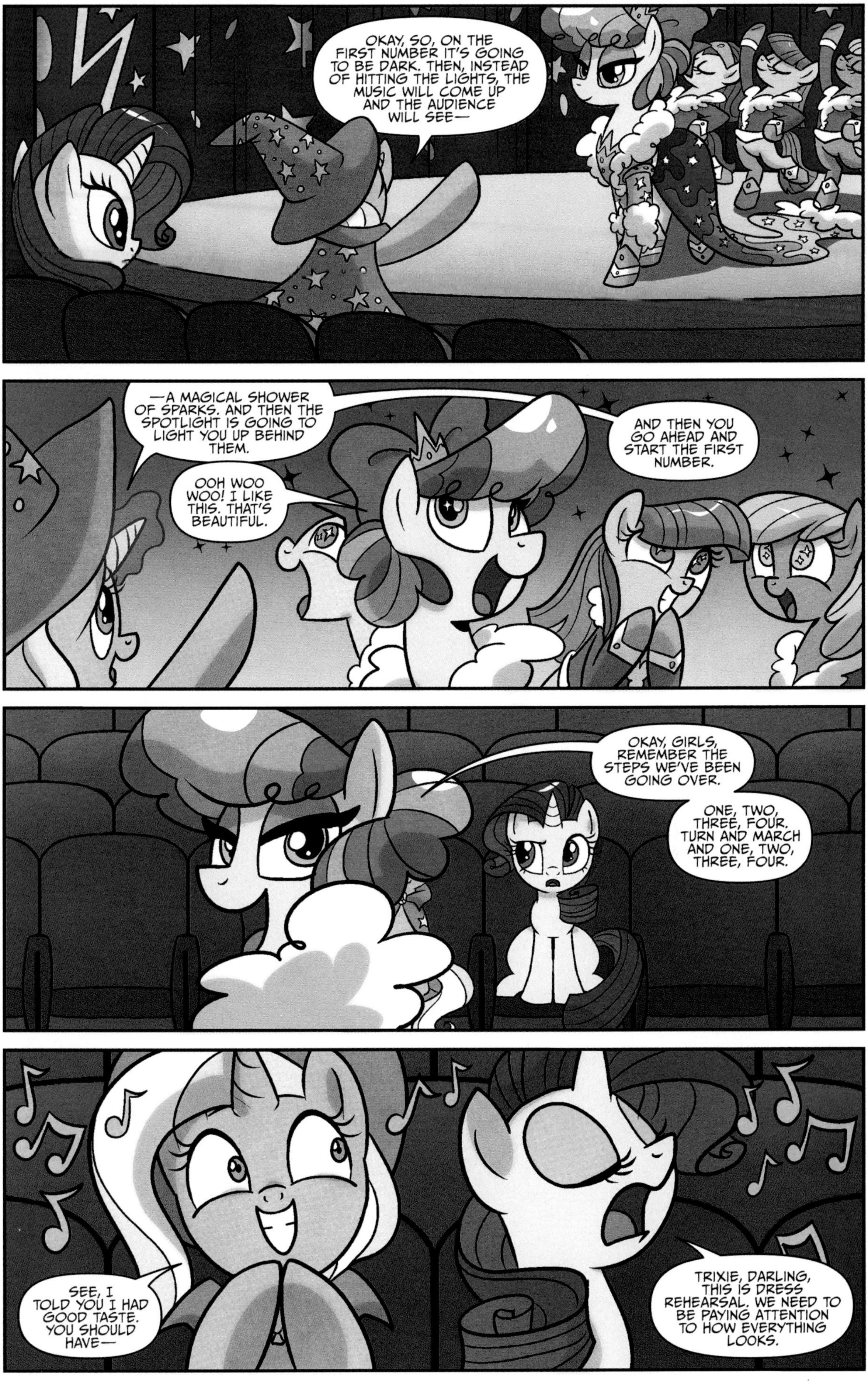
OKAY, SO, ON THE FIRST NUMBER IT'S GOING TO BE DARK. THEN, INSTEAD OF HITTING THE LIGHTS, THE MUSIC WILL COME UP AND THE AUDIENCE WILL SEE—
—A MAGICAL SHOWER OF SPARKS. AND THEN THE SPOTLIGHT IS GOING TO LIGHT YOU UP BEHIND THEM.
OOH WOO WOO! I LIKE THIS. THAT'S BEAUTIFUL.
AND THEN YOU GO AHEAD AND START THE FIRST NUMBER.
OKAY, GIRLS, REMEMBER THE STEPS WE'VE BEEN GOING OVER.
ONE, TWO, THREE, FOUR. TURN AND MARCH AND ONE, TWO, THREE, FOUR.
SEE, I TOLD YOU I HAD GOOD TASTE. YOU SHOULD HAVE—
TRIXIE, DARLING, THIS IS DRESS REHEARSAL. WE NEED TO BE PAYING ATTENTION TO HOW EVERYTHING LOOKS.

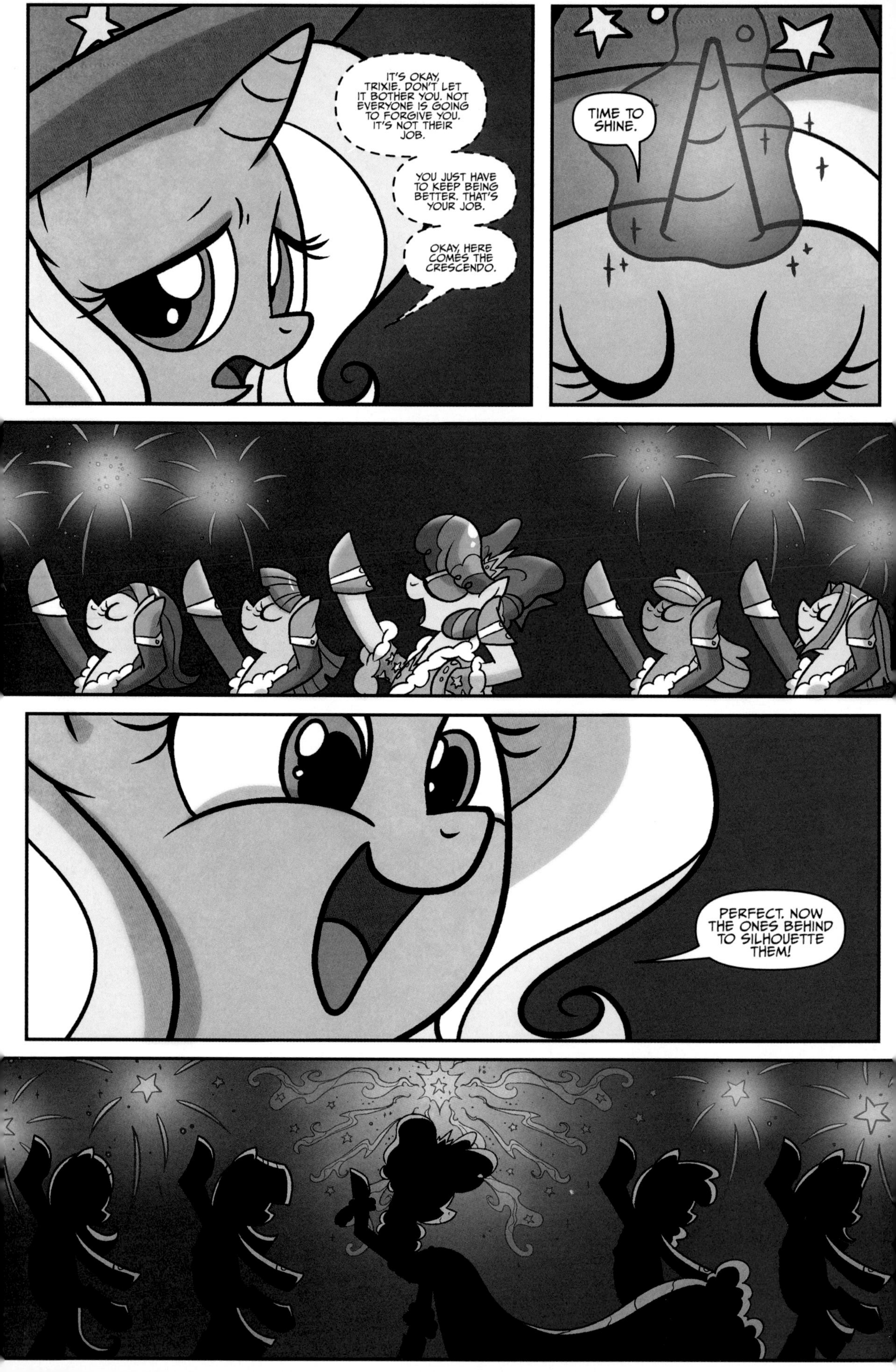
IT'S OKAY, TRIXIE. DON'T LET IT BOTHER YOU. NOT EVERYONE IS GOING TO FORGIVE YOU. IT'S NOT THEIR JOB.
YOU JUST HAVE TO KEEP BEING BETTER. THAT'S YOUR JOB.
OKAY, HERE COMES THE CRESCENDO.
TIME TO SHINE.
PERFECT. NOW THE ONES BEHIND TO SILHOUETTE THEM!

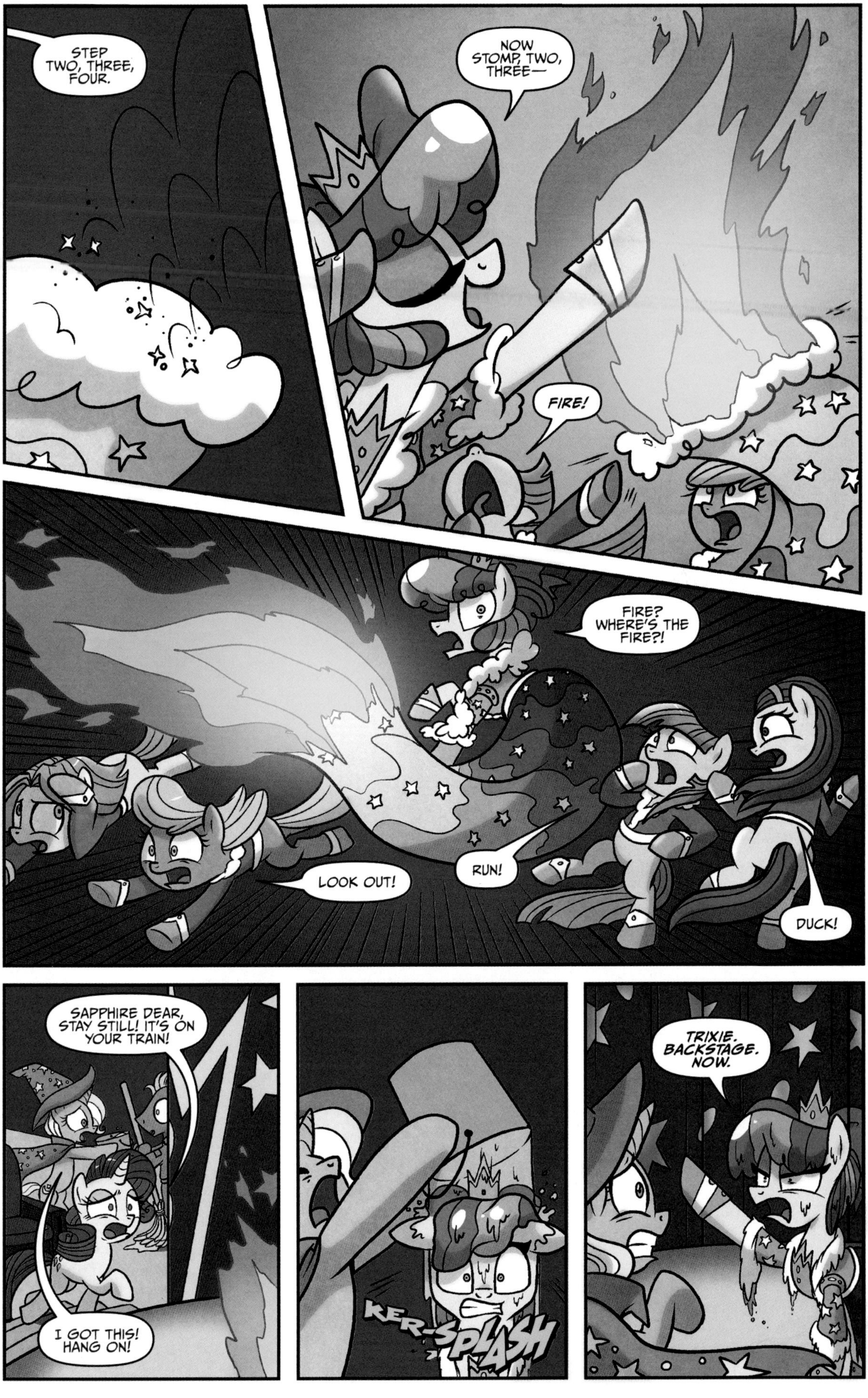
STEP TWO, THREE, FOUR.
NOW STOMP, TWO, THREE—
FIRE!
FIRE? WHERE'S THE FIRE?!
LOOK OUT!
RUN!
DUCK!
SAPPHIRE DEAR, STAY STILL! IT'S ON YOUR TRAIN!
I GOT THIS! HANG ON!
KER-SPLASH
TRIXIE. BACKSTAGE. NOW.

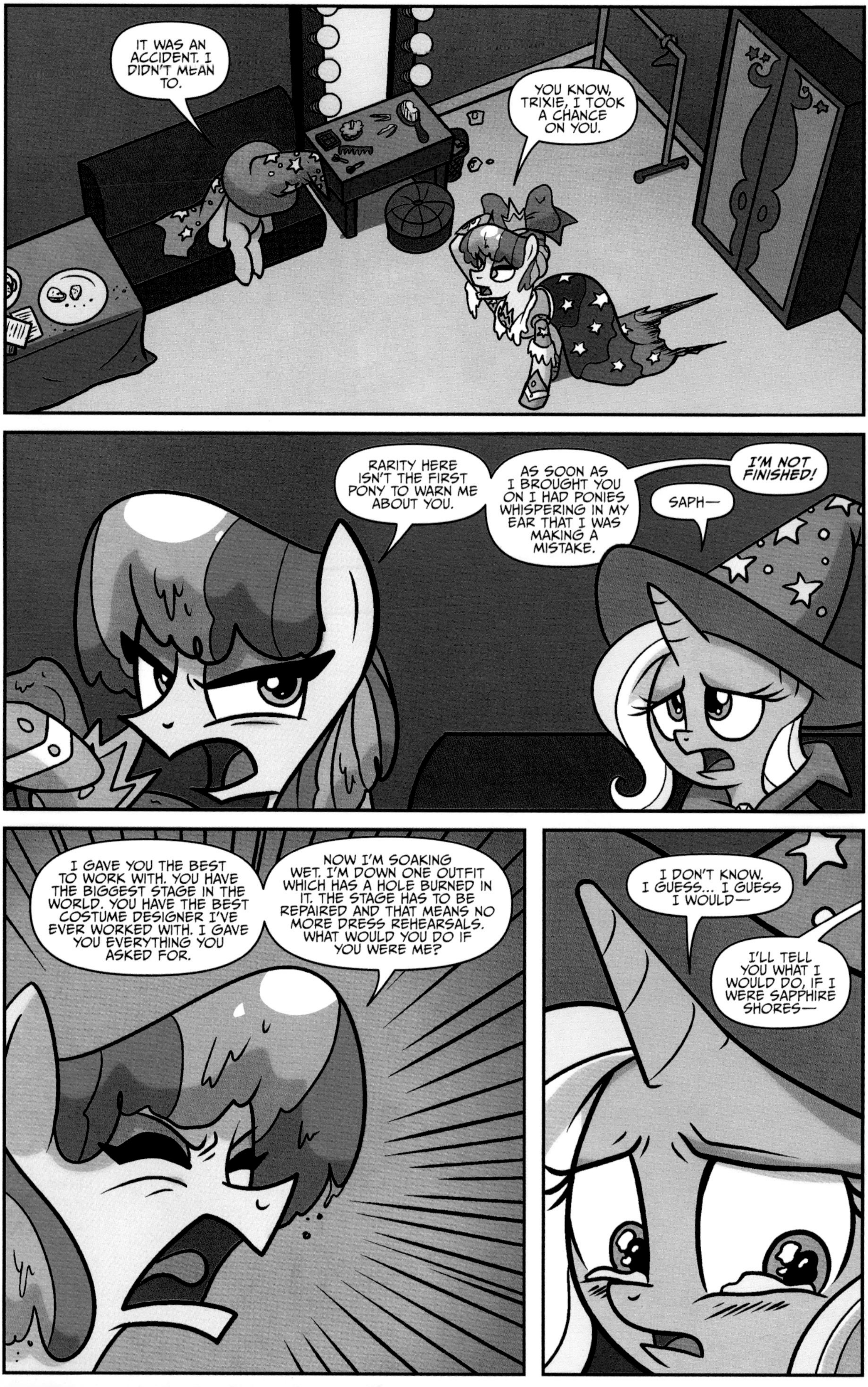
IT WAS AN ACCIDENT. I DIDN'T MEAN TO.
YOU KNOW, TRIXIE, I TOOK A CHANCE ON YOU.
RARITY HERE ISN'T THE FIRST PONY TO WARN ME ABOUT YOU.
AS SOON AS I BROUGHT YOU ON I HAD PONIES WHISPERING IN MY EAR THAT I WAS MAKING A MISTAKE.
SAPH—
I'M NOT FINISHED!
I GAVE YOU THE BEST TO WORK WITH. YOU HAVE THE BIGGEST STAGE IN THE WORLD. YOU HAVE THE BEST COSTUME DESIGNER I'VE EVER WORKED WITH. I GAVE YOU EVERYTHING YOU ASKED FOR.
NOW I'M SOAKING WET. I'M DOWN ONE OUTFIT WHICH HAS A HOLE BURNED IN IT. THE STAGE HAS TO BE REPAIRED AND THAT MEANS NO MORE DRESS REHEARSALS. WHAT WOULD YOU DO IF YOU WERE ME?
I DON'T KNOW. I GUESS... I GUESS I WOULD—
I'LL TELL YOU WHAT I WOULD DO, IF I WERE SAPPHIRE SHORES—

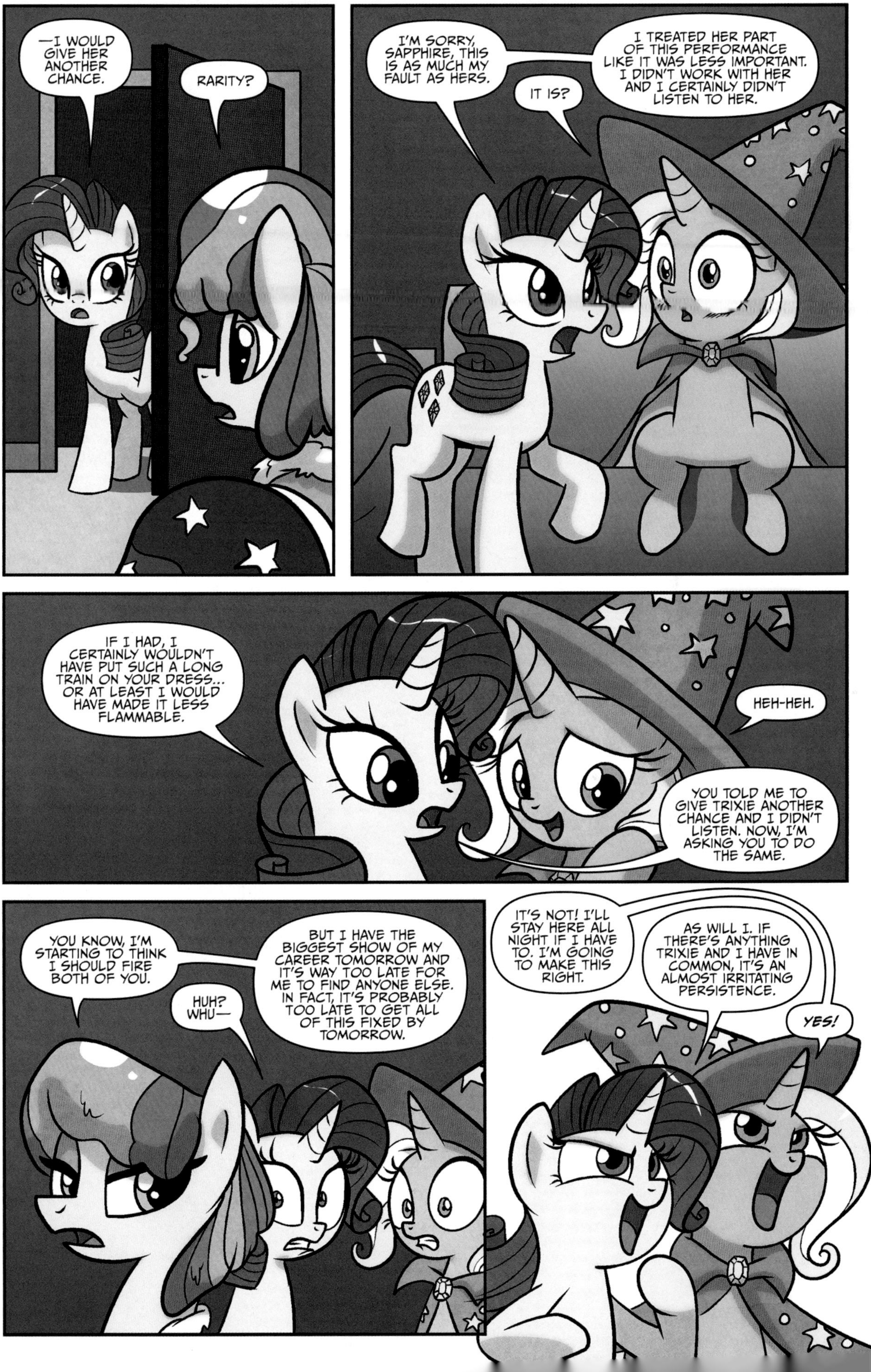
—I WOULD GIVE HER ANOTHER CHANCE.
RARITY?
I'M SORRY, SAPPHIRE, THIS IS AS MUCH MY FAULT AS HERS.
IT IS?
I TREATED HER PART OF THIS PERFORMANCE LIKE IT WAS LESS IMPORTANT. I DIDN'T WORK WITH HER AND I CERTAINLY DIDN'T LISTEN TO HER.
IF I HAD, I CERTAINLY WOULDN'T HAVE PUT SUCH A LONG TRAIN ON YOUR DRESS... OR AT LEAST I WOULD HAVE MADE IT LESS FLAMMABLE.
HEH-HEH.
YOU TOLD ME TO GIVE TRIXIE ANOTHER CHANCE AND I DIDN'T LISTEN. NOW, I'M ASKING YOU TO DO THE SAME.
YOU KNOW, I'M STARTING TO THINK I SHOULD FIRE BOTH OF YOU.
HUH? WHU—
BUT I HAVE THE BIGGEST SHOW OF MY CAREER TOMORROW AND IT'S WAY TOO LATE FOR ME TO FIND ANYONE ELSE. IN FACT, IT'S PROBABLY TOO LATE TO GET ALL OF THIS FIXED BY TOMORROW.
IT'S NOT! I'LL STAY HERE ALL NIGHT IF I HAVE TO. I'M GOING TO MAKE THIS RIGHT.
AS WILL I. IF THERE'S ANYTHING TRIXIE AND I HAVE IN COMMON, IT'S AN ALMOST IRRITATING PERSISTENCE.
YES!

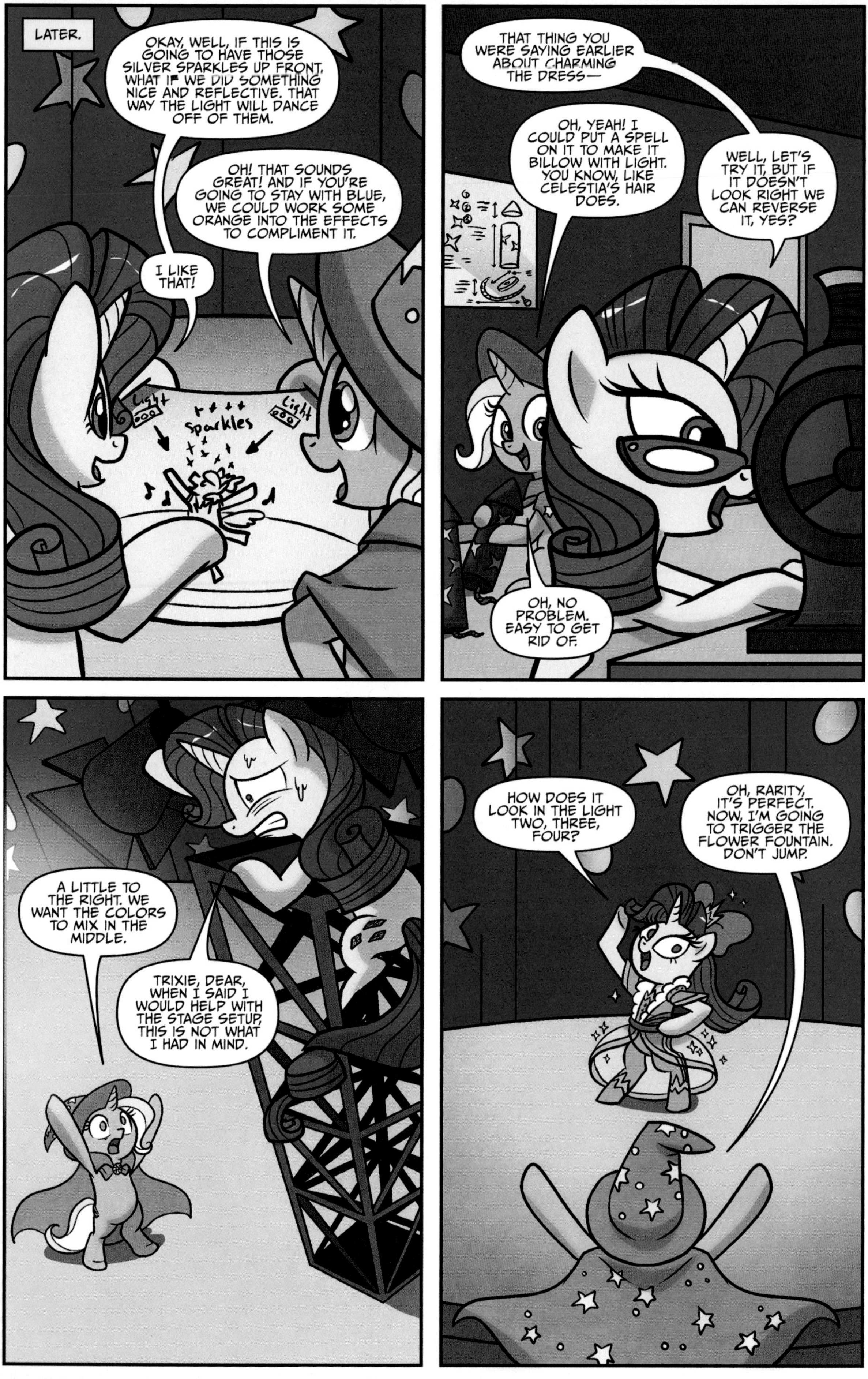
LATER.
OKAY, WELL, IF THIS IS GOING TO HAVE THOSE SILVER SPARKLES UP FRONT, WHAT IF WE DID SOMETHING NICE AND REFLECTIVE. THAT WAY THE LIGHT WILL DANCE OFF OF THEM.
OH! THAT SOUNDS GREAT! AND IF YOU'RE GOING TO STAY WITH BLUE, WE COULD WORK SOME ORANGE INTO THE EFFECTS TO COMPLIMENT IT.
I LIKE THAT!
Light
Light
sparkles
THAT THING YOU WERE SAYING EARLIER ABOUT CHARMING THE DRESS—
OH, YEAH! I COULD PUT A SPELL ON IT TO MAKE IT BILLOW WITH LIGHT. YOU KNOW, LIKE CELESTIA'S HAIR DOES.
WELL, LET'S TRY IT, BUT IF IT DOESN'T LOOK RIGHT WE CAN REVERSE IT, YES?
OH, NO PROBLEM. EASY TO GET RID OF.
A LITTLE TO THE RIGHT. WE WANT THE COLORS TO MIX IN THE MIDDLE.
TRIXIE, DEAR, WHEN I SAID I WOULD HELP WITH THE STAGE SETUP, THIS IS NOT WHAT I HAD IN MIND.
HOW DOES IT LOOK IN THE LIGHT TWO, THREE, FOUR?
OH, RARITY, IT'S PERFECT. NOW, I'M GOING TO TRIGGER THE FLOWER FOUNTAIN. DON'T JUMP.

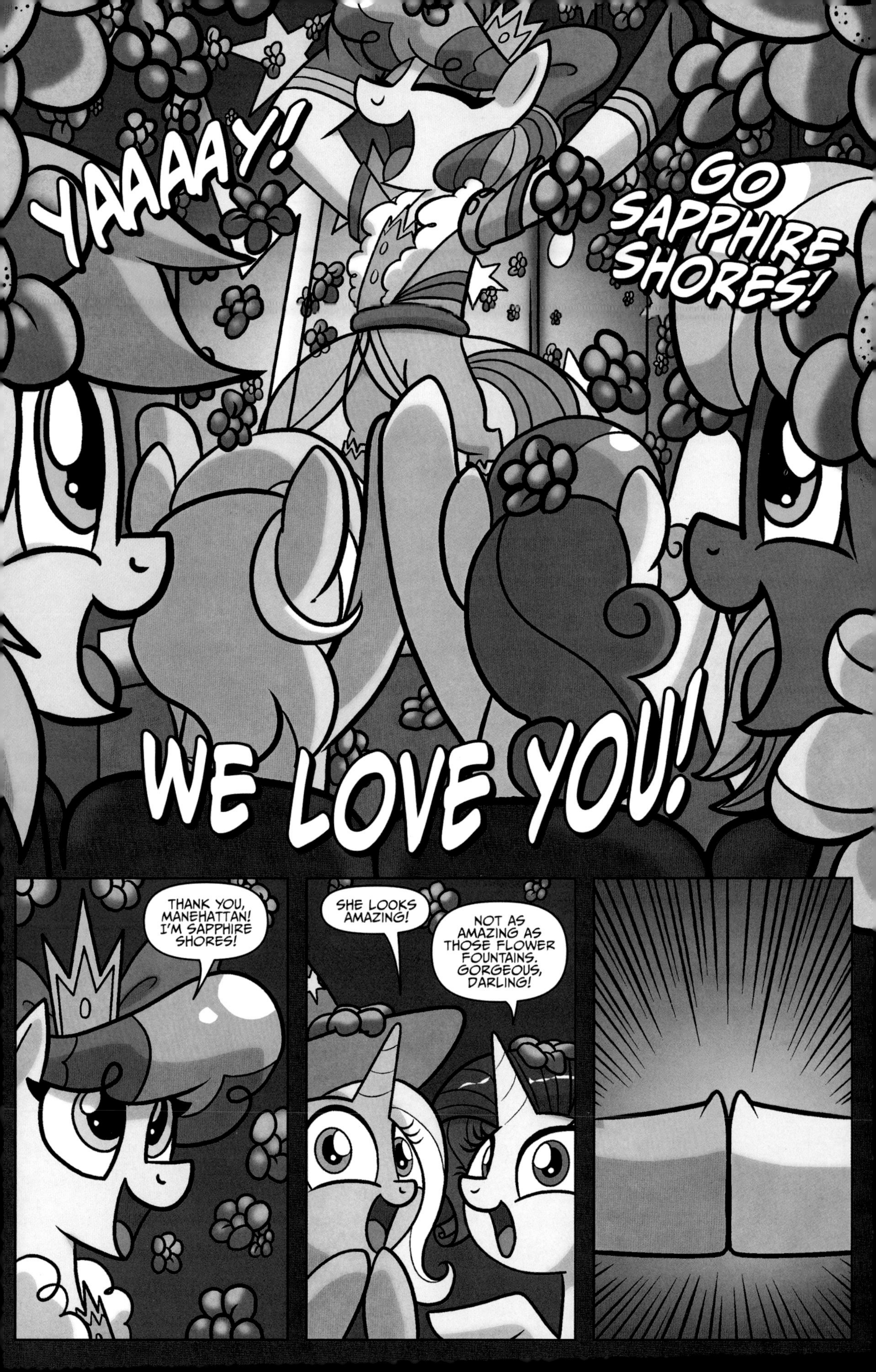
YAAAAY!
GO SAPPHIRE SHORES!
WE LOVE YOU!!
THANK YOU, MANEHATTAN! I'M SAPPHIRE SHORES!
SHE LOOKS AMAZING!
NOT AS AMAZING AS THOSE FLOWER FOUNTAINS. GORGEOUS, DARLING!

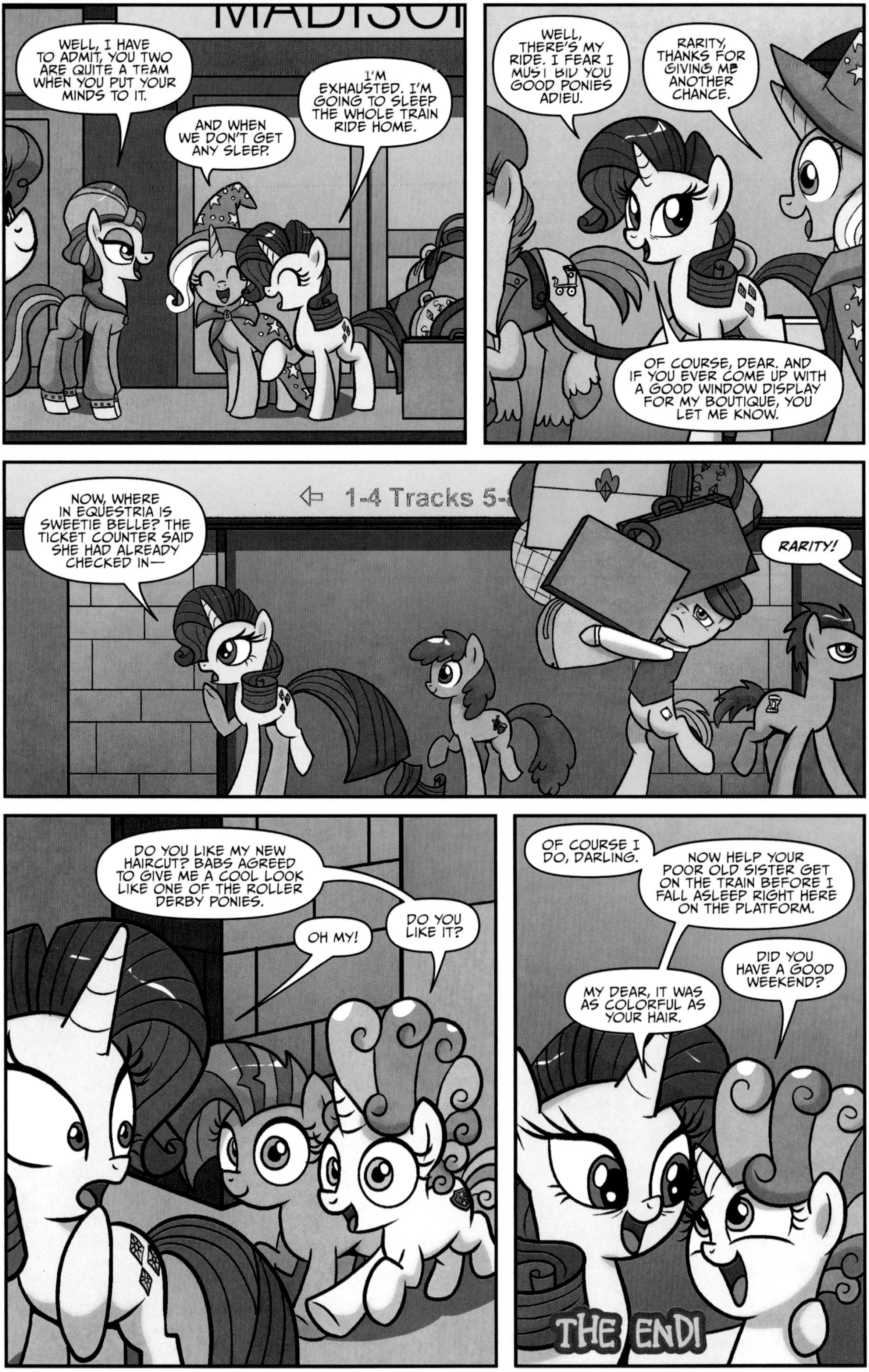
MADISO
WELL, I HAVE TO ADMIT, YOU TWO ARE QUITE A TEAM WHEN YOU PUT YOUR MINDS TO IT.
AND WHEN WE DON'T GET ANY SLEEP.
I'M EXHAUSTED. I'M GOING TO SLEEP THE WHOLE TRAIN RIDE HOME.
WELL, THERE'S MY RIDE. I FEAR I MUST BID YOU GOOD PONIES ADIEU.
RARITY, THANKS FOR GIVING ME ANOTHER CHANCE.
OF COURSE, DEAR. AND IF YOU EVER COME UP WITH A GOOD WINDOW DISPLAY FOR MY BOUTIQUE, YOU LET ME KNOW.
1-4 Tracks 5-
NOW, WHERE IN EQUESTRIA IS SWEETIE BELLE? THE TICKET COUNTER SAID SHE HAD ALREADY CHECKED IN—
RARITY!
DO YOU LIKE MY NEW HAIRCUT? BABS AGREED TO GIVE ME A COOL LOOK LIKE ONE OF THE ROLLER DERBY PONIES.
OH MY!
DO YOU LIKE IT?
OF COURSE I DO, DARLING.
NOW HELP YOUR POOR OLD SISTER GET ON THE TRAIN BEFORE I FALL ASLEEP RIGHT HERE ON THE PLATFORM.
DID YOU HAVE A GOOD WEEKEND?
MY DEAR, IT WAS AS COLORFUL AS YOUR HAIR.
THE END!

art by
Tony Fleecs

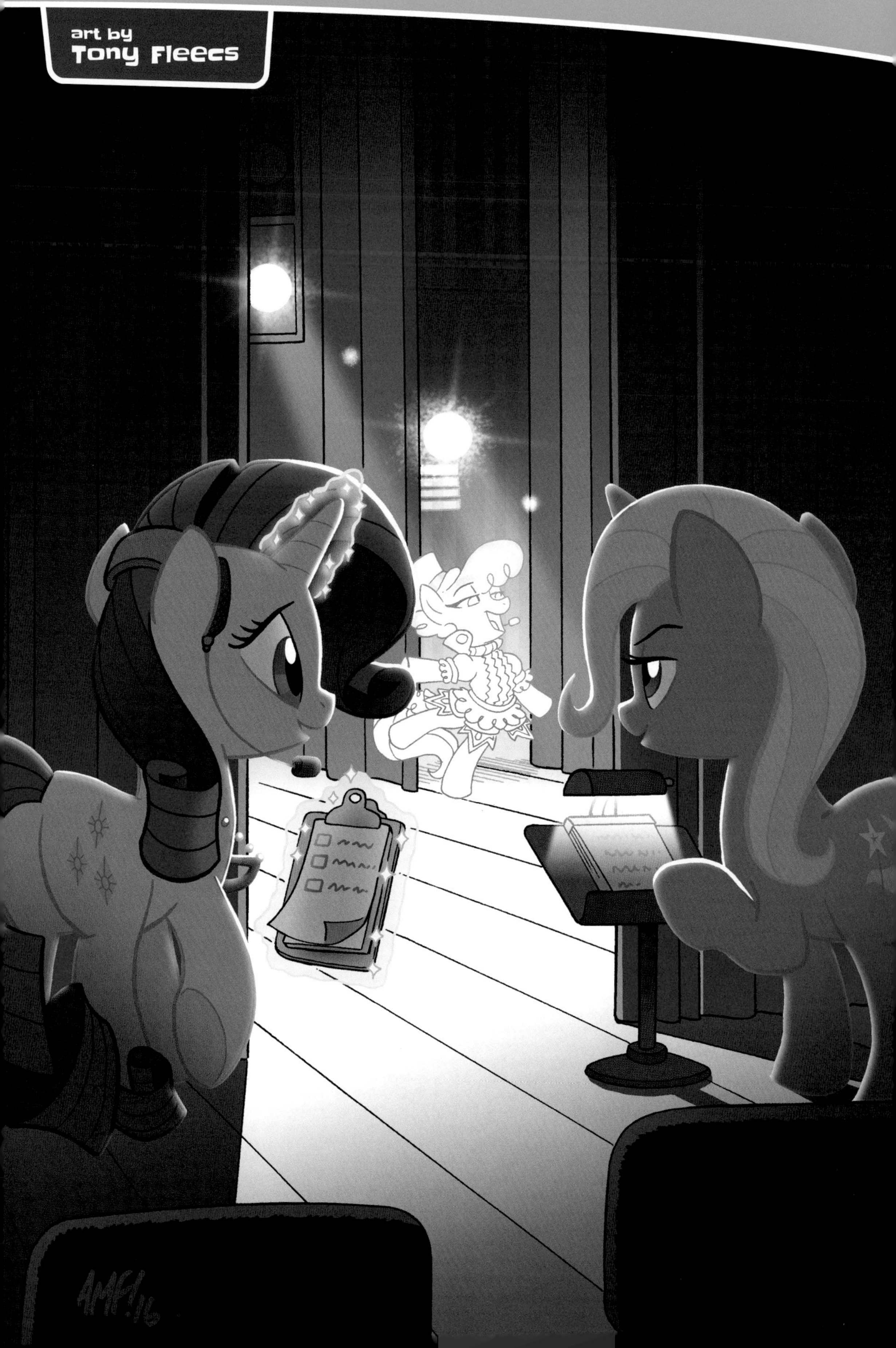

Princess Celestia & Princess Luna

art by
Andy Price

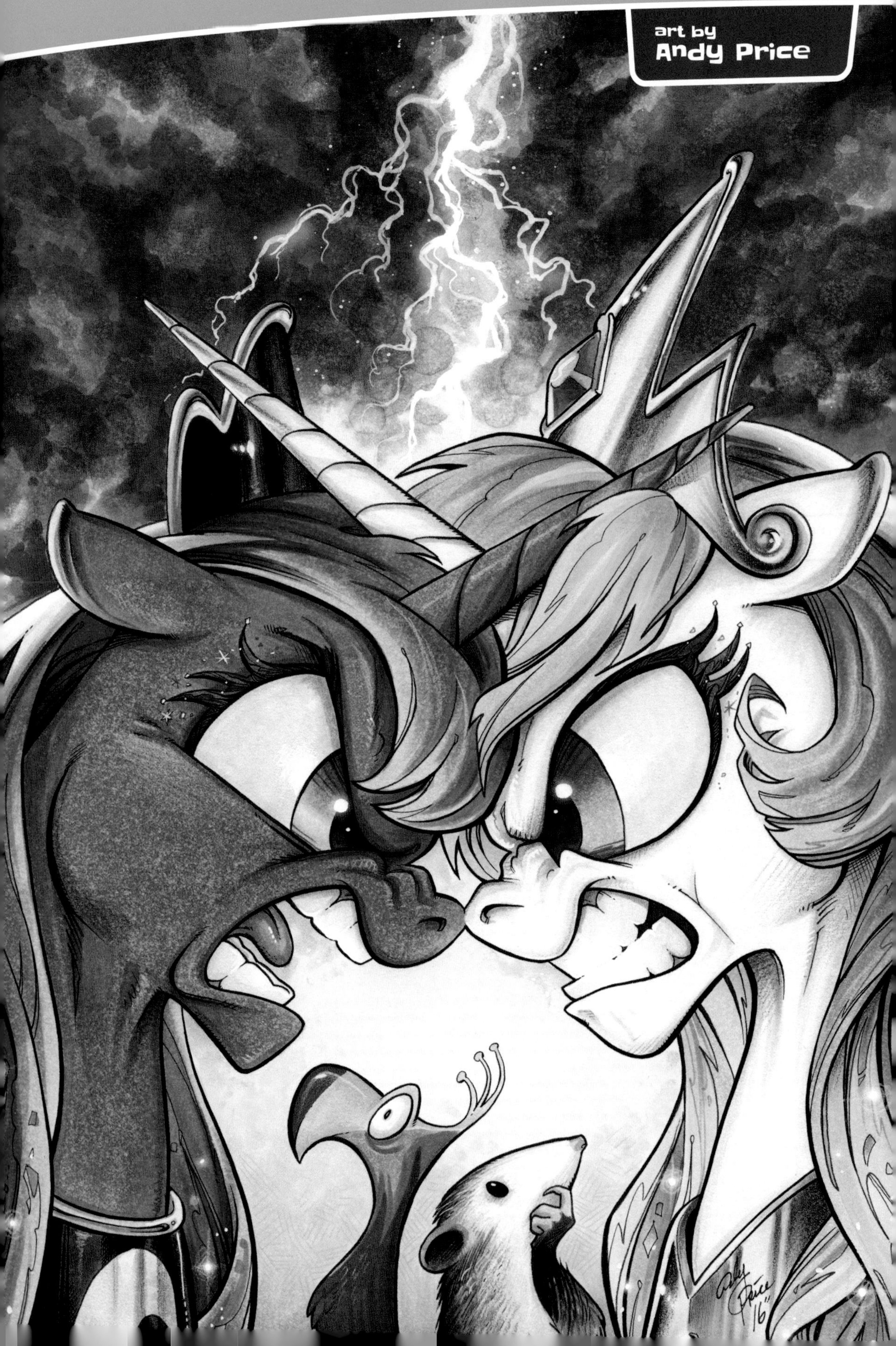

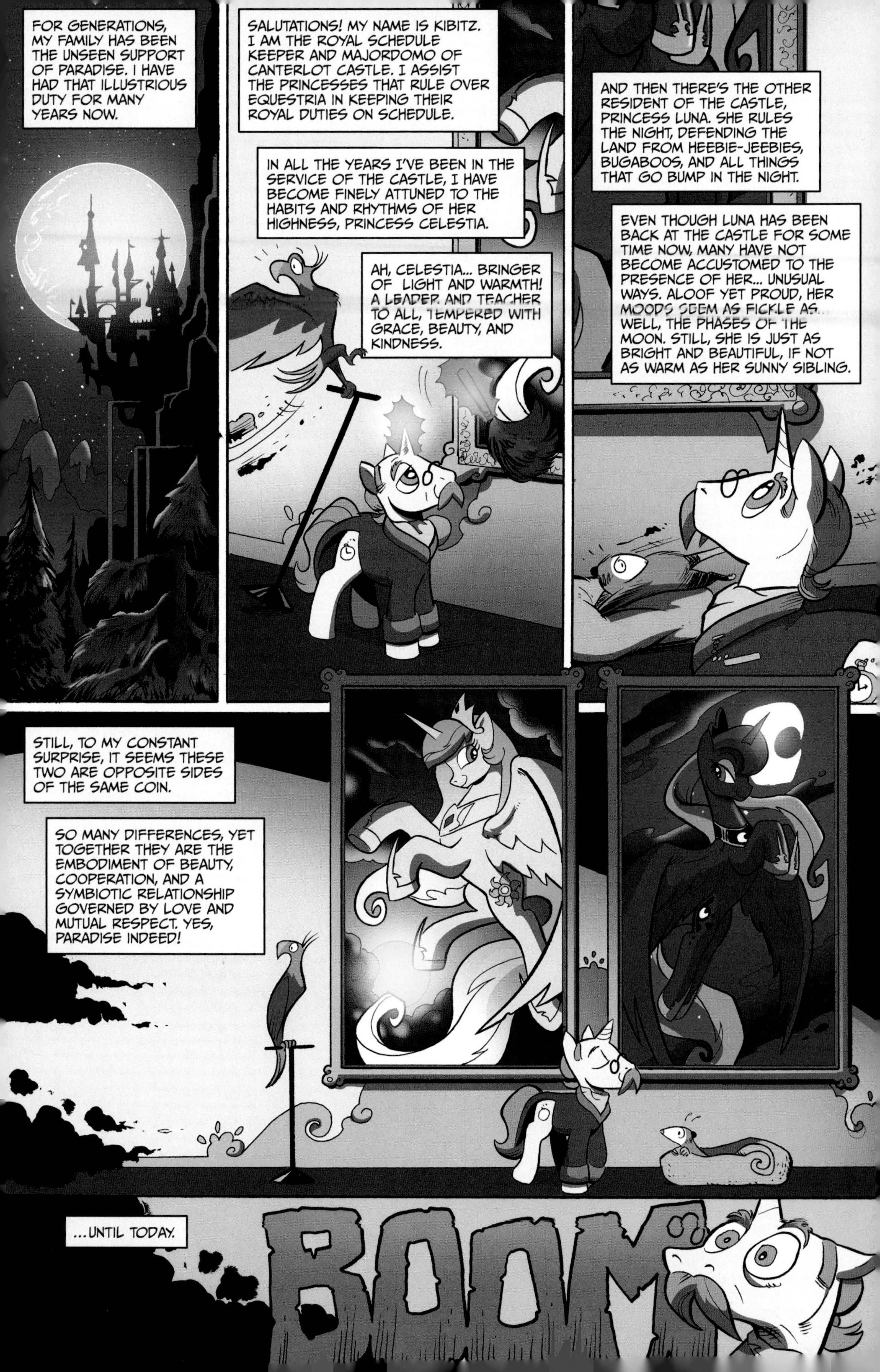
FOR GENERATIONS, MY FAMILY HAS BEEN THE UNSEEN SUPPORT OF PARADISE. I HAVE HAD THAT ILLUSTRIOUS DUTY FOR MANY YEARS NOW.
SALUTATIONS! MY NAME IS KIBITZ. I AM THE ROYAL SCHEDULE KEEPER AND MAJORDOMO OF CANTERLOT CASTLE. I ASSIST THE PRINCESSES THAT RULE OVER EQUESTRIA IN KEEPING THEIR ROYAL DUTIES ON SCHEDULE.
IN ALL THE YEARS I'VE BEEN IN THE SERVICE OF THE CASTLE, I HAVE BECOME FINELY ATTUNED TO THE HABITS AND RHYTHMS OF HER HIGHNESS, PRINCESS CELESTIA.
AH, CELESTIA... BRINGER OF LIGHT AND WARMTH! A LEADER AND TEACHER TO ALL, TEMPERED WITH GRACE, BEAUTY, AND KINDNESS.
AND THEN THERE'S THE OTHER RESIDENT OF THE CASTLE, PRINCESS LUNA. SHE RULES THE NIGHT, DEFENDING THE LAND FROM HEEBIE-JEEBIES, BUGABOOS, AND ALL THINGS THAT GO BUMP IN THE NIGHT.
EVEN THOUGH LUNA HAS BEEN BACK AT THE CASTLE FOR SOME TIME NOW, MANY HAVE NOT BECOME ACCUSTOMED TO THE PRESENCE OF HER... UNUSUAL WAYS. ALOOF YET PROUD, HER MOODS SEEM AS FICKLE AS... WELL, THE PHASES OF THE MOON. STILL, SHE IS JUST AS BRIGHT AND BEAUTIFUL, IF NOT AS WARM AS HER SUNNY SIBLING.
STILL, TO MY CONSTANT SURPRISE, IT SEEMS THESE TWO ARE OPPOSITE SIDES OF THE SAME COIN.
SO MANY DIFFERENCES, YET TOGETHER THEY ARE THE EMBODIMENT OF BEAUTY, COOPERATION, AND A SYMBIOTIC RELATIONSHIP GOVERNED BY LOVE AND MUTUAL RESPECT. YES, PARADISE INDEED!
...UNTIL TODAY.
BOOM

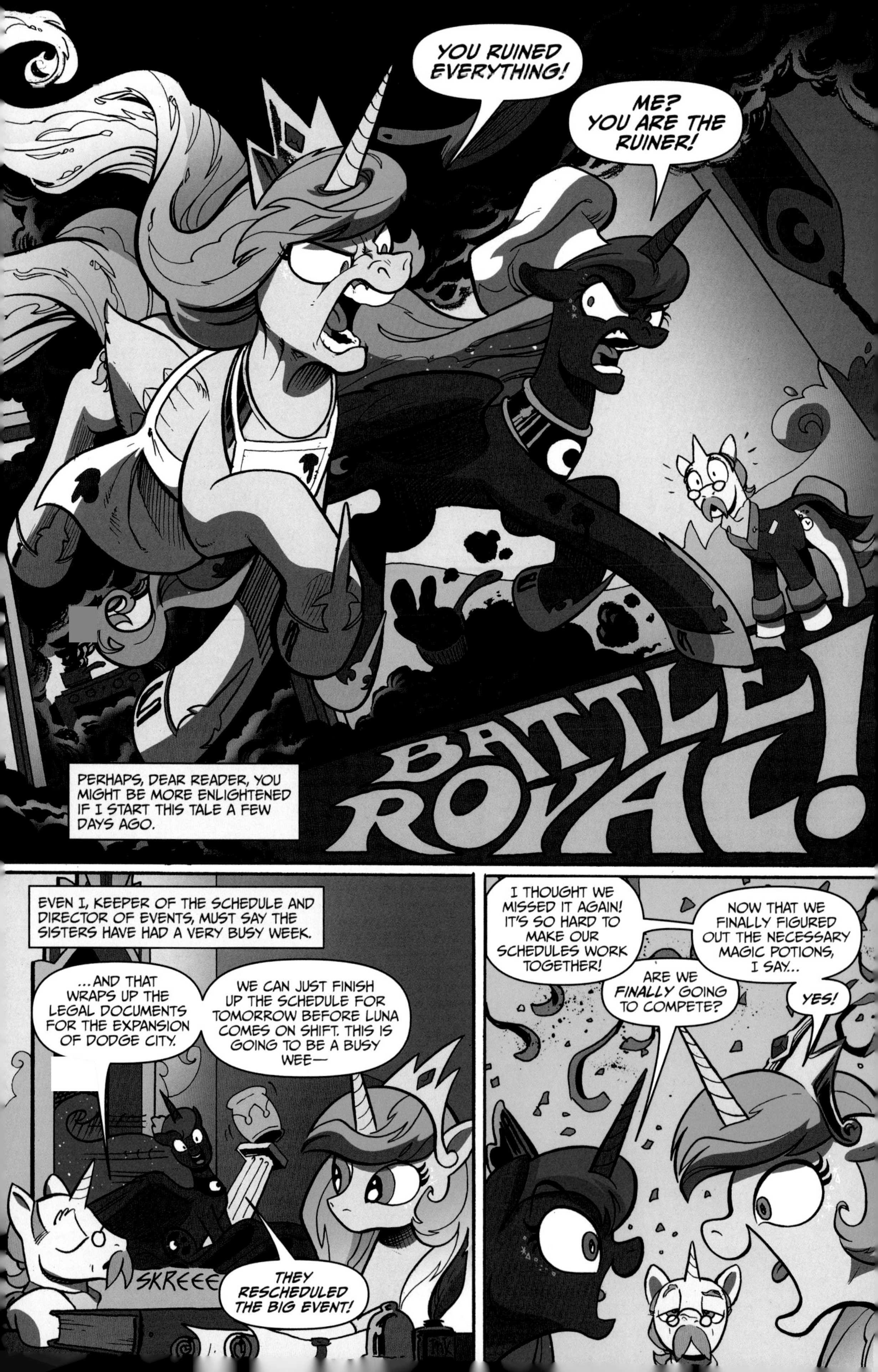
YOU RUINED EVERYTHING!
ME? YOU ARE THE RUINER!
PERHAPS, DEAR READER, YOU MIGHT BE MORE ENLIGHTENED IF I START THIS TALE A FEW DAYS AGO.
BATTLE ROYAL!
EVEN I, KEEPER OF THE SCHEDULE AND DIRECTOR OF EVENTS, MUST SAY THE SISTERS HAVE HAD A VERY BUSY WEEK.
...AND THAT WRAPS UP THE LEGAL DOCUMENTS FOR THE EXPANSION OF DODGE CITY.
WE CAN JUST FINISH UP THE SCHEDULE FOR TOMORROW BEFORE LUNA COMES ON SHIFT. THIS IS GOING TO BE A BUSY WEE—
SKREEE
THEY RESCHEDULED THE BIG EVENT!
I THOUGHT WE MISSED IT AGAIN! IT'S SO HARD TO MAKE OUR SCHEDULES WORK TOGETHER!
NOW THAT WE FINALLY FIGURED OUT THE NECESSARY MAGIC POTIONS, I SAY...
ARE WE *FINALLY* GOING TO COMPETE?
YES!

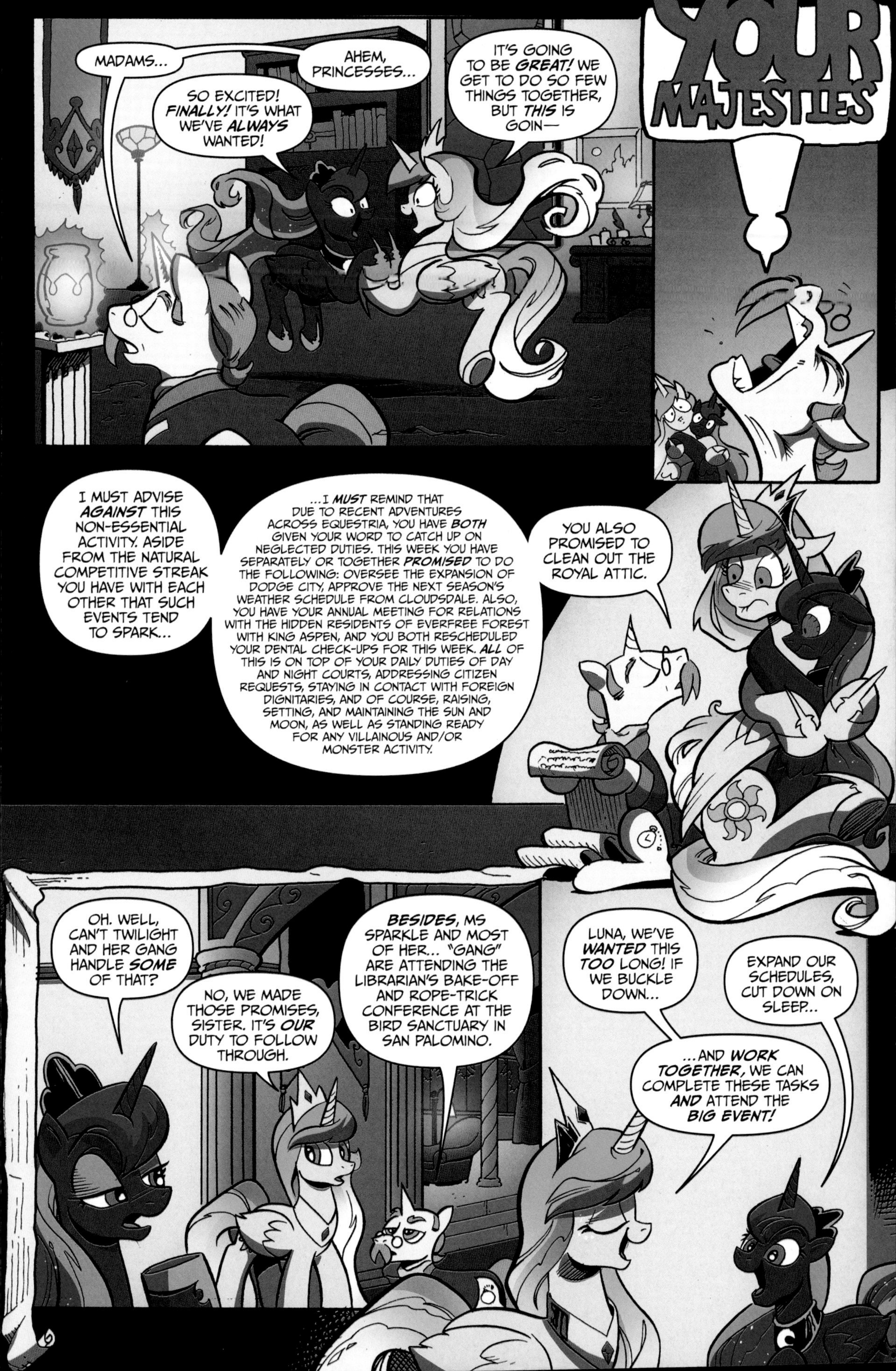

MADAMS...
AHEM, PRINCESSES...
SO EXCITED! FINALLY! IT'S WHAT WE'VE ALWAYS WANTED!
IT'S GOING TO BE GREAT! WE GET TO DO SO FEW THINGS TOGETHER, BUT THIS IS GOIN—
YOUR MAJESTIES!
I MUST ADVISE AGAINST THIS NON-ESSENTIAL ACTIVITY. ASIDE FROM THE NATURAL COMPETITIVE STREAK YOU HAVE WITH EACH OTHER THAT SUCH EVENTS TEND TO SPARK...
...I MUST REMIND THAT DUE TO RECENT ADVENTURES ACROSS EQUESTRIA, YOU HAVE BOTH GIVEN YOUR WORD TO CATCH UP ON NEGLECTED DUTIES. THIS WEEK YOU HAVE SEPARATELY OR TOGETHER PROMISED TO DO THE FOLLOWING: OVERSEE THE EXPANSION OF DODGE CITY, APPROVE THE NEXT SEASON'S WEATHER SCHEDULE FROM CLOUDSDALE. ALSO, YOU HAVE YOUR ANNUAL MEETING FOR RELATIONS WITH THE HIDDEN RESIDENTS OF EVERFREE FOREST WITH KING ASPEN, AND YOU BOTH RESCHEDULED YOUR DENTAL CHECK-UPS FOR THIS WEEK. ALL OF THIS IS ON TOP OF YOUR DAILY DUTIES OF DAY AND NIGHT COURTS, ADDRESSING CITIZEN REQUESTS, STAYING IN CONTACT WITH FOREIGN DIGNITARIES, AND OF COURSE, RAISING, SETTING, AND MAINTAINING THE SUN AND MOON, AS WELL AS STANDING READY FOR ANY VILLAINOUS AND/OR MONSTER ACTIVITY.
YOU ALSO PROMISED TO CLEAN OUT THE ROYAL ATTIC.
OH. WELL, CAN'T TWILIGHT AND HER GANG HANDLE SOME OF THAT?
NO, WE MADE THOSE PROMISES, SISTER. IT'S OUR DUTY TO FOLLOW THROUGH.
BESIDES, MS SPARKLE AND MOST OF HER... "GANG" ARE ATTENDING THE LIBRARIAN'S BAKE-OFF AND ROPE-TRICK CONFERENCE AT THE BIRD SANCTUARY IN SAN PALOMINO.
LUNA, WE'VE WANTED THIS TOO LONG! IF WE BUCKLE DOWN...
EXPAND OUR SCHEDULES, CUT DOWN ON SLEEP...
...AND WORK TOGETHER, WE CAN COMPLETE THESE TASKS AND ATTEND THE BIG EVENT!

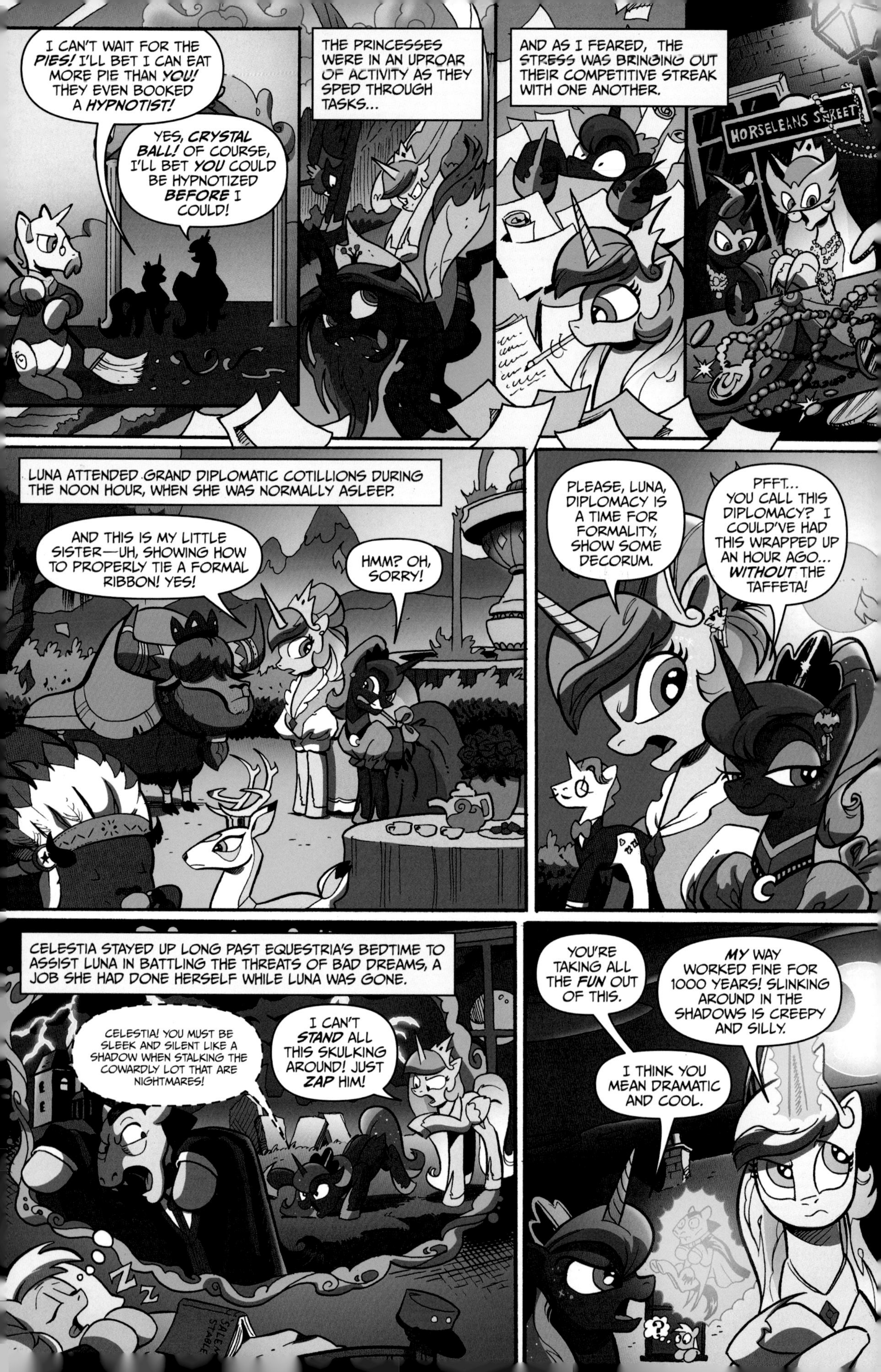

I CAN'T WAIT FOR THE PIES! I'LL BET I CAN EAT MORE PIE THAN YOU! THEY EVEN BOOKED A HYPNOTIST!
YES, CRYSTAL BALL! OF COURSE, I'LL BET YOU COULD BE HYPNOTIZED BEFORE I COULD!
THE PRINCESSES WERE IN AN UPROAR OF ACTIVITY AS THEY SPED THROUGH TASKS...
AND AS I FEARED, THE STRESS WAS BRINGING OUT THEIR COMPETITIVE STREAK WITH ONE ANOTHER.
HORSELEANS STREET
LUNA ATTENDED GRAND DIPLOMATIC COTILLIONS DURING THE NOON HOUR, WHEN SHE WAS NORMALLY ASLEEP.
AND THIS IS MY LITTLE SISTER—UH, SHOWING HOW TO PROPERLY TIE A FORMAL RIBBON! YES!
HMM? OH, SORRY!
PLEASE, LUNA, DIPLOMACY IS A TIME FOR FORMALITY, SHOW SOME DECORUM.
PFFT... YOU CALL THIS DIPLOMACY? I COULD'VE HAD THIS WRAPPED UP AN HOUR AGO... WITHOUT THE TAFFETA!
CELESTIA STAYED UP LONG PAST EQUESTRIA'S BEDTIME TO ASSIST LUNA IN BATTLING THE THREATS OF BAD DREAMS, A JOB SHE HAD DONE HERSELF WHILE LUNA WAS GONE.
CELESTIA! YOU MUST BE SLEEK AND SILENT LIKE A SHADOW WHEN STALKING THE COWARDLY LOT THAT ARE NIGHTMARES!
I CAN'T STAND ALL THIS SKULKING AROUND! JUST ZAP HIM!
Z Z
SALEM STABLE
YOU'RE TAKING ALL THE FUN OUT OF THIS.
MY WAY WORKED FINE FOR 1000 YEARS! SLINKING AROUND IN THE SHADOWS IS CREEPY AND SILLY.
I THINK YOU MEAN DRAMATIC AND COOL.

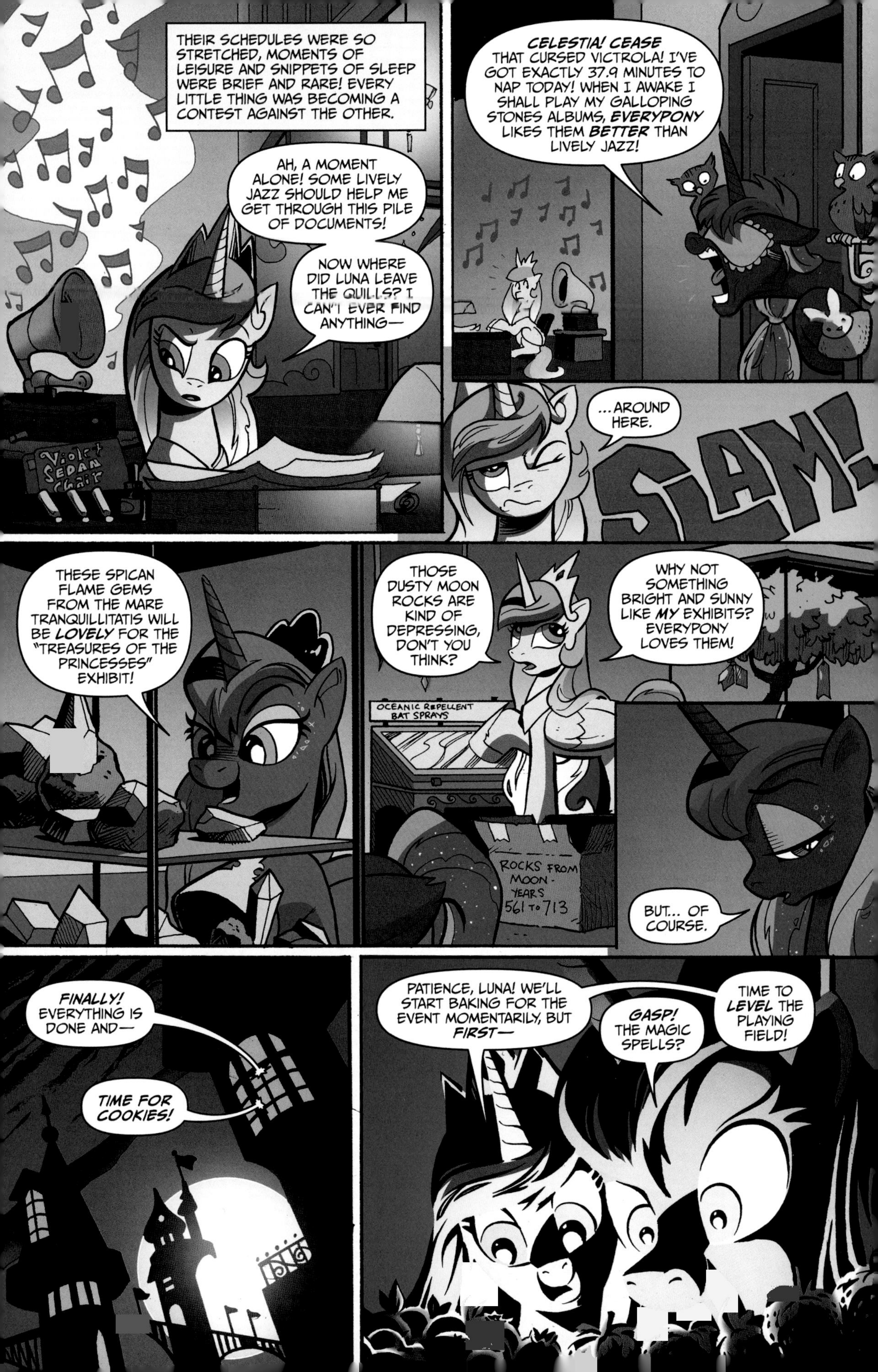
THEIR SCHEDULES WERE SO STRETCHED, MOMENTS OF LEISURE AND SNIPPETS OF SLEEP WERE BRIEF AND RARE! EVERY LITTLE THING WAS BECOMING A CONTEST AGAINST THE OTHER.
AH, A MOMENT ALONE! SOME LIVELY JAZZ SHOULD HELP ME GET THROUGH THIS PILE OF DOCUMENTS!
NOW WHERE DID LUNA LEAVE THE QUILLS? I CAN'T EVER FIND ANYTHING—
Violet SEDAN Chair
CELESTIA! CEASE THAT CURSED VICTROLA! I'VE GOT EXACTLY 37.9 MINUTES TO NAP TODAY! WHEN I AWAKE I SHALL PLAY MY GALLOPING STONES ALBUMS, EVERYPONY LIKES THEM BETTER THAN LIVELY JAZZ!
...AROUND HERE.
SLAM!
THESE SPICAN FLAME GEMS FROM THE MARE TRANQUILLITATIS WILL BE LOVELY FOR THE "TREASURES OF THE PRINCESSES" EXHIBIT!
THOSE DUSTY MOON ROCKS ARE KIND OF DEPRESSING, DON'T YOU THINK?
WHY NOT SOMETHING BRIGHT AND SUNNY LIKE MY EXHIBITS? EVERYPONY LOVES THEM!
OCEANIC REPELLENT BAT SPRAYS
ROCKS FROM MOON - YEARS 561 TO 713
BUT... OF COURSE.
FINALLY! EVERYTHING IS DONE AND—
TIME FOR COOKIES!
PATIENCE, LUNA! WE'LL START BAKING FOR THE EVENT MOMENTARILY, BUT FIRST—
GASP! THE MAGIC SPELLS?
TIME TO LEVEL THE PLAYING FIELD!

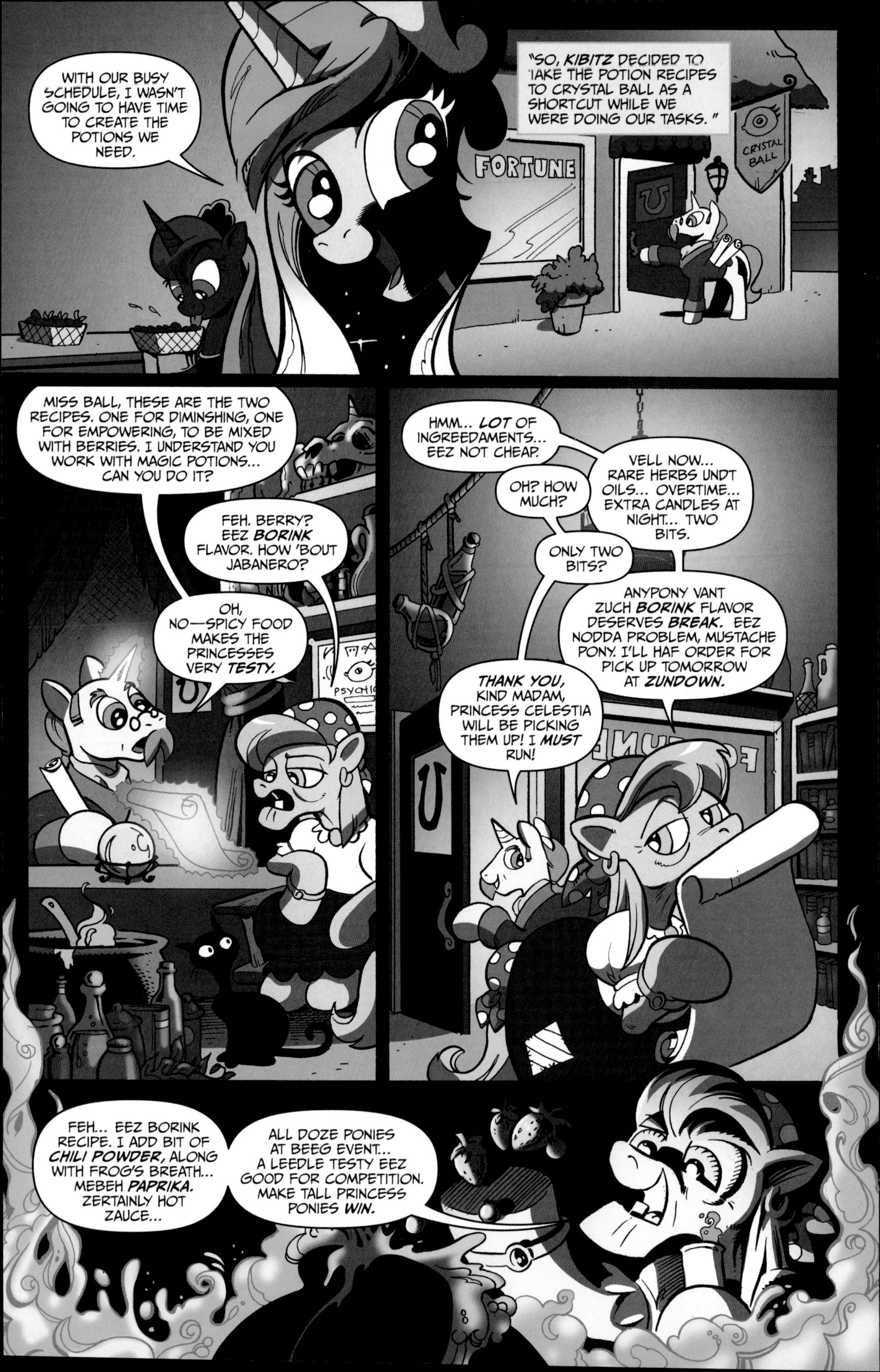
WITH OUR BUSY SCHEDULE, I WASN'T GOING TO HAVE TIME TO CREATE THE POTIONS WE NEED.
"SO, KIBITZ DECIDED TO TAKE THE POTION RECIPES TO CRYSTAL BALL AS A SHORTCUT WHILE WE WERE DOING OUR TASKS."
FORTUNE
CRYSTAL BALL
MISS BALL, THESE ARE THE TWO RECIPES. ONE FOR DIMINSHING, ONE FOR EMPOWERING, TO BE MIXED WITH BERRIES. I UNDERSTAND YOU WORK WITH MAGIC POTIONS... CAN YOU DO IT?
FEH. BERRY? EEZ BORINK FLAVOR. HOW 'BOUT JABANERO?
OH, NO—SPICY FOOD MAKES THE PRINCESSES VERY TESTY.
PSYCHIC
HMM... LOT OF INGREEDAMENTS... EEZ NOT CHEAP.
OH? HOW MUCH?
VELL NOW... RARE HERBS UNDT OILS... OVERTIME... EXTRA CANDLES AT NIGHT... TWO BITS.
ONLY TWO BITS?
ANYPONY VANT ZUCH BORINK FLAVOR DESERVES BREAK. EEZ NODDA PROBLEM, MUSTACHE PONY. I'LL HAF ORDER FOR PICK UP TOMORROW AT ZUNDOWN.
THANK YOU, KIND MADAM, PRINCESS CELESTIA WILL BE PICKING THEM UP! I MUST RUN!
FEH... EEZ BORINK RECIPE. I ADD BIT OF CHILI POWDER, ALONG WITH FROG'S BREATH... MEBEH PAPRIKA. ZERTAINLY HOT ZAUCE...
ALL DOZE PONIES AT BEEG EVENT... A LEEDLE TESTY EEZ GOOD FOR COMPETITION. MAKE TALL PRINCESS PONIES WIN.

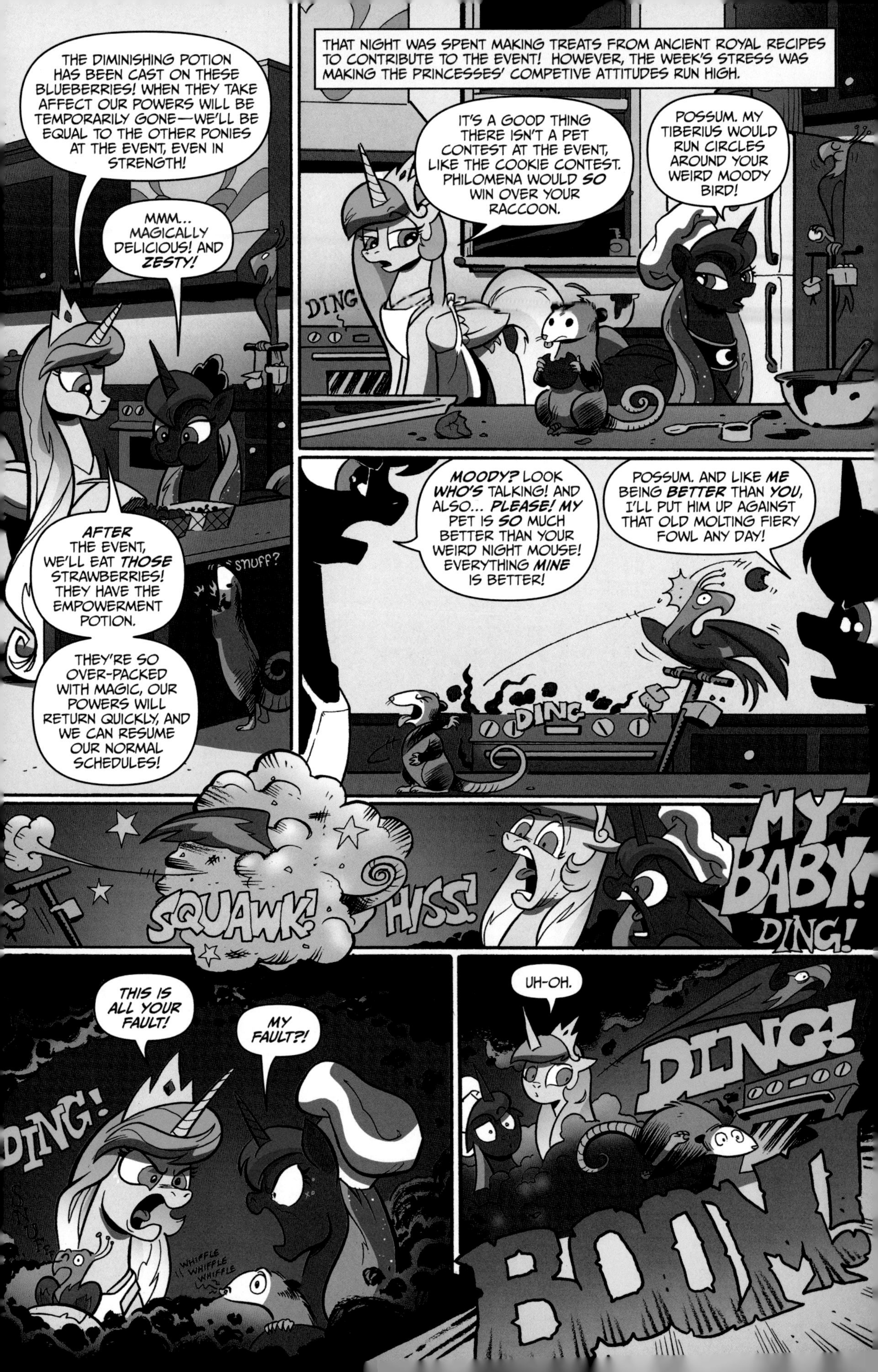
THE DIMINISHING POTION HAS BEEN CAST ON THESE BLUEBERRIES! WHEN THEY TAKE AFFECT OUR POWERS WILL BE TEMPORARILY GONE—WE'LL BE EQUAL TO THE OTHER PONIES AT THE EVENT, EVEN IN STRENGTH!
MMM... MAGICALLY DELICIOUS! AND ZESTY!
AFTER THE EVENT, WE'LL EAT THOSE STRAWBERRIES! THEY HAVE THE EMPOWERMENT POTION.
THEY'RE SO OVER-PACKED WITH MAGIC, OUR POWERS WILL RETURN QUICKLY, AND WE CAN RESUME OUR NORMAL SCHEDULES!
SNUFF?
THAT NIGHT WAS SPENT MAKING TREATS FROM ANCIENT ROYAL RECIPES TO CONTRIBUTE TO THE EVENT! HOWEVER, THE WEEK'S STRESS WAS MAKING THE PRINCESSES' COMPETIVE ATTITUDES RUN HIGH.
IT'S A GOOD THING THERE ISN'T A PET CONTEST AT THE EVENT, LIKE THE COOKIE CONTEST. PHILOMENA WOULD SO WIN OVER YOUR RACCOON.
POSSUM. MY TIBERIUS WOULD RUN CIRCLES AROUND YOUR WEIRD MOODY BIRD!
DING
MOODY? LOOK WHO'S TALKING! AND ALSO... PLEASE! MY PET IS SO MUCH BETTER THAN YOUR WEIRD NIGHT MOUSE! EVERYTHING MINE IS BETTER!
POSSUM. AND LIKE ME BEING BETTER THAN YOU, I'LL PUT HIM UP AGAINST THAT OLD MOLTING FIERY FOWL ANY DAY!
DING
SQUAWK!
HISS!
MY BABY!
DING!
THIS IS ALL YOUR FAULT!
MY FAULT?!
DING!
WHIFFLE WHIFFLE WHIFFLE
UH-OH.
DING!
BOOM!

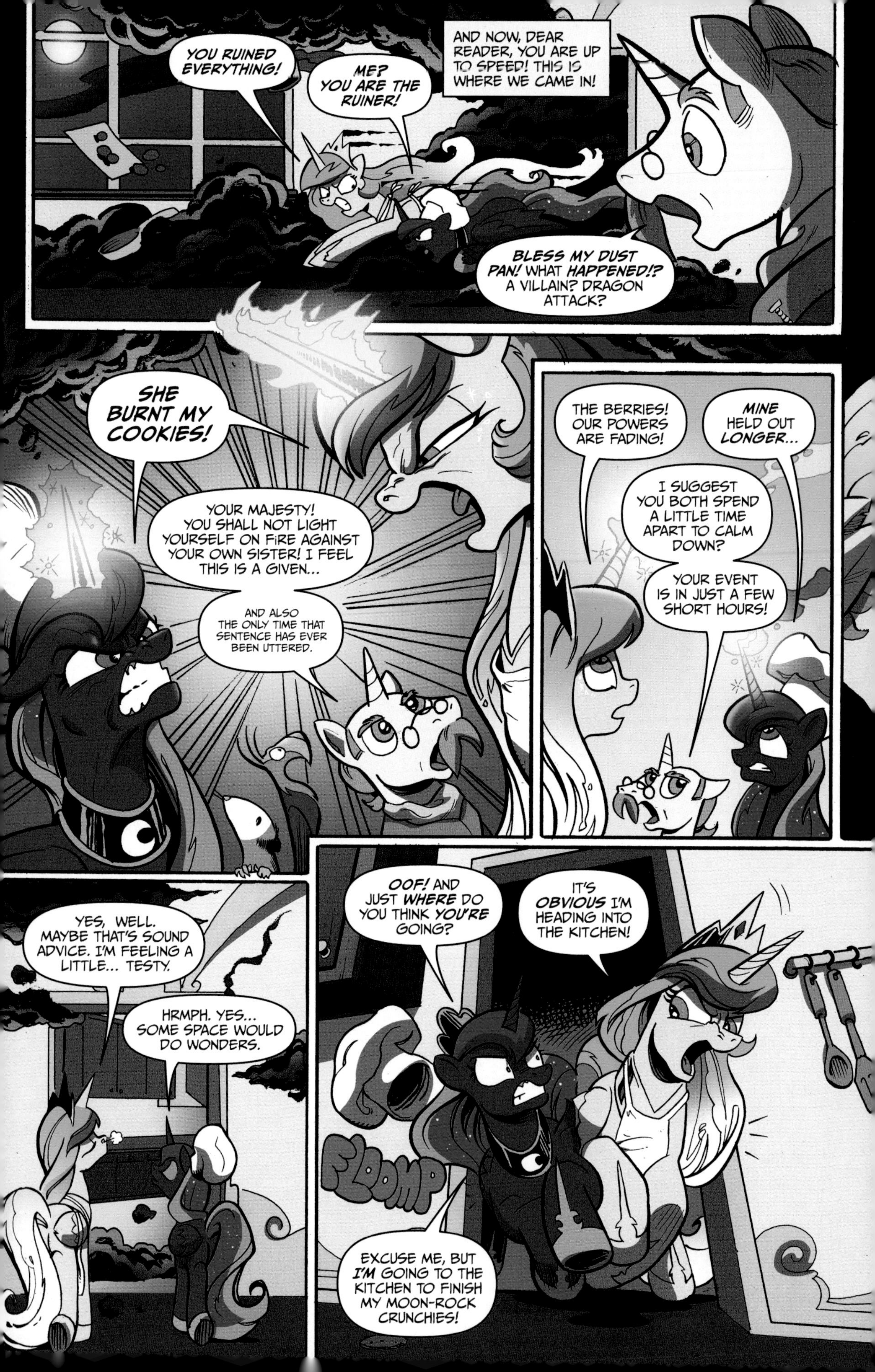

YOU RUINED EVERYTHING!
ME? YOU ARE THE RUINER!
AND NOW, DEAR READER, YOU ARE UP TO SPEED! THIS IS WHERE WE CAME IN!
BLESS MY DUST PAN! WHAT HAPPENED!? A VILLAIN? DRAGON ATTACK?
SHE BURNT MY COOKIES!
YOUR MAJESTY! YOU SHALL NOT LIGHT YOURSELF ON FIRE AGAINST YOUR OWN SISTER! I FEEL THIS IS A GIVEN...
AND ALSO THE ONLY TIME THAT SENTENCE HAS EVER BEEN UTTERED.
THE BERRIES! OUR POWERS ARE FADING!
MINE HELD OUT LONGER...
I SUGGEST YOU BOTH SPEND A LITTLE TIME APART TO CALM DOWN?
YOUR EVENT IS IN JUST A FEW SHORT HOURS!
YES, WELL. MAYBE THAT'S SOUND ADVICE. I'M FEELING A LITTLE... TESTY.
HRMPH. YES... SOME SPACE WOULD DO WONDERS.
OOF! AND JUST WHERE DO YOU THINK YOU'RE GOING?
IT'S OBVIOUS I'M HEADING INTO THE KITCHEN!
FLOOMP
EXCUSE ME, BUT I'M GOING TO THE KITCHEN TO FINISH MY MOON-ROCK CRUNCHIES!

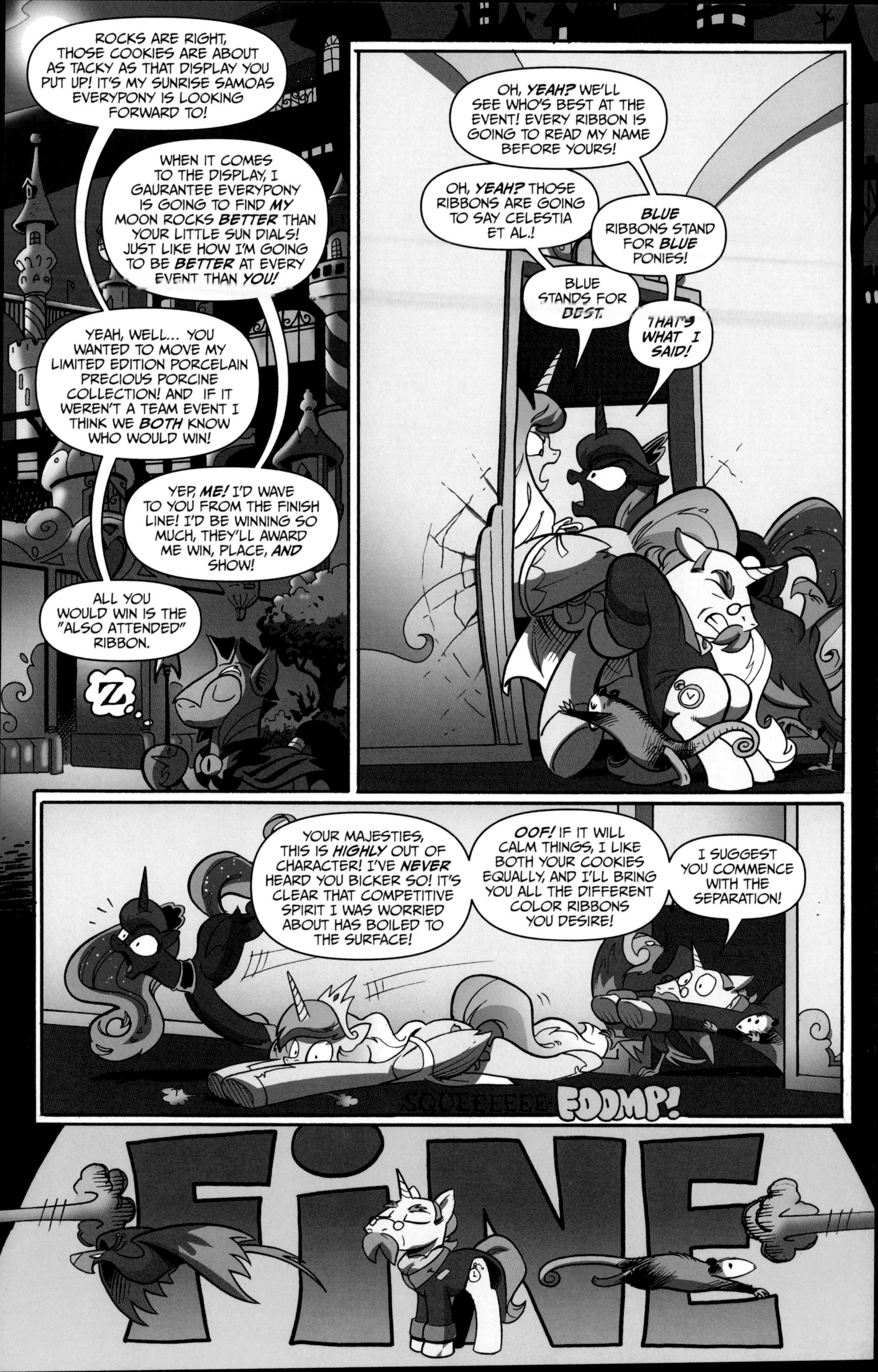
ROCKS ARE RIGHT, THOSE COOKIES ARE ABOUT AS TACKY AS THAT DISPLAY YOU PUT UP! IT'S MY SUNRISE SAMOAS EVERYPONY IS LOOKING FORWARD TO!
WHEN IT COMES TO THE DISPLAY, I GAURANTEE EVERYPONY IS GOING TO FIND MY MOON ROCKS BETTER THAN YOUR LITTLE SUN DIALS! JUST LIKE HOW I'M GOING TO BE BETTER AT EVERY EVENT THAN YOU!
YEAH, WELL... YOU WANTED TO MOVE MY LIMITED EDITION PORCELAIN PRECIOUS PORCINE COLLECTION! AND IF IT WEREN'T A TEAM EVENT I THINK WE BOTH KNOW WHO WOULD WIN!
YEP, ME! I'D WAVE TO YOU FROM THE FINISH LINE! I'D BE WINNING SO MUCH, THEY'LL AWARD ME WIN, PLACE, AND SHOW!
ALL YOU WOULD WIN IS THE "ALSO ATTENDED" RIBBON.
Z
OH, YEAH? WE'LL SEE WHO'S BEST AT THE EVENT! EVERY RIBBON IS GOING TO READ MY NAME BEFORE YOURS!
OH, YEAH? THOSE RIBBONS ARE GOING TO SAY CELESTIA ET AL.!
BLUE RIBBONS STAND FOR BLUE PONIES!
BLUE STANDS FOR BEST.
THAT'S WHAT I SAID!
YOUR MAJESTIES, THIS IS HIGHLY OUT OF CHARACTER! I'VE NEVER HEARD YOU BICKER SO! IT'S CLEAR THAT COMPETITIVE SPIRIT I WAS WORRIED ABOUT HAS BOILED TO THE SURFACE!
OOF! IF IT WILL CALM THINGS, I LIKE BOTH YOUR COOKIES EQUALLY, AND I'LL BRING YOU ALL THE DIFFERENT COLOR RIBBONS YOU DESIRE!
I SUGGEST YOU COMMENCE WITH THE SEPARATION!
SQUEEEEEE-FOOMP!
FINE

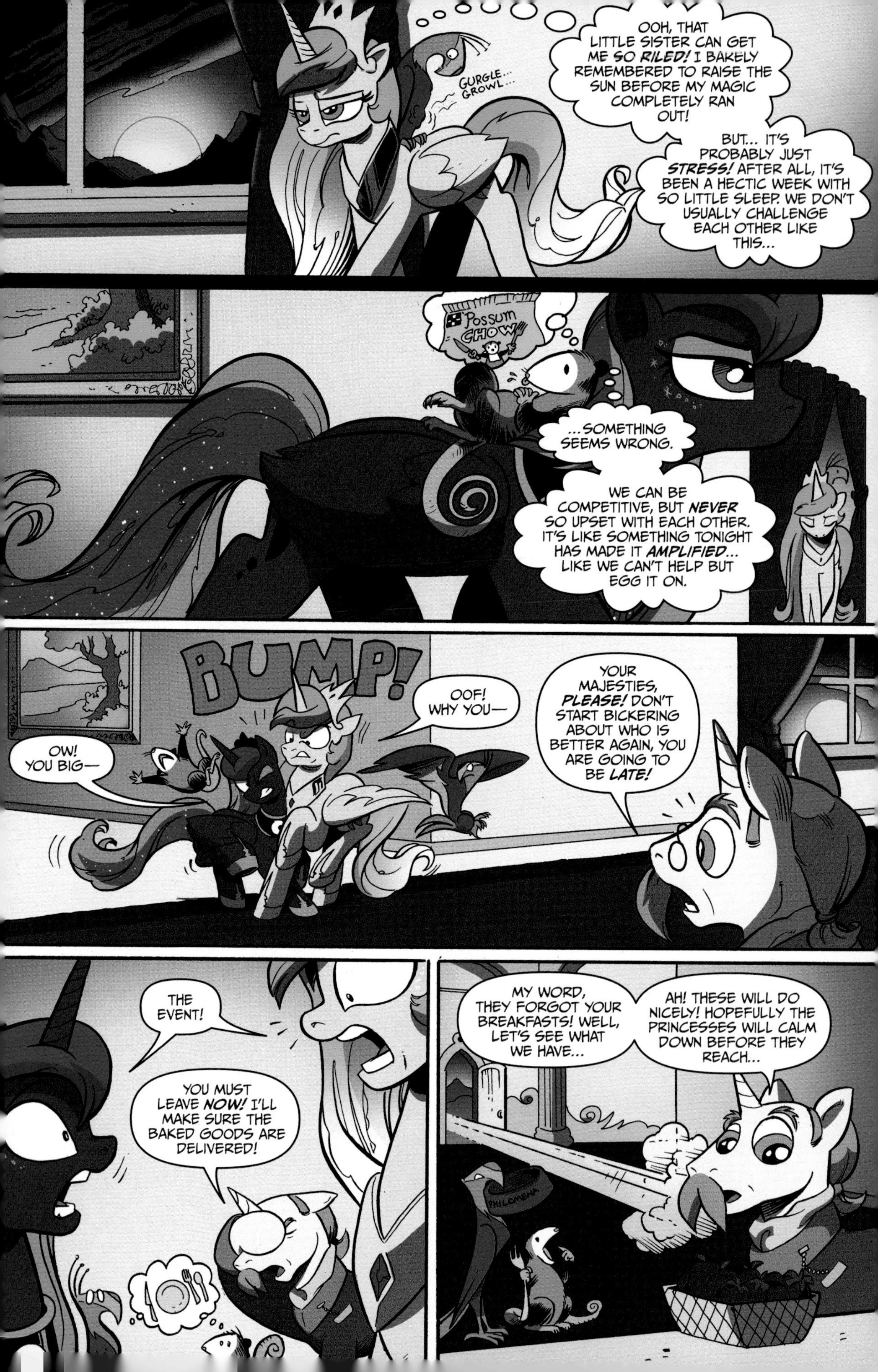
GURGLE... GROWL...
OOH, THAT LITTLE SISTER CAN GET ME SO ***RILED!*** I BAKELY REMEMBERED TO RAISE THE SUN BEFORE MY MAGIC COMPLETELY RAN OUT!
BUT... IT'S PROBABLY JUST ***STRESS!*** AFTER ALL, IT'S BEEN A HECTIC WEEK WITH SO LITTLE SLEEP. WE DON'T USUALLY CHALLENGE EACH OTHER LIKE THIS...
Possum CHOW
...SOMETHING SEEMS WRONG.
WE CAN BE COMPETITIVE, BUT ***NEVER*** SO UPSET WITH EACH OTHER. IT'S LIKE SOMETHING TONIGHT HAS MADE IT ***AMPLIFIED...*** LIKE WE CAN'T HELP BUT EGG IT ON.
BUMP!
OW! YOU BIG—
OOF! WHY YOU—
YOUR MAJESTIES, ***PLEASE!*** DON'T START BICKERING ABOUT WHO IS BETTER AGAIN, YOU ARE GOING TO BE ***LATE!***
THE EVENT!
YOU MUST LEAVE ***NOW!*** I'LL MAKE SURE THE BAKED GOODS ARE DELIVERED!
MY WORD, THEY FORGOT YOUR BREAKFASTS! WELL, LET'S SEE WHAT WE HAVE...
AH! THESE WILL DO NICELY! HOPEFULLY THE PRINCESSES WILL CALM DOWN BEFORE THEY REACH...
PHILOMENA

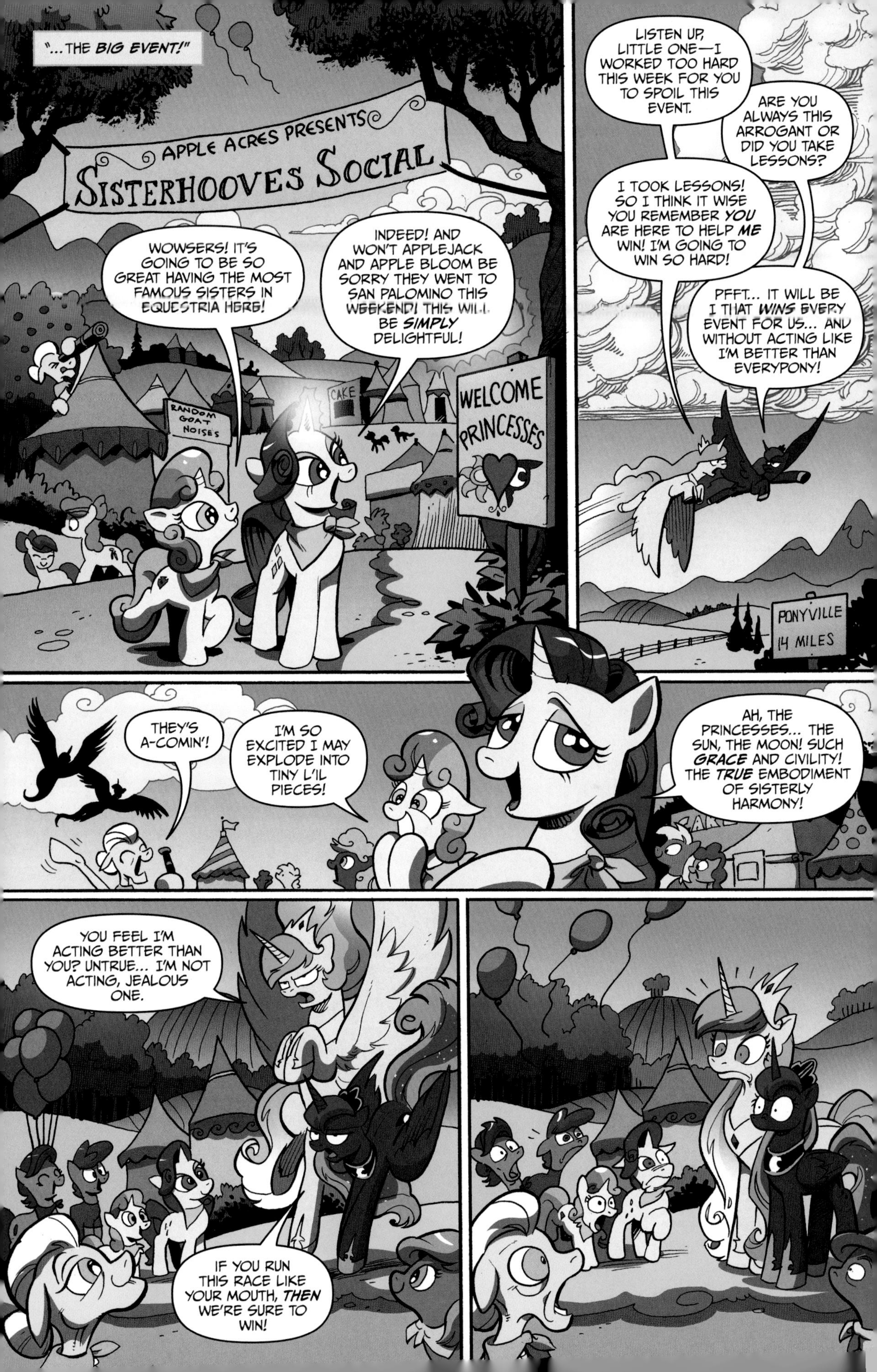
"...THE BIG EVENT!"
APPLE ACRES PRESENTS
SISTERHOOVES SOCIAL
WOWSERS! IT'S GOING TO BE SO GREAT HAVING THE MOST FAMOUS SISTERS IN EQUESTRIA HERE!
INDEED! AND WON'T APPLEJACK AND APPLE BLOOM BE SORRY THEY WENT TO SAN PALOMINO THIS WEEKEND! THIS WILL BE SIMPLY DELIGHTFUL!
RANDOM GOAT NOISES
CAKE
WELCOME PRINCESSES
LISTEN UP, LITTLE ONE—I WORKED TOO HARD THIS WEEK FOR YOU TO SPOIL THIS EVENT.
ARE YOU ALWAYS THIS ARROGANT OR DID YOU TAKE LESSONS?
I TOOK LESSONS! SO I THINK IT WISE YOU REMEMBER YOU ARE HERE TO HELP ME WIN! I'M GOING TO WIN SO HARD!
PFFT... IT WILL BE I THAT WINS EVERY EVENT FOR US... AND WITHOUT ACTING LIKE I'M BETTER THAN EVERYPONY!
PONYVILLE 14 MILES
THEY'S A-COMIN'!
I'M SO EXCITED I MAY EXPLODE INTO TINY L'IL PIECES!
AH, THE PRINCESSES... THE SUN, THE MOON! SUCH GRACE AND CIVILITY! THE TRUE EMBODIMENT OF SISTERLY HARMONY!
YOU FEEL I'M ACTING BETTER THAN YOU? UNTRUE... I'M NOT ACTING, JEALOUS ONE.
IF YOU RUN THIS RACE LIKE YOUR MOUTH, THEN WE'RE SURE TO WIN!

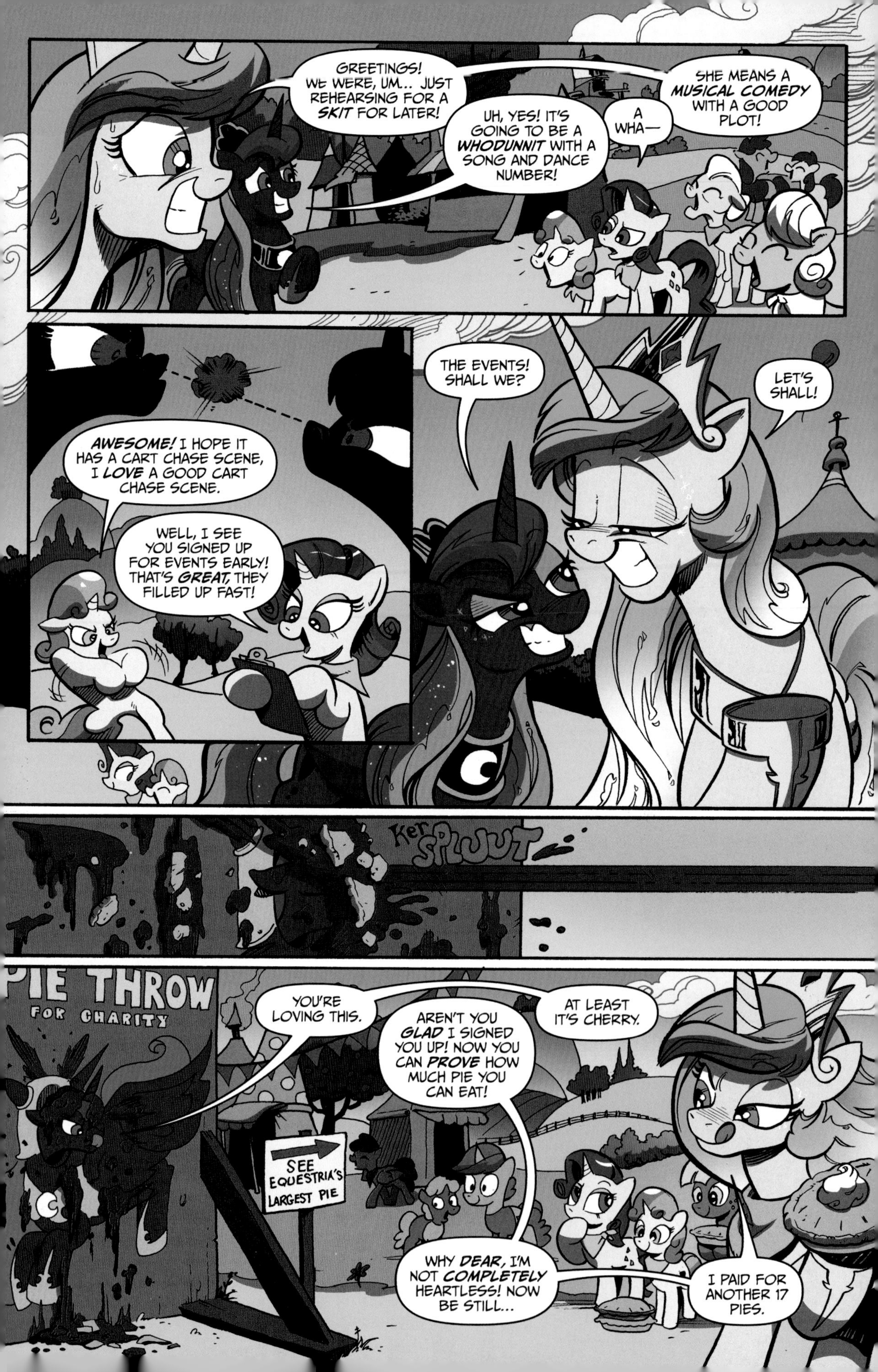
GREETINGS! WE WERE, UM... JUST REHEARSING FOR A SKIT FOR LATER!
UH, YES! IT'S GOING TO BE A WHODUNNIT WITH A SONG AND DANCE NUMBER!
A WHA—
SHE MEANS A MUSICAL COMEDY WITH A GOOD PLOT!
AWESOME! I HOPE IT HAS A CART CHASE SCENE, I LOVE A GOOD CART CHASE SCENE.
WELL, I SEE YOU SIGNED UP FOR EVENTS EARLY! THAT'S GREAT, THEY FILLED UP FAST!
THE EVENTS! SHALL WE?
LET'S SHALL!
Ker SPLUUT
PIE THROW
FOR CHARITY
YOU'RE LOVING THIS.
AT LEAST IT'S CHERRY.
AREN'T YOU GLAD I SIGNED YOU UP! NOW YOU CAN PROVE HOW MUCH PIE YOU CAN EAT!
SEE EQUESTRIA'S LARGEST PIE
WHY DEAR, I'M NOT COMPLETELY HEARTLESS! NOW BE STILL...
I PAID FOR ANOTHER 17 PIES.

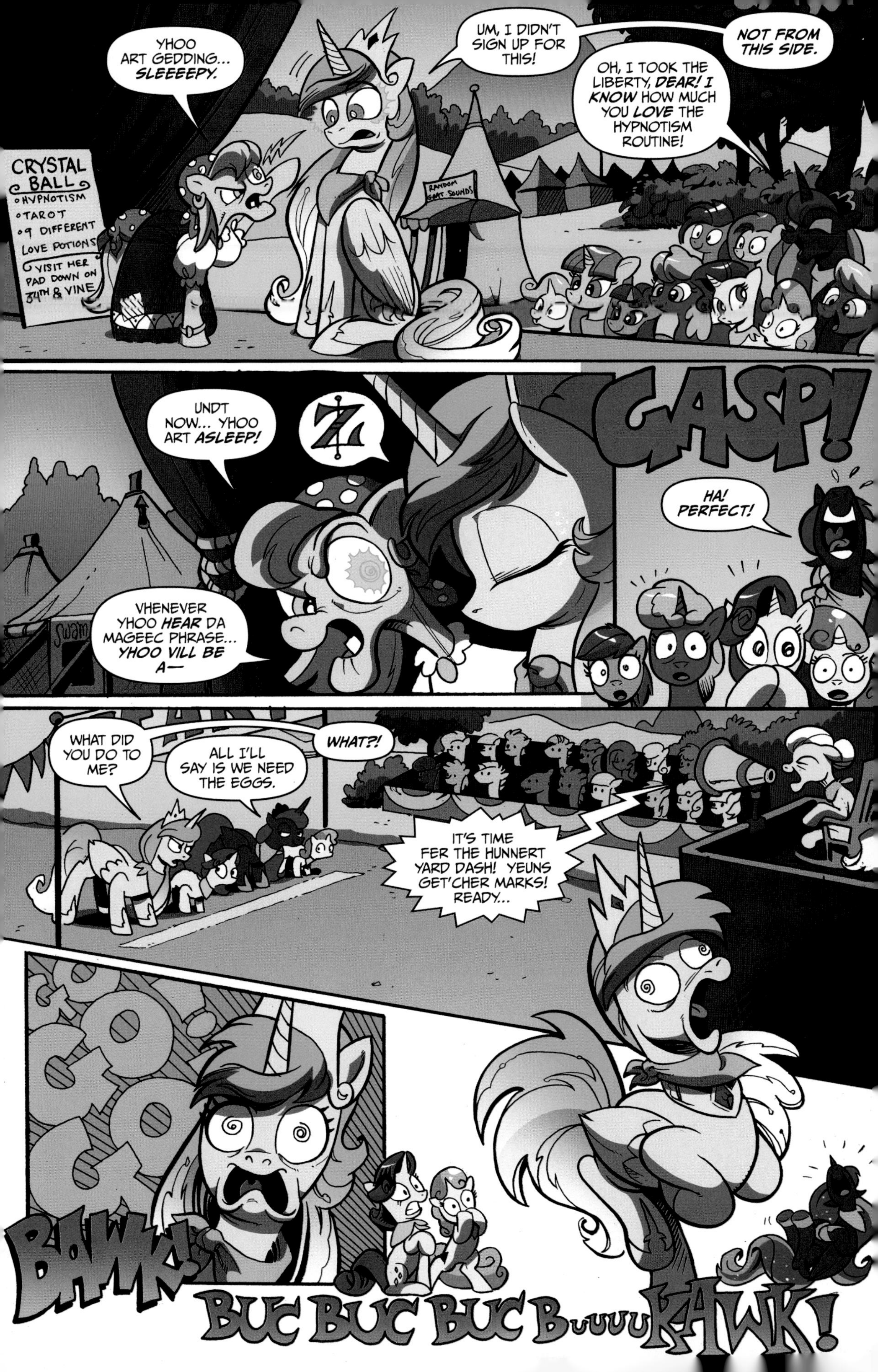
YHOO ART GEDDING... SLEEEEPY.
UM, I DIDN'T SIGN UP FOR THIS!
NOT FROM THIS SIDE.
OH, I TOOK THE LIBERTY, DEAR! I KNOW HOW MUCH YOU LOVE THE HYPNOTISM ROUTINE!
CRYSTAL BALL
HYPNOTISM
TAROT
9 DIFFERENT LOVE POTIONS
VISIT HER PAD DOWN ON 34TH & VINE
UNDT NOW... YHOO ART ASLEEP!
Z
GASP!
HA! PERFECT!
VHENEVER YHOO HEAR DA MAGEEC PHRASE... YHOO VILL BE A—
WHAT DID YOU DO TO ME?
WHAT?!
ALL I'LL SAY IS WE NEED THE EGGS.
IT'S TIME FER THE HUNNERT YARD DASH! YEUNS GET'CHER MARKS! READY...
GO
BAWK!
BUC BUC BUC BuuuuKAWK!

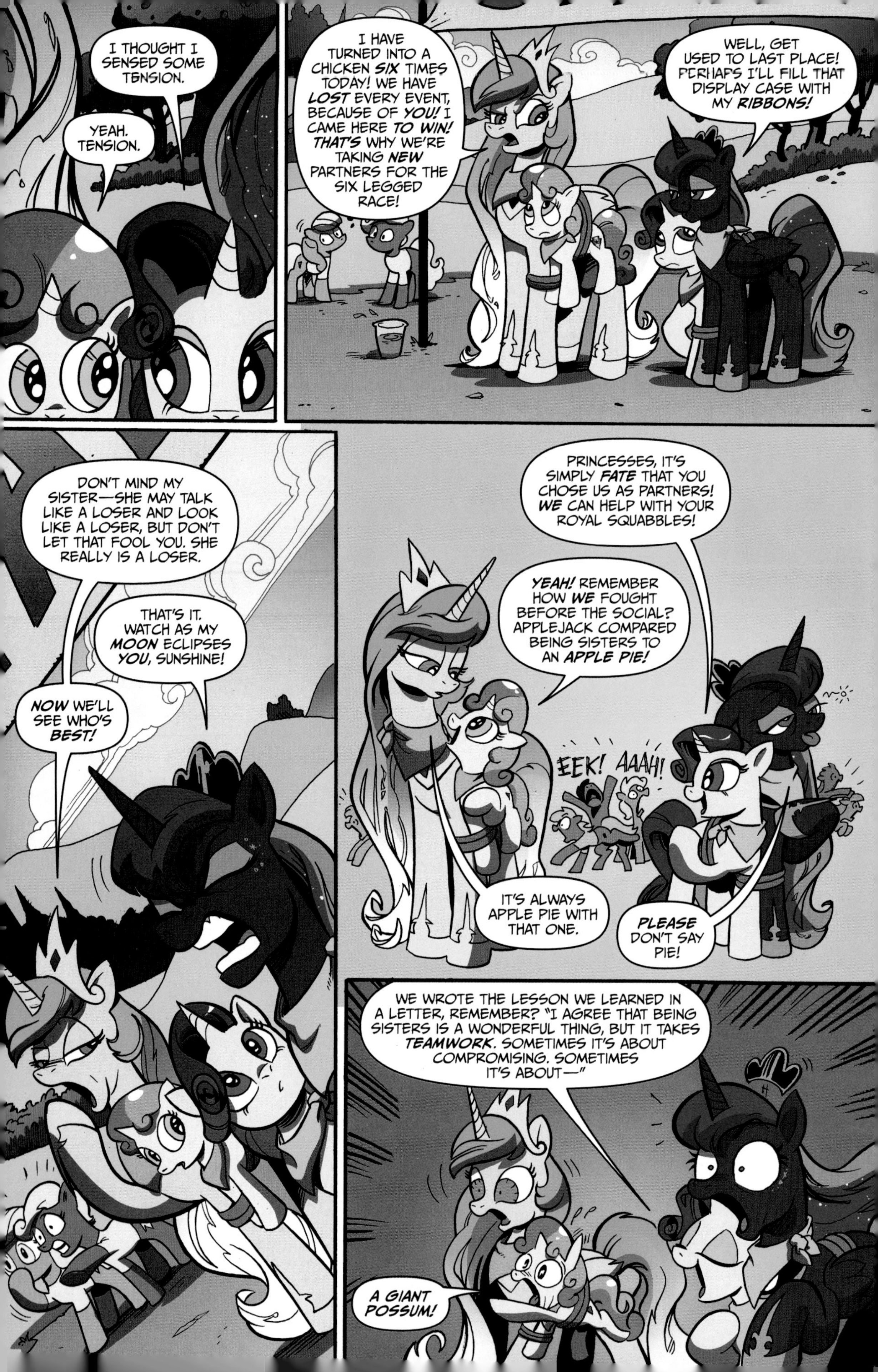
I THOUGHT I SENSED SOME TENSION.
YEAH. TENSION.
I HAVE TURNED INTO A CHICKEN *SIX* TIMES TODAY! WE HAVE *LOST* EVERY EVENT, BECAUSE OF *YOU!* I CAME HERE *TO WIN! THAT'S* WHY WE'RE TAKING *NEW* PARTNERS FOR THE SIX LEGGED RACE!
WELL, GET USED TO LAST PLACE! PERHAPS I'LL FILL THAT DISPLAY CASE WITH MY *RIBBONS!*
DON'T MIND MY SISTER—SHE MAY TALK LIKE A LOSER AND LOOK LIKE A LOSER, BUT DON'T LET THAT FOOL YOU. SHE REALLY IS A LOSER.
THAT'S IT. WATCH AS MY *MOON* ECLIPSES *YOU*, SUNSHINE!
NOW WE'LL SEE WHO'S *BEST!*
PRINCESSES, IT'S SIMPLY *FATE* THAT YOU CHOSE US AS PARTNERS! *WE* CAN HELP WITH YOUR ROYAL SQUABBLES!
YEAH! REMEMBER HOW *WE* FOUGHT BEFORE THE SOCIAL? APPLEJACK COMPARED BEING SISTERS TO AN *APPLE PIE!*
EEK! AAAH!
IT'S ALWAYS APPLE PIE WITH THAT ONE.
PLEASE DON'T SAY PIE!
WE WROTE THE LESSON WE LEARNED IN A LETTER, REMEMBER? "I AGREE THAT BEING SISTERS IS A WONDERFUL THING, BUT IT TAKES *TEAMWORK*. SOMETIMES IT'S ABOUT COMPROMISING. SOMETIMES IT'S ABOUT—"
A GIANT POSSUM!

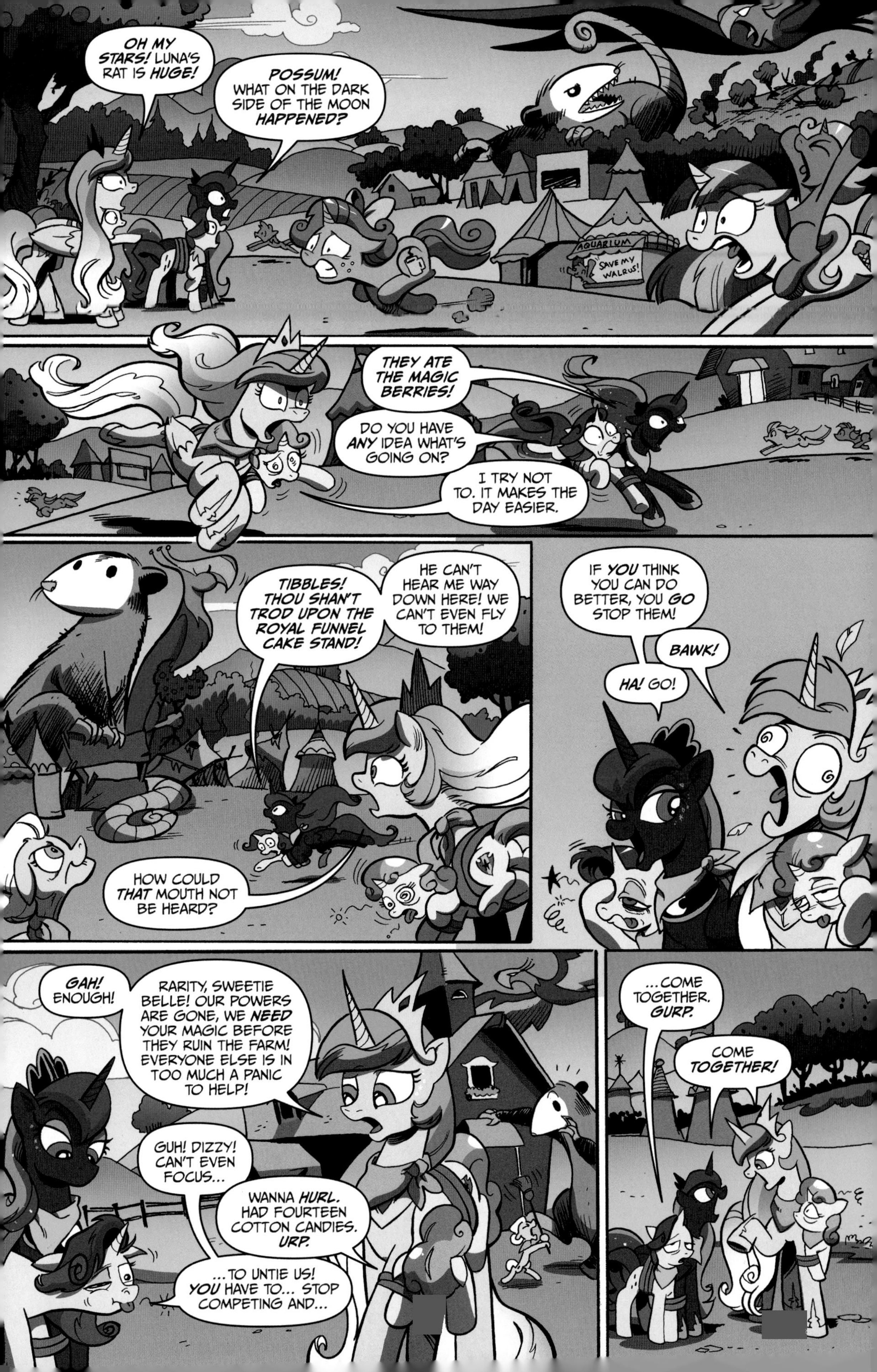

OH MY STARS! LUNA'S RAT IS HUGE!
POSSUM! WHAT ON THE DARK SIDE OF THE MOON HAPPENED?
AQUARIUM
SAVE MY WALRUS!
THEY ATE THE MAGIC BERRIES!
DO YOU HAVE ANY IDEA WHAT'S GOING ON?
I TRY NOT TO. IT MAKES THE DAY EASIER.
TIBBLES! THOU SHAN'T TROD UPON THE ROYAL FUNNEL CAKE STAND!
HE CAN'T HEAR ME WAY DOWN HERE! WE CAN'T EVEN FLY TO THEM!
HOW COULD THAT MOUTH NOT BE HEARD?
IF YOU THINK YOU CAN DO BETTER, YOU GO STOP THEM!
BAWK!
HA! GO!
GAH! ENOUGH!
RARITY, SWEETIE BELLE! OUR POWERS ARE GONE, WE NEED YOUR MAGIC BEFORE THEY RUIN THE FARM! EVERYONE ELSE IS IN TOO MUCH A PANIC TO HELP!
GUH! DIZZY! CAN'T EVEN FOCUS...
WANNA HURL. HAD FOURTEEN COTTON CANDIES. URP.
...TO UNTIE US! YOU HAVE TO... STOP COMPETING AND...
...COME TOGETHER. GURP.
COME TOGETHER!

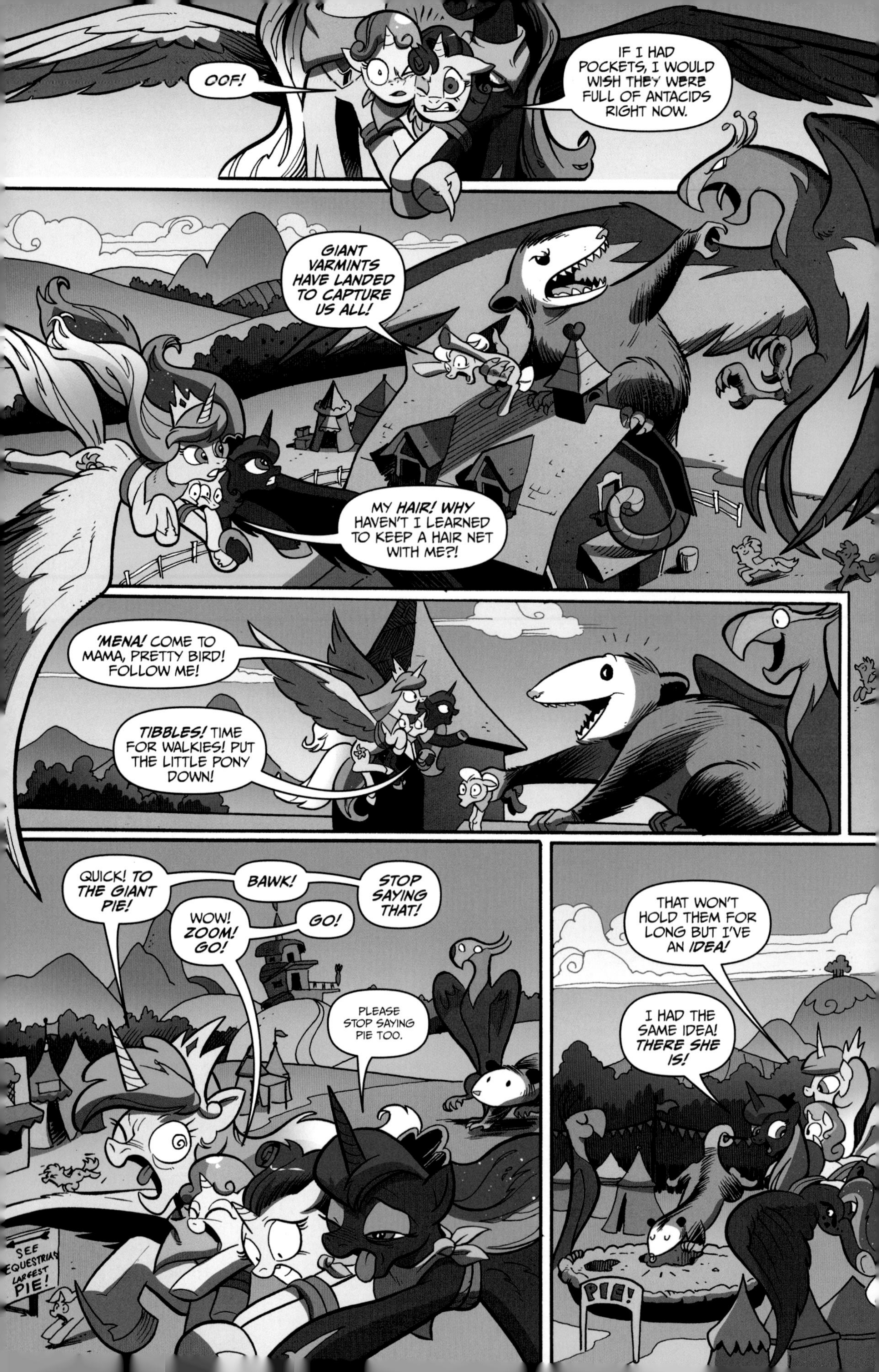

OOF!
IF I HAD POCKETS, I WOULD WISH THEY WERE FULL OF ANTACIDS RIGHT NOW.
GIANT VARMINTS HAVE LANDED TO CAPTURE US ALL!
MY HAIR! WHY HAVEN'T I LEARNED TO KEEP A HAIR NET WITH ME?!
'MENA! COME TO MAMA, PRETTY BIRD! FOLLOW ME!
TIBBLES! TIME FOR WALKIES! PUT THE LITTLE PONY DOWN!
QUICK! TO THE GIANT PIE!
BAWK!
STOP SAYING THAT!
WOW! ZOOM! GO!
GO!
PLEASE STOP SAYING PIE TOO.
SEE EQUESTRIA'S LARGEST PIE!
THAT WON'T HOLD THEM FOR LONG BUT I'VE AN IDEA!
I HAD THE SAME IDEA! THERE SHE IS!
PIE!

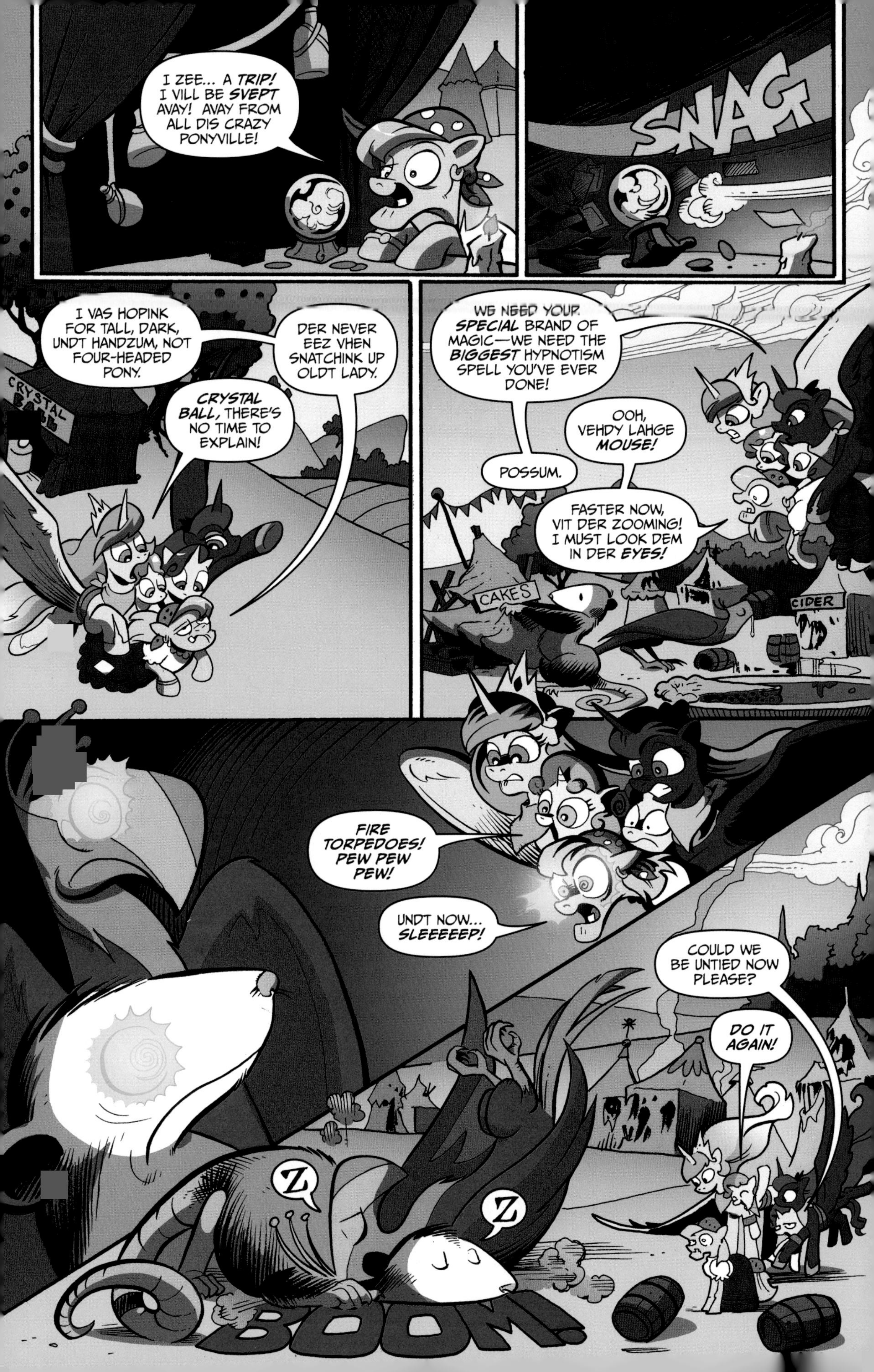
I ZEE... A *TRIP!* I VILL BE *SVEPT* AVAY! AVAY FROM ALL DIS CRAZY PONYVILLE!
SNAG
I VAS HOPINK FOR TALL, DARK, UNDT HANDZUM, NOT FOUR-HEADED PONY.
DER NEVER EEZ VHEN SNATCHINK UP OLDT LADY.
CRYSTAL
CRYSTAL BALL, THERE'S NO TIME TO EXPLAIN!
WE NEED YOUR *SPECIAL* BRAND OF MAGIC—WE NEED THE *BIGGEST* HYPNOTISM SPELL YOU'VE EVER DONE!
OOH, VEHDY LAHGE *MOUSE!*
POSSUM.
FASTER NOW, VIT DER ZOOMING! I MUST LOOK DEM IN DER *EYES!*
CAKES
CIDER
FIRE TORPEDOES! PEW PEW PEW!
UNDT NOW... *SLEEEEEP!*
COULD WE BE UNTIED NOW PLEASE?
DO IT AGAIN!
Z
Z
BOOM

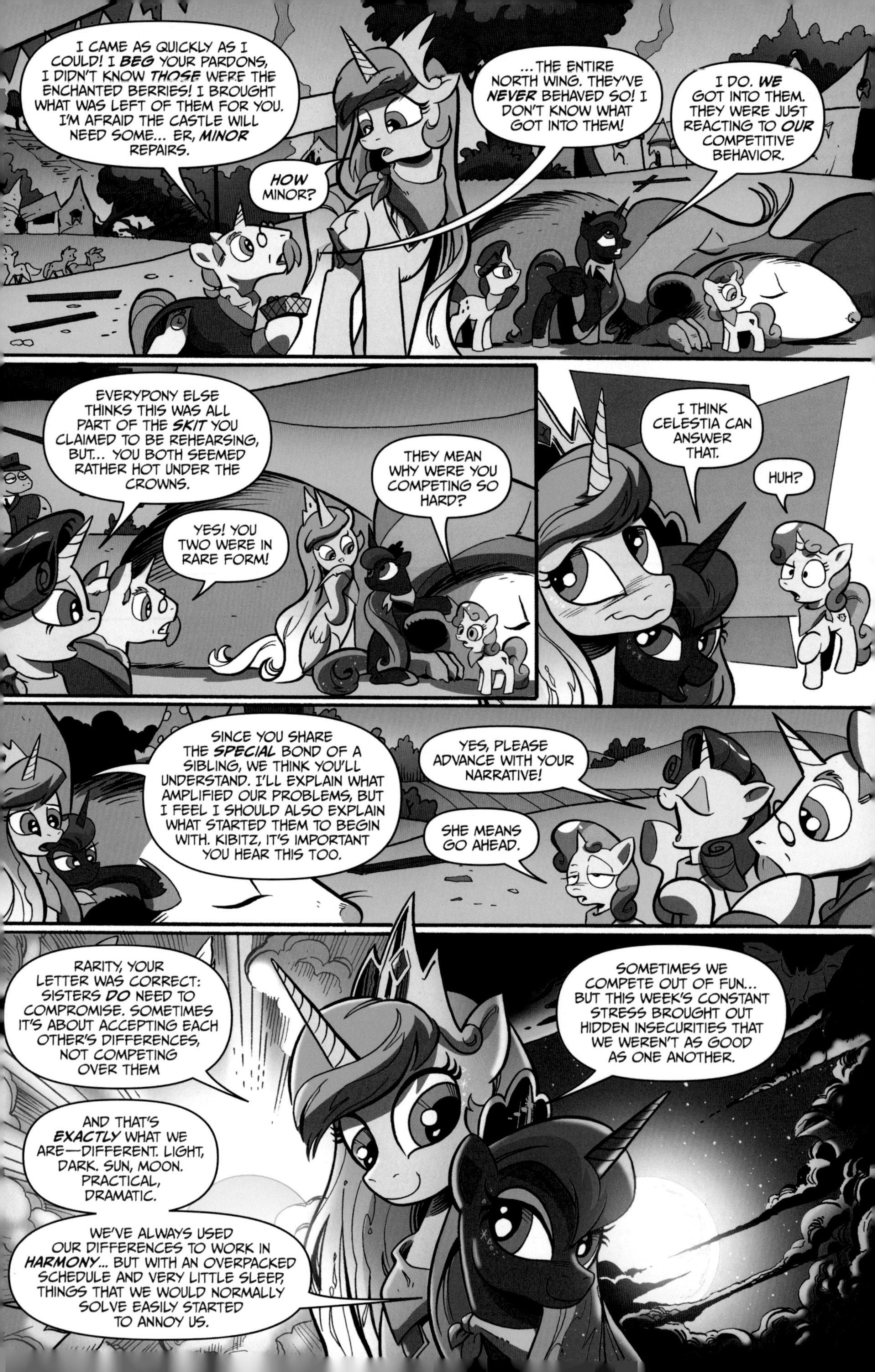
I CAME AS QUICKLY AS I COULD! I BEG YOUR PARDONS, I DIDN'T KNOW THOSE WERE THE ENCHANTED BERRIES! I BROUGHT WHAT WAS LEFT OF THEM FOR YOU. I'M AFRAID THE CASTLE WILL NEED SOME... ER, MINOR REPAIRS.
HOW MINOR?
...THE ENTIRE NORTH WING. THEY'VE NEVER BEHAVED SO! I DON'T KNOW WHAT GOT INTO THEM!
I DO. WE GOT INTO THEM. THEY WERE JUST REACTING TO OUR COMPETITIVE BEHAVIOR.
EVERYPONY ELSE THINKS THIS WAS ALL PART OF THE SKIT YOU CLAIMED TO BE REHEARSING, BUT... YOU BOTH SEEMED RATHER HOT UNDER THE CROWNS.
YES! YOU TWO WERE IN RARE FORM!
THEY MEAN WHY WERE YOU COMPETING SO HARD?
I THINK CELESTIA CAN ANSWER THAT.
HUH?
SINCE YOU SHARE THE SPECIAL BOND OF A SIBLING, WE THINK YOU'LL UNDERSTAND. I'LL EXPLAIN WHAT AMPLIFIED OUR PROBLEMS, BUT I FEEL I SHOULD ALSO EXPLAIN WHAT STARTED THEM TO BEGIN WITH. KIBITZ, IT'S IMPORTANT YOU HEAR THIS TOO.
YES, PLEASE ADVANCE WITH YOUR NARRATIVE!
SHE MEANS GO AHEAD.
RARITY, YOUR LETTER WAS CORRECT: SISTERS DO NEED TO COMPROMISE. SOMETIMES IT'S ABOUT ACCEPTING EACH OTHER'S DIFFERENCES, NOT COMPETING OVER THEM
SOMETIMES WE COMPETE OUT OF FUN... BUT THIS WEEK'S CONSTANT STRESS BROUGHT OUT HIDDEN INSECURITIES THAT WE WEREN'T AS GOOD AS ONE ANOTHER.
AND THAT'S EXACTLY WHAT WE ARE—DIFFERENT. LIGHT, DARK. SUN, MOON. PRACTICAL, DRAMATIC.
WE'VE ALWAYS USED OUR DIFFERENCES TO WORK IN HARMONY... BUT WITH AN OVERPACKED SCHEDULE AND VERY LITTLE SLEEP, THINGS THAT WE WOULD NORMALLY SOLVE EASILY STARTED TO ANNOY US.

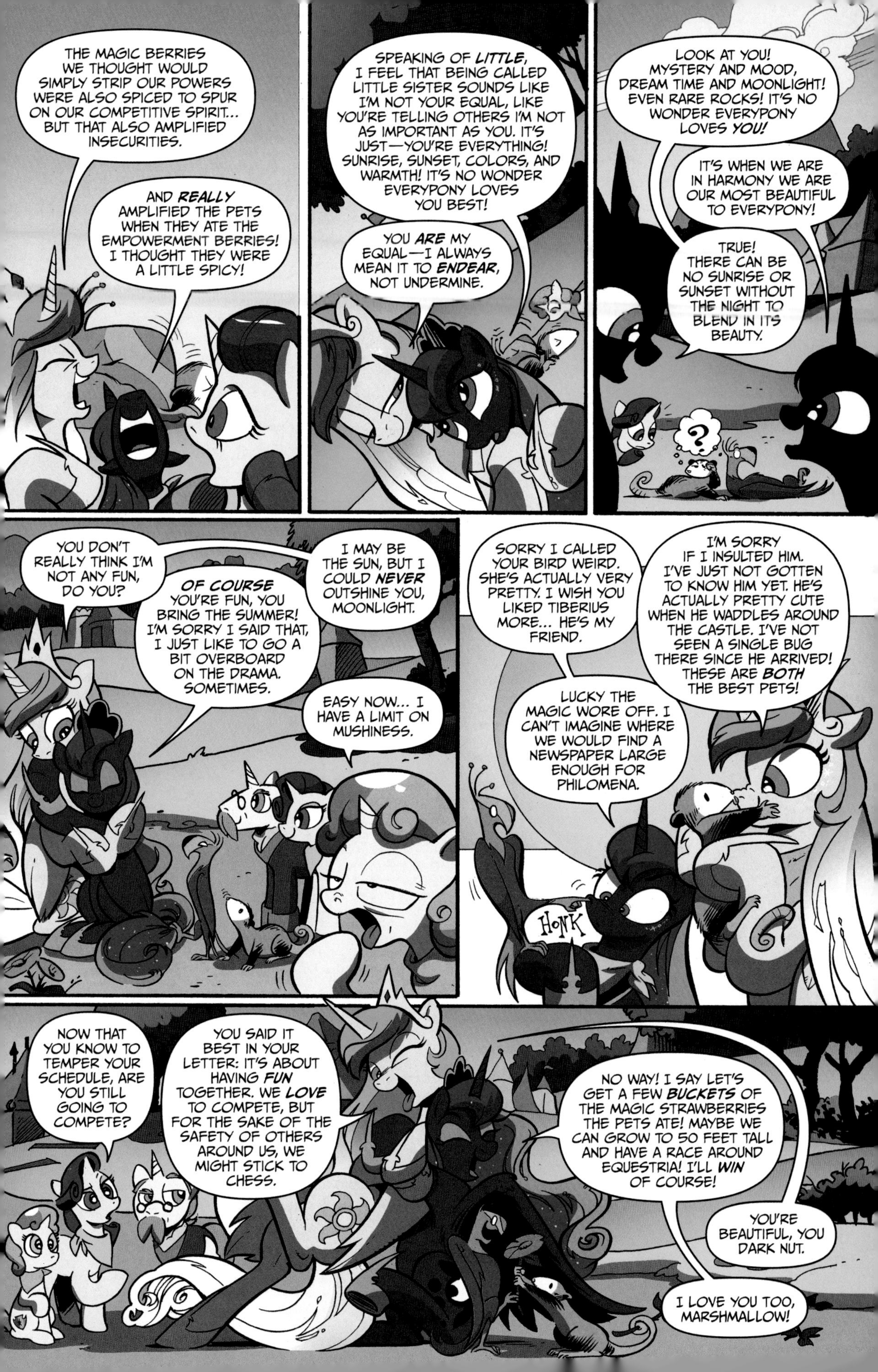
THE MAGIC BERRIES WE THOUGHT WOULD SIMPLY STRIP OUR POWERS WERE ALSO SPICED TO SPUR ON OUR COMPETITIVE SPIRIT... BUT THAT ALSO AMPLIFIED INSECURITIES.
AND REALLY AMPLIFIED THE PETS WHEN THEY ATE THE EMPOWERMENT BERRIES! I THOUGHT THEY WERE A LITTLE SPICY!
SPEAKING OF LITTLE, I FEEL THAT BEING CALLED LITTLE SISTER SOUNDS LIKE I'M NOT YOUR EQUAL, LIKE YOU'RE TELLING OTHERS I'M NOT AS IMPORTANT AS YOU. IT'S JUST—YOU'RE EVERYTHING! SUNRISE, SUNSET, COLORS, AND WARMTH! IT'S NO WONDER EVERYPONY LOVES YOU BEST!
YOU ARE MY EQUAL—I ALWAYS MEAN IT TO ENDEAR, NOT UNDERMINE.
LOOK AT YOU! MYSTERY AND MOOD, DREAM TIME AND MOONLIGHT! EVEN RARE ROCKS! IT'S NO WONDER EVERYPONY LOVES YOU!
IT'S WHEN WE ARE IN HARMONY WE ARE OUR MOST BEAUTIFUL TO EVERYPONY!
TRUE! THERE CAN BE NO SUNRISE OR SUNSET WITHOUT THE NIGHT TO BLEND IN ITS BEAUTY.
?
YOU DON'T REALLY THINK I'M NOT ANY FUN, DO YOU?
OF COURSE YOU'RE FUN, YOU BRING THE SUMMER! I'M SORRY I SAID THAT, I JUST LIKE TO GO A BIT OVERBOARD ON THE DRAMA. SOMETIMES.
I MAY BE THE SUN, BUT I COULD NEVER OUTSHINE YOU, MOONLIGHT.
EASY NOW... I HAVE A LIMIT ON MUSHINESS.
SORRY I CALLED YOUR BIRD WEIRD. SHE'S ACTUALLY VERY PRETTY. I WISH YOU LIKED TIBERIUS MORE... HE'S MY FRIEND.
I'M SORRY IF I INSULTED HIM. I'VE JUST NOT GOTTEN TO KNOW HIM YET. HE'S ACTUALLY PRETTY CUTE WHEN HE WADDLES AROUND THE CASTLE. I'VE NOT SEEN A SINGLE BUG THERE SINCE HE ARRIVED! THESE ARE BOTH THE BEST PETS!
LUCKY THE MAGIC WORE OFF. I CAN'T IMAGINE WHERE WE WOULD FIND A NEWSPAPER LARGE ENOUGH FOR PHILOMENA.
HONK
NOW THAT YOU KNOW TO TEMPER YOUR SCHEDULE, ARE YOU STILL GOING TO COMPETE?
YOU SAID IT BEST IN YOUR LETTER: IT'S ABOUT HAVING FUN TOGETHER. WE LOVE TO COMPETE, BUT FOR THE SAKE OF THE SAFETY OF OTHERS AROUND US, WE MIGHT STICK TO CHESS.
NO WAY! I SAY LET'S GET A FEW BUCKETS OF THE MAGIC STRAWBERRIES THE PETS ATE! MAYBE WE CAN GROW TO 50 FEET TALL AND HAVE A RACE AROUND EQUESTRIA! I'LL WIN OF COURSE!
YOU'RE BEAUTIFUL, YOU DARK NUT.
I LOVE YOU TOO, MARSHMALLOW!

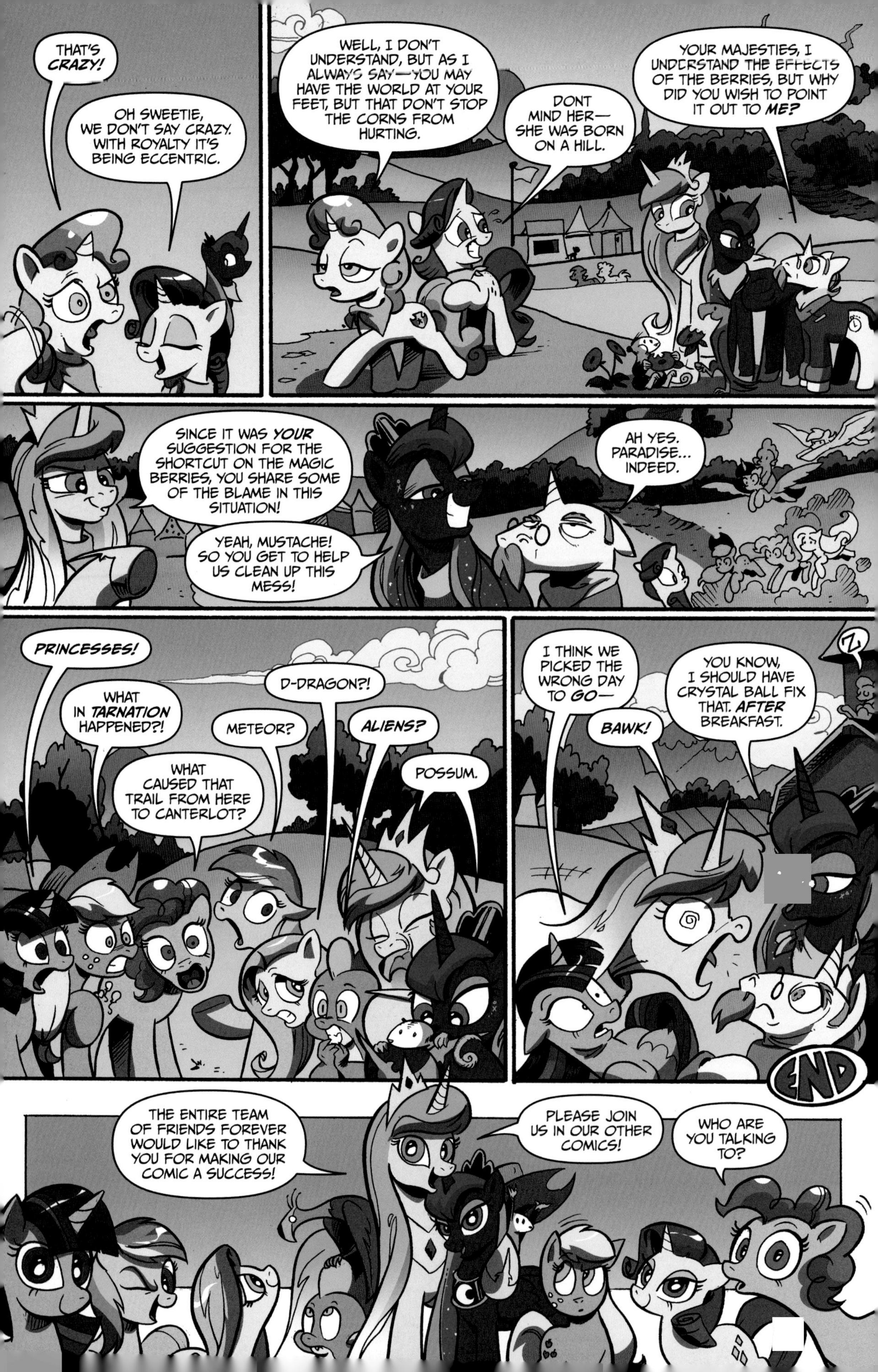
THAT'S *CRAZY!*
OH SWEETIE, WE DON'T SAY CRAZY. WITH ROYALTY IT'S BEING ECCENTRIC.
WELL, I DON'T UNDERSTAND, BUT AS I ALWAYS SAY—YOU MAY HAVE THE WORLD AT YOUR FEET, BUT THAT DON'T STOP THE CORNS FROM HURTING.
DONT MIND HER— SHE WAS BORN ON A HILL.
YOUR MAJESTIES, I UNDERSTAND THE EFFECTS OF THE BERRIES, BUT WHY DID YOU WISH TO POINT IT OUT TO *ME?*
SINCE IT WAS *YOUR* SUGGESTION FOR THE SHORTCUT ON THE MAGIC BERRIES, YOU SHARE SOME OF THE BLAME IN THIS SITUATION!
YEAH, MUSTACHE! SO YOU GET TO HELP US CLEAN UP THIS MESS!
AH YES. PARADISE... INDEED.
PRINCESSES!
WHAT IN *TARNATION* HAPPENED?!
WHAT CAUSED THAT TRAIL FROM HERE TO CANTERLOT?
METEOR?
D-DRAGON?!
ALIENS?
POSSUM.
I THINK WE PICKED THE WRONG DAY TO *GO*—
BAWK!
YOU KNOW, I SHOULD HAVE CRYSTAL BALL FIX THAT. *AFTER* BREAKFAST.
END
THE ENTIRE TEAM OF FRIENDS FOREVER WOULD LIKE TO THANK YOU FOR MAKING OUR COMIC A SUCCESS!
PLEASE JOIN US IN OUR OTHER COMICS!
WHO ARE YOU TALKING TO?

my LITTLE PONY

FRIENDS FOREVER

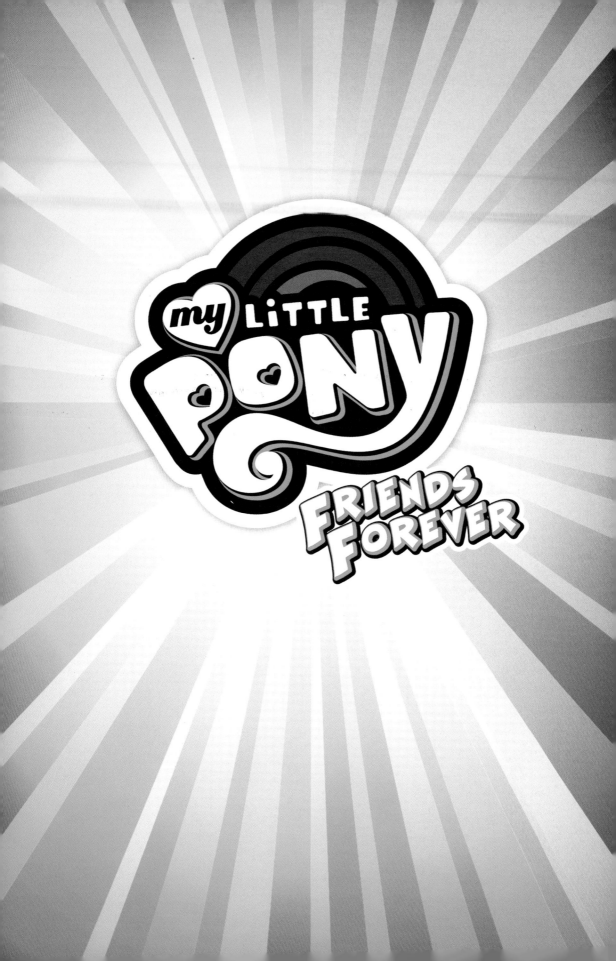

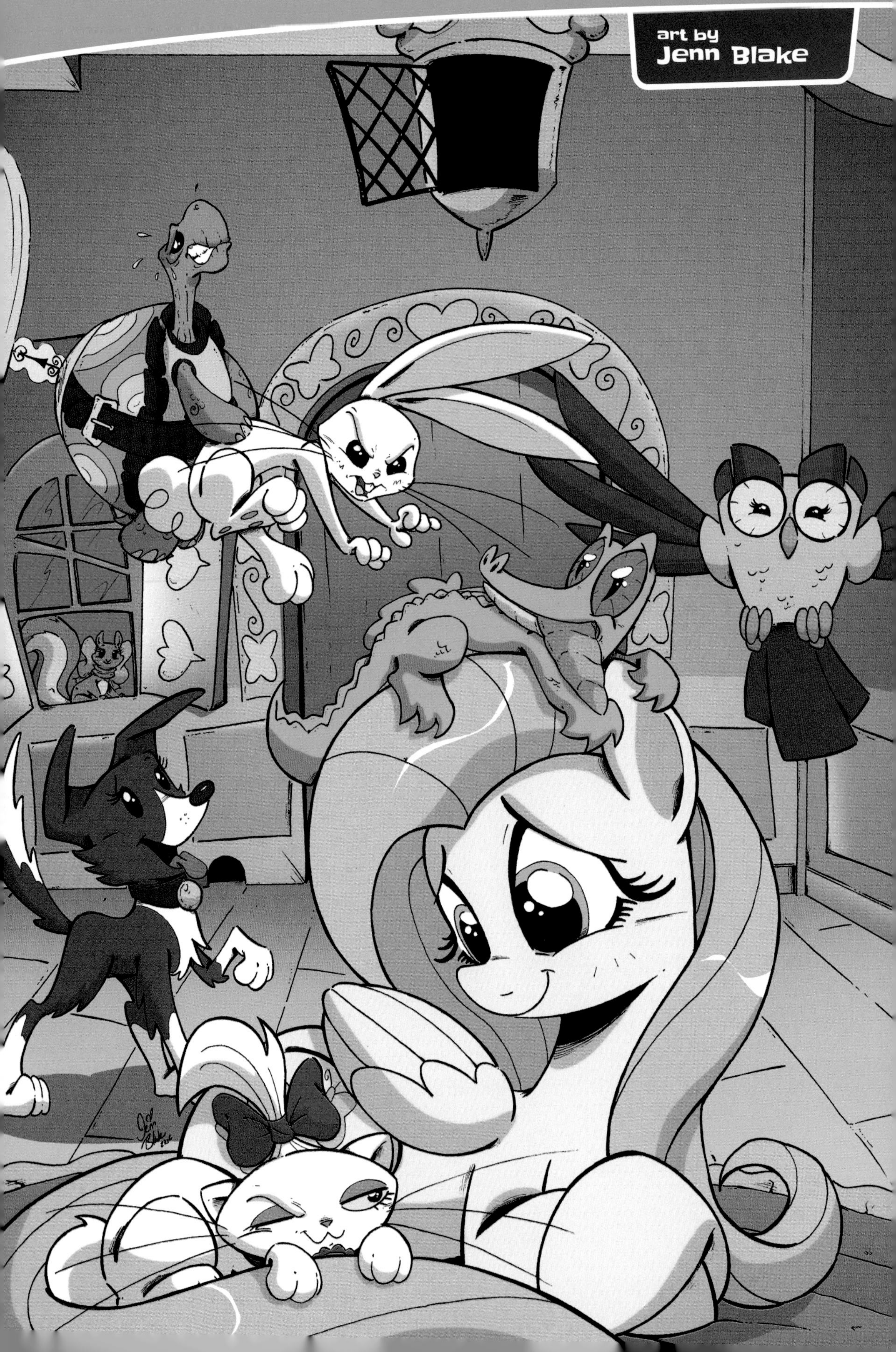
art by
Jenn Blake

art by
Nidhi Chanani

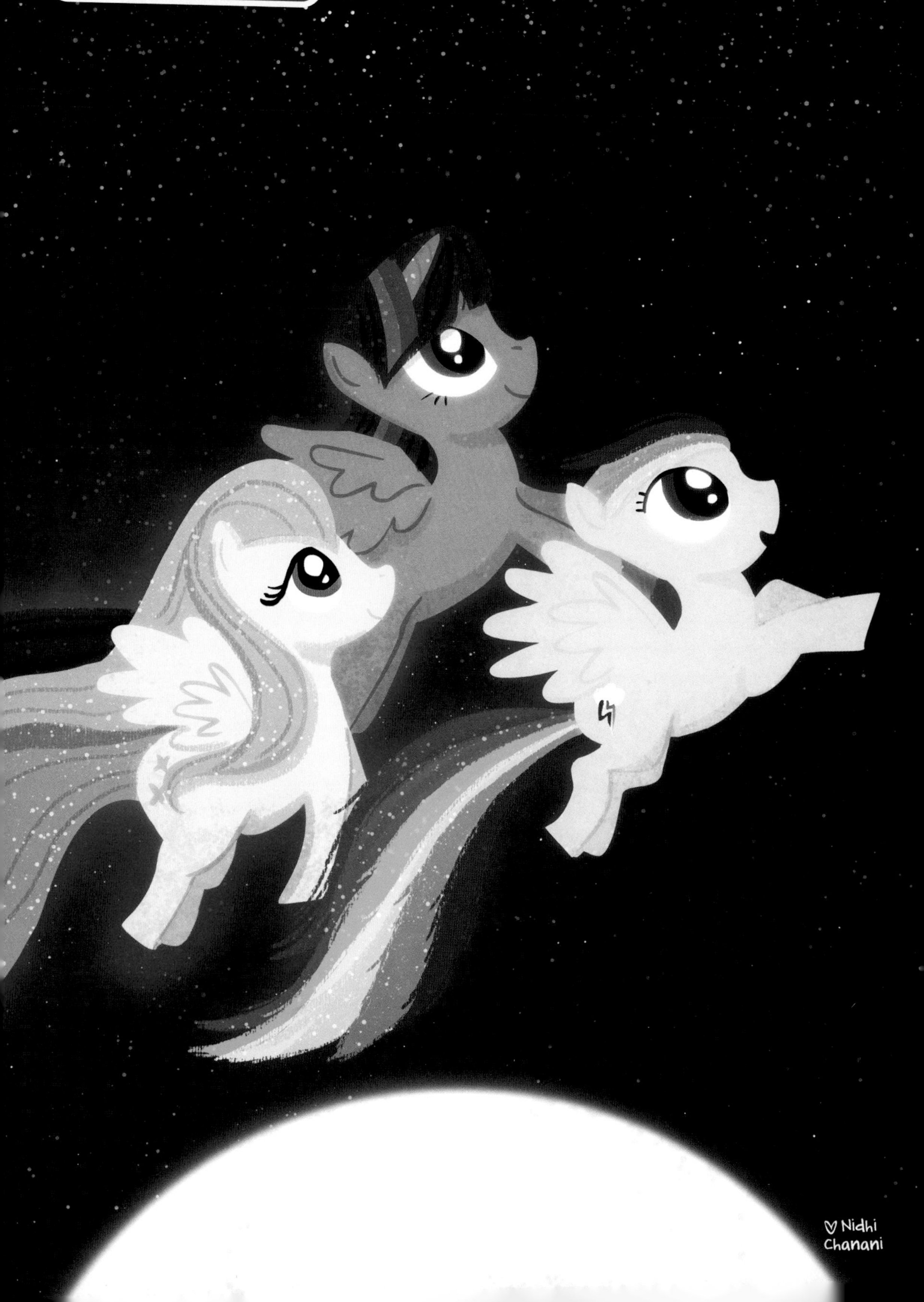
Nidhi
Chanani

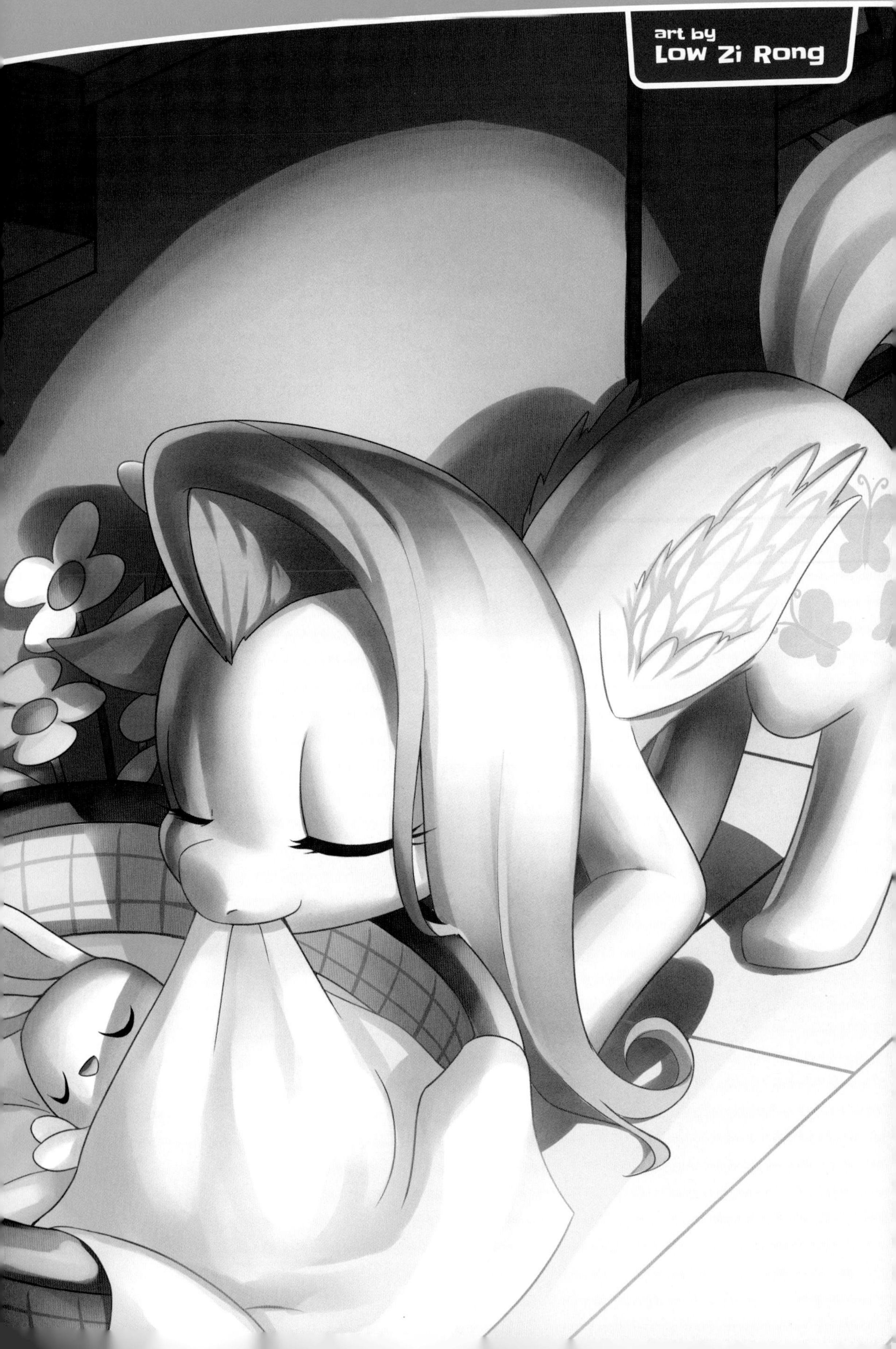
art by
Low Zi Rong

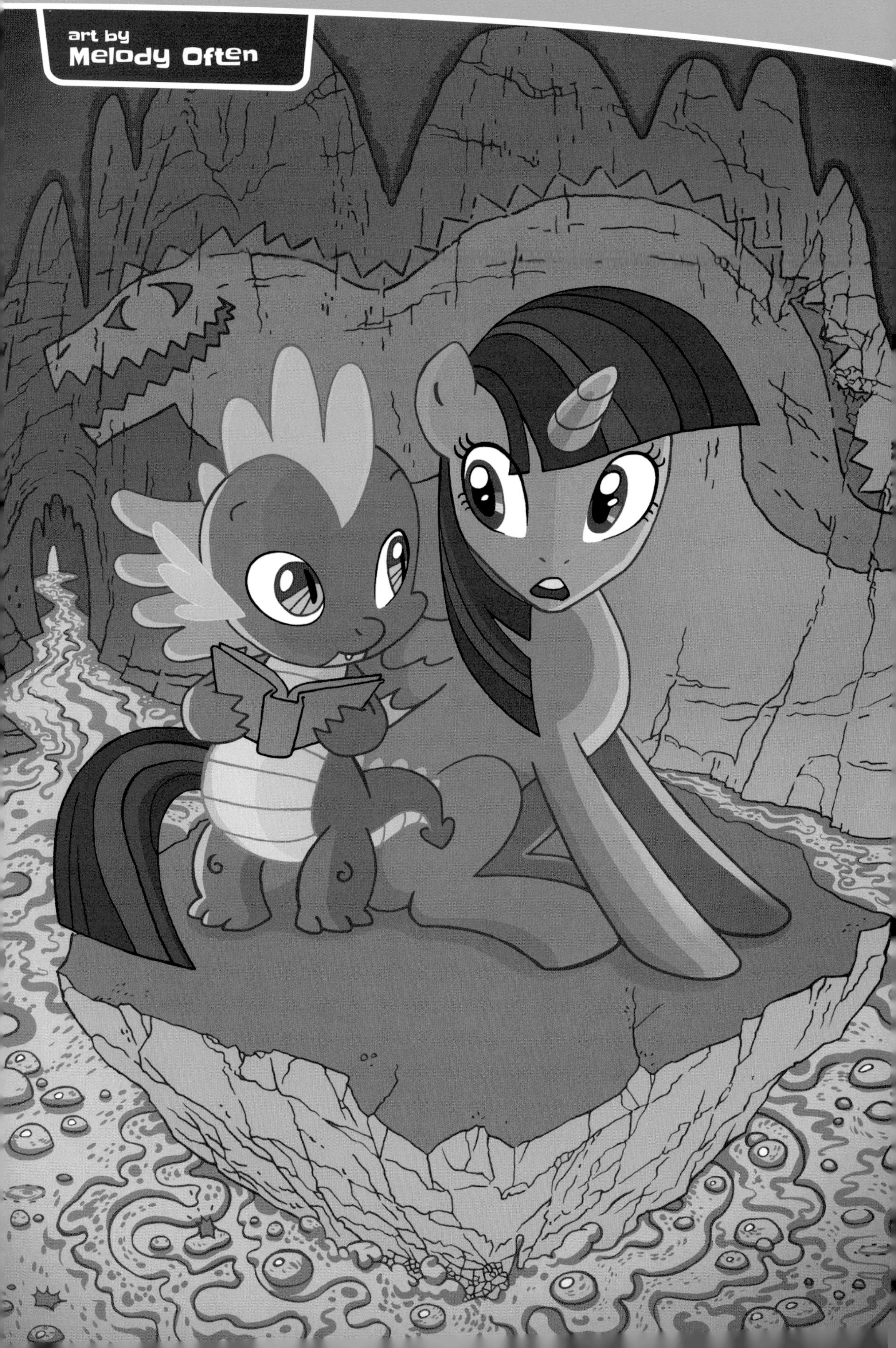
art by
Melody Often

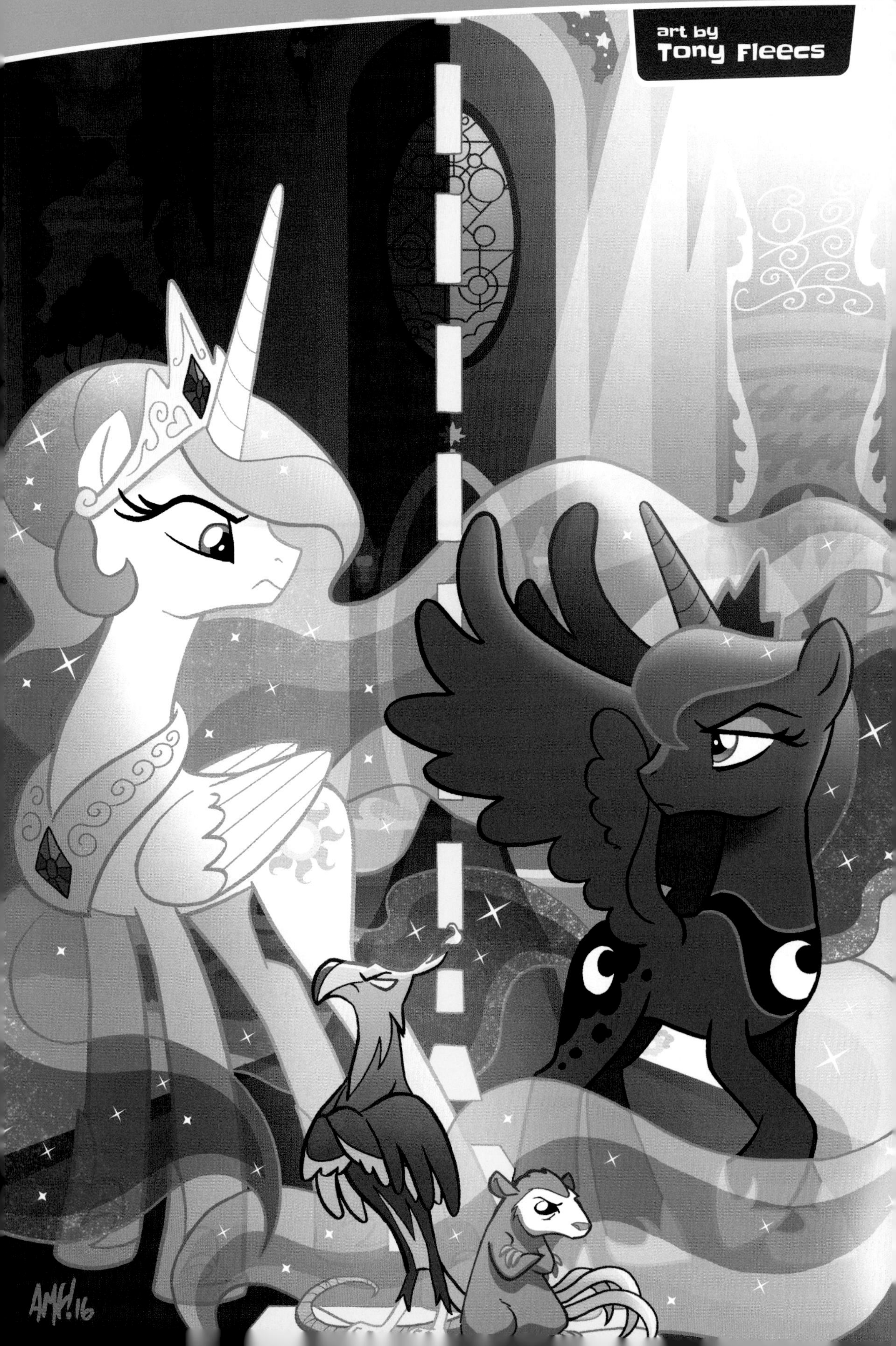
art by
Tony Fleecs
AMF!16